JUNKIE

by

Robert P. French

Michael,

*Thanks so much
for your support*

Robert

Junkie.

Published by Robert P. French, Vancouver, Canada.

www.robertpfrench.com

This book is a work of fiction. Characters, incidents, names and places either are fictitious or are used fictitiously. Any resemblance to actual persons, living or dead, or to actual events, is entirely coincidental.

ISBN 978-0-9876896-2-7

Acknowledgements

This book would not have been possible but for the help and encouragement of many wonderful people and if I have forgotten anyone, I sincerely apologize: Gillian Maxwell who introduced me to people who understand the world of drugs; Mark Hayden of Addiction Services, Vancouver Coastal Health; Richard Utendale who told me about the life of a heroin addict and walked me through the streets; Bob Woodroff who showed me the inside of an SRO; Hank Reiner of the Crown Prosecutor's office; an anonymous former Vancouver Police Department detective; and Roy Kuchma, the best read man I have ever met. I would also like to thank the Vancouver Public Library for providing the perfect location for any writer.

My very special thanks go to Lisa Rector-Maass of Third Draft Editing in New York, who supported and mentored me from day one through all the drafts.

Dedication

To my wife Penny who believed in me when I
had stopped believing in myself.

Chapter 1

I didn't die last night.

The sandpaper sound of Roy's voice tells me I wasn't that lucky. Another day to fight my way through.

The pain is deep in my bones. My toenails hurt. My hair hurts.

A claw bites into my shoulder, sending a new tsunami of agony crashing through me.

"Hey, Rocky. It's Saturday. We gotta getcha well."

Saturday! And Roy's here to get me through.

His Sally Ann boots, one brown and one black, are stamping the cold out of his feet. "Come on, man," he croaks. "It's nearly seven. I gotcha stuff here."

I kick off the rancid quilt—left here by some crack head —and the feeling of disgust at its touch fights with my burning need. I push myself up and feel my bones shatter.

Visible between Roy's stamping legs, the green dumpster tagged with a swastika confirms it. We're in the alley, the one that terrifies me. I can feel my heart racing in my throat.

My eyes take in the morning detritus strewn across the pavement: garbage bags; crusts of bread; broken glass; rotted fruit; and, of course, the usual assortment of used needles. The human feces, not six feet from where I slept, assail my senses. It's been a thirty-eight year struggle and I have finally arrived at the bottom.

But the stench, the filth and my irrational fear of this alley are an inconsequential backdrop to what Roy has in his hands. "D'you want me to help ya with it?" He always offers and I always refuse. I let him hold on to it for me on Friday

1

nights, to make sure I've got it for Saturday morning, but I don't trust anyone. Not even Roy. Roy's my only friend in this life. And I hate the bastard.

I reach up with both hands and snatch the eight items from him.

In my lap, they are all that exist in the world.

***

The urgency in Roy's voice cuts through the haze. "Rocky, man. It's gone quarter past seven. Come on. Time to get ready, eh." Deep breath. It feels good... I feel good. That twenty minutes on the nod went by way too quickly. But it's twenty past. I spent too much time. Roy must have woken me late. That's not like him. Damn, I have got to get moving *right now*.

His filthy hands grab me and pull me to my feet. God, why does he do that? I know he's trying to help but I hate being grabbed by him.

As I stand up, my old denim jacket drops to the ground. I scoop it up fast. It's stained. Looks like blood; it is blood, a lot of blood. Blood is a part of the scenery around here— encrusted on faces, arms and legs, smeared on clothes and sidewalks—but I have some residual memory of a knife, a memory filtered through last night's haze. The blood is fresh, but no longer wet. *In the last six hours,* a tendril of my old self thinks. But my old self is gone; too painful to contemplate. I have to let it go...

Who am I kidding? I can never let it go.

Roy hands me a plastic Safeway bag, wrapped up tightly, and I push it as deep as I can into the pocket of my jacket, knowing I need the contents and hating that I want them. "Thanks, man," I say and really mean it.

I need to rush now. Right now. But there is a sadness on his face that holds me. Why does he do that? He knows it's

Saturday and I have to get going. It's probably just Roy being dramatic. Again.

I start to head out of the alley but, damn it, the image of his face pulls me back. I can't just leave the poor old devil looking like that.

He is standing, leaning against the dumpster, forlorn in his long brown coat, several sizes too large for his tall, stringy frame. His face shows no trace of the streak of malice that sometimes lurks below the surface. The baldness, about which he is so sensitive, is covered by the ever present, battered, leather cowboy hat perched on the top of his head, the chin strap tied at his throat. With his straggly gray hair falling to his shoulders, he looks like an ancient Jessie James. He would like the simile just fine... except for the ancient bit. He's sensitive about his age too.

"You OK?" I check my nine dollar watch. Seven twenty-five. I'm cutting it fine.

The watery blue eyes peer down over his beak of a nose. He cleans his hornlike fingernails with the wicked looking switchblade he always carries. Come on, Roy, come on.

"Sure." No eye contact. Now I know something is wrong, something serious. Unlike me, he's chipper in the mornings—a rare condition for an alcoholic as far gone as Roy—but today he looks deflated. Diminished.

"What's up man?" I ask. I recheck the time; maybe I can spare just one more minute.

He shakes his head. "Nothing, you go." There are streaks down his dirty old face.

I rein in my need and wait the aeon, stretching some twenty seconds, until he speaks.

"Tommy died last night."

"What?" I feel the blood drain from my face then look down at the blood on my jacket and strain to remember... but can not.

I look up. I don't think Roy has noticed it.

He nods, his head hanging. "Yeah. Bad drugs."

The loss bites hard. People die all the time in these alleys but Tommy's death is a blow. Tommy Connor was a life long alcoholic but he was both a gentleman and a gentle man. A man with an unwavering sense of humor and an optimism wildly at odds with the reality of his life.

My old self is trying to burst through with questions. I crush it down and push the questions out of my mind; it's better that way. I just say, "I'm sorry to hear that, man. I know you and Tommy were real close." I note the poor grammar which I often affect with Roy and the guys on the street. A survival mechanism, I guess.

I reach out to touch him, comfort him, but don't know how. I grip his shoulder, shake it once, pat it and shake it again. Hoping that somehow just the contact will console. He shrugs off my hand and turns his back to me. "Anyways, ya gotta go. Tell her Roy sends his love." There is a catch in his voice.

I reply with the unvarying formula. "I will Roy. She always loves to hear from you."

As I hurry away, he says, "Maybe I'll get to meet her some time soon." There is no mistaking the bitterness.

"Sure," over my shoulder, "that would be great. I'll arrange something."

I feel the flood of guilt. We both know that it will never happen but what can I say? It's the ritual we observe every Saturday morning.

"Later!" he shouts after me, his voice angry now. "Ya know where to find me when ya get back."

I turn up the collar of my jacket and pull the peak of my baseball cap down over my eyes. A futile camouflage but I need a low profile on the streets because of how I used to make my living and, more to the point, how I make my living now. There are people who will kill me if they recognize me.

Kill me very slowly and painfully. With a shiver, I hurry off toward the buses.

Then one of the quashed questions bubbles to the surface. Tommy was an alcoholic like Roy. Why would he die from an overdose? No, not an overdose. What did Roy say? Bad drugs?

Chapter 2

The first bus driver must have seen the blood on my jacket. He wouldn't stop to pick me up—one or two of them are like that driving through the downtown east side—then the second bus took forever to arrive. Only two more months. I can't blow it by being late now. I just can't.

Kevin's doorbell chimes the first four notes of the 1812 overture. It's the only doorbell I've ever heard that plays Tchaikovsky and in my past life I rang a lot of doorbells.

There is no reply.

Kevin is the only one of my old friends who will have anything to do with me. His loyalty to me has not wavered despite the thousand ways I have betrayed it.

I ring again. Da da da daaaa. If Kevin's not home, I am screwed.

One more ring… nothing. Try the door handle… locked. I *am* screwed.

Last night was my first night of actually sleeping outside on the streets and I've already absorbed the fragrance of the alley. I can't go like this, it would not be fair to her, but if I cancel she would really be hurt. Even though a part of me wants to go back to the downtown east side and look into Tommy's death, I can't let her down. I have to swallow my shame and go like this: dirty, smelly and covered in blood. Maybe she *should* see me as I really am, even though the thought disturbs me.

I head down the three steps from the front door, three paces, through the gate and start down the street.

"Cal. Here, Cal." It sounds like someone calling their dog. But it's not. I breathe out and feel the tension wash out of my shoulders. Thanks to Roy I'm known as Rocky on the streets so it's always a bit strange to hear my real name being used.

I turn and jog back to Kevin's door.

Usually, he greets me with his wide, quirky grin but today he seems distracted, harried maybe. For some reason it makes me feel uncomfortable. He grabs my arm, pulls me through the door and envelopes me in a bear hug. I hate being hugged by guys but Kevin's the exception; with him it just feels natural. He's like a brother, in fact, much more than a brother, to me. He holds the hug much longer than usual and when he lets go, his face is lined. He is worried about something. Again I get a feeling of discomfort.

He is wearing a silk robe, in a paisley design, and is holding a cup of coffee. He checks his watch. "Whoa. You'd better go get ready," he says. I pause for a second, trying to read what is wrong from the lines on his face.

"Go," he says, forcing a smile. If I weren't already late... But I am, so I head towards the back bedroom where he lets me keep my stuff, inhaling the faintest redolence of sandalwood that says Kevin's place.

"Cal." His voice stops me; his smile still seems forced. "Can you hurry it up because I really need to talk to you before you go."

"Sure Kev." I was right.

He nods and heads upstairs, giving me no clue to what he wants to talk about. It worries me a lot but I don't know why.

On the bed he has laid out my good clothes, toiletries and a clean bath towel. On the bedside table are two two-zone bus tickets and a twenty dollar bill. Kevin knows that there is always a high risk that I will divert the money but he always leaves it just the same and never asks. That twenty dollars could get me off the street and put a roof over my head tonight. Maybe... But no, I couldn't. One day I must

7

tell Kev that, although tempted to the contrary, I have always used the money as he intends.

***

I've rushed through my ablutions and I'm ready to go. I check my watch. It's after eight thirty and I am going to have to push it to get to West Van on time.

He is waiting for me in the hallway.

He comes straight to the point. Kevin always comes straight to the point. "Cal, I need your help on something… It's a bit difficult to talk about this but…" His voice tapers off.

Rather than let him finish, I cut in, "Listen Kev, I really want to help but you know I can't be late. Wouldn't it be better if we talked when I get back, when we've got more time?"

A look of both frustration and annoyance morphs onto his face. "Hell, Cal. I've got a real problem here." There is an unexpected anger in his tone. It chides me that he has gone to bat for me a thousand times and has supported without once judging me. I owe him my time… and much more. I will just have to risk it.

"Sorry, man." I am trying to keep the frustration out of my voice. "It'll be OK if I'm a few minutes late. What's the problem?" I sneak another quick look at my watch.

I can see that he is balancing his own need against mine and, being Kevin, my need wins out. He sighs. "Don't worry about it. You go. You've only got a couple of months left and I don't want to screw it up by making you late. Let's have a beer and talk about it when you get back this afternoon."

I will betray Kevin if I leave and myself if I stay.

I nod and smile at him and head out with two of Shakespeare's lines, I forget from where, forcing themselves into my head:

8

He that is thy friend indeed,
He will help thee in thy need.

I ignore the urging of the words, somehow knowing that leaving is absolutely the wrong decision.

Chapter 3

I hear a high pitched scream from inside the five million dollar home.

It is exactly ten o'clock. I just made it on time. This is the one thing for which I am always on time. "Mommy, Daddy's here," she shrieks. I love that voice, full of joy and innocence. The sound of her running feet on the hardwood floor brings a big grin to my face. "Mommy, Mommy. I can't open the door. Quick, Daddy's here." I crouch down seeing her in my mind, jumping up and down in anticipation, frustrated at being not quite tall enough to open the top deadbolt. "Mommeeee-eeeee!" After what must seem an age to a seven year old—and to a thirty-eight year old for that matter—the door flies open and she launches herself into my arms.

We hug like we've been parted for a year. All my cares dissolve. She grips me tight around the neck for ten wonderful seconds and then lets go and wriggles out of my grasp. "Look Daddy, look." She pirouettes. "Don't you just love my new hair?" Her blond hair is cut in a bob and, although I liked her hair long, I have to admit it looks very cute. Sam probably had it done in some tony West Van salon.

"Wow, Ell, it's great, I *do* love it." My grin is so big it is hurting my cheeks.

"Me too, don't I Mommy?" She looks up at Sam for confirmation. I follow her eyes up to the soon-to-be Samantha Walsh, formerly Sam Rogan, my ex-wife. She looks great. I can see why I fell in love with her. She is

10

wearing jeans and an old plaid work shirt over a tight, white tee. On her, it is just plain chic. Her brunette hair has been cut to her shoulders and looks a bit like Ellie's. The cut emphasizes her long neck and slim face and the watery sunlight catches the hair's natural red highlights. The 'Kiss the Cook' apron and the smudge of flour on her cheek do nothing to mar her quintessential elegance. She smiles down at us, enveloping me in her warmth and for an instant I am transfixed by those green eyes.

"Listen, Cal, could we make a bit of a change today?"

The euphoric moment is extracted by the augur turning in my gut. A couple of times she has tried to cancel my visits with Ellie and it has been nasty. Sam sees the concern written on my face. "No, no," she reassures me, "it's just that George and I are having a dinner party tonight and I have loads to do. Would you like to take Ellie out by yourself?"

I'm good at hiding my feelings—I've had a lot of experience—but I can't pull it off now. The custody part of our divorce stipulates that I can only have unaccompanied visits with Ellie after a two year period. The two years will be up nine Saturdays from now.

This is the first time Sam has suggested an unaccompanied day and I'm praying it might portend an easing of the rules. "Sure, that would be great."

Ellie bounces up and down and hugs me again. "Come on Daddy, let's go out on the dock and look for seals."

"Sure, sweetie. Get your coat and boots on." She runs into the house, giving me a moment with my ex-wife.

"Thanks, Sam. I really appreciate it."

She smiles and nods.

My curiosity overcomes my fear of blowing it. I know the excuse of a party would never cause a change like this. "Can I, uh, ask why?"

After five seconds of internal debate, which is a very long time period in the circumstances, she shrugs, "Ellie

11

asked to have the time with you alone and I told her no." She pauses and I hold my breath. "But when she asked why, I discovered I didn't have a good reason to refuse her. So, there it is." Then, an afterthought. "But Cal you've got to understand this is not a regular change. It's a one-off, right?"

For some unknown reason I don't buy her explanation; I'm sure there's more to this than she is letting on. "You've never let—" the look on her face freezes the next words on my lips. I've blown it by pushing too far.

I cover with, "Sure Sam, absolutely." I feel like a jerk.

After a long look, she shakes her head and smiles, then checks over her shoulder for a second and slips her hand in the pocket of the apron. Taking a step forward, she stumbles but before I can reach out to steady her, she catches herself by grabbing the door frame. "Cal, no stupid pride here, OK? Here's twenty-five bucks. I know you always bring money when you come to see Ellie but it's just a little bit extra; maybe take her out for a nice lunch."

My amazement overcomes my stupid pride.

"Thanks, Sam. I… uh… well…" I have a Masters degree in English Lit so it's not often that words escape me… but when they do it's usually with Sam. I put the money in my pocket and have a twinge of guilt when I think about how I could use it. It makes me determined to spend every penny on Ellie.

Sam smiles again and kisses me gently on the cheek as Ellie comes bouncing out of the house.

"Come on, Daddy, let's go." She grabs my hand and drags me down the drive. I look over my shoulder and wave at Sam, who is still standing in the doorway, still holding on to the frame. With her other hand she waves back and I realize that I wish she were coming too.

Ellie talks non-stop on our way to the dock. She's been in grade two at her private school for two months now and is telling me about all her friends and teachers and Puffy the hamster and how she is doing so well in math and, oh yes, Mrs. Tanaka said that the picture she drew of me and Mommy was very, very good.

I love listening to her but I find my mind drifting.

We are only a five minutes from George's and Sam's five million dollar home, so far removed from the squalor of the downtown east side, but distance does not blunt the thoughts or the pain of Tommy's death. Why would an alcoholic die from an overdose? I'm going to miss his cheery optimism, even though of late it has become increasingly difficult to share it. And Roy, how will he fare without his best friend? He will disappear into a world of drink, of course, but will he emerge this time? Although I hate what Roy has done to me, I would be lost without him.

"Daddy, you weren't listening." Ellie tugs on the arm of my jacket and, as I look down at her lovely little face, the dark thoughts evaporate. "I said I dreamed about Uncle Kevin last night. When am I going to see him again, I haven't seen him for aaaages." She giggles. "He always brings me a stuffy whenever he comes."

Her sheer joy and enthusiasm make me laugh out loud and my heart is eased. "Soon sweetie," I promise. I immerse myself in her chatter and, just as we are stepping on to the Dundarave dock, she says, "Daddy?"

I sense another switch in direction coming and I can't help the chuckle that comes bubbling up. "Yes, sweetie," I grin down at her.

"A junkie's a good thing, right Daddy?"

The blood drains from my face as a hand twists my stomach into a knot.

I stop and crouch down so that our eyes are level. "Where did you hear that word, Ellie?"

During the pause, my clenched jaw muscles start to hurt.

"It's OK, sweetie, you can tell me."

She reads my expression and looks down at the wooden decking, her voice a whisper. "I heard George tell Mommy that you were a junkie now." She looks up into my eyes, "That's good, right? Like being a policeman and helping people."

I force my jaws to relax for fear of shattering my teeth, weakened by five years of heroin use. I want to run back to George Walsh's five million dollar house and knock some teeth out of his smug five million dollar face; except that he is out; there was no sign of his dark green Bentley Continental parked in its place of pride under the porte cochère. Instead, I take a deep breath and force myself to smile. I have to tread with caution here. I can't bad mouth George because anything I say to Ellie will surely get back to Sam.

And I'm not about to lie to Ellie.

In this instant I know, without any doubt, that this is the defining moment. This very second must be the beginning of the end of my addiction. I have used my terror of the excruciating pain of withdrawal as an excuse. Detox and rehab don't have a stellar record of success but somehow, I *must* make them work for me. I have to do this for Ellie, no choices, no excuses, no more junkie rationalizations. It stops now.

I only pray that I can do it.

"Ellie, sweetie, you're getting to be a big girl now, so I am going to talk to you like you were already a grown up. OK?"

She gives a serious nod.

"Do you remember when you were sick with the chicken pox a couple of months ago, just before your birthday?"

"When I was itchy all the time?"

"Yes. Well, I have a sickness too?"

"Does it make you itchy too, Daddy?"

I almost grin because it does indeed make me itchy, "Well, yes. But it makes me sick and it's because I took this

14

very bad medicine, which I have to keep taking." I feel unworthy of her. It is like I am doing the usual junkie trick of making excuses but I don't know how else to tell a seven year old about the effects of heroin.

With incontrovertible logic, she asks, "If it's bad, why do you keep taking it?"

I fall back on the parent's perennial answer to a tough question. "It's difficult to explain, sweetie." Her look tells me she needs more. I think for a bit and then finish up with, "Anyway, Daddy has got this sickness and lots of other people do too. Some people call us junkies." I feel bad this is not good enough and frustrated that I do not know how to explain the reality of my degraded life to my innocent daughter.

Ellie considers this for a moment and looks out across English Bay. I have no idea whether or not she has understood anything I have tried to explain.

"Junkies are not bad people, honey. They've just made some bad decisions." My own rationalization makes me sick. I reeks of *it's not my fault*, the junkie's vintage whine.

Suddenly her face breaks into a broad grin. "Look, Daddy. Out there. Is that a seal?"

She skips along the dock and her innocent joy makes my heart brim with a real physical pain.

This is it. I have two months to sort myself out. In two months I have to be ready.

But can I give up heroin or am I deluding myself? Will I ever be worthy of my little girl's unconditional love?

She turns back to look at me and, bouncing with excitement, points out towards the inquisitive harbor seal bobbing in the water but, through some perverse trick of the mind, thoughts of Roy's buddy, Tommy, intrude upon my moment of joy.

Why would an alcoholic die from 'bad drugs'?

Chapter 4

I breath a sigh of relief as Ellie runs in. I trust Cal the father but what Cal the junkie might do has always worried me. She throws off her coat and hops along the hall on one foot, struggling with her boot. "Mommy, we had Italian food for lunch at the tractoria. Why is it called that? There weren't any tractors there." She vanishes, giggling, into the downstairs bathroom.

I laugh—the joke sounds like one of Cal's—and call after her, "That's great, sweetie."

Cal gives a big goofy smile. He looks like the man I fell in love with. Despite what I have to do, I can not stop myself from grinning back. A big part of me will always love this man although life would be so much simpler if I could just hate him. But I can't. Cal was my rock; the enthusiasm and idealism he brought to his job was an inspiration for me in my own work. I loved his ready laugh and gentle sarcasm when I took myself too seriously.

Then he ruined everything with drugs.

George is my rock now, a much more reliable one at that, and he is a bit more serious about things than Cal ever was. He provides a wonderful, stable environment for my darling Ellie and anyway serious is good.

"Same time next week?" he asks.

"Cal. Listen." I do not want Ellie to hear this. I check over my shoulder, move out onto the step and pull the front door closed behind me. I can not avoid a slight stagger and I pray that I won't lose my balance and fall. I fell last week on

16

a photo shoot; it took me several minutes to get back up again.

"Are you alright?" he asks, concerned.

"Sure. A bit too much sampling of the wine while I was cooking."

I don't think he buys it. A big part of me wants to tell him the truth; it would be such a comfort to have him on my side. I have never lied to him before, not even a lie of omission. I don't want to start now. For an instant I can't decide. But, as much as it would be an enormous weight off my mind to tell him, I shouldn't let him know the truth. Not yet. It might spur him into the right action for the wrong reasons. Does that make sense? I don't know any more. Maybe…

He starts to say something but before he can pursue the matter, I decide. I need to do this fast before I have another incident. "I know you're trying to be a good father," I cut him off. "I mean you *are* a good father. Ellie loves you and you're really wonderful with her. And she is the one person who trusts you completely because you're always on time when you come to visit her and you have never missed a visit in the two years since we signed the custody agreement."

I pause. He knows there is more coming and stands there with trepidation. Damn it, why do I want to hug him right now?

"The thing is, there are things in my life that… I mean…" I have to say this right but I don't want to hurt him. "Look, when we did the custody agreement, the idea was that you had two years to sort yourself out and stop taking drugs so you could have a more normal relationship with your daughter. But you haven't done anything, have you?" He just looks at me. "Have you, Cal?" He shakes his head and looks down.

Years of built up frustration overcome my feelings for him, causing the words to come tumbling out. "Oh, Cal.

17

Ellie needs more than a four hours a week Dad. She's always saying she wants to see you or call you. She asks why she can't go over and stay at your house. Last Wednesday in the middle of watching a TV show, she said, 'I want to watch Dora the Explorer. I want Dora to help me find the way to Daddy's house,' and she burst into tears.

"George is a good man and he has a great relationship with Ellie. He always says that after we're married in February, he would love to adopt her. But *you're* her father, Cal. Please, please stop using, get a job and start living a normal life for God's sake. Seeing your daughter for four hours a week is just not good enough. She deserves more." I can feel the anger burning inside and I am frightened that my body will react and let me down.

Cal is very still. He looks like a condemned man, holding his breath waiting for the ax to fall.

It breaks my heart but I can't stop now; I have to put Ellie first. "You're either in or you're out. If you're not clean by the New Year, I'm going to cut you out of her life and have George adopt. I'm truly, truly sorry but that's the way it is."

The hurt on his face is awful but I can't waver now; too much is at stake. If Kevin lives up to his promise and does his part, maybe, just maybe, it will be another lever to force Cal to stop using. Kevin can be a big softy, bless him, but I really hope he doesn't chicken out this time; maybe I'll phone and remind him.

With a firm grip on the door handle, I step back into the hallway. I don't want to hear any excuses or promises. I just need him to take the ultimatum on board and do the right thing: take action, not talk. Please Cal, no more talk.

But before I can get the door closed, he speaks. "Sam. Listen." He puts his hand out to stop it closing and my heart drops; I know what he is going to say, maybe not the words but the intent. "Listen... When I was out with Ellie today, she said a couple of things that touched me, deep down. Frightened me… I made the decision. I know you've heard this before and I know I've put it off for too long but I am absolutely going to stop using. Ellie means more to me than anything. I promise you and I promise Ellie that by New Year's day, I will be clean. Nothing will stop me this time."

The familiarity of the words is painful. I heard them over and over and over and over and over again when we were married. The same words that always preceded a total lack of action.

"Oh, Cal," I say and, as I step backwards to close the door, my foot catches on the rug. Somehow I manage to right myself and push the door closed before he can see the tears of frustration. Frustration at my illness and frustration at him and his promises.

He has *got* to get straight before I become too sick to cope.

Chapter 5

Pain.

Whatever choice I make will lead to pain.

I am going to have to suffer the crippling physical pain of detox or bear the unbearable agony of losing Ellie from my life. And, even now, I can feel the worm of heroin withdrawal drilling into my bones. I shot up at seven this morning in the alley and then again at nine thirty in the restroom of a coffee shop in West Van, twenty minutes before seeing Ellie. I hate to do it twice so close together. It's a sure fire way to deepen the habit but I need that second fix to get me through my four hours with her.

And again there is no reply to the ringing of Kevin's doorbell.

I remember that Kevin wants to speak to me about something. Sam's ultimatum drove it from my mind. And what was the matter with her? She almost fell, twice come to think of it. I don't buy that 'sampling the wine' excuse for a moment. Not Sam. Unless she's changed since she's been with George...

I try the bell again. I can maybe get through for another hour before the pain becomes too bad to manage.

I try the door handle.

It opens.

"You home, Kevin?" I call. Silence. Louder, "Kev?" He must have gone out and left the door open for me. I'll do my laundry while I wait for him. I head towards the spare bedroom.

I reach for the door handle and something stops me. Fear slithers through my gut. Every house has a distinct smell; Kevin's smells of sandalwood. But this is different. Primal. An odor with which I am all too familiar. And it reminds me of…

"Kevin." I fly up the stairs. "Kevin!" I hear the note of panic in my voice. At the top, I glance left to the kitchen, immaculate as ever, then turn right into the living room.

He is on the couch.

A jolt of electricity fires up my spine and all the hair on my body is bristling. I can feel the pump of adrenaline in my veins. Breathing is difficult.

Kevin is wearing the paisley robe from this morning. It is thrown open revealing royal blue boxers. The black and yellow handle of a fishing knife is sticking out of his stomach. High, just under the ribcage, it is angled, so the blade must be close to the heart. He is drenched in blood.

I am shocked by the wave of detachment which breaks over me; it holds my emotions in check as my old training takes over. My fingers search for the carotid artery but find no pulse. I try the other side of his throat but the cold flesh tells all. I have touched more than a few dead bodies though never the body of someone I have known well, the body of a friend whom I love. I take his wrist and try to move his arm. It's just going into rigor. He's probably been dead since very soon after I left. Even this thought doesn't break the unnatural calm that has descended on me.

I scan the body. There are no other stab wounds. There's a lot of blood, so I'm guessing that maybe the blade didn't find the heart but severed a major blood vessel, allowing the heart to keep pumping blood, and Kevin's life, out through the wound.

I direct my attention to the details of the scene. It's not a robbery. Kevin's wallet is right there on the coffee table, uncharacteristically messy right now, so is his prized Rolex, a graduation present from his father.

Something has switched inside me. My training and instincts as a detective, suppressed for so long, have taken over and I can not deny the guilty pleasure that it feels freeing, wonderful. Has it taken the death of my closest friend to make me alive?

On the floor under the coffee table is a ring; it looks like an engagement ring. Wait a minute, Sandi's not here! The calm that descended on me disappears and I rush upstairs. As much as I detest Kevin's girlfriend, I dread what I know I am going to find.

But she is not in the bedroom. Or the bathroom. A wave of relief washes through me. The bed is unmade and the quilt is thrown back. Only one pillow holds the indentation of a head. A quick scan of the room reveals nothing that is obviously out of place.

Back to the main floor and it is starting to sink in that he is actually dead but I rein in my rising panic. I can't let my feelings in. Not yet.

I go into the kitchen and pick up the phone on the wall beside the fridge. I dial nine, one... and then stop. As quickly as he appeared, the detective vanishes and is replaced by the junkie.

If I call the police now, I will become the prime suspect: the junkie friend. I need to go back downstairs, get my stuff, slink back to the downtown east side and get the fix that I now so desperately need to wash away the pain in my body and the grief in my heart. Leave it to someone else, probably Sandi, to find Kevin.

I wipe my fingerprints from the phone, go downstairs and head for the front door. I can be back on the east side in half an hour and, as soon as I find Roy, I can get well. I freeze at the front door. My clothes. I have to take them with me. I head for the bedroom and again the smell of Kevin's blood stops me.

For a moment I am paralyzed by indecision, rooted to the spot.

Then, as the familiar smell of blood stirs up memories from my former life, I know that the moment upstairs, when the cop rose to the surface, was real. In spite of all that has happened to me in the last five years, I am still a detective; a junkie, yes, a failing father, yes, but above all I am a detective. The dormant longing to be back on the job bursts through the layers of emotion under which I have buried it. For a moment, I even believe that I could give up heroin if I might just...

Now the indecision is gone; I have no choice.

I return up the stairway to the living room and recheck the scene. There are no signs of a struggle. Kevin's body is sitting upright, well back on the sofa; his body is not slumped but his chin is on his chest. The sofa has nothing on it except the body but I see a piece of paper lying, half hidden, underneath it.

I know that I should not disturb a crime scene but it does not bother me, I have to know the truth; I owe it to Kevin. I remove my handkerchief from my pocket and wrapping it around my fingers, grip the edge of the paper and pull it out. But instead of sliding free, it tears on something under the couch. I have crossed a line and this time it *does* bother me. Now I'm tampering with evidence, changing it, perhaps doing something that will confuse the crime scene techs when they get here. The paper is blank except for four words at the top of the page: 'Mom & Dad I'. The other side is completely blank. Feeling a sliver of guilt, I try to slide it back, part way under the sofa but I can not get it into the exact position.

Now the ring. It is an engagement ring and not a cheap one. A quick examination reveals no telltale engraving. This time, I am able to return it to its exact position.

Keeping my good jacket from touching the body, I lean over and look at the knife and the wound it has made. It's Kevin's fishing knife, I have seen it a hundred times on the many fishing trips Kevin, Brad and I took over the years. It is top quality. I should know; I bought if for him, almost twenty years ago, and it cost me over a hundred bucks back then. I take in the things littered over the coffee table and check that there is nothing out of place or odd in the room.

It is now way past the time to call the police, but first I need to take care of one more detail.

Clearly, I won't be using Kevin's place any more to store my good clothing. So I am going to stay dressed as I am, in my good clothes, for when the police come. It would not do to change back into my street clothes, especially with the blood on my jacket from last night. Although not Kevin's blood, it would be a complication when the police arrive, enough to make them detain me. That mustn't happen. I'm thinking like a cop but am going to act like a criminal.

I take a couple of garbage bags from the kitchen and hurry downstairs. I get my other good clothes—pitifully few of them, left over from my previous life—and fold them into the bottom of the first garbage bag. Then I cover them with the second garbage bag, add my toiletries then stuff my dirty old street clothes on top, including the blood stained jacket; I will not be washing it in Kevin's machine today… or ever again. I leave the townhouse and as I hasten up the street, I think I see the curtains twitch at Mrs. Komalski's house, next door. Just what I want is Kevin's nosy neighbor observing my movements. I take a quick look round and stuff my garbage bag in the bushes between the end of the row of townhouses and the back of the gas station.

I force in a deep breath and return to the townhouse—without seeing any noticeable curtain twitches—lock the door behind me and head up to the kitchen.

I make the nine-one-one call then go back to the sofa and stand, looking down at Kevin's body, knowing these are our last moments together. I draw myself up to full attention.

"I promise you Kev, no matter what, I will find out who did this to you," I whisper. "I promise you and I promise your parents." But my voice breaks and now, at last, the tears can come.

And through my tears, I think again of Brad.

Kevin, Brad and me, christened the three amigos by our grade eleven classmates after we pulled a prank which, twenty years after it happened, is still talked about at Magee High School. Although we have not spoken in a while, too long a while, we have a bond, the bond of a friendship that was forged in eighth grade and tempered though our turbulent adolescence. I need to be the one to tell him of Kevin's death.

I sniff twice but not from the tears. Sniffing is one of the withdrawal symptoms. The aches have already started creeping into my bones and I know that in less than an hour the pain will be unbearable.

When I make good on my promise to Ellie and Sam of going into detox, this agony will be magnified daily, getting worse and worse as my body adjusts. Through the eternity of a week the torture will reach its excruciating climax, then ease and slowly fade to a memory. But then come the weeks of rehab, weeks of learning to live one's life without succumbing to the craving for that purest moment of bliss which only heroin can bestow.

Now comes the cruelest joke of all: the system spits you out, back on to the streets of the downtown east side, with no money, no job and no home. Thus seventy percent of the graduates are drawn back into the life and are using again within three months.

The thought draws my eyes to the coffee table and Kevin's Rolex. I guess its value at somewhere north of twenty grand. It would fetch a few thousand from one of the east side's many crooked pawnbrokers. That would give me enough money to come out of rehab and take a good try at getting off the street; get a small apartment away from the east side, find a job…

Of course, this is all crap; it's my junkie mind in full delusional mode. You can't buy your way out of addiction. Everyone knows that. With a few thousand dollars, I would be getting high five, six times a day for a couple or three weeks and then it would all be gone.

Besides, Kevin's dad gave him that watch; I could never face him again if I stole it, which is way too high a price to pay.

I hear the scream of a police siren and without thinking —it feels like I am not moving under my own control, or is that just one more junkie rationalization?—I take out my handkerchief again, wrap it around my hand and grab Kevin's wallet. I open it and am surprised to see that in addition to the credit cards and the various identity cards which normal people carry, it is bulging with cash: hundreds, fifties and twenties. Why would Kevin be carrying around so much cash?

I don't have time for speculation. I take all but twenty five bucks and stuff it in my pocket, then close up the wallet and place it back on the table in the same place. "Sorry buddy," I whisper to the inert flesh that used to be my best friend… but I still look with longing at the Rolex.

By taking the cash I've crossed a line I have never crossed before. I have crossed another line by tampering with the evidence. Now that I have crossed those lines, maybe two or three thousand dollars from that watch would help me get back on my feet when I get out of rehab. Maybe I'll just…

I teeter on the edge but fortunately, I am interrupted before I get to find out just how low I might sink.

The bell rings and knuckles hammer on the front door. I run down and let them in. Two uniformed officers. One looks like he's just out of the Justice Institute with red hair and bright red cheeks covered in peach fuzz. I'm betting he doesn't shave much more than once a week. He's short too. Whatever happened to the height requirements for cops?

His partner is a hoary old timer with three chevrons on his sleeve. His craggy face has real character written all over it. The four inch scar on his right cheek speaks of his history. His uniform fits well over his ample girth. Our eyes lock and a wealth of knowledge passes between us.

"Hi Cal." He is the very picture of wariness. "You're the one who called this in." It's not a question.

"Hi Sarge. Yeah. I did… The body's upstairs."

I go to lead the way but the young cop grabs my bicep and pulls me to one side. "You wait here sir," he says in a deep voice, a voice wildly at odds with his size and appearance. Sarge looks at me, half smiles and raises his eyebrows as if to say, 'Kids eh?'

We troop up the stairs, the kid in the vanguard. The shock of seeing Kevin's body hits me all over again and I shake my head in an attempt to banish the tears that want to flow. Knowing that I have stolen money from Kevin's wallet makes me flush with shame.

The kid makes his way towards the body but Sarge stops him with, "Wait a minute, Dave. This may be a murder scene." *May* be? A dead body with a knife in the gut and soaked in blood? But then Sarge always was conservative. "You checked he's dead?" This is addressed to me.

"Yeah. For quite a few hours."

27

He nods and keys the radio on his shoulder. The model of efficiency, he confirms the death, adds that it is suspicious and requests a crime scene unit and a detective team. While he is doing this, the kid takes out a notepad and asks me for my name and address. "Cal Rogan," I say, "no address."

He looks me up and down, sees how I am dressed and his confusion turns to anger making his face redden even more. "This is no joking matter, sir," he says, "I need your address and I need it now." He's an officious little twerp and I'm starting to dislike him. Sarge is catching our conversation while he is listening for a response from his radio. He's trying very hard to suppress a grin. I suspect he's not too fond of this kid either.

"I already told you, kid. No fixed abode." The use of the word 'kid' gets a big reaction. He stuffs the notepad back into his pocket and moves toward me, his hand reaching behind him, probably for handcuffs. I straighten up and he realizes that not only am I at least eight inches taller than him but also, despite five years of heroin use, I am still built like the proverbial brick shit house. He hesitates and I think that one day, in a dangerous situation, a hesitation like that may cost him dearly.

"Back off, Dave." Sarge rumbles. "He's OK and he's telling you the truth. Just wait 'til the detectives get here." It feels good to have Sarge in my corner right now.

Dave however is definitely not a happy camper but screw him.

Sarge keys off his radio. "Who's the vic?" he asks, more out of interest than need to know.

"His name's Kevin Wallace. My best friend."

"Sorry to hear that," he says and he means it. "How'd you find him?"

"Well I came over here to see him and got no reply, so I tried the door and it was open. I came in and here he was." The truth, as far as it goes.

"The door was locked when we got here." Said evenly with no hint of guile but Sarge never misses much.

"Yeah, I locked it behind me when I came in." I'm hoping that I'm not giving any tell that I'm hiding something.

Sarge just nods. "Detectives should be here soon. Dispatcher says they're pretty close by. Your old buddies, Waters and Stammo: the gruesome twosome," he chuckles.

I draw in a deep breath and let it out slowly.

"Did Steve make sergeant yet?" I ask.

Sarge gives me a long, hard look and shakes his head.

Steve Waters and I worked a lot of cases together on the downtown east side but I dread facing him. Just over three years ago, he found out I was using. He tried to cover for me but when it all came out, they fired me and his imminent promotion to sergeant was put on hold. I doubt he will ever be able to forgive me for that.

Steve is a good guy and a great cop and I'm glad it will be him looking into Kevin's murder.

On the other hand, his partner today, Nick Stammo, is an A-1 prick.

Chapter 6

I am now well into withdrawal, sniffing every few seconds and my gut hurts. My neck muscles are sore and the pain is worming its way into my bones. Worst of all I am feeling edgy and kind of twitchy. I can not stop myself from scratching. Soon my concentration will dissipate. I'm good for about a half hour max, then I'm going to be in a bad way.

Sarge and the kid have gone, the forensic team are upstairs and I am in the downstairs bedroom with Steve and Stammo. I have just finished telling them about everything that happened today, leaving out only the details of the money I have stolen from Kevin's wallet and the fact that I have a blood stained jacket stashed in a garbage bag behind some bushes. Either would just raise too many questions and put me in the frame.

Both of them know what my sniffing and general twitchiness are about. I feel ashamed that Steve can see me like this and I can see he is disgusted but, despite how he must feel about me, I think he is at least a little sympathetic. If it were up to him, he would let me go now. Stammo, however, wants to take advantage of my situation and try and catch me in a lie. He and I have a history and he would love to have the upper hand. Nick Stammo is everything that a cop should not be. He's a bully and cares more about closing a case than about catching the right offender. He's also lazy and I am surprised that Steve and he are working this together. Stammo is tall and skinny, a bit like Roy but without the charm.

He questions and re-questions me trying to find a hole in my story, but as I am telling the truth he can not catch me in a lie. His weasel face is showing his frustration and it angers me that he is so bad at his job. If I were doing this interrogation there are a host of questions I would ask that he does not even come close to thinking about.

He keeps hammering away for about fifteen minutes and then, to my surprise, he says, "Well I don't think we need keep you any longer, Rogan."

They walk me to the door and Steve asks, "Where will you keep your good clothes now that you won't be coming here any more?"

I haven't had time to think about that and I tell him so.

"So Cal, where are your other clothes?" he asks.

My mind races.

If I tell them the truth, it will seem suspicious that I hid my clothes in a garbage bag up the street. They will want to look at them and will see my blood stained jacket. Even though it is not Kevin's blood, they will not know that until they have it tested, so it is an odds on certainty that they will arrest me if they see that jacket.

If they arrest me, in my pocket they will find the cash I took from Kevin's wallet providing a ready made motive. Then, on top of that, I'm going to have to go through the agony of withdrawal in a holding cell. The horror of it makes me break into a cold sweat and ratchets the pain up a notch. My breathing is heavier and I can feel a pulse in my neck but, despite the fear, the cop, who has been buried inside me for so long, wants to speak up. The only way I can rid myself of the unclean feeling that has enveloped me from the instant I snatched Kevin's money, is, like Juliet, *to make confession and to be absolved*. Maybe I can also use this to make good on my promise to Ellie and Sam, my promise to get clean; maybe I can tough it out in a cell. There is no evidence tying me to Kev's murder, they'll have to let me go

31

eventually and, when they do release me, the heroin will be flushed from my system. I make a snap decision: I am going to go for it.

"My clothes are in—"

Then it hits me: if they arrest me, they will stop looking for Kevin's actual killer. Less than half an hour ago, I stood by the body of my best friend and made an oath to him and to his parents that I would find out who killed him. If I let them arrest me, he and his parents will not get the justice they deserve. Nothing can come ahead of this oath; Kevin's death must not go unavenged.

So what am I going to tell Steve and Stammo? My mind, made sluggish by the pain, can only come up with, "—uh, in the laundromat. You know, that one on Fourth, where the woman will do your clothes for you. I've got to go and pick them up now. Good job you reminded me."

"I thought that they'd stopped doing people's laundry for them." Steve says evenly.

Oh shit. "No, they still do it." But I know he's going to check on it—I would in his shoes—and then he will know that the laundromat on Fourth stopped doing washes for people over a year ago. "They started again a few months back," I add.

There is a long silence.

"Why don't we drive you there?" Steve offers.

I look at my watch. "My stuff won't be ready yet. Not for another forty-five minutes or so." I'm getting in deeper.

Stammo joins in, "We can take you there now. It'll be better than waiting here with your dead friend upstairs."

"I've got something else to do first."

"What?" asks Stammo with a smile which shows his cigarette stained teeth. No one ever taught him how to do a smile that wasn't creepy.

My mind somehow cuts through the pain in my body and goes into overdrive. I have to come up with something

32

plausible. Quickly. Then, out of nowhere, I remember a course in undercover work; one thing stuck in my mind: *Make all your lies as close to the truth as possible.*

"Isn't it obvious? You know I'm an addict and unless you're blind or stupid," I let my eyes linger on Stammo, "then you'll know that I am in real need of a fix right now. So what do you think I am going to do? Shoot up here in front of you? Go shoot up in the fucking laundromat?" I rein in my rising temper. "I need to go somewhere quiet and take care of business."

Steve looks hard at me. "OK, Cal." He knows I am lying about the laundromat but can not quite decide why, so he makes the compassionate choice for me and the more comfortable choice for himself. If he thinks I'm going to shoot up now, he wants me out of this house and out of his sight. The thought floods me with shame. Junkies feel stabbed by shame every day but the look in Steve's eyes sharpens the blade for me.

It is Stammo's turn again. "So where can we get hold of you if we need to ask you any more questions?"

I look him in the eye and I can see he is enjoying this. I can't hold back. "Listen, you smug bastard. You know where I'm at. I'm living on the street or in flophouses on the downtown east side. If you want me, get your lazy ass in gear and come and find me." He tenses and his hands are balling into fists. This close, I can smell the stale cigarette smoke on his clothes. I look him straight in the eye and in that instant I know he will not try anything. He must remember the last time we had a run in like this. But I was a cop back then, not just some junkie.

Steve defuses the situation. "Do you still hang with Roy?" he asks calmly.

Without taking my eyes off Stammo, I nod.

"OK, no problem. We can find you through Roy." He hands me his business card. "Give me a call first thing

Monday morning, we'll probably want to talk to you some more. I'll see you, Cal. Take care." I am dismissed.

"Yeah. See you Steve." I hold Stammo's gaze for a moment longer, then bestow a false smile on him, turn and take off.

I wonder how quickly they will go and visit the laundromat and what they will do when they confirm the lie.

Chapter 7

The pain is unbearable. I have got to get well and, for a few blessed moments, I need to blot out the horror of Kevin's dead body on the couch. And Roy's friend Tommy, what about his death? There's no way it's connected to Kevin's. But on the other hand, I just don't believe in coincidences.

Where's Roy, I *need* him now. Is he drinking away the memory of Tommy's death?

Roy has always been my link. I give him the money to buy my drugs and in return, I pay for his booze. A strange symbiosis.

But where the fuck *is* he?

He is not at Beanie's Eatery on Hastings Street. Despite its cutesy name, it is a hole but it is his favorite place; he is always there on Saturday when I get back from seeing Ellie. Always there, ready with my drugs. Where is he? A grim thought fights its way through the pain into my consciousness. What if Roy is dead too, like Tommy? *Is* there some link between Tommy's and Kevin's deaths? Is there a link to Roy? And to that blood on my jacket.

I can't think clearly and I can't take the time to think it through. I can not even take the time to mourn Kevin. I have to take the risk and go and make the buy myself. I think about my promise to Sam that I will stop using. As soon as I can, I will get into detox and break out of this cycle. But I can't think of that right now. My whole world has shrunk to one screaming need.

I make my way towards the Carnegie library at Hastings and Main, I probably won't be recognized there. I keep my

35

face covered by buttoning my jacket over my chin and pulling the peak of my Chicago Cubs cap down over my face.

The steer spots me before I am halfway along the block. "Whatcha looking for man? Down?" From a mile off, he can spot a heroin addict in withdrawal. His ravaged face tells me he's been a user for a long time. Is this where my face is headed?

"Yeah."

He walks me into the alley beside the library and leads me to another ravaged face slouching beside a dumpster. A frisson of fear passes through me. I drop my head further forward, the better to cover my face. Street dealers work in groups of three or four: the steers who guide customers to the dealer; the dealer who holds the drugs and does the actual transaction; and the money man—who is often the muscle too—he holds all the cash. I do not care if the dealer sees me; it is the guy holding the money that I worry about. I do not know which of the people hanging in the alley is the money man—a quick glance does not reveal any familiar faces—but if he sees me and recognizes me, I am screwed.

I offer the dealer five of Kevin's twenties. "Gimme ten points."

He does not take the cash. He looks long and hard at me. Maybe an ex-cop gives off a vibe that these guys can sense; it's one of the two reasons I get Roy to buy for me. Maybe he is going to refuse to sell to me. As if in anticipation, the pain ratchets up a notch and I hear myself groan.

He too is a junkie. He recognizes the groan and knows it is genuine but still he holds back. I want to grab him, shake him and scream my need into his face.

He looks up and down the filthy alley and turns back to me.

"Fuck off," he says.

Hating myself for it, I plead, "Please man, I really need it."

No reaction.

"Please."

He looks up the alley again and makes a small gesture towards me with his head. He is signaling the muscle. I've got to go. Fast.

All choice is gone. I have to go to the dealer in the alley where I woke up this morning. The alley fills me with dread and the man who holds the money there knows that I have stolen from him. But I have no choice. I shuffle down Hastings trying to avoid any movement that exacerbates the pain. It is impossible but I try. I ignore the Guatemalan and Salvadoran dealers who control this block. No matter what I offer, they are not going to sell to me. They deal only with their own and anyway they mostly deal in coke.

Finally I make it to the maw of the alley. It beckons me in and for an instant my fear almost overcomes my need. Who am I kidding? Nothing overcomes this need. I plunge in and make my way to the dealer standing beside the dumpsters. He looks askance at me; he is searching his memory.

I brandish the hundred dollars, still clutched in my hand —it's a miracle that someone did not see it and mug me en route—"Gimme ten points."

He looks long and hard. "Hundred fifty." Bastard! So much money for a gram of powder that started life in the poppy fields of Afghanistan and sold for a hundred and fifty bucks a *kilo*. Only criminal enterprises can make markups of one hundred thousand percent.

I don't want to show that I have more money on me. "OK, how about seven points?"

He shrugs. The money and the seven flaps of precious powder change hands. As I push past the dealer, I notice that he is looking at a big guy, dressed all in black, standing about twenty yards away. The money man. He is looking at me and talking on a cell phone. I recognize the face. He knows me and he knows Roy.

I run out of the alley as fast as I can.

The need to be indoors and off the streets is warring with my burning need to get well. I am only three blocks from the Lion Hotel, staggering from the pain as I walk there.

Then I see him, standing outside Sunrise Market. Roy. My relief at seeing him safe is eclipsed by my anger. Where the fuck was he when I needed him to buy me my drugs? He sees me and says something but I can not catch what he is saying. I don't have time for him now. Saturdays he likes to cross examine me about my visit with Ellie.

He looks agitated. "Rocky—"

"Not *now* Roy." I do not have time for his drama. I push past him. "Come and see me in an hour."

He grabs my arm. "Rocky, you gotta listen to me—"

"In an hour Roy." I order as I snatch my arm from his grip.

I run past Sunrise and through the door to the Lion Hotel.

Only a few minutes now. Hang on. Hang on.

***

The room is bleak. Four walls, dirty and battle scarred from the drunks and junkies who are the only denizens that the once respectable hotel has known in its recent past. But at least it will provide me shelter for a week, thanks to ninety of the dollars that I withdrew shamefully from Kevin's wallet.

I'm slouched on the rickety old bed. The place provides clean sheets but the bed beneath them…

But right now my mind is focused on the eight items in my lap.

There is no world outside this room. No daughter. No friends, dead or alive. Nothing but me, my need and my heroin.

As always, I force myself to do it right, subjugating the burning need to be rid of the pain to the consequences of screwing up. I slip off my jacket and roll up my left sleeve, over the elbow and halfway up my bicep.

Tear open the first package, remove the swab, find a good site—they're getting fewer and fewer—and rub the alcohol over the target. Wipe my fingers with the swab.

Now the rubber tie. Tie it tight over the muscle and grip the long end with my teeth.

My avowal to Sam inserts itself into my consciousness. *I promise you and I promise Ellie that by New Year's day, I will be clean. Nothing will stop me this time.* What if they could see my now? What would they think? Will I ever be able to rid myself of this need and follow through with that promise? Somehow I must.

Can I stop now? Go cold turkey in this ruined room?

Maybe I can...

But not now. I can't think about that now.

Open the little pill box of filters, place one on my right knee. Remove the safety cap and balance the needle with great care on my left knee.

Hang on, the pain will soon be gone.

Force my hands to be steady, open four flaps and pour the precious contents into the spoon; I shouldn't be using four points, it's too much but I need it right now. Rip the plastic container with my teeth and pour half of the sterile water over the white powder.

Soon, baby, soon.

Fumble for the lighter. Why does it take four tries to light for God's sake?

Heat up the spoon. Come on, come on, COME ON.

A junkie's a good thing, right Daddy?

Through the pain, I burn with shame. If Ellie could see me here, doing this, what would she think?

The liquid is bubbling. It's ready. Don't rush at the end.

Put the spoon on the bed beside me and hope it doesn't scorch the blanket but I can't worry about that now. Drop in the little cotton filter.

As I reach for the needle, the tremor in my hands causes me to fumble and knock it. It falls and lands point down in the floor, spearing a wad of dried bubble gum spat on the disgusting carpet by a previous inhabitant. Revulsion rises in my gorge as I carefully pull it out.

I can't find the antiseptic swab. I need it to clean the needle.

Where the *fuck* is it?

Careful not to spill the precious liquid cooling in the spoon, I scrabble among the things around me but it's nowhere to be seen.

A fresh wave of pain runs through me. Cal would never use this contaminated needle but Rocky can only think of getting well. I'll have to risk it, even if it kills me.

Spike into the filter, beveled side up, draw back on the plunger.

Almost there, almost. Needle at the proper angle, try not to think about the saliva in the bubble gum or the mouth from which it came, slide it into the vein, pull back a little on the plunger.

No blood in the needle. Damn it, I'm not in the vein.

Try again. No go. Shit. *Shit.* It's getting harder and harder to find veins.

Again.

Blood, thank God, got it.

Yank off the rubber tie with my teeth.

Push the plunger home slowly, slowly, slowly.

Pull out the needle, drop it to the floor and press where the little spot of blood has formed.

In a moment it's coming. Release, comfort, bliss. If I can get clean for Ellie and for Sam I will never experience it again. How will I live without...

Oh... Oooh... Oooooooh.

The world slows as a warm and gentle wave suffuses me and washes the pain out of every cell and every care out of my soul. Oooooooooh, God, that's good. I look up for a second and smile as my head nods forward.

Just floating...

Chapter 8

The yellow and black handle protruding from his chest is all that I can think about; the fishing knife that I bought for him was the instrument of his death. But wielded by whom? Who would ever think of murdering Kevin?

The note under the couch—"Mom and Dad I"—was a clumsy attempt to make it look like suicide. I do not even know for sure if it was Kev's handwriting.

The ring on the floor was an engagement ring. Was Kevin planning to propose to Sandi or had he already done so and she turned him down? Or did they have an argument and she threw it back at him? I wonder if she was there in the morning when I got there; she usually was on Saturday mornings. But I remember that in the afternoon, when I ran upstairs to the bedroom, there was only the indentation of a head on one of the pillows.

If I were running the investigation, I would start with Sandi and then talk to the neighbors, especially Mrs. Komalski who is right next door to him; she misses nothing. If I were running the investigation... The thought gives me a physical pain. Kevin's death has triggered my longing to be back in the department, a longing that I have suppressed for years.

But what if I *did* investigate his death? What if I could find the killer? *And* get clean? Would that give me a shot at getting back into the VPD? All my logic tells me that they would never rehire a former addict but dreams are not always beaten down by logic.

My thoughts are interrupted by a double knock on the door that has to be Roy. He doesn't ever live in flop houses. He says they make him feel caged. He lives out in the open air, under bridges, in doorways or under trees, and he prefers it that way. I have observed how twitchy he can get indoors. I'm surprised that he is here at all. It must be important.

I can not help feeling a bit guilty about the uncharitable thoughts that I had for him earlier and about the brusque way I treated him outside the Sunrise market. I'm glad he's here, maybe he can tell me more about Tommy's death too.

I put a welcoming smile on my face as I unlock the door and open it wide.

The guy dressed in black from the alley steps into the room. His fist is headed towards my face and he's as big as me. But slow. I slam him with the door and push him off balance. His ham-sized fist sails past my ear as I grab his arm and spin him hard into the room. His head adds another insult to the poor, abused wall opposite the door and in that instant, while he is still dazed, I grab his lapels and drive my forehead hard into his nose. It gives out a satisfying crunch.

Before I can complete the ballet by bringing my knee up into his groin, I hear, or maybe just sense, that he is not alone. Springing to my left, I spin back to face the door, just in time to see the end of a four foot length of rebar, which was being aimed at my back, finish its arc and make contact with the elbow of the man in black. The crack of splintering bone is quite satisfactory; the screech of pain which follows, not so much.

The wielder of the re-bar is not an inch less than six foot eight and he is veritable Goliath from hell. His tightly tattooed arms, which are fifty percent thicker than my thighs, have completed the second wind up with the re-bar and he is stepping into the swing like an oversized Barry Bonds.

He looks very tough and he scares the hell out of me. These guys are not here to beat me up. The re-bar tells it all.

They are here to kill me.

And I have just one shot; if it fails, I'm dead, or worse, crippled for life.

I pivot to my left, shoulder to the wall, and drop into a crouch bringing my right knee up to my chest. Braced against the wall and with every ounce of my strength, I drive my right heel hard into his kneecap as the re-bar whistles over the top of my head.

For a normal man, the kick would demolish the knee joint, leaving everything below the femur hanging like wet spaghetti. But for Goliath it does not. However, it has, at the very least, shattered the patella, inflicting enough damage to drop him backwards, bellowing, onto the bed, which promptly gives up the ghost and falls apart under his weight.

I grab both the window of opportunity and the garbage bag with my clothes. In three seconds flat I am out of there. Members of drug gangs are sometimes armed and I doubt Hell's Goliath would have any qualms at shooting me.

Trying to ignore the pain in my foot from the kick I delivered, I hare down the hallway, tensing my back against the almost inevitable thwack of a bullet and praying that the injury to his knee will spoil his aim. Bob, the manager of the Lion, is coming out of his office, drawn by the noise from the room. He is carrying a baseball bat and blocks my way. He knows me well enough as a good, regular tenant so I should be able to talk my way out of this.

"A couple of dealers tried to kill me." I say, "I'd leave it alone if I were you."

I look back. There is no one in the corridor and the noise from the room is changing. The shrieks of the man in black have turned into sobbing and Goliath is now shouting profanities. I hear him bellow, "I'll fuckin' kill you Rogan." Shit! How the hell does he know my name?

Bob's a good guy. He takes a long look at me then says, "OK. Get outta here. But don't you think of coming back any time soon. I can't have 'em coming back for you." He goes back into the office and I hear the click of the lock and the sliding of the bolt but by then I am halfway down the stairs on my way back to the streets.

As I push through the door of the hotel, I almost knock over an old man in sneakers and a beige gabardine raincoat who is running on the spot in front of the hotel. It is Nelson, a regular fixture on the downtown east side. Nelson can be seen at all times of the day, running anywhere and everywhere. No one has ever seen him walk. Nelson is not playing with a full deck and should be in care but, like so many others, the health care system has abandoned him to the streets. He is an old-timer whom Roy and I have always helped when we can. Right now he is in a state of high agitation.

I do not have time for Nelson right now; I have got to get far away from this location. But before I can run off he says, "Rocky, it's Roy, come on, quick." He takes my arm and starts a fast shuffle down Powell Street towards Oppenheimer Park, dragging me after him. The sentence was a great effort for the usually monosyllabic Nelson. I tighten my grip on the garbage bag and jog along beside him.

On the corner of Dunlevy is an ambulance, red and blue lights strobing. The paramedics are lifting a body on to a stretcher. I sprint past Nelson and get to the ambulance as they are wheeling the stretcher towards the open back doors. Roy is conscious and they have a clear plastic oxygen mask over his face. I lean over him and he mouths the word "Sorry." Now I know how Goliath and his buddy were able to find my accustomed hang out and how they knew my name.

The paramedics slide Roy into the back of the ambulance.

"Can I come with him?" I ask.

"You a relative?" the female of the duo asks.

"No, but—"

"Sorry, sir. Only relatives."

"Where are you taking him?" I ask.

"St. Paul's."

Her partner closes the back doors, gets in the cab and drives off.

My strategy for survival on the streets has claimed another casualty. But now I know what I need to do.

Chapter 9

"You have *got* to be kidding me." I am stunned by what they are saying.

"The forensics don't lie, Cal."

It is Monday and we are sitting in an interview room in the Main Street police station. It is hard to be here again. It makes me think of the good times that I had working here and makes the loss of my job in the VPD so much more painful. I try to deny it when I am on the streets but in this building there is no escape from the fact: I was and always will be a cop. It is in my DNA, programmed at the deepest level. The fact that I no longer have a detective's badge is the most devastating aspect of my spiral into addiction.

Steve's bombshell has shattered my one faint hope of getting back into the VPD, a hope that has been growing in me since Saturday: solve Kevin's murder and be welcomed back into the fold. I long to be back in this building and part of the team again, doing the one thing that gave the most meaning to my life, but Steve's bizarre pronouncement that Kevin's death was suicide has ripped that hope away, leaving a profound sense of despair.

"I wish to hell the forensics did lie, Rogan," Stammo is saying, "Because if it *was* murder, I would go full blast after you."

I ignore him. "What was the TOD, Steve?"

"As close as they can figure it, he died at around 9:30, give or take a half hour."

"So you could have done it before you left there." Stammo can't resist taking another shot.

47

I turn on him. "Make up your frigging mind, Stammo. What are you saying? It's suicide or murder?"

"The pathologist says it's suicide," he gives me that creepy smile again, "but I've got a couple of questions about that." He glances at Steve and I feel uneasy at the silent communication which passes between them.

"First thing is we want to know why you tampered with the crime scene." He leaves the statement hanging.

They know about the money. I work hard to keep the mixture of shock and guilt off my face. If they search me, I still have most of it in my pocket. It is the perfect motive for murder. Is this talk of suicide a ploy to catch me out in something?

"What?" I try to cover my fear by sounding incredulous. "How d'you figure that?" It comes out with more of a squeak than a ring of righteous indignation.

"He left a note. It was on the floor, part way under the couch. Did you happen to notice it?"

I keep the relief off my face. I can not see any downside in going for the truth here. "Yes, I did. And, before you ask, yes, I did move it to look at it. It was snagged on something under the couch and it tore when I pulled it out. I'm sorry."

"We're wondering if maybe you touched anything else," Steve says.

"I admit I looked at the diamond ring that was on the floor and I put it back in exactly the same position but that's it. I didn't touch anything else."

"What about the knife?" Stammo asks.

"Definitely not."

They are silent. It's an obvious move to see if I will talk and volunteer anything else and I am gripped by a mad desire to fill the void by telling them about the money; it has weighed on my conscience from the moment I took it. But instead, I push down the guilty feelings and ask, "Why does the pathologist say it was suicide?" I direct the question to Steve.

48

His face is blank. "We checked with the laundromat, Cal," he says. "They haven't offered a do-your-laundry service for over a year. So where the hell were your good clothes on Saturday and why did you lie to us?"

Fortunately, I expected this question and have a plausible lie at hand. I start with the truth, "They were in a garbage bag. I hid them in the bushes at the end of the street."

"Why'd you do that, Rogan?" Stammo demands.

I put on a sheepish look. Now for the lie. "Because I had heroin with me. I couldn't run the risk that you would find it and seize it and maybe arrest me, so I put it in the bag with my clothes and hid it."

Again they exchange looks. "Give us a minute, Cal," Steve says and he and Stammo leave the interview room.

I suppress a strong desire to slide my garbage bag under the chair but I dare not draw attention to it; they will be watching me in the two way mirror. After the incident at the Lion Hotel, I moved into a hostel and I am not allowed to leave anything there during the day. With Roy in the hospital, I have no one to leave my good stuff with so I've had to bring it with me. I am wearing my good jacket for this meeting but my street jacket, with the blood on it, is in the bag.

I look at the mirror. I know they are there but what are they discussing? Are they going to leave me waiting here for an hour? Or two? Will they keep me until withdrawal starts? Is this whole suicide theory part of a plan to put me at my ease and then entrap me with some damning evidence?

The door slams open and they walk back in. I can sense a tension between them.

"OK, Cal," Steve says. "We are still treating this as a suicide. There was no sign of a struggle. His Rolex and his wallet full of credit cards and some cash were there in full view, so it wasn't a robbery."

Again I suffer a twinge of guilt as I think of the money from Kevin's wallet that is in my pocket.

"The knife was his own knife," Steve continues, "with only his prints on it. The slight blurring of the prints indicate that he pulled the knife into his chest himself. The only prints in his apartment were his, his girlfriend's and his mother's. Oh, and yours. But they were only downstairs and on the phone in the kitchen. On top of that, there was the note. As you know, it said, 'Mom and Dad I.' We think he started to write a suicide note and then abandoned the idea and just went ahead with it."

Although I feel an element of relief that maybe they are not thinking of accusing me, this suicide theory feels wrong. When I think about it, I know in my heart that Kevin would never kill himself. I start to say this but Steve cuts me off. "We talked to his parents and his mother said that he had been depressed lately and this was corroborated by his girlfriend. She works with him and said that he was having some difficulties with the project he was working on.

"Because of who his family is, the Coroner got Dr. Marcus to come in on Sunday and do the autopsy. She couldn't find *anything* that points to murder. She's even released the body to the funeral home, in deference to his parents, who still carry a lot of weight in City Hall. I'm sorry Cal, your buddy Kevin killed himself."

I look across the bare table. In the two way mirror, I can see myself and the backs of their heads. I wonder if there is anyone on the other side of the mirror. *Is* this all an elaborate trap to catch me out and try to make me for the murder? Or is that just junkie paranoia?

I think back to the crime scene. The body, the knife, the things on the table and the note do all point to suicide, except... Why didn't he finish writing the note? Why stop after four words? I remember the note... and I think I know what's wrong with it.

"Steve, Nick," I use Stammo's first name to try and get him on side. "I knew Kevin well. We've been friends since eighth grade. We've been through a lot together and I see him every week, every Saturday. I can tell you right now that he did *not* commit suicide. His mother is not the best person to make that judgment; she has always been a borderline depressive herself. And I wouldn't take the word of that bitch of a girlfriend on anything. Kevin just would not kill himself, especially not over something at work. It doesn't make sense."

They have made up their minds. "Listen, Cal. We have no evidence. If the Coroner's office says it's suicide, we can't do anything more. I know it's hard when a good friend has killed himself but you need to accept—"

"Christ, Steve, save me the counselor speech. I'm telling you that Kevin *didn't* kill himself and if you guys won't take the time to prove it, then I sure as hell will." My earlier despair disappears. Kevin *was* murdered; I'm sure of it and I'm going to prove it and rub their noses in it.

Stammo stands and leans over towards me, his white fists placed knuckle down on the table's surface. "Stay out of this Rogan. Just remember that you're not a cop any more. When you were one, you weren't much of one, so just stay the fuck away from this."

His cheap shot at me is so weak that I don't even think about taking the bait. He wants me to lose it and take a punch at him. As sweet as that would be, I just smile at him. If I hit him it's assaulting a police officer; if he hits me it's police brutality. So I say, "It's probably a good job that you're too lazy to pursue this case Stammo, because you're sure as hell too stupid to solve it."

"OK. That's enough." Steve cuts in, grabbing Stammo's arm before this whole thing escalates out of control. "We met with you to discuss this as a courtesy, Cal. We've told

51

you where we stand and that's it. I think you'd better go now."

I nod to him. I shouldn't have put him in the position of choosing between Stammo and me. With as much dignity as I can muster, which is not much, I pick up my green garbage bag and head for the door.

"Wait a minute, Rogan."

Stammo is looking at the bag.

"Lemme see that."

"For Christ's sake Stammo, there are no drugs in there now. I wouldn't bring drugs into a police station."

He takes the bag from me, empties it out on the table and starts rummaging through my things. I am embarrassed that this is the sum total of my possessions and angry that Stammo is pawing through them. A pair of underpants fall onto the floor. I glance at Steve and his look of pity cuts into me.

Stammo lifts up the jacket, looks at the blood stains and smiles at me "Maybe we should take your advice and look into this a bit more. I'll take this. I wanna test that blood on it."

"Fuck off, Stammo. I woke up on Saturday morning like this. It was on there when I went to Kevin's."

"Whose blood is it, Cal?" Steve asks. He looks embarrassed; he knows where Stammo is going with this.

"I don't know Steve. When I woke up it…" Then it all comes back in a rush. "Wait a minute, I *do* remember. It's Roy's. He was drunk the night before, got belligerent and threatened some other old drunk. The dumb bastard drew that stupid great knife that he loves so damn much, then cut himself on it. I got his blood all over my jacket when I dragged him out of Beanie's."

Stammo is calm now; he sports the smug smile of success. "Well, that's OK then." His voice is oozing sarcasm.

"But I'm sure you won't mind if we verify that will you Mr. Rogan?"

Steve intercedes for me. "Nick, do you really think—"

"You know the law here, Rogan." Stammo continues as if Steve had not spoken. "We do have the right to seize that jacket as possible evidence."

I look at Steve, knowing that he won't let Stammo get away with this. After a couple of seconds staring at Stammo, he just shrugs. *Et tu Brute*.

I have no choice. I want to tell them that it is cold outside at nights and I need the jacket but that would just be too demeaning.

I start to stuff my things back into the garbage bag.

However, maybe I can eke an advantage out of this situation. Now it's *quid pro quo* time.

"Steve. Will you do just one thing for me?"

"Sure." Said cautiously.

"Can you give me a copy of the suicide note?"

Stammo is in there like a cat after a bird. "What the fuck for?"

I just stand and wait for Steve to answer. He glances back and forth between Stammo and me, looking for a way out. I think Stammo's glare tips him over. "Sure. Why not?"

When he brings me the copy, warm from the Xerox, I am sure that I'm right. Kevin was murdered.

And I am going to find his killer.

Chapter 10

I hate this fuckin' place. Full of freakin' yuppies with their flashy clothes and cell phones. These days ya can't tell if someone's talking to themselves 'cause they're looney toons or 'cause they're on a phone with one of them ear things. The whole freakin' world's gone crazy.

I feel real out of place here. I wouldn'a come here at all but Rocky likes it. He used to come here with that bastard Kevin and some other friend, Brad I think his name was. But I gotta say that they do brew a nice beer and I got a real thirst on me after two days in the hospital.

"Thanks for bringing me, Rock." I take a long swig of the lager. "And thanks fer gettin' me outta St. Paul's. Them walls was closing in on me."

"No prob, Roy." Rocky takes an equally long swig of his I.P.A. It's too bitter fer my taste but he just loves it. "It was difficult finding you in there, not knowing your last name…"

He leaves it hanging. I've never told nobody on the street my last name, not even Rocky, and I'm not about to start now. I kinda like that it bugs him.

He looks at me over his beer and I know that look, it's his cop look. I ain't seen that in a long while; it's good to see, it reminds me of the old Rocky, but I wonder where it's coming from.

"While you were in the hospital Roy, I made a big decision," he says.

"What's that, Rock?"

"You've heard me talk about my buddy Kevin?"

Oh fuck!

"Yeah." I say, keeping my voice real even.

"I was at his place on Saturday, you know to change my clothes before going to see Ellie, but when I got back there in the afternoon, he was dead. I found the body. Someone had stabbed him."

I feel my eyes open up wide. I gotta keep control now. I can't let him guess what I know or how I feel. 'Specially how I feel.

"What happened?" I ask, still keeping my voice nice and even.

"This morning, I met with my old buddy at VPD, Steve Waters. You remember him, right? They said the forensics point towards suicide, but I can't accept that. I knew Kevin. He would never kill himself."

I know why he would.

"I decided that I'm going to look into it myself and find out who killed him."

I take another long drink of my beer to give myself some thinking time and, as a thousand things spin through my mind, there's one thing I know fer sure: nothing good can come of him investigating Kevin's death. I got to head him off from this and I think I know how to do it.

"Well, *I* been doing some thinking too, Rock." I can hear the sarcasm in my voice and so can he. "The reason I was in the hospital in the first place was 'cause of you." I stop to let that sink in and from the guilty look he's giving me I guess it does.

I take a quick look around; ya gotta be careful, even in a place like this. I drop my voice to a whisper. "You can't go on supporting your habit like you have been, eh. It was OK to roll the odd dealer here and there. Stealing from drug dealers ain't really stealing anyway. And you was smart, ya never picked the same guy twice and ya didn't restrict yourself to the downtown east side neither. Ya kept a sense of proportion too. Never rolled no one for more than three or four grand. Never hit the same gang too often. Never nothing to draw serious attention. That was smart.

"But this last time ya blew it. Ya picked the wrong guy to roll. He was too well organized. He had backup. And worst of all, he got a good look at the both of us, eh. When he came after you at the Lion, you was just plain lucky to get away with it." I look hard at him. "I wasn't so lucky."

"Yeah, I'm sorry about that, Roy, but—"

"But nothing. While you're on the street you're a liability to me. What you need to do now is forget this whole thing. If the cops say it's suicide then that's what it is. You ain't a cop no more Rocky, they fired your ass two and a half years ago," I can see that hurts him but I gotta press on, "so just leave it alone. Now's the time for you to get into detox and right after that into rehab."

Before he can argue with me, the food's delivered by a snotty looking waitress. I drink down my beer and order another one. She gives me a look like I'm something she just stepped in.

"You're right, Roy."

What!

A sadness comes into his face. "Do you know what Ellie said to me on Saturday?" he asks. "She said, 'A junkie's a good thing, right Daddy?' Right there and then I knew I had to get straight for her."

God bless little Ellie. If we can get him off the streets before he learns too much…

"'Course you do," I say. "It's gonna be hard but you gotta do it. For yourself and for that cute little girl of yours. You'll be able to get back on your feet, get a place and maybe have her live with you on weekends or something. You can take her to a fancy Italian restaurant anytime you want. Maybe invite me to come and stay sometimes so that I can meet her, just like you've always promised. I'd like that. I would." I think I'm getting through to him.

"This morning I called the help line for the detox center on East Second," he says, "They're full at the moment but they put me on their waiting list. Said that they should have a place for me in a week or ten days. I've got ten days to solve Kevin's murder."

"You sure they can't get you in there sooner?" I ask.

He nods.

Well, that's it. Rocky's never lied to me; the only person he ever lies to is himself. I just gotta find a way to stop him doing any investigating. Maybe even...

"How did Tommy die, Roy?" he asks out of the blue.

I feel the sadness coming on just like a wave washing over me. Tommy's death has really got to me, especially seeing as it was all my fault. I have to look up and blink so as I don't start bawling. If I hadn't'a... Ahh, what the fuck! There's no point in dwelling on it. What's done is done, even though it never should have happened. It's brought home to me how life on the streets is, whatja call it?... fragile, that's it, fragile.

I really wanna tell him... Maybe I should... Get it off my chest and tell him the truth, the whole truth.

"Well, it's like this..." As I get my thoughts together, it hits me as to what the truth will do to Rocky; I don't wanna be the one to tell him, it'll tear him apart *and* it will make him even keener to look into Kevin's death. "Not now, Rock. It's too soon. I can't talk about it right now. Maybe later." I hope he ain't gonna push it.

I can tell he's not satisfied with the answer but he just lifts his glass and chinks it against mine. "Here's to Tommy. And here's to you, Roy," he says. The beer feels good going down. I have to work hard to stop myself from finishing it all in one go. I wonder where he got the money to bring me here.

Oh, no. Don't tell me he's...

"Rocky," I lean towards him and whisper, "where didja get the money for all this? You haven't been..." from habit, I look around again for dangerous faces, "y'know."

"No Roy. After what that dealer and his pit bull buddy did to you on Saturday night, I've retired from that game." He has a guilty look on his face now. "When I found Kevin, his wallet was on the table with a load of cash in it." Now he's blushing. "Before the police arrived, I took most of it. Left just enough so that it wasn't empty. What was strange was that when I got round to counting it, there was over a thousand bucks. Why would Kevin have that much cash on him?"

I choke on a piece of pizza trying not to laugh. We're eating and drinking on Kevin's thousand dollars! There's a word for this. What is it? Rocky'd know; he's full of big words. What is it?... Ironic. That's it. For a minute, I think about telling him but I'm still sober enough not to, thank God. He wouldn't find it funny.

"I dunno, Rock. But look at it this way. If Kevin had known that you've made the decision to get clean and get off the streets, he'd have wanted you to have that money." I can't hold back a smile. "Even if we are blowing some of it on beer and pizza." I take another long drink. "Sometimes it's nice to have money to burn."

His face has taken on a funny look. Like a kid who just got slapped by his Ma. Now what have I done?

"Rocky. What is it? Was it something I said?"

"No Roy. I was just remembering something. You didn't say anything wrong."

"What is it?"

He looks off like he's looking out to sea. He's deciding if he's gonna tell me something.

Still not looking at me, he says, "When you said about having money to burn, you reminded me of when I was a kid. I found this envelope on the front step. I must have

58

been about ten years old at the time. I opened it and it was full of money. I counted it. It was a lot of money; for us it was anyway. I ran into the kitchen laughing. 'Mom,' I shouted, 'we don't have to move again. Look what I found out front. You can pay the rent and we can stay here.'

"Without a word, my mother took it from me, looked at her name, hand written on the envelope, then removed the contents. One by one, she tore each banknote and dropped the halves in a saucepan, then lit the last two notes on the red hot element of the electric stove and set fire to the lot. Nine hundred and thirty dollars, three months rent in those days, burned to ashes.

"As a kid, I couldn't work out why she would do that. I still can't." He shakes his head.

It's the first time in the seven years since I first walked up to Rocky in his unmarked cop car, that he has ever talked about his childhood and it has answered a question that I have always wondered about. It makes me sad all over again.

Chapter 11

The mansion is the most beautiful home I have ever been in; it has always been a haven of peace for me, warm, loving and welcoming. Approaching the threshold today makes my stomach churn.

It was for Kevin alone that I attended the funeral where I avoided the judgement in the eyes of my fellow mourners by keeping my head bowed. If I had to make eye contact— as I did with a tearful Brad when we raised the casket to our shoulders—I gave the half-smile, nod, avert-eyes routine which one adopts at funerals.

But here it will be different. I am here not for Kevin but for his parents—*if* they will allow me in—and I will be on view to many who knew me before my very public descent into a life of drugs.

Before I can succumb to my rising desire to turn tail, the imposing front door is opened by the ramrod straight Arnold, Mr. Wallace's personal assistant. "Mr. Rogan," he has called me that since we first met, when I was twelve. "Come in."

He takes my jacket and hangs it on the rack in the corner of the hallway. It looks out of place beside the expensive furs and cashmere coats and, although it is my 'good' jacket, I am acutely aware that my definition of good has eroded. I glance down at what I am wearing and feel shamed, which feeling is then magnified tenfold as I place my garbage bag of belongings under my jacket.

"My condolences," Arnold enunciates in his very British accent; I assume it is for Kevin's death, not for the nadir to which I have fallen.

"And mine to you Arnold." I say gratefully, for I can not yet detect any indication of a changed attitude toward me.

"Thank you, sir." He has known Kevin since he was born and must feel his loss sharply. I look into his eyes. It is the first time that I have really looked at him, looked at the lithe, whipcord thin man in the expensive Harry Rosen suits, the man who has been with the Wallaces since long before I was born. I wonder how he feels about Kevin's supposed suicide. Does he accept the story or does he know, like me, that Kevin would never take his own life? Now is not the right time but at some point I must question him about what he knows or thinks.

For the first time in my life, I offer him my hand and, after a moment's hesitation, we shake; I wonder if the presence of death sharpens the need for physical contact between those still living. His hand is cold and the shake is long and beyond firm; I almost wince.

I extricate my hand and before taking the four marble steps down from the entrance lobby, I scan the large reception room for Mrs. Wallace. I catch the glances of several of the mourners and can read the emotions from discomfort to disdain to disgust. One elderly matron, one of Kevin's aunts I think, nudges her companion and points in my direction. Again I feel like turning tail and running out of this house and back to the solace of the familiar faces on the downtown east side.

Then I see her, the woman who was as much a mother and more of a role model to me than my own mother had the ability to be. I hurry down to join the end of the line of people who are waiting to offer their condolences.

As I wait my turn, I sense a presence move in behind me and feel compelled to turn round. I am face to face with the

Mayor, a not unexpected guest. I did not notice him at the graveside although I recognized several Federal MPs, a cabinet minister, two senators and a smattering of provincial politicians. All are here out of respect for Kevin's family and, perhaps, for the healthy campaign contributions which they are known to bestow. Like most cops, or ex-cops, I have a healthy distrust of politicians of any stripe but the current Mayor of Vancouver is the exception.

Yet he is an enigma to me: law and order has always been a big part of his political platform—which has garnered the support of almost everyone in the VPD—but, in complete opposition to that platform, he has stated more than once that he strongly supports the legalization of drugs: all drugs, not just marijuana. It is a position that, as a cop, or rather as an ex-cop, makes no sense at all to me. Why make drugs more available than they already are?

"Mr. Mayor." I extend my hand. "Cal Rogan."

He obviously recognizes me but he can not put a context around me, something every politician hates.

"Mr. Rogan." His shake is firm. "I'm pleased to meet you again, even if on such a sad occasion. You were a friend of Kevin's, of course." It is said in such a way that it could be a statement or a question.

"Yes, sir. Since we were at Magee High School together."

Somehow, my reply triggers his memory. "Of course, I remember that Kevin and his family were at the ceremony we had for you and Detective Constable Waters at City Hall, right after you sent those gang members to jail."

His smile is warm but I sense a wariness. His clever control of the publicity around the big gang bust that Steve and I made helped to reinforce the law and order side of his platform and was a contributing factor to his re-election. However, my fall from grace into my current life caused him some embarrassment. I feel myself flushing with embarrassment of my own.

He resolves the conflict in a manner foreign to most politicians: by being straightforward. "I was sorry about what happened to you. You were a good detective and you had the potential to be a great one. What is your, uh, status at the moment?"

The junkie in me wants to lie about how great I am doing but under the scrutiny of those clear blue eyes I say, "To tell you the truth sir, I've pretty much hit rock bottom. I think I'm ready to quit now. I know I am. But what I don't know is if I have the strength to do it." I am shocked at my own candor.

He looks hard at me, delving beyond my eyes. "I think you do, Cal." He puts his hand on my shoulder and I feel the electric charge of his charismatic personality. "If you ever straighten yourself out, maybe…" He hesitates for a long moment, wishing perhaps that he had not spoken so quickly. "I can't promise anything but when you're *sure* the time's right, come and talk to me anyway."

I am overwhelmed by what he is saying but before I can formulate a response, Kevin's mother's hand closes over mine and she pulls me to her side. I hungrily take this as a sign of her acceptance of my presence here. "Mr. Mayor," she says. "How good of you to come."

As they talk cordially, like the old friends they are, I feel that yearning deep in my soul to be a cop once again. It is a yearning that I have suppressed since the day they fired me. I swallow and my eyes prickle. Was he saying that if I sort myself out, I can get back in? He would somehow smooth the road back to the department? Can he do that? If so, why would he? And why would he say so now, today, the day of Kevin's funeral?

Maybe his attitude towards the drug problem is part of this. Maybe he thinks that as an addict I am in favor of legalization and that, if I were to return to the VPD, I would become an inside supporter of his position. But maybe I'm more of a cop than an addict, because legalization has never made any sense to me; I just can't see how it would work.

Even so, the Mayor is a man with a reputation for doing the right thing. If I could be a cop again... No, I must be reading something into what he said. But what if...

He moves on to make room for the next person who wants to pay her respects to Kevin's mother. He holds me in his gaze for a moment, then nods and walks away. I stay beside Mrs. Wallace, her hand tight on mine, while she receives the condolences of one person after another.

I let my eyes sweep the room but this time, they are the eyes of a cop rather than those of a junkie. I know many of the people here. Could one of them be responsible for Kevin's death? It comes as a shock to me that it is more than likely. Murders are almost invariably committed by someone known by the victim and all of the people here fall into that category. In fact, if I think about it, it is almost certain that Kevin's murderer is in this room at this very moment. The realization makes my spine tingle and I find myself looking in a very different way.

Kevin's mother is still holding my hand and I feel her tense. I can sense how she feels about the next, and last, person in line, an opportunistic, beady-eyed and overweight Provincial politician whom I detest.

"Please excuse me; I must rest for a moment." She turns to me, "Cal, please give me your arm and take me into the library."

Feeling the daggers coming from those piggy political pupils, I give her my arm and lead her into the library. It is a large, imposing room with an almost uncountable number of books on a labyrinth of shelves. In my youth, I spent many happy hours here, learning the love of literature; now I feel like I should not be here, as though somehow I am unclean or unworthy. As soon as the door closes behind us, she stops leaning so heavily on me and says, "I had to get away from that little worm. He hated Kevin for some reason. I'm surprised that he had the temerity to come to the funeral."

She leads me to a corner of the room where there are two overstuffed leather chairs, sits and indicates for me to follow suit. "Cal, it has come to my attention that you have been saying that it is your belief that Kevin did not kill himself. Is that correct?" How did she know that?

"Yes Ma'am. You know that it was me who found him and I just can't believe that he did it. First—"

She cuts me off with a graceful gesture and fixes a daunting gaze upon me.

"Now you listen to me, California Rogan." Her use of my full name is an indication that she is both serious and disapproving. "I know it is difficult for you to accept that Kevin killed himself. He was my son and I loved him; I loved him dearly and I knew him better than anyone." She swallows twice and looks up at the ceiling, eyes blinking, struggling for control. It is a struggle that she wins, for now. Her voice has taken on a commanding air, words stilted and precise. "He was suffering from depression. He always has. You didn't know that, did you? He confided in me that he was having some serious problems and it was weighing very heavily on him. I tried to get him to put it in perspective but I'm afraid that it just overcame him. I can assure you Cal, it was suicide."

I feel a strong need to tell her otherwise. "But Mrs. Wallace, I saw him every week, every Saturday. He never seemed to be depressed, or at least not depressed enough to kill himself. On that last day, he was worried about something and he wanted to speak to me about it but I put him off until later." A lump has now formed in my throat as I remember how I failed to respond to Kevin's need. "I know I should have taken the time to talk to him but nevertheless—"

Again she cuts me off. "Yes Cal. You should have taken the time." Her eyes drill through me. "Then you might have learned what was bothering Kevin and you'd understand why he chose to take his own life."

Guilt knifes through me. If I had taken the time to talk to Kevin and listen to his problem, would he still be alive today? I ask the question, dreading what the answer might be. "What was it?"

She looks at me, her face obdurate. "Believe me Cal, you don't want to know. No one must ever know, not even my husband; especially not my husband. It is something I intend to take to my grave. "

What could possibly be so bad that it would make Kevin commit suicide? Sure, he looked a bit down when I saw him on Saturday morning, but *kill* himself? I just don't buy it. Or am I trying to convince myself? Salve my conscience because I didn't take the time to talk to my best friend when he needed my help. I have to know what was bothering him so much.

"Please Mrs. Wallace, I have to know. What was it?"

The vehemence of her reply is unprecedented, her voice harsh. "You must let this go, Cal. If you don't, you may unearth something, something terrible, something that will shame Kevin and ruin this family. Just accept that he killed himself for God's sake."

She takes two deep breaths to calm herself. "You don't understand depression." Her voice is almost back to its normal timbre. "You can't possibly. I have suffered from it my whole life. Look!"

She rolls back her left sleeve and thrusts her wrist at me. There are two white scars, one more prominent than the other. It embarrasses me to see them. I feel like some depraved voyeur. As I stare at them, I feel an insistent itch in the crook of my left arm. "Those are the result of my own lost battles," she says. "There are others. Kevin inherited it from me. I try to tell myself it is not my fault but…" a single tear runs down her cheek. "Please Cal. Leave it alone. No good can come of you trying to prove otherwise. Promise me you will leave it alone." She shakes my arm roughly. "You have always been like a son to me and I am asking you to promise me now, as a son."

The tears making furrows in the makeup on her cheeks are mirrored on my own. I tell her. "Of course… I promise Mrs. Wallace."

"Thank you, Cal. Thank you."

But as she takes my hand and kisses it in gratitude, I know, like Hamlet, that my words may prove *as false as dicers' oaths*.

Chapter 12

I know what Sandi thinks of me and it is nothing good. About a month ago I overheard her ask Kevin, 'Why do you let that junkie loser come here anyway?'

Sandi Palmer and I have detested each other from the get go. I think she is a cold, calculating bitch who was never good enough for Kevin but, right now, I am not looking at her through junkie's eyes. She is tall and leggy with a fantastic figure and the long black hair, pale skin and blue eyes that speak of Irish ancestry. Her face is spoiled by her mouth which has a mean set to it and that, I believe, sums her up; except for the fact that she is a PhD in biochemistry and, according to Kevin, is one of the most brilliant people he ever knew. They met at Kevin's employer, QX4, where she is a scientist in the research department that Kevin manages. Or managed.

She was Kevin's girlfriend for about six months and was pretty much living with him. I am surprised that she was not there on Saturday morning.

But then again, maybe she was. When I went there in the morning, Kevin took a hell of a long time to come downstairs and open the door. She could have been upstairs. They might even have been... I make a mental note to find out. Now I'm thinking like a cop again.

And, of course, there is the question of the engagement ring on the living room floor.

She is talking to Brad when I walk over from the library.

It is almost four hours since my last fix and I feel myself getting jittery. I have some heroin with me but it would feel disrespectful to shoot up here in the Wallace's home. I guess I still have some scruples. Scruples or not, Rocky will need to get well in an hour but there are things Cal needs to do first: for one, interview Sandi.

Brad and Sandi are standing at an angle to each other, both facing away from me, both holding small plates of canapés. I stop a few paces away from them and listen in on their conversation.

"I don't think it would have made any difference if he had known," Brad is saying. "What's important here, Sandi, is that Kevin left a legacy: his work. You have to take that and make it bigger, better, more successful than even Kevin could have." I can not help but smile with affection for him. This is classic Brad: the quintessential positive thinker. He has attended every positive thinking seminar known to man and has read everything from Horatio Alger and Napoleon Hill to Tony Robbins and Deepak Chopra. Only Brad could find a positive in the horror of Kevin's death.

I return to an earlier thought: Kevin's killer is somewhere in this room; it could even be Sandi or Brad. My conversation with Mrs. Wallace has hardly dented my belief that Kevin was murdered.

"Hi guys," I say.

They turn towards me and Brad beams in counterpoint to Sandi's sour expression which falls a soupçon short of a sneer.

"Hey, Cal. Great to see you." Brad gives me a hug and pats me on the back. I reciprocate uncomfortably although feeling grateful for his acceptance of me. He releases me and holds me at arm's length. I watch his face grow serious. "How was Mrs. Wallace?" he asks.

"Pretty bad. She is adamant that Kevin really did kill himself and she has found a way to blame herself for it."

Sandi nods but addresses herself to Brad making a point of not recognizing my presence. "People tend to blame themselves when a loved one dies by their own hand. It's natural. I keep asking myself why I didn't see it coming. Or did I see it coming but pushed it out of my psyche and buried my head in the sand. I just can't help thinking that if I had just paid a bit more attention, maybe…" Her voice trails off and I have to admit that she seems sincere, even if way off the mark.

I try to offer some consolation. "Sandi, maybe you didn't see it coming because it didn't happen that way. Have you considered that they may have got it wrong and that it wasn't suicide?"

Her mouth tightens like she has bitten into a lemon and her eyes flare at me. "What, you think he was *murdered*?" She is having difficulty modulating the volume of her voice and a few of the guests, including the Mayor, turn in our direction. "You knew him. Why would anyone want to kill Kevin?"

I do not want to attract the attention of the Mayor by getting involved in a scene with Sandi. I drop my voice to just above a whisper. "You're probably right Sandi but I really need to know one way or the other," I say. As soon as the words are out of my mouth, I realize that I have already broken my promise to Mrs. Wallace. Pushing down my feeling of guilt, I continue, "All I can say is that all my instincts tell me that he didn't kill himself. And those instincts rarely let me down when I was a detective."

"Oh, right. The cop…" Her tone and the dismissive look on her face ricochets around in the emptiness that I feel at no longer being in the VPD.

"Hey, guys," Brad the peacemaker interjects, "let's not argue. Kev wouldn't have wanted that. He would have wanted us to, I dunno, like… well, celebrate his life, accept his death and move on."

I ignore Brad's words and take a different tack with Sandi. "I know that I'm not your favorite person in the world and let's face it, I've never done anything to merit your respect. But one thing we do have in common is we both loved Kevin." I pause and she acknowledges me with a half nod. Quarter nod, really.

"Everyone may be right that he committed suicide but I just need to verify that for myself. I can't live with the thought that Kevin killed himself and that I never saw it coming. You must feel the same way." Another pause but I can see that I have struck a chord.

I press on, "Here's not the place but I want to have a talk with you. His mother says that he was worried about something. I'd like to ask you about it but not here. Would it be OK if I dropped by your office and had a chat?"

In the silence I look to Brad for support.

"Cal," he says, "I think that Sandi is in enough pain that she's not going to want you rooting around and making matters worse. I think you should just drop this whole thing. You're not a cop any more and the detectives on the case *and* the Coroner's office agree it was a suicide. Let's leave the dead in peace, eh? We need to move forward here."

I feel the frustration turn in my gut. I must not let the creeping pain of withdrawal push me into anger.

I look at Sandi and realize that she has been scrutinizing me while Brad was speaking. She seems to come to a decision and throws me by putting a hand on my arm. "Listen, Cal. I can't imagine how Kevin could be a murder victim. But you were his friend and I know he loved you like a brother," she puts her other hand on Brad's arm. "You were both like brothers to him. I guess I owe it to him to give you the benefit of the doubt. Why don't you come by my office on Thursday morning at nine. We can talk then."

She reaches into her purse and brings out an elegant gold case from which she slides a business card. She hands me the card and, with a dismissive gesture, she turns her attention back to Brad.

I am stunned at her acquiescence. I felt sure that she would turn me down. I can't help wondering what made her agree; knowing her, it was well thought out. And Brad. Why did he try and derail my attempt to meet with her? What does he think I might unearth?

Rather than delve into these questions now, I decide to devote my time to the main reason that I came here today and do it before the cravings get unbearable.

Chapter 13

The hand is stark white with a road map of blue blood vessels meandering under the parchment that once was skin. It is emaciated, stiff and cold to the touch. I take hold of it gently, wary in case it should snap off from the withered arm. I think back a quarter century to the first time I shook this hand and was pulled into a world that I had read about in books and only dreamed existed in life.

Without letting go, I sit beside the bed. "How are you sir?" I ask. I have never called him anything other than sir. He is a wonderful man; my respect for him is absolute. My withdrawal causes me to sniff twice and I feel deeply ashamed that the evidence of my addiction is open for him to observe.

"Hello, Cal. It's good to see you." Kevin's father is frail from the ravages of the cancer that is eating him alive but the disease has not yet robbed his voice of the strength, warmth and a charisma that not even the Mayor can match.

"It's good to see you too, sir. I'm sorry that it is under such circumstances."

"Indeed. A man should not outlive his son. Even if he will soon be following him to the undiscovered country."

I complete the quote. "...*the undiscovered country from whose bourn no traveler returns.*"

He smiles. "Your mother did well by you, Cal."

"Yes, sir. I know."

"A man who loves Shakespeare will never be alone."

We sit in silence, his hand in mine, his eyes closed.

I think he has fallen asleep. I do not have the heart to wake him but I know that I must. There is one thing I need to know before I have to leave to deal with the encroaching pain. I can not hold in the groan as a wave of it washes through me. The sound stirs him and he again quotes Hamlet. "*When he himself might his quietus make with a bare bodkin.*" He is silent for a moment. "Cal, I don't want to believe that my son stabbed himself but they tell me he did. Even my wife believes he did it."

He leaves the unasked question hanging in the air but I do not answer it. Instead I ask, "If he didn't kill himself, who did? And why, why would anyone want to kill Kevin?" Will the father tell me what the mother will not?

His hand tightens on mine. "That is what *you* must find out, Cal." His intensity sends a shiver down my spine. Again I think of my promise to Mrs. Wallace and again regret my cowardice in giving it so readily, knowing that I would betray it on one word from this man.

"I know he didn't do it, sir. I'm going to prove that he didn't *and* find out who did."

He squeezes my hand. "I want you to do just that. If there is *anything* you need, any help that I can give, you are to call this house and speak to Arnold. I will see to it that he gets you whatever you want. He has been with me for over forty years. He is *completely* loyal to this family. He will do *anything and everything* that is necessary to help you find Kevin's murderer. Find out who did this, Cal, no matter what the consequences."

"I intend to, sir."

His hand relaxes on mine. "And I intend to postpone shuffling off this mortal coil until you come back here and sit beside me and tell me that you have brought my son's killer to justice."

My voice trembles as I say, "I will sir, I promise you."

And now my stomach is in turmoil. Partly because I dread that I may not still have the chops to carry through on this promise and partly because I must now own up and face the music by telling Mrs. Wallace that I have already proven false to the promise that I made to her less than an hour ago.

And it is all overlaid with my screaming need for heroin.

Chapter 14

I fell again today.

It was at Pigeon Park. I crouched down to take a picture of three elderly drunks, sitting on a park bench, passing a bottle in a brown paper bag. It was a wonderful shot. It captured a moment of carefree joy in three careworn lives and will be perfect for the dust cover of the book. But as I straightened up, my right leg—it's always the right leg—folded under me. As I rolled my body to protect the camera, I fell on my right shoulder but the pain that stabbed through me was eclipsed by a sudden rush of fear.

A huge, tattooed man, whom I have seen several times recently, hanging around near where I have been photographing, was suddenly looming over me, projecting a sense of menace. A five thousand dollar Hasselblad would buy a lot of drugs. He changed his grip on his crutch and reached down for the camera but with a surge of anger, I clutched it to myself vowing that I would not give it up, not for the camera itself—George would happily buy me a replacement—but for the perfect shot I had just taken; *that* I refused to surrender.

But I was surprised.

"Let me help you up," he said with a Chinese accent. "Give me your hand." I examined his face and could see no ill intent. He gave me a broken toothed smile. "It's OK," he said. "My mother has falls all the time."

I had difficulty getting up and so he leaned his crutches against a wall and, balancing on one foot, he crouched down, picked me up and sat me on a bench: quite a feat of strength.

He sat beside me for a moment. "Why you take photos of drunks and junkies?" he asked.

"It's for a book, a photo essay about addiction."

He stared into my eyes. "Why?"

All the clever rationale, that my agent and publisher had lauded and encouraged, floated out of my mind under the gaze of this giant. And the truth flooded in. "I guess I want to understand why people become addicts."

He grunted as he hauled himself to his feet, hopped over and retrieved his crutch. "It's because they a bunch of lowlifes," he said as he limped away and stationed himself outside the art gallery across the street, not looking directly at me but kind of scanning the crowd.

Now three hours later, I feel a frisson of fear as I park the Porsche. Several pairs of eyes swivel in my direction. Cal always says that the people on the streets of the downtown East side are harmless but it's easy for him; he's big and he's tall and he's tough. When *I* look at them, all I can feel is an undertow of violence flowing beneath their resentful looks.

I don't know whether to leave my camera equipment in the back of the SUV or bring it with me. If I bring it, I risk someone grabbing it from me and maybe pushing me over or hitting me or worse. If leave it, I am inviting someone to smash the back window and grab it anyway.

The ever present specter of my MS decides it for me. Carrying the heavy camera cases could easily throw me off balance. Anyway, I am parked right outside the coffee shop where Cal agreed to meet me, so I can keep an eye on the car from there.

My heartbeat triples as, without warning, my door flies open. I was *sure* it was locked. I can not suppress the gasp of fear as I spin to my left and grab at the door's arm rest, hoping that I can slam it shut before whoever—

"It's OK, Sam. It's only me."

"Cal." I breathe a huge sigh of relief, tinged with anger at him for scaring me and at myself for being scared. "You frightened the life out of me."

He smiles and shakes his head. I know what he's thinking. *Scared-ee-cat.* I should be mad but I can't suppress a laugh from bubbling up.

I get out of the car and take his arm in case I stumble. I hold on tight and then am aware that this is the closest we have been physically since we separated and, unexpectedly, I find that I like it. This makes me feel awkward and I can sense that he feels it too. He looks at me and smiles that goofy Cal smile. I don't want to give him the wrong idea but I can't explain why I am holding his arm so tightly. I need to keep the knowledge of my MS from him. The decisions he needs to make now must be made because *he* wants to make them, not out of pity for me. I pray that the news I have for him will be the lever that decides him to do the right thing. If it doesn't, well…

He leads me into the coffee shop. It is remarkably up-market for this part of town; it's warm and cozy and the coffee smell is strong. We order and I pay.

I follow Cal to a table. It's low and there is a love seat beside it, its back to the wall. Cal sits and I have to choose between sitting opposite him and talking loudly or sitting beside him which feels just a bit too intimate. I opt to sit beside him but avoid any physical contact by sliding as close to the arm as I can.

After the moment of silence he asks, "So what did you want to talk to me about? When I called last night to talk to Ellie, you said it was urgent."

Now that the moment is here, I find myself avoiding it for fear that I will lose my temper and precipitate the opposite of what I want to happen.

"How was Kevin's funeral yesterday?" I ask.

"Pretty grim."

"I'm sorry I didn't come." I can't tell him why: that I felt so sick I couldn't even drive. "I can't believe he's gone. It was only last Saturday; you were with Ellie and he was probably doing it right then. Oh my God, I didn't think of that before. Why would he kill himself, Cal?"

"He didn't."

"But it said in the Sun that he—"

"Yes, I know. But I knew Kevin. He wouldn't do that."

"But Cal—"

"And I have evidence. I'm going to check it out tomorrow morning. Then I'll be sure."

I can feel the old sadness hit me. To Cal, solving a murder was always more important than anything, more important than Ellie, more important than me. Even though heroin took it all away from him, he is still driven by the need to be a cop. It was that drive and the sheer dedication that he had to solving crime that first attracted me to him so many years ago. I guess I am attracted to men with that kind of drive. George certainly has it for business. Will George's drive to do the next deal, and then the next and the next, eventually distance me from him too?

The barista calls out our order and Cal goes to fetch it. He is not dressed in the clothes that he normally wears when he comes to see Ellie; these are more worn and stained. I am seized by a strong desire to go and get my camera and photograph him, to look into his soul through the camera lens which always reveals the truth. Just to know why.

But now is not the time, damn it.

He sets the coffees down on the table. "How are things looking for getting into detox, Cal?"

"I'm on the waiting list. They're full right now and with the winter coming on people are going into detox just to get off the streets. They said that they won't have a place for me for another week or ten days. There just aren't enough detox beds in Vancouver." I recognize his tone of voice. It's the addictive voice talking. The whiny one that rationalizes why he has or hasn't done something. God knows I heard it enough times when we were married. I look at him and I know he recognizes it too.

"I'm afraid that's not good enough, this time, Cal." He opens his mouth to object but I forestall him with an irritated gesture. "I got called into Ellie's school yesterday afternoon, called into the Principal's office. There was a problem in class. Mrs. Tanaka, her teacher, was asking the children what their parents did for a living and when Ellie's turn came, she stood up and said proudly, 'My Mommy's a photographer and my Daddy used to be a policeman and now he's a junkie.' Some of the less innocent kids in the class sniggered at her and one boy said something about *his* Dad showing him 'filthy junkies begging for money on street corners.' This caused the kids to laugh even more and, before Mrs. Tanaka could do anything, Ellie flew across the room and started hitting and kicking the boy. She pushed him out of his chair and he hit his head on the desk of the kid next to him. He had to be taken to Lions Gate emergency and have stitches in his forehead."

Cal's face has gone white. He just sits there, saying nothing, running the fingers of his left hand through his hair, a gesture I remember him doing whenever he was worried about something.

"Anyway, the school has a zero tolerance policy when it comes to violence. They told me she is no longer welcome there and that I have to find another school for her."

"There's gotta be something we can do to get the school to change their minds."

"I tried that. George came with me and he can be very persuasive but the school would not budge an inch. It's a private school; they can do it."

"Sam, I am so sorry." He is clearly devastated by what I have told him but I need to press on.

"I'm afraid sorry is not good enough, Cal. There are two things you need to do. First, you have to commit to going into detox. Today's the third. If what you say is true about getting in,—"

"It is, I—"

"—you have until the thirteenth of this month. If you are not in by then, as much as I hate the thought, I am going to court and quashing our custody agreement."

"OK, Sam. You have my word." He looks beaten but I have to go the next step.

"Second thing, you need to talk to Ellie and explain to her why violence is never an option when people say nasty things to her. Then you need to explain to her what your addiction is all about and what you are going to do about it. OK?"

He looks off into the distance, through the windows of the coffee shop and out onto Main Street. I can not tell what is going on in that clever mind but I can see that my news is weighing heavily upon him. After what seems an age, but is probably only thirty seconds, he reaches a decision. He nods to himself and the frown lines wash out of his face.

"When can I see her," he says. "I have a lot to put right."

"Tomorrow evening, George will be in Toronto for a meeting. Why don't you come over to the house and have dinner with Ellie and me. You can speak to her then."

"Thank you Sam. I won't let you down about this."

His choice of words is an echo of the past and brings tears to my eyes. When he first started taking drugs, he would use those very words right before he let me down. Again and again and again.

Chapter 15

"This is Kevin's office."

Sandi cuts me a sharp look, reacting to the note of accusation in my voice. "When Kevin died, I was promoted to Director of Research of QX4, so it's mine now. Do you have a problem with that?"

I am invaded by a desire to make some remark about not waiting long for the body to cool but I rein it in. I must not blow this meeting.

We sit on opposite sides of her very messy desk; Kevin would have a fit if he could see it. Under the white lab coat she is dressed in jeans, shirt and a sweater, a plain ensemble that understates her figure. Every visible item of clothing is either black or white. She is without makeup and her jet black hair is tied back in a severe ponytail.

"Look, Sandi. I'm sorry." She maintains the best poker face I have seen in a while. "The fact is that you and I have never got on that well and we both know it. But one thing is for sure, we both loved Kevin and we both have a right to know how he died. I'm sure that the coroner and the police and Kevin's mother are all wrong when they say he committed suicide and when I talked to you after the funeral on Tuesday, I felt pretty sure that you agree. I think that's why you said you'd see me here today, isn't it?"

"No, Cal, it isn't." No crack in her expression.

Did I misread her that badly? "Then why *did* you agree to see me?"

"Isn't it obvious? To try and dissuade you from pursuing this crazy idea that Kevin was murdered. It can only cause more grief for his mother, for me and, for that matter, for this company." The words come out stilted, like she is reading from a script.

In the brief silence, I can hear a buzz of conversation from the adjacent office.

"Sandi, do you have a sample of Kevin's handwriting here?"

"Why?" Her brow is furrowed and her mouth is pursed in annoyance; it is a very Sandi expression.

"Please, Sandi. Do you?"

"Yes, I do."

"Can you show me, please?"

"Why?" She asks. If she will not show me I might as well pack up shop and go.

I stand up and reach down for my green garbage bag, so out of place in the plush surroundings. It works. There is a momentary look of panic in her eyes.

"Sit down, Cal." She says it like she is talking to a recalcitrant teenager. I take my time doing so.

She takes a hardcover notebook from the credenza behind Kevin's desk—I guess I need to accept that it is her desk now—and hands it to me. I open it at random. My heart rate increases as right there in front of me is the confirmation I was seeking. About half way down the page is a section headed 'Indications of Addiction' followed by a numbered list. I look at a couple of other pages and the pattern is consistent.

I let her stew for a moment before speaking. "The police found the beginnings of a letter, supposedly a suicide note, that read 'Mom and Dad I.' You know that it was me who found the body?" She nods. "Well I remember seeing the note and something seemed wrong so I got the police to give me a copy."

I take it from my pocket and hand it to her. "Well, straight away you can see that the 'and' is not spelled out; it's an ampersand. You know how precise Kevin was; he was almost pedantic. He would never write a suicide letter to his parents starting Mom & Dad? He would start it out with 'Dear' or 'My dear' and he would write out the word 'and' in full. Plus he would have started a new line before writing the 'I' or at least put in a comma. But the real clincher is if you look at his notebook, see, here, halfway down the page. You see the word 'Indications'? See how he writes the letter I? It has little lines at the top and bottom of the letter. But underneath there is the number one which he writes as a straight vertical line with no serifs.

"Kevin wasn't writing 'Mom and Dad I' he was writing 'Mom & Dad 1', like he was making a list, maybe his Christmas shopping list. Who would write a Christmas list if they were thinking of committing suicide?"

Sandi laughs and it is not a pleasant sound. "That's it?" she sneers. "That's the proof that he didn't kill himself? If that's all you've got, you might as well—" she stops herself in mid sentence. What was she about to say? *You might as well* go? So, why would she cut herself off like that?

I drop my plan to try and convince her that Kevin's death was murder and just sit looking at her. It works.

She rises from her chair, walks over to the door, opens it and checks the hallway outside. After closing the door, she returns to the desk with a look of indecision on her face. She sits, then gets up and walks to the window. She stands motionless looking across the parking lot.

From the next door office I hear a peal of laughter. Sandi cuts a glance at the adjoining wall and, for the first time, I see a real, unscripted emotion in her face. It is fear.

I find myself holding my breath, letting her decide by herself to talk to me about whatever is on her mind. After about thirty seconds she takes a deep breath, shakes her head, walks back to the desk and perches herself on the corner. Her face is softened by an unbearable sadness.

"OK." Her voice is just above a whisper. "I am going to have to tell you this. But I need to know that I can trust you to keep it confidential and not mention it to anyone, not the police, not even Brad, in fact, especially not Brad. If word of this got out, it could ruin this company and put a lot of people out of work. Worst of all, it would shatter Kevin's reputation beyond repair and be devastating to his parents.

"The reason I'm telling *you* is that if you continue to stir up trouble by claiming Kevin's death was a murder, it might all come out and cause a lot of pain to a lot of people. So, Cal, can I trust you on this?"

I quash the feeling that she has rehearsed this little speech. I don't want to make the promise because I may have to break it. But then again, I have made three other promises in the past three days. I have already broken one and I know I may have to break them all.

I hold her eye. "Yes, Sandi. I give you my word." Sincerity: once you can fake that you've got it made.

"How much do you know about what we do here?" she asks.

"Not a lot. For some reason, Kevin never talked to me about his work." In retrospect, it seems strange; why *did* he always avoid the subject?

"We are on the brink of a breakthrough with a product that Kevin devoted his working life to developing. His thesis was that addiction is a genetically triggered, neurochemical imbalance and that addicts are born with it. He discovered that the imbalance can be changed by drug therapy."

"What, you take a pill and bingo, you're cured? You're not an addict any more? You can not be serious." I can not control the laughter that bubbles to the surface.

Sandi shushes me and, again, I see the look of fear slither across her face.

"I'm deadly serious." She leans forward as her voice returns to a whisper. "Kevin was a genius. He decided to

85

start by dealing with addiction to depressants: alcohol, heroin, Valium. He once told me that the decision to start there was in part technical but was also because of you. He wanted to develop a drug that would cure you. He never came to terms with the fact that his best friend was a jun— an addict. He worked like a man possessed, six days a week, twelve, fifteen, sometimes twenty hours a day. The only day he ever took off was Saturday and the reason for that was so *you* had somewhere to go to prepare for your visits with your daughter." Her voice is laced with bitterness at this last.

I had no idea that Kevin was so driven and I am humbled that he sacrificed his one day off to help me.

"Do you know anything about the pharmaceuticals business?" she breaks in on my thoughts.

"No, I… No. Nothing."

"Well, when you are developing drugs for use by humans, the government monitors your every move. As you go forward you have to get permissions for every phase of development. The most time consuming is getting authorization to do human trials: to test the drug on real human subjects. The submission for running a human trial can make a stack of paper five feet high. You send it in to the federal government and they can, and sometimes do, take years to authorize you to proceed."

There is silence from the office next door. She leans forward and drops her voice even lower. "Kevin did animal trials. We gave heroin or Valium or alcohol to rats and later to pigs. We got them addicted then made half of them quit cold turkey and gave the drug to the other half. And the drug seemed to work just fine, with no ill effects. Of course, we were able to check our results by examining the behavior and the brains of the rats and pigs but they can't relate their experiences, so he was very impatient to begin human trials.

"He submitted the request for human trials as soon as we started testing on animals but one of the bureaucrats in

Ottawa kept raising objections to various elements of the submission. He kept asking for more and more data and would then delay months before coming back and asking for even more. Kevin became more and more frustrated. He presented them with all the details of the animal trials but felt he was being stonewalled by Health Canada. He took it *very* personally.

"On top of that, senior management and the major investors were getting antsy. Investing in a bio-tech company is a bit like dropping cash into a black hole. It sucks it up and then tries to drag you in after it. The investors were talking about forcing management to cut back staff to a very minimum until the government approvals came through. They were hinting that they thought it was Kevin's fault, that he hadn't handled the submission properly or that he had made enemies of some bureaucrats who were now paying him back."

Sandi worries her bottom lip with her teeth. She is coming to the punch line. I catch a merest hint of her perfume. It is the same one that Sam always wears and I can feel myself reacting to it.

"So... three months ago—"

Without any knock, the door bursts open.

"You coming to the meeting San—?"

Sandi, whose face is inches from mine, straightens up with a look of guilt.

The intruder smiles. He is an overweight guy in a black suit with a slicked down comb over. He looks back and forth between Sandi and me, a salacious expression growing on his face.

"Oh, Chet. This is Cal Rogan. He's a friend of Kevin's. He brought me some papers that Kevin had left at his house." Sandi delivers the lie without hesitation. I'm impressed. It is as though she anticipated the possibility of being interrupted and had a prepared excuse for my presence. "Give me a minute. I'll join you in the meeting."

But Chet is not about to be fobbed off so easily. "What papers would those be?" Salacity has given way to slyness.

I look at Sandi and can see that she has not prepared for being questioned on her lie.

"Kevin forgot this. Left in my kitchen," I say, picking up the notebook that I used to check on his handwriting. "I thought I'd better bring it in, in case it was something important."

Without asking, he takes it from my hand and flicks through the pages as though looking for something specific.

"I see," he says. "OK." His tone indicates that it is anything but OK. "Nice to meet you, Cal." He can not come close to faking sincerity.

He takes a too long look at me before tucking the notebook under his arm and leaving, closing the door behind him.

Sandi lets out a loud breath. She is spooked, no doubt about it.

"You'd better go," she says. "That was the CEO. If he knew I was discussing company matters with you, I'd be in big trouble. I'm sorry, Cal. I can't." She gets up and walks to the door.

Screw Chet. Now I'm never going to discover what she was working up to tell me: what it was that happened three months ago.

Chapter 16

I know, deep down, that if I do not get the story now, I am never going to get it.

"Sandi, wait."

Her hand is on the door handle. She turns to me. "I can't." She shakes her head.

I have about two seconds to persuade her.

"Look, Sandi, if you don't tell me what this is all about. I am going to have to speculate on what it was you were going to tell me. Either way, I am going to put all my efforts into investigating Kevin's death and I am going to be asking all sorts of questions about QX4, Kevin's drug and anything else that I can unearth."

She opens the door and signals me to leave. I'm flying by the seat of my pants here. I drop my voice. "And I will certainly have to tell the police what you have told me so far."

This gets to her. I can see that she is frightened by what I am saying. I need one thing to tip the balance.

"I'll also have to contact the feds, Health Canada I think you said, and ask them what they know about all this."

She closes the door fast and leans back against it. Now she is terrified, which seems like a huge overreaction to me.

"You bastard, Cal! You said that you would keep this confidential."

"I will. I will." I force a smile. "*If* you tell me what happened three months ago."

She knows she is beaten and my elation at getting her to continue talking is dirtied by my feelings of guilt that I have blackmailed her like this. She walks away from the door and sits back on the edge of her desk. I stay standing. The first few tendrils of pain have started. I am on a new descent into the pit of withdrawal.

"Three months ago, Kevin got so frustrated by the government's stalling that he did the unthinkable. He started clinical human trials without waiting for the approvals to come through. He kept it secret, he didn't even tell *me* and I was his deputy director *and* the woman he was sleeping with." The hurt of betrayal sits in her eyes.

"Anyway, with the help of someone he knew, someone outside the company, he went out on to the streets and started administering the drug to alcoholics and heroin addicts. He recruited thirty of them. He paid them money, cash out of his own pocket, to keep them in the program and he conducted his tests. He was very thorough. He observed all the correct protocols, except that he didn't date the results he was documenting. He was planning to fill in the dates later, after he had the government approval for the trail.

"Things were going well, unbelievably well. Addicts and alcoholics were reporting that both the physical and psychological cravings were disappearing. They were saying that they were sure that they would be cured. It was like a miracle.

"Three weeks before he died, Kevin took an evening off and cooked dinner for me at his place and he told me what he was doing. He was so excited; he was like a kid. He said that he had made a major breakthrough. He even said that he was thinking of putting you on the drug; more than anything else, he wanted to see you cured.

"I was stunned. I couldn't believe what he was saying. What he was doing was completely unethical and totally illegal. If he were found out, the government would step in and shut down the company. Everyone would lose out, staff, management and the investors. His career would have been ruined. He could have gone to prison for God's sake.

"I pleaded with him to stop but he was gripped by a kind of madness. He kept insisting that it was the only way. He was obsessed with finishing the trials; obsessed with the thought of curing addiction. He made me promise to keep his secret and even though every fiber in me was screaming to tell company management what he was doing, I couldn't betray him. The consequences for him were too dire. If only I'd known what was about to happen…"

I hardly hear her last few sentences. My whole world is spinning. No junkie wants to be a junkie. A drug that can cure addiction is our holy grail. That Kevin had developed it and proven it is a miracle. I have got to persuade her to get me into the trials for this drug when they get government approval. Before even, if she—

My reverie is broken by the choking sound coming from Sandi. She is still sitting on the edge of the desk and she is sobbing. I walk over to her and tentatively put an arm around her shoulder. Although it is awkward, I feel a strong need to comfort her—perhaps it is an attempt to assuage my guilt at forcing her to tell me this story—but she shakes off my touch and I draw away. To hide the embarrassment, I cross the room and stare out the window at the parking lot below, savoring the idea of a drug to cure addiction. This is the answer to my prayers. As if in agreement, a sudden pain makes my bowels clench and I sniff, twice. If I can get on this drug and kick heroin, I can start to reestablish my life and be a proper father to Ellie.

The thought of Ellie restarts the tape I keep playing and replaying in my head: my meeting with Sam yesterday afternoon. The shame sits in my stomach like lead. My actions and my choices have once again forced themselves into Ellie's life. *A junkie's a good thing right Daddy?* My inadequacy in answering that innocent question has resulted in her being separated from the school and the teacher that she loved. For each hurt a junkie causes himself, he visits a dozen hurts on the people who love him. I have to break out of the cycle of addiction.

My train of thought is broken by a sigh from Sandi and then the sound of tissues being drawn from a box. As I turn back, I look at her desk. Kevin would have a fit. He was excessively neat. In the few days that Sandi has been in this office she has turned the desktop into a war zone.

There are papers, open text books, computer printouts, hand written notes on squared paper. White Post-it notes are everywhere, on books, on papers and on the small percentage of the desk's surface that is still visible. The writing on them is in a tiny script written in black pen. Everything is black and white except, sticking out from under the box of tissues, is a business card with only the logo visible. It comprises three bright slashes of color: yellow, green and purple. It stands out in contrast to the monochrome background.

Sandi blows her nose. She sits up straight and I can see that she is steeling herself for the next part of her story.

"A few days after he first told me, Kevin confided that one of the addicts that he was treating had died. He didn't believe that *Addi-Ban*, our drug, was a contributing factor but he was sad at losing a patient. Then, within a week, one more addict and two of the alcoholics died. Of course, he stopped the trials straight away but in the following few days there were another three deaths. Seven of the thirty subjects had died."

I am stunned at the contents of the Pandora's box that I have forced Sandi to open. The junkie part of me wants to run away, back to the familiarity of the downtown east side, where heroin can wash away the pain that is taking hold of me and erase the memory of what I have just learned. In the search for Kevin's killer, I have found that he was one himself.

"Kevin was beside himself," She continues. "On top of the guilt, he knew that it would all come out, that he would be ruined and that the company would be too. He became very depressed. He took time off work, which was unheard of for Kevin, and he pretty well cut me out of his life. That hurt... a lot.

"The next thing I knew, there was a phone call from his mother telling me that he had committed suicide." She breaks down into tears again.

A million thoughts tumble through the cop part of my brain.

This is the problem that Mrs. Wallace claims was the cause of Kevin's suicide. Of course, a man like Kevin would be devastated to find out that he had killed people but he was also the type of man to stand up and face the music, to accept his responsibility regardless of the consequences. Despite what Sandi has told me, my gut refuses to accept that suicide was the cause of death.

One mystery may be solved: the thousand dollars in his wallet has been bugging me. Kevin was a great user of plastic; I have seen him use his credit card to pay for a two dollar cup of coffee. Maybe the money was there to pay the addicts for their cooperation. There was enough to pay each addict about thirty bucks. A junkie will do almost anything for thirty bucks,

No, wait. The increasing pain of withdrawal is stopping me from thinking straight.

He had stopped giving out the drug right after the second round of deaths, so the cash wouldn't be for his subjects.

Regardless of the money issue, something doesn't add up but I can't put my finger on it. I don't believe every part of

Sandi's story. I have a strong sense that she is not telling me everything.

"Doing illegal trials just doesn't sound like Kevin. You mentioned that the investors and your management people were getting antsy. Is there any possibility that they were coercing him to push ahead with the trials, without waiting for government approval?"

"Not the investors. They were very much in the background, I don't even know their names. But maybe someone in management. The delays in approvals were a real problem. R&D companies eat cash like ravenous wolves. If the investors were unhappy with progress, some senior people, including Chet, who you just met, might get fired and in the process lose some juicy share options."

One of the rules of criminal investigation is 'follow the money'. She seems to be pointing the finger too quickly at the management group, the slimy CEO in particular. It makes me interested in the investors whom she dismissed too easily.

"How much money have the investors put into QX4?"

"Over fifteen million in all. More than half of it from one person, I understand."

"What's his name?" I ask.

I can not read the look that passes across her face. "I told you I don't know. They keep it pretty tight around here."

They may do but that look tells me that somehow I need to shake that bit of information loose later.

"Who helped him?" I ask.

"What?" She doesn't understand the question.

"You said that he had the help of a guy he knew, someone outside the company, when he went out to administer the drug to his guinea pigs. Who was he?"

"I don't know. Kevin never told me."

"How did Kevin know him?"

"I don't know. Why would I know that and what does it matter anyway?"

She is getting irritated at my questions. A fair sign that she has not been completely forthcoming.

"Sandi, do you have a list of the names of the people who were taking the drug?"

"No, why?"

"Kevin didn't leave any notes or computer files or anything?"

"No." She is getting irritated with my questioning. She looks at her watch.

Maybe Roy can help confirm my strong suspicion that I have solved the mystery of Tommy's death.

I need to keep her cooperative, for a while at least, until I have had all my questions answered. "I know that these questions may seem irrelevant and a bit upsetting but if you could just hang in there and answer a couple more. OK?"

She relents a little. "Sure."

"On the Saturday Kevin died, I was at his house in the morning. Were you there too?"

She looks at me with not the ghost of a tell on her face. For no apparent reason, I think of the red haired young cop that accompanied Sarge to Kevin's house that afternoon. The kid would be talking his head off right now, asking and re-asking the question. I know to keep quiet. Seconds pass in complete silence until she says, "No."

I think it's a lie. I go with my intuition. "What were you arguing about?"

"Who said we were arguing?" Worded like that, her question confirms that they were. Again I just keep quiet, leaving my question hanging in the air.

She is flustered now. "I wasn't there and I'm not prepared to talk to you about it, Cal." She looks at her watch again and glances towards the door. "You had better go now."

If I were still a cop, there would be all sorts of things I could do to pressure her into an answer. Now all I can do is ask, "Was it something to do with that engagement ring that I saw on the floor?"

"I told you, I'm not going to talk to you about my relationship with Kevin."

Time to tack onto another course. "So when did you take over Kevin's job?"

Her eyes cut away from me and back. She pauses for a moment too long. "Why?"

"When did you?"

"On Monday."

"What? The first working day after he was killed? That was pretty clinical wasn't it?"

"Oh, for heaven's sake, Cal. Do you have any idea what Kevin's death could do to the company? When we announced Kevin's death we had to show that we had a contingency plan. The Company needed to appoint a new Director of Research straight away and I was the logical choice. For what it's worth, I didn't even want the damn job. I'm a scientist, not a manager. I took it to save the company. Even so, our stock took a dive of almost *sixty percent.*"

"So, are you telling me that Kevin's desk got that messy in just one week?"

"Go to hell, Cal. Now it's really time for you to go." She gets up and opens the office door.

Sometimes, I just can not keep my big mouth shut.

She leads me in silence out of the office and back down to the lobby. At the front desk, she pulls off my visitor's badge, throws it into the box from which it came and stands motionless, disdain etched on her face. "Not a word of this, Cal," she says.

I shake my head; there is no way I would let this information become public after my encounter in the library with Mrs. Wallace when she showed me her wrist; I would never run the risk that she might succeed where previously she failed

Sandi's story has backfired on her. She told it to me to convince me that Kevin committed suicide but it has had the reverse effect. And I wonder how much of it is true? Or more to the point, what might she have left out? As I think back, I get the feeling that in some way she has been trying to manipulate me but I can't work out how or why.

I have nine days before I can check into rehab. Nine days to get to the truth.

But right now my one need, my only need, is to shoot up and staunch the pain that is coursing through me.

Chapter 17

Before I can say anything, Cal preempts me, "Brad, one of the reasons that I wanted to see you was that I need to talk to you about how Kevin died."

I glance around and drop my voice to a whisper. "Keep your voice down, Cal." I shouldn't have brought him here. Sciué is way too up-market. It's packed full of businesspeople—eating gourmet pizza, sipping Chardonnay or expensive Italian bottled water and dabbing cappuccino foam from their upper lips—and if one of them should overhear this conversation…

"You mean your theory that he was murdered?" I whisper.

"Yes and it's more than just a theory, Brad." His voice is showing his irritation and is still too loud for my liking.

I have to steer him away from this. He was a good cop, a great cop in fact, and despite the drugs and being on the streets, I'm betting that his mind is a sharp as it ever was. If he starts digging into Kev's death, he may uncover—

He breaks my chain of thought. "First thing," he says, "is that Kevin wasn't the type to kill himself. We both know that. We both knew him since we were kids. No matter what his mother says now, he was never that depressed. Plus he idolized his father and even if something drove him to think about ending it all, he would *never* have done it while his father was still alive."

His voice is starting to get louder again and I signal him to keep it down. The guy at a table to my right and behind Cal is looking at us with interest. Maybe it's because we look like the odd couple—although Cal is in his 'good' clothes, they are more than a little shabby and are in sharp contrast to me in my favorite Zegna suit—or maybe the guy has caught the drift of our conversation and is trying to eavesdrop.

Cal is really fired up by his theory, I have not seen such a gleam in his eye since before he got hooked on heroin. It is not going to be easy to persuade him but I have to try.

"But what about the suicide note he started, that—" I whisper.

"I saw it, Brad," he interrupts. "It wasn't a suicide note, it was a shopping list."

"What?"

He pulls a rumpled piece of paper from his jacket and hands it to me. I listen in silence as he relates his trip to Sandi's office and his theory about the note being a shopping list.

"Yes, but—"

He cuts me off again. "There's another thing. When I met with Sandi this morning, she did everything she could to try and convince me that Kevin killed himself. It made me even more certain that he didn't."

I try to keep the concern off my face. "What did she say?"

"She said that Kevin was conducting illegal tests of their drug."

Shit! She told him. The stupid bitch, why the hell would she do that?

He's watching me like a hawk. Cal knows me well and he's looking for a tell on my face. To give myself time, I furrow my brow in puzzlement and I stare off into the distance before turning to him.

The guy at the next table glances at us again.

I lean in towards Cal. "Sandy told you that Kevin was conducting illegal drug tests?" I put as much amazement and disbelief as I can muster into the whispered words.

"Yes. I think she said it to convince me that Kevin was overcome with guilt and that was why he killed himself. She told me not to tell you about it."

I buy some more time by taking a bite of the lox and artichoke pizza in front of me. "Illegal drug tests?"

"Yes." Cal leans in towards me. At least he's keeping his voice down now. "She said that they went wrong and that some of the addicts that were the guinea pigs died. She said that Kevin couldn't live with the fact that he had killed people."

Now which way do I go? If I support Sandi's story, it provides a good reason for Cal to accept that Kevin's death was suicide and it may be enough to stop him from pursuing his murder investigation? On the other hand, Cal may not have a badge and he may be living on the streets but he is still a cop in his very soul. Even if he stops investigating the murder idea, he will start investigating the testing itself and who knows what he will unearth then? I have to chose the lesser of two evils.

"Kevin killed people by doing illegal drug tests on them?" I say. "That's crazy. Sure, it would be a good reason for Kevin to have killed himself but I just don't buy him doing anything that illegal. He wouldn't play with people's lives. I'm wondering why Sandi would say something like that."

"I don't know. Maybe she knows who killed Kevin and is trying to protect them. It was one of the reasons I wanted to talk to you."

"It's crazy, Cal. I just don't believe it. Could you see Kevin doing anything like that? I don't buy it." My voice drops a few more decibels. "Cal, you mustn't talk like that. Imagine what it would do to Kevin's parents if a rumor like that got out." Cal idolizes Mr. Wallace. It might just be enough for him to keep the story under wraps.

"OK, OK. Don't worry. I won't say anything," he assures me but I still worry that the cop in him will not hesitate to use this information if he has to.

He digs with enthusiasm into his pizza. "So, Brad," he says, "you're in the business world. What do you know about QX4? What sort of people are on the management team over there? Could they have known about what Kevin was doing and decided to get rid of him permanently?"

I feel on firmer ground now. "I don't think so. They're a small player in the pharmaceutical business but they have a promising product. As a big part of their public relations, they had billed Kevin as the genius behind their addiction drug, *Addi-Ban*, so when word of Kevin's death hit the press, their shares took a huge dive."

"How well do you know them?" he asks.

I make a snap decision. It's better to stick with as much of the truth as I can and try and control what Cal knows rather than have him dig around where he shouldn't. "Pretty well." I admit. "It was my firm that took them public."

"*Your* firm?" That caught him by surprise.

"The original investors had put in seventeen and a half million dollars, most of which had been spent on developing the drug. Six months ago we sold fifty percent of the company on the Toronto Stock Exchange for twenty five million dollars and the shares have done fantastically well; they pretty near doubled in price. Made a lot of people rich. On paper anyway.

"But when they released the news of Kevin's death on Monday, the share price dropped sixty percent by the end of trading yesterday. The investors lost all their profits and then some. Overnight, management's stock options were worth nothing. That's why I'm sure they would never kill Kevin. It would be in their absolute worst interest."

He nods. Cal never had much of a head for finance but he gets what I'm saying.

"Sandi said that there was one major investor. Who was that?" he asks.

"Sorry Cal. I can't tell you." If I did, that would put the cat among the pigeons.

"Why? It's public knowledge isn't it? Doesn't a public company have to file reports about who their major shareholders are?"

Hmmm. Maybe he knows more about the corporate world than I thought. "Yes. But if you look, you will find that the major shareholder is an off-shore corporation. You'd never find out who's behind it."

"OK. But you know, right?" He looks eagerly at me.

I can use his faith in my being in the know. "No I don't. No one in my firm knows who the actual investors are. And believe me, if we can't find out with our resources, nobody can. But I can tell you one thing: no one involved with the company would have a motive to kill Kevin; he was key to the company's success. Anyway, think about it, in all the time you were a cop when did you ever arrest someone for a business related murder? That's the stuff of fiction."

He is silent as he digests this. He is rubbing the inside of his arm and I see a slight nodding of his head. Now is the time to get him thinking in a different direction. He's not going to budge from this murder idea so maybe I can send him down a road to nowhere.

"When someone's murdered, who do you look at first, Cal?" I ask.

Despite the years of heroin, his mind is still as sharp as a tack. He gets where I'm going.

"The spouse, most of the time. Brad, are you saying that Sandi might have killed him?"

"No. I'm just saying that it's far more likely than a bunch of businessmen from QX4."

"What would be her motive?" he asks.

If I pull back now, it will make him all the more keen to investigate Sandi. He always was a contrarian.

"Forget it Cal," I say. "It was stupid of me to say that. It doesn't make sense. Not Sandi. She may not be the nicest person in the world but killing Kevin…" I shake my head.

"Just humor me," he takes the bait. "Let's say Sandi did it. What motive could she have?"

I shrug, "Maybe he dumped her. Or maybe she thought he was cheating on her. Maybe he *was* cheating on her. We both know that Kevin was a real ladies' man. It wouldn't be the first time he'd done it to someone he was seeing, would it? I don't know, maybe she was after his job."

He doesn't seem to be convinced.

"It's pretty lame isn't it?" I say.

"What?"

"This whole murder idea." His face is neutral. "Sandi's a bitch, sure, but a murderer? Come on. And the idea of someone at QX4 killing him just doesn't fly. Why would they put their own shares in the toilet? Why don't you just drop it, Cal?"

"I don't know," he says. "Maybe it doesn't make sense that Sandi or someone from work would kill him but can you think of anyone else who might have a motive?"

"Well yeah. There is someone."

Now he's all ears.

"Who?" he asks.

"You."

For a moment he is too dumbfounded to reply.

"Me?" he takes a deep breath. "Me? Why in God's name would *I* want to kill Kevin?"

"I think you know the answer to that Cal," I say.

"Brad, I swear I don't have the faintest idea what you are talking about."

I'm sure he's not faking his response. Maybe Kevin didn't tell him. "You mean you don't know?" I say.

"Don't know *what?*" His voice has risen in exasperation and three chic businesswomen at another table turn to stare their disapproval.

I drop my voice again. "About a week or so before he died, Kevin had decided to stop letting you keep your clothes at his place and going there every Saturday to change."

"That's ridiculous. Why would Kevin do that? Did *he* tell you that?"

"No."

"Then who did?" The famous Cal Rogan temper is rising.

"In the mood that you're in, I don't think I should tell you."

"Brad. You can't just tell me that Kevin was going to cut me loose and then not tell me why or how you know this. Please." The exasperation is strong in his voice.

I wait a beat. "Sandi told me. At the reception after the funeral. She said that Kevin had decided that he should stop enabling your addiction by making it easy for you to keep using drugs while still seeing Ellie."

He is silent, staring into the distance. A lot of things are churning through that clever mind of his but the end product is confusion.

Finally he speaks. "Even if this were true *and* if I knew it, I wouldn't kill Kevin. I couldn't. I think you know that."

"I'd like to think that, Cal. But you know better than anyone what drugs can do to a person and you do still have that famous temper of yours."

Now it is my turn to be surprised because instead of objecting, Cal just nods.

"Cal, why don't you just quit. You're a strong guy, I know you can do it. You just got to have a positive mental attitude about it."

"Come on Brad, you don't know what the fuck you're talking about."

The famous temper is brewing but I'm not going to let him wriggle out of it that easily. "As a matter of fact, I *do* know what I'm talking about." I keep my voice quiet. "I've never told you this before because, well, when you were a cop I didn't want to compromise you, but I use a little blow now and again. Y'know, just at parties and things and maybe before going on a date." I almost laugh at his dumbfounded expression but I keep a straight face and press my case. "But I don't let myself get addicted. I know I can stop at any time. You just need to believe the same thing. It's all a matter of attitude and changing your belief systems. There are courses that you can go on where you can get your mind working in a positive direction and actualize all your inner strength to banish the addiction from your life."

He sits motionless looking at me and I can not tell what is going on in his head but I see a tear form in his right eye. It swells in size and trickles down his cheek. With an awkward movement, he wipes it away and stands. "I'd better get going," he says.

Now I feel guilty about trivializing his addiction; maybe it's not so easy for him to change his mental attitude.

Now he is making me doubt my own beliefs just when I need them most.

Chapter 18

On the restaurant's sidewalk patio Brad and I say our uncomfortable goodbyes. He makes his way back to his office and I, trailing my bag of possessions, head along Pender Street back towards the east side. It's a gray day. The low clouds feel like they are crushing me and I can sense the first tendrils of my four-hourly need for heroin stir the depression that is taking hold. I check my watch and see that it is only three hours since my last fix. Not good. I'm feeling like a street person again.

Kevin's words come flooding back. *Cal, I need your help on something... It's a bit difficult to talk about this but...* Was Kevin going to tell me I could no longer use his place on Saturdays? It hurts. I feel betrayed, betrayed by the one person who stood by me, never judging me through my downward spiral, then wanting to abandon me at the end, just when I am ready to turn my life around.

I feel a sardonic smile come unbidden to my lips. *Turn my life around.* Every junkie says that at least once a week. Who am I kidding? Kevin would have been right to cut me off... but acknowledging the fact does not reduce the hurt.

The lunch with Brad was surreal. His revelation that he uses coke stunned me but what really upsets me is the unfairness of it all. Why should he be able to use drugs whenever he wants without getting addicted? I was hooked from the first moment I used heroin. Why me? It's the junkie's mantra and it brings back Sandi's words from this morning. *Kevin's thesis was that addiction is a genetically triggered, neurochemical imbalance and that addicts are born with it.* Is the fact, that I'm a junkie and Brad isn't, all one huge, unfair, cosmic joke, an accident of birth?

However, I need to put all that behind me—before the pain of withdrawal clouds my ability to think—and analyze what really went on during my lunch with Brad.

He definitely had an agenda but what was it? I need to force myself to look at it through a cop's eyes. First, he wanted to convince me that Kevin's death was suicide. Then his reaction to Sandi's bombshell about Kevin's illegal drug testing was odd. He denied knowing about it and he didn't give any obvious tells that he might be lying but he just worked too hard to repudiate that Kevin would do such a thing. Yet would Sandi make up a story like that? She's way too smart not to know that I could easily disprove a lie that was so enormous.

Then Brad wanted to divert me away from investigating the people at QX4. I've got to admit that it doesn't make sense for any of them to kill Kevin if it's going to make their share price drop sixty percent but somehow Brad was just a little too keen to turn me away from the management or shareholders, even to the extent of pointing me at Sandi as a suspect. My gut tells me that Brad is up to his ears in this whole thing. There's no way he would have done anything to hurt Kevin but he is hiding something big and I need to find out exactly what that is.

And I need to talk to Roy. I spent most of yesterday looking for him but I guess he didn't want to be found. I want to see if he's ready to talk to me about Tommy's death. Assuming Sandi's story is true, it seems just beyond coincidental that Tommy died at the same time as Kevin's guinea pigs were dropping like flies.

My thoughts are interrupted by a very British voice behind me. "Can I buy you a postprandial coffee, Mr. Rogan?"

I turn to face Arnold, Mr. Wallace's personal assistant. His tall and powerful frame is dressed in an immaculate, charcoal gray, pinstripe suit, a dazzling white shirt and a military tie. He makes me feel shabby.

"Arnold… hi." I am surprised and, for some reason, pleased to see him here in the downtown core. Is this a chance encounter and, if it is not, how in heaven's name did he track me down? "What are you doing here?" I ask.

"Let's get a coffee and talk." Without saying more, he crosses Pender and leads me down to an organic coffee shop half a block north on Granville. He rebuffs my attempts to engage in conversation and the peremptory way in which he strides ahead of me stirs an irritation. He does not say a word until we are seated at a table with giant take-out cups of pungent Kenyan steaming in front of us.

Without any pleasant preamble he says, "I quite literally owe my life to Mr. Wallace and I repay my debt with loyalty to him and his family. Absolute loyalty, Mr. Rogan. I will do anything to protect them and the honor of their family name. So when he asked me to help you find Kevin's supposed murderer, I of course complied. You, however, should know that I do not do so with any great enthusiasm."

Arnold is displaying a hard edge that I have never before encountered in him, a sign of a sea change in our relationship.

"My instructions from Mr. Wallace are clear. I am to help you in any way that I can except that I am not to give you money, but that I may buy items for you that you might need. He has further instructed me that I am to get regular updates from you on your progress. That is why I am here now."

He takes an incongruously delicate sip of his coffee and eyes me over the brim. His raised eyebrows indicate that it is my turn to speak now.

Suppressing my irritation, I tell him a very abridged version of what I know or suspect and he takes it all in without breaking eye contact for an instant, which I find disconcerting. He is sitting, leaning forward with one elbow on the table, his thumb under his chin and his fingers beating a silent tattoo on his lower lip; I find myself rubbing the itchy spot in the crook of my left arm in unison. It has become infected and I think back to the Lion Hotel and my needle sticking out of that wad of used bubble gum.

Arnold lets me finish my explanation without interruption, asks no question, offers no comment. He is silent for a long time.

"So, to summarize, Mr. Rogan: Kevin was killed five days ago and all you have are some suspicions. The girlfriend"—the word comes out as a sneer—"is a possible suspect; Brad knows more than he is telling you and you do not have a viable theory of the crime." I feel my face flush. Put that way it makes my efforts sound pathetic and I am not sure if the flush that comes to my face is from shame or anger.

"So what's *your* theory of the crime?" I counter. It comes out more aggressively than I intended.

"*My* theory?" His voice betrays nothing but I sense an anger in his eyes. "My theory is that there was no crime. Kevin quite simply killed himself."

"Oh, come on, Arnold! You know as well as I do that Kevin would never kill himself while his father was still alive," I protest.

"There are things that you don't know. Things that I'm not prepared to discuss with you, or with anyone for that matter, but they provide a very real motive for suicide."

"Oh, you mean the illegal drug testing?" I can not keep the gloating at my knowledge out of my voice.

His eyes harden and I see his nostrils flare. He's going to hit me! My hands ball and my shoulders tense. Arnold may be twenty years my senior but he is powerful and hard; he would certainly give me a run for my money in a fight.

But before I can push my seat back, the moment passes and he seems to force himself under control. Seems to.

"Where did you hear about it?" he asks.

"I'm not prepared to tell you." If I did tell him, in the mood he is in, he might go to Sandi's office and kill her.

To my great surprise, he seems to accept my refusal. "That information must *never* be passed on to Mr. Wallace. Do you understand? He could not bare to know that Kevin had betrayed the family's honor like that. If you ever tell him, Mr. Rogan, you will live to regret it."

I do not need his threats to agree with this. "Believe me Arnold, neither he nor Mrs. Wallace will ever hear it from me."

We look at each other and the tension between us subsides.

He removes a business card from the breast pocket of his suit jacket. The obverse has an elegant and simple crested design with the name Wallace Investments in copperplate script. Arnold's name is not in evidence but there is a phone number. On the reverse is a name and address written in an obsessively neat hand.

"That is your new address. It is a clean and functional rooming house. Go there and the owner will give you keys. The rent will be paid for as long as you live there and it will provide you with a good base from which to conduct your investigation."

There is a condescension in his tone that irritates me. I suppress my immediate reaction. "Arnold, I have known you for over a quarter of a century and yet I don't know your last name. What is it?"

In his eyes, there is confusion at the abrupt change of subject then a sudden flare that reveals a blade of anger. "I hardly see the relevance of my surname," he says in that haughty manner that only the Brits can affect. "What is being offered here is—"

"Yes, Arnold. I know what is being offered." I can feel my temper rising, irrational but real. "But you know, you are one of two people in my life whose last names I don't know. It bugs the hell out of me. I'll probably never know the other one's but I want to know yours… now."

"One other thing Mr. Rogan." I might just as well not have spoken. "Mr. Wallace asked me to tell you that whether or not you solve Kevin's murder, when you decide to stop your use of heroin, he will support you in any way that he can. So… do *not* do anything stupid. Do we understand each other?"

My irrational side is now in full-on mode. "You know what Arnold? I am going to solve Kevin's murder but I am going to do it my way. Please tell Mr. Wallace that I really appreciate his support, but that I don't need a rooming house or promises of future help. *I* will contact *you* if there's anything I need and I'll give you updates when and if I think they are appropriate. Please give my very best regards to Mr. and Mrs. Wallace."

I stand and slip the business card back into the breast pocket of his jacket, turn and leave the coffee shop with as much dignity as allowed while hauling a green garbage bag of clothes in one hand and a giant cup of hot coffee in the other.

I am nursing the feeling that both Sandi and Brad have tried to manipulate me and that Arnold has tried to buy me.

But I *am* going to solve the mystery of Kevin's murder and I *am* going to do it my way and on my terms. For the first time in years, I feel like the cop I used to be: in charge and confident in what I am doing. Except that I need to find a quiet alley in which to shoot away the pain that is worming into my bones.

Chapter 19

Roy is pissed. In both senses of the word. It is not a good combination.

I have finally tracked him down. We are sitting at a table in Beanie's Eatery. It smells of stale beer and cigarette smoke, despite the city's no smoking bylaws. A hundred drunks are either hunched over their beer glasses, whining at their lot in life or talking and laughing aggressively. The word fuck, in all its conjugations and declensions, swirls through the air. An unpleasant place to be at any time but it's Roy's favorite hang out. Don't ask me why.

He has consumed way too much alcohol for rational conversation but I want to confirm that Kevin was conducting illegal tests of his wonder drug. Then I realize, with a shock, that, more than anything, I want Roy to deny it, to prove Sandi a liar, to provide definitive proof Kevin did not do this thing that killed Tommy Connor and six others.

With Roy in his present state, I need to come at it obliquely.

"Are there plans for a service or anything for your buddy Tommy?" I ask.

"No. He's still in the morgue. They're doin' an autopsy on him but they ain't rushin' it. They don't care so much when the body's a homeless person. Wouldn't do it at all if the law didn't say they gotta." He sighs. "Poor bastard. It's pure luck that I ain't lying there beside him." His face contorts into an angry frown.

"Roy, when you told me about Tommy's death you said something about bad drugs."

"Did I now?" Roy at his most ornery.

"Yes, you did. But Tommy didn't use drugs did he? He was a drinking man, like yourself." 'Drinking man' sounds nicer than alcoholic or any one of a long list of sobriquets that could be applied.

"What of it?" Arms crossed, still intransigent.

"Well, why would Tommy die of bad drugs, if he didn't use drugs?" I keep my questions quiet and gentle.

He shrugs and calls for another beer.

"So what did happen to Tommy, Roy?" I say it in my most reasonable voice.

"Why the fuck do you care, eh?"

"Because I liked Tommy and I care about what happened to him."

"That the only reason?"

"No. I also think Tommy's death may be connected to Kevin's murder."

He turns his battered old face to me, the bleary eyes focusing with difficulty. I see the malicious side of Roy darting to the surface like a Great White. *Something wicked this way comes.*

He spits out the words. "Your asshole buddy Kevin wasn't murdered, you stupid fucker. *He* was the murderer! Him and his stupid fuckin' drug. He's what happened to Tommy. And to a bunch of others. But he didn't have the guts to own up to what he done, did he? He fuckin' killed himself instead."

The hairs on the back of my neck come to attention as his words sink in. I have been hoping against hope that Sandi's story about Kevin's illegal drug testing would prove false, despite Arnold's confirmation. Now that faint hope is gone. But the bigger questions are how did Roy know that there were other people killed by Kevin's drug and why is he so sure that Kevin killed himself? How could he possibly know that?

"Roy, what do you—"

My question dies in my throat as I look at him. Tears are streaming down his face and he is racked by sobs. "And God forgive me... I helped... I helped the bastard... I helped him find his guinea pigs."

What! *Roy* was the one helping Kevin? The one Sandi referred to as *someone outside the company.* How the—

"I did it 'cos I knew he was ya friend and because he told me that he wanted to use the drug to cure ya. Is that what ya wanted to hear? Are ya happy now? Are ya?"

He lurches to his feet and sneers down at me.

He spits as he speaks, an unholy gleam in his eye. "I'm glad the bastard's dead. I hope he rots for ever in hell. He was a fuckin' murderer."

There is an icy ring of truth to what he has said. From the maelstrom of thoughts that are assailing me one pushes to the fore. I have to know. "Roy, how do you know that Kevin killed himself?"

But I have taken my eye off the ball. Roy lifts the other side of the table and pushes it over on top of me. As I go over backwards in my chair, I see him turn on his heel and head for the door.

I flail about for several seconds, getting the heavy table off me and rolling out of the downed chair onto the filthy carpet, so that by the time I am on my feet, the door is swinging closed behind him. I have to catch him right now and get the truth out of him. I start for the door but am brought up short by a powerful hand on my arm. It is Beanie's Eatery's bouncer. "What the hell are *you* doing?" He booms.

I try to pull away from his grip and follow Roy through the door but his hand is enormous; it is in proportion to the rest of him. He is holding my left arm at the elbow and the pain is much greater than it should be. "Look, I'm sorry, I have to catch my buddy." I indicate the door with my head.

He shakes his head. "Roy's a regular here," he says. "We take care of our own."

The noise level has dropped and a dozen pairs of malevolent eyes are focused on me. A couple of guys get to their feet and stand either side of me giving questioning looks to the bouncer. Survival moves to the top of my list of priorities. I weigh the odds. I could take any one of them, probably all three. The bouncer first. Use his grip on me, pull away and use his reaction to add force to the head butt. With him down, the other two will be easy. Then I sense that there are others standing behind me. Seconds pass. He smiles for a long moment, then lets go of me and walks to the bar.

I turn and five men are standing between me and the exit. They wait a beat then pull apart just enough to let me push between them. I walk through the doors onto Hastings Street but I am too late. It is dusk and Roy is not visible on any horizon.

The questions come flooding back in. How the hell did Roy know Kevin? I have never talked to him about Kevin other than that he was a friend who let me keep my good clothes at his house and I'm sure that I never told Kevin about Roy. Why would I?

Like Arnold, Roy seemed so sure that Kevin killed himself. Could my murder theory be wrong? If it is, then my secret plan, to solve it and prove my worth to the VPD, just went up in smoke.

I had pinned so much on getting justice for Kevin and yet, if Roy is right, justice has, in a weird way, been served: Kevin has paid for the lives he took with his own life.

My world has collapsed around my ears.

Chapter 20

It is a long time since I have felt such a warmth. I struggle to suppress a veil of depression at the knowledge that it has been lost from my life; in the last three years, heroin has been my only solace, my last fix only two hours ago.

I have had a long, hard, confusing day, which started this morning when I walked into Sandi's office—was it really only ten hours ago?—yet Sam and Ellie have cleansed me of the slings and arrows of outrageous fortune with nothing more than Sam's homemade Osso Buco, a fine Chianti taken from George's cellar and Ellie's laughter. We are sitting on bar stools around the butcher-block table in Sam's kitchen. I asked if we could eat in here because the kitchen is Sam's domain and, unlike the rest of the house, it bears no reminders of her fiancé George Walsh, which allows me to pretend for a moment that we are a family again, having a normal family meal. We have, as though by mutual consent, avoided all the subjects that would bare this illusion but I know the illusion is about to be shattered.

Sam gets up and starts to clear away the plates; it is my cue. I feel my gut tense; the time to pay the piper has arrived. I have to put some things right. Now.

I reach over and pick Ellie up from her stool, settle her on my knee and glance at Sam, rinsing dishes at the sink. She smiles encouragement at me. I think of all the ways that I have let down Sam and Ellie and know that this can not be one more.

I put my arm around Ellie's shoulder. "Mommy told me about what happened at school, sweetie." I say.

116

She says nothing but I feel a slight shrug of her shoulders.

"I want you to know that it was my fault—"

"No it wasn't Daddy. It was Nate. He said mean things about you. He said you were filthy. He said you—"

I put my finger gently to her lips. "Listen to me, sweetie," I interrupt. "It *was* my fault because I didn't explain to you what a junkie is. I'm going to tell you now, so that you know, OK?"

Another shrug.

This is the fundamental truth of my life.

"There are two types of drugs, sweetie. There are medicines that the doctor gives you or that you buy in a drug store and those are drugs that make you better when you're ill. You know about those, right?"

She looks up at me a nods.

"But there is another kind of drug that you don't get from a doctor. People take them because it makes them feel good; sometimes very good." I pause to let that sink in.

"Like chocolate?" she asks.

"Kind of, except that it makes them feel a hundred times better than chocolate does."

"A *hundred* times?"

"Maybe more, sweetie, but the problem is that when some people start taking these drugs, they can't stop, even if they really want to; they have to take more and more and then more—"

"Oh, you mean like cigarettes," she interrupts. "George smokes cigarettes but Mommy only lets him smoke them outside. I heard him tell Mommy that he really wants to stop but he can't, right Mommy?"

Sam looks uncomfortable. "It's not the same, Ell," she says. "Listen to what Daddy is telling you."

"The drugs I'm talking about are called heroin and cocaine and crack. When some people *start* taking these

117

drugs they can't *stop* taking them. People like that, who can't stop, are called drug addicts or junkies.

"Ellie, I take a drug called heroin and... well, I'm a drug addict." With a shock, I realize that I have never before said those exact words to anyone, not even to myself.

I feel a hand on my shoulder and turn to look at Sam. The words have brought tears welling in her eyes but before either of us can say anything, Ellie says, "If it's a thousand times better than chocolate, it must be *really*cool, Daddy." The enthusiasm in her voice makes my blood run cold and I feel Sam's hand tense. I don't want to make drugs sound interesting or glamorous but I have to tell Ellie the truth.

"Yes, they do make you feel really good Ell but the problem is that they are very, very bad, not cool at all."

"They can't be good *and* bad, Daddy?" she chuckles.

I sense that Sam wants to jump in and say something but I turn and plead, "Let me explain it, Sam. Please." She looks hard at me, then nods uncertainly.

I turn back to Ellie. "I take a drug called heroin and it makes me feel good when I take it but if I don't take it every four hours, I get pains in my body; they are very bad pains and I get them everywhere. Sometimes if I can't get heroin in time, the pain is so bad that I can hardly walk and all I can think about is stopping the pain. Sometimes the pain makes me scream. But then, when I take the heroin, all the pain goes away until four hours later, when it comes back again."

I pause to let Ellie absorb this. She looks up at me then hugs me and kisses me on the cheek. "Poor Daddy."

"Anyway, sweetie. In nine days I am going into a place like a type of hospital where they are going to help cure me of my addiction, so that I won't have to take any more heroin and I won't be a junkie any more."

A claw of fear squeezes my gut as I think about the pain I am going to have to live with for four or five sleepless days in the detox center: one hundred and twenty solid hours;

seven thousand, two hundred and twenty long minutes of agony; a time longer than any sadist could continuously torture his victim.

Sometimes Sam can read me like a book. She puts her arm around me, "You can do it Cal. I know you can," she whispers as she brushes her lips against my cheek. I look into her eyes, wanting to kiss her and realize, with a shock, that her lips are parted and she is leaning in towards me. I feel the pressure of her breast on my arm and her fragrance catches in my nose and throat. My heart is beating a tattoo.

"When you stop being a junkie are you and Mommy going to be married again?"

The smolder dissipates and wafts away in the breeze of Ellie's innocent question.

Sam pulls back and clears her throat. "No Ell," she says, "But we'll always be friends and we'll always be your Mommy and Daddy. We both love you very much."

Ellie looks disappointed for a second then takes another tack. "If George is a junkie for cigarettes, is he going to that hospital place too?"

"No Ell," Sam answers, somewhat abruptly. "Cigarettes are different. People who smoke them aren't junkies." I sense in her voice that George would be most upset if Ellie called him a cigarette junkie. I have to bite the inside of my cheeks to keep the smile from my lips.

"Why?" The eternal kid question.

"Well…" Sam is searching for a right answer and her frustration is obvious. She catches the look on my face and says, "Daddy will explain it."

I let the grin out. "The reason is that some drugs that people can get addicted to, like cigarettes and wine or beer, are legal but others like heroin and cocaine are against the law; the people who buy them and sell them can go to jail. They only call people addicts or junkies if their drugs are against the law."

119

"Why?"

I shake my head. "I honestly don't know, sweetie." And I don't.

"Well, I *do*," interjects Sam. "It's because we don't want our children using them. By making them illegal it makes them harder to buy."

Oh that it were that simple, Sam. "That's not quite right. Every cop in North America knows that it is easier for a kid to buy a rock of crack cocaine from someone at school than it is to buy a six-pack of beer from a liquor store." Sam starts to object but I stop her with, "I'm making an important point here, Sam." I turn Ellie's face so that she is looking directly into my eyes. Her look tells me that she can see that I am deadly serious. "Ell, I want you to promise me something. If a boy or girl at school ever tries to give you a pill or some powder or a cigarette or anything like that, I want you to promise me that you will say *No* to them and, straight away, you will go and tell your teacher. Will you promise me that sweetie?"

"Yes, Daddy," she whispers.

"It's important sweetie, because that pill or powder or cigarette could make you very, very ill, even kill you." Her eyes widen and she nods.

Sam comes and puts her arm around Ellie. "No need to frighten her, Cal," she says, her voice gentle. "Remember, this is West Van, it's a *good* neighborhood."

"It's a *rich* neighborhood. That makes it an ideal target for the drug gangs. They make so much money they can afford to pay high school kids to distribute for them. Maybe even some elementary school kids too."

Maybe if drugs were legal, they would be harder for school kids to get; the gangs and their teenage hoodlums would be out of the drug business. But then, who *would* be selling drugs, the tobacco companies? Heroin Lite and Crack Menthol?

Anyway, it's time for a change of subject and my second salvo.

"Sweetie, we need to talk about something else. When that boy called me a filthy junkie, he was only using words. He probably doesn't even know what a junkie is. It was wrong of him to try to hurt you by saying that, but it was *more* wrong of you to hit him. I want you to promise me something else: if anyone calls you a name or says something to hurt you, instead of hitting them all you have to do is say, '*sticks and stones may break my bones but names will never hurt me.*' My mommy taught me that."

"She was my grandma, right Daddy?"

"Yes sweetie, she was."

"OK, Daddy, I will. I'm sorry I hit Nate."

"That's good sweetie."

She nestles comfortably on my lap and slips her thumb into her mouth. I didn't know she still sucked her thumb: the ignorance of the absentee father.

"OK, Ell," Sam chimes in. "Time to go have a bath and get ready for bed… and take that thumb out!"

Without complaint, Ellie slides off my lap and skips out, leaving Sam and me in the kitchen together with the elephant of that almost kiss. Sam is making Americanos with her fancy automatic espresso machine. "Thanks for doing that, Cal. I really appreciate it."

"No prob. I appreciate you letting me explain it. Especially over such a great meal. Thank you Sam, I really am grateful."

She smiles, almost shyly. She looks at me and the smile morphs into something more intense. "Cal, you will go into detox and rehab like you promised?"

"Yes Sam, of course I will." I note the irritation in my voice but then remember all the failed promises that I have made to her over the years. "Sorry."

She hands me an Americano and leads me out of the kitchen. I want to enjoy the sway of her hips as I follow her, except that there is something wrong. Incongruously, Roy comes to mind; Sam is walking like Roy when he is trying to hide the fact that he is drunk: walking in an exaggeratedly careful manner. She has had a glass and a half of Chianti but that is not enough to make her tipsy. Was she drinking before I arrived, I wonder?

I follow her into the living room with its spectacular view of English Bay, still pretty impressive at night. The room makes me uncomfortable. It is full of reminders of George: photos of him sailing, riding a Harley Davidson, shaking hands with politicians and sports figures—the rich man's vanity gallery. There are no pictures of Sam or Ellie which seems very strange to me.

"Is there anything that I can do to help you with detox Cal?" Sam asks as we settle on the leather furniture, far more George's style than hers.

"No thanks, Sam. It's going to be five days of hell but I'll get through it somehow. Then I'm scheduled for three weeks of rehab, learning to live my life without drugs. But you know what really frightens me?"

Sam shakes her head. She looks lovely.

"What do I do after rehab? A lot of people who go through rehab end up using and back on the streets within two, three months. I can't handle the thought of that. I'll need to find a job, but as what? I have a Masters in English Lit and twelve years experience as a cop. It doesn't qualify me for much. A security guard, maybe, but no one would hire me once they do a background check and learn my drug history."

"Do you think there's any hope that you could get back on the police force, maybe in a civilian role at first?" she asks.

Although I feel a thrill at the thought, I just shrug. "That might be *where hope is coldest and despair most fits*." I ask myself, not for the first time, if I am becoming bitter. Still, the line that came unbidden to my mind is from *All's Well that Ends Well*, so maybe it's a good omen. "My one chance is that if I could solve Kevin's murder, it might, just might, buy me a pass back into the department."

She makes no attempt to rein in the frustration in her voice. "Do you honestly think that Kevin was murdered *and* that you can prove who did it in the next nine days, Cal?"

"I have to, Sam. I have to."

She looks at me for a long moment. "I know you do," she says, "It's part of you, a part of you that—"

Her words are cut off as Ellie bursts into the room, still dripping from a lighting-quick bath.

"Daddy, Daddy, I have this great idea. Why don't you have a sleepover here and we can have breakfast together tomorrow and you can come with me and Mommy and see the new school that I might go to. Can you, Daddy, can you? Pleee-eeease."

I look at Sam. She is smiling... and she doesn't say no. She looks at me but, for all my cop's intuition, I can not read what is behind those lovely green eyes.

"Tell him Mommy. Tell him."

I want so much to hear Sam ask me to stay that it hurts. But, by the same token, it will be way more painful to hear her say *No*... so I preempt, "I'd love to, sweetie, but I have to go. There is a man I have to meet early in the morning."

Ellie is vocal in her disappointment and Sam, cheeks flushed, can not meet my eye.

Chapter 21

The smells and snores of sleeping men in the dorm of the backpackers' hostel are keeping me awake... or is it really the thought that I could have been sleeping at Sam's house? In a clean bed in a warm, sweet smelling guest room, or perhaps in... but I dare not even think that.

My garbage bag of possessions is in the bed with me, safe, I hope, from a thief in the night. My refusal of Arnold's offer of a bed in a clean rooming house feels pretty silly right now. A roof over one's head should never be taken for granted.

We're moving. Today.

How I hated those words.

For as far back as I can remember, every six to nine months, as inexorable as the passing of the seasons, my mother and I would move. My objections were dismissed, countered by harsh commands to pack my things into boxes and garbage bags. We would load our meager possessions into a truck that my mother had begged, borrowed or rented and we would make a series of trips back and forth from one home to the next until, long past midnight, we fell into our beds, exhausted.

As a child it was a source of great puzzlement to me. As a youth, a thing of embarrassment and anger. Until the day I understood. Then it became a beacon of pride.

It was the Monday of the long weekend in September, nineteen eighty-nine. The night before my first day in grade twelve. She had cooked a special meal: lobster soup, thick porterhouse steaks with fries and Caesar salad, followed by strawberries and cream. An unheard-of extravagance and I marveled at what it might portend.

After I had done the dishes, she asked me to sit with her in the living room. She sat on our old winged chair, the floral pattern of its slipcover faded from years of washing. My mother was a striking woman with steel gray hair curled into the same style that she had worn since as far back as I could remember. She smoothed her plain gray dress over her knees and locked her gaze on me.

I could sense momentous events in the wind.

"Tonight, Cal," she said, her voice redolent with the flavor of her European roots, "we will talk about University. You will need to choose where you are going and what it is you want to study."

With the conceit of youth in full bloom, I said, "No need, Mom. I'm gonna join the police force. I've decided to apply to the Justice Institute."

To my amazement, my rigid, forceful and stern mother did not object, either to my goal or to my use of the word gonna. "That is very good, Cal." She nodded. "Even from age six, you have said that you want to be a policeman. You will be a good policeman because you are a good man." It was the first time that she had ever referred to me as a man.

"So tell me," she continued, "what do you want to achieve as a policeman?"

I rambled on about helping people and making the world a safer place, the idealism of youth—betrayed so profoundly by me now—pushing me to heights of hyperbole. When I ran out of steam, she nodded and said, "Good. These are worthy goals. Noble ones. In order to achieve such things you will need to move into a position of power and influence within the police force, no?"

I agreed, stunned that she had any idea of my ambitions. She let the colloquy of my goals and dreams run its course before saying, in a voice so quiet that I had to lean forward to hear, "In the old country, I grew up in a time of great political unrest and I did not receive the education that my parents planned for me. By the time you were twelve, you knew more than I did. A thing of pride for me but also a hard thing for a parent to digest."

I remember feeling embarrassed by this, thinking about the ways I must have hurt her by flaunting my teenage knowledge. I wondered why she was baring her soul to me and was uneasy about where this conversation might lead.

"But one thing I *do* know for sure is this. I have cleaned many, many offices of big-time doctors, lawyers and businessmen and I have noticed that the bigger and better the office, the more certificates are on the walls. I have studied those certificates. The more powerful the man the more degrees he has. I have seen with my own eyes the value of education.

"And so have you. Mr. Wallace, Kevin's father is a very important man isn't he? And didn't you once tell me that he has three degrees?" I remembered the time I told her about Mr. Wallace's accomplishments and blushed at how I had tried to rub her nose in it. I feel myself blushing now at what Mr. Wallace would think if he knew.

"Yes, but—" She held one finger to her lips but it was her intensity that silenced me.

"It has been difficult for you, moving once, sometimes twice a year, hasn't it?"

I hesitated, wrong footed by the change in subject. "No, Mom. I understand. Really."

"I appreciate you saying that, Cal. But, it's not true. It *was* difficult for you, I know. And you didn't understand. You still don't. But now it is time for you to learn the truth."

She lit a cigarette—her one vice that she restricted to just two a day, home rolled fourteen at a time, every Sunday night —and inhaled deeply and gratefully.

I too inhaled; I had been holding my breath.

"I always knew your father would leave me," she sighed. I sat very still, scared to break the spell. She had always refused to talk about my father. I knew nothing about him. Perhaps this was about to change.

"I knew that I would be faced with having to bring you up on my own. So from the moment of your birth, before even, I was determined to make sure that you got the very best education, no matter what. But how? I was unskilled and uneducated so I had to make do with minimum wage jobs."

Her lips pursed. "I've never talked to you about your father and maybe that was wrong, I don't know. But this I will tell you. When he walked out on us, I swore that I would never let you be contaminated by him. I would never accept *anything* from him. He offered money and tried to bribe me to let him see you but I refused and I had the law on my side. I had a restraining order forbidding him to come near either of us."

I was amazed to hear her talk to me about my father. I wanted to know more but did not dare to interrupt, lest I shattered the moment.

"So it was up to me to provide for your education. I tried to save. I made budgets and plans but I could never begin to save enough. Then one day, it came to me." She looked off into the distance, shaking her head.

"What, Mom?" The mention of my father presaged more revelations, maybe keys to some of the puzzles of my youth.

"All the budgets told the same story. We only had enough money for rent, food and clothing. I remember thinking, 'If we didn't have to pay rent, the problem would be solved.'

"So I stopped paying rent." She said it casually, with a shrug, as if this was the obvious solution. "The landlord called me up and I told him that I was having a little difficulty and that I would pay him soon. The next month, he was a little more forceful, but I made more promises and he didn't do anything. It wasn't until halfway through the third month that he lost patience and served me with an eviction notice.

"So I looked for a new apartment and we moved in the middle of the night. A midnight flit, I called it. I put the three months rent that I hadn't paid into a savings account.

"From the time you were seven years old until last summer we did the same thing a total of fourteen times. Every year it got more difficult to find a landlord that would take us. But I always found a way. Always." There was a bitterness in her voice, that I did not dare try to interpret or ask about, for fear that I would learn what no child should know about his mother.

"The year we didn't move was the year you started at Magee. I wanted you in that school so badly. Just before the school year started, I moved us to that little house in Marpole, just inside the Magee catchment area, and stayed there a year so that you would be able to establish yourself at the school. We had to move twice the next year to make up for it."

She looked at me hard, her face at its most uncompromising. "Every penny of rent money that I saved is still in that account together with interest. By the time you graduate from Magee next summer there will be over thirty-five thousand dollars, which is plenty enough for you to take two degrees and you *will* spend every penny of it on your education."

My mouth hung open at her revelation. With the selfishness of youth, I had always considered the inconvenience and embarrassment that our constant moves caused me and I heaped the blame on her head, mainly in silence but sometimes openly and with great acrimony. Now all I could do was try to fathom the enormity of the sacrifice that she made for me. A proud woman, she subjected herself to great humiliation in the eyes of our landlords and her friends and neighbors to do this thing for me. Her goal was a better life for her son.

Her son, who has betrayed her sacrifice by living like this.

Hidden in the darkened room, my face burns with humiliation and shame.

Chapter 22

I have to find Roy. I have to get to the bottom of his furious outburst at Beanie's. He's somehow at the epicenter of Kevin's death and I have to know what he knows. I have been searching for him all morning: Beanie's, the bottle recycling depot, the Savoy pub and all of his preferred hangouts. I talked to a couple of his drinking buddies but they were clammed up. They have been told not to talk to me; Roy does not want to be found.

I have combed the downtown east side and now I have to do it all over again.

Then I see the peripatetic Nelson, running in his flat-footed gait along the other side of Pender Street, on a vital mission known only to himself. It is the first time that I've seen him since the incident with black shirt and Goliath at the Lion Hotel, when he took me to where Roy was being loaded into an ambulance. Although he hardly speaks, he sees everything in his travels. If anyone knows where Roy is, it is Nelson. I just have to find out how to get the information out of his addled old brain.

"Nelson!" I call. But then I remember that he hardly ever responds to anyone or anything; Roy is the only one who can communicate with him. I start running along Pender, waiting for a break in the traffic so that I can cross. "Nelson!"

Without warning, he turns and crosses Pender towards me, ignoring the traffic, the tails of his shabby gabardine raincoat flapping in the wind. Two cars screech to a halt and I wince at the sound of an SUV plowing into the back of one.

To my surprise he runs straight at me and I say, "Hi Nelson."

Without breaking pace, he gives me a fleeting glance, an instant of eye contact, and I can tell that he is terrified. "C'mon, quick."

I jog along beside him, car horns honking behind us. I want to stop him but he becomes very agitated when stationary. "Nelson, have you seen Roy?" I ask in my most reasonable tone.

Without any warning, he turns right on to Carrall and I overshoot, skid to a halt and run to catch up to him.

I resist the urge to grab hold of him. "D'you know where Roy is, Nelson?"

"Huh."

Roy can often interpret his grunts but I have no idea what he means, except that I can smell the fear.

"Is that a yes or a no, Nelson?" I ask, trying to keep my voice reasonable.

"Huh."

His fear transfers to me; it's got something to do with Roy.

I follow him across Hastings.

"Nelson! Have you seen Roy?" I want to calm him but I sound like I'm talking to a fractious child.

"Huh."

His grunt pushes me over the edge. I grab his arm, pull him to a halt and turn him so he is facing me. I shake him. "Nelson, I need to find Roy," I enunciate slowly.

He squirms in my hands and I feel like I am abusing a wounded child; it feels wrong but I have to know where Roy is. "Nnnn… Nnnn…" he says and, with a burst of unexpected strength, he twists out of my grip and darts into an alley.

I follow him and the hairs on the back of my neck become erect. It is the same alley that I woke up in almost a week ago, the day Kevin died. I don't know why it has always been a place of dread for me. Even when I was a cop, with a badge and a gun, I was terrified of it. My skin creeps as I follow Nelson into its maw.

I would turn and run right now, except for what I see: a lone figure about three quarters of the way down. He is standing beside two green dumpsters which are overflowing with garbage bags.

Roy.

Nelson stops. I stop. He jogs on the spot for a three second beat and then turns and hares out of here.

We look at each other over the forty yards that separate us and I wonder what was the source of Nelson's fear. I am rooted to the spot. Something is wrong. Different. It is the silence. This time of day, the alley is normally teeming with crack heads, one of their many spots, but right now it is empty, quiet, unnatural.

I shake off my rising panic. It is, after all, just Roy and me.

I force my shoulders to relax and I smile. "Hey Roy," I call and walk slowly towards him. He does not move an inch. "I just need to talk to you... about Kevin." I keep my voice even and reasonable, as much to calm me as to calm him. I check the recessed doorways of the buildings that back on to the alley. They too are empty, no one sleeping in them, no one shooting up or on the pipe.

Roy stands frozen until I am about half way towards him.

Then, as if on command, he turns and dashes down the alley. His wiry frame was built for speed and despite his age, he is fast. I am going to have to go hard to catch him.

As I accelerate after him, four men step out from between the dumpsters.

One is dressed in black and has his arm in a sling; another is a giant on crutches. The other two are big and tough looking. I weigh the odds, one against two and two halves. My chances are about fifty-fifty but I must not discount Goliath's crutches or his colleague's feet. I need to talk to Roy, not deal with these bozos.

I shall side with Tacitus. *He that fights and runs away, may turn and fight another day.* A tendril of my mind wonders if I am using this logic to rationalize my fear of the alley. I spin around to dart after Nelson and stop dead.

Blocking the end of the alley, are three more men, big, hard, fit looking men, making their way toward me. I remember the rest of the quotation. *But he that is in battle slain, will never rise to fight again.* The revised odds may make those words prophetic.

I turn back the other way. Two of the four are advancing, leaving Goliath and his buddy as full backs. Behind them, standing at the far end of the alley, is Roy, wearing an unreadable expression. He fishes in his coat pocket and pulls something out. I can't see what it is. Thirty pieces of silver perhaps? He looks up at me for the briefest instant and then runs off, out of my line of sight.

I walked into this one. Maybe I'm not as street smart as I thought; no cop goes in without backup. That's it. Think like a cop, Cal. I remember the words of my combat instructor at the Justice Institute, a canny old Scot. *Let your training conquer your fear. Act and react. Don't think.* I center myself and although I'm outnumbered seven to one, my blood starts to sing with the anticipation of battle.

I have just about three seconds to act. I throw my garbage bag of possessions into a doorway; if I survive this encounter, I may be able to get back and retrieve it before it becomes the property of some crack head.

The first group is split two and two. Attack the weaker front. I would love to have the advantage of a weapon but a quick glance around reveals nothing. Except for one small item...

I take three steps towards the advancing pair and drop to one knee, a genuflection to my attackers that gives me a brief element of surprise. I hear running footsteps behind me. My right hand darts down, grabs the discarded needle and, in one fluid motion, I surge up and forward and bury it in the neck of the smaller, but far more dangerous looking man on my right. For a tiny fraction of a second, I realize the enormity of what I have done. I may have set this man on the road to his death with an infected needle. I remember shooting up with the dirtied needle at the Lion Hotel and I wonder who might die first. Him or me?

My victim yells out and his hands claw up to his throat.

For an instant, his partner glances towards him, diverting his attention away from me; it is just enough time for me to jab my left fist into his nose.

It is not much of a punch but it *is* accurate. He is blinded long enough so that he does not see the powerful right uppercut that snaps his head back and fells him like an ox.

Less than three seconds have passed since my first move and all that stands between me and the far end of the alley are two injured men. I feel a burst of elation at my two fast won victories.

I leap over the fallen body and race forward.

Footsteps are on my heels.

Snap decision: take out the one with the sling. His injury is the easiest to attack and it is better to disable the more mobile of the pair. A piece of cake. I feint towards Goliath but, at the last moment, veer towards the man in black. I approach him from his injured side and move in close.

I push down on his elbow while grabbing his wrist and wrenching it up and away from his body. He shrieks and spins away, trying to escape from my grip. I give a victory whoop as I push him towards Goliath and leap past.

I made it! Home free. I'm sure I can outrun my pursuers and, if I really push it, I can catch Roy.

And all the air explodes out of my lungs as I hit the ground.

I hear the crack of a breaking rib an instant before the pain lances through my chest. Goliath is keeping his aluminum crutch pushed hard between my legs and, try as I might, I can not writhe away from it. I grunt in frustration as I try to roll on my back to give me a shot at his injured leg.

Then it's all over.

Hard hands haul me to my feet. They slam me against the stone wall of one of the old buildings that back on to the alley.

I take stock of my situation.

Two of the three who followed me into the alley have iron grips, one on each bicep; they have me pinned to the wall. In front of me is the third man, clearly the leader, flanked, to the left, by the man I stabbed with the hypodermic—hand cupped over his throat, he is wearing a very unpleasant look—and to the right, by Goliath with a broken-toothed grin like the battlements of a medieval tower. The man in black is leaning against the far wall, nursing his elbow and whimpering and the last member of the somewhat less than magnificent seven is still unconscious.

As fast as it came, my battle lust is gone. Now I need to use my brain.

I think I know why I'm here and I know how they got me here but what are their plans for me?

Drug gangs do not have a tendency to leave their enemies alive.

The leader of the group is in no hurry. He stands silent and immobile staring at me. He knows how to use silence. In most cases his victims will fold under his scrutiny and start blabbing, confessing or begging. It's an old interrogation strategy and a good one. I have used it myself with great effect and, despite knowing I'm being played, it still daunts me.

However, every second that he waits is a second in which I can recover and regain my strength, a second more in which I might be able to seize an opportunity. *Remember to find the advantage hidden in the disaster, laddie,* a Scottish voice in my head says.

The leader is wearing a crisp, white t-shirt under a soft leather jacket that must have cost a couple of grand. I do not recognize the brand of his jeans but I am betting that the designer is a household name in West Van. I *do* recognize his shoes. They are Ferragamo loafers. Once upon a time, I splurged half a week's salary on a similar pair. He is tall, about my height, and has long, well groomed, blond hair. He looks more like a movie star than the leader of a drug gang. He is worrying some object in his jacket pocket and I have a nasty feeling I know what it is.

He guesses that I am not going to be the first to speak.

"So… Cal Rogan? Right?"

How the hell does he know my name? He got to me through Roy so I guess Roy told him. But 'Cal'… Roy never calls me anything other than Rocky.

I would shrug but his boys have me too well pinned.

"Do you know why we're all here today?"

"Because last time you sent two brainless morons to do a man's job?"

Goliath's grin turns into a scowl. I am probably going to pay for my smart mouth.

"No, not exactly." He chuckles but I do not find it encouraging. "You see Mr. Rogan, I can *not* have junkies, especially junkies who are ex-cops, stealing from my associates and therefore from me.

"I know for a fact that you attempted to steal from my friend over there and from one or two others. I am even wondering if you might be the bad boy who has been relieving some of my colleagues of their hard earned dollars from all over the city.

"Anyway, it doesn't matter. Your short career as a thief has come to an end."

He takes the object he has been fondling from his pocket and slides it over the fingers of his left hand. Brass knuckles rip open skin and deform bone. My skin crawls at the image of what my face will look like after his ministrations. He steps forward with a big smile on his face and I know I have just one chance to get out of this, one chance to save my life.

My right leg jacks up and my foot buries itself in his solar plexus. It's not as debilitating as a kick to the groin but much easier to deliver accurately; a kick to the groin rarely connects.

As he doubles over and staggers backwards, I try to twist out of the grip of his henchmen. My arm pulls away from the one on my right and I swing my free fist towards the one on the left. The dangerous looking thug, the one I stuck with the needle, steps in from the side, blocks my punch without any difficulty and jabs a fist hard into my face making my head slam back against the wall.

I spit out bits of a tooth, weakened by five years of heroin use.

A punch to my solar plexus empties my lungs and makes me retch. A second punch to the chest connects with my newly broken rib and I scream.

I am thrown to the ground and from a distance I hear a different type of scream. A scream with which I am familiar. Feet and fists pummel my body as the sirens get louder. I know now that my fear of this alley is prescient of my death here.

Then the pounding stops and Blondie is kneeling beside me. His cohorts have backed off. He bends down close and whispers to me through the pain.

"Your kid's next. Pretty little thing... but not for too much longer." It is the last thing I hear as his brass knuckled fist descends.

Chapter 23

I shouldn't be here. Rocky'd fucking kill me if he knew. Plus I feel real out of place. I always wanted to come but now I'm here, I'm worried that she'll take one look at me, dirty and dressed like this, and be scared or something.

The door looks real expensive. The knocker is a friggin' great brass lion head with a ring in its mouth. It's gleaming in the sun; someone puts a lot of time into polishing it, that's fer sure. I better not touch it. It will take a fingerprint real easy and ya gotta be careful. I press a knuckle on the bell and hear a shriek from right on the other side of the door, "Mommy! Daddy's here."

The door swings open and there's Ellie standing on her tippy toes, just managing to reach up to the top latch. This is the closest I ever seen her and she is even prettier than I thought. She don't seem the least bit frightened. Maybe Rocky *has* told her about me.

I crouch down to her height. She smells of Johnson's baby shampoo; I haven't smelled that fer a while, eh. "Hi Ellie. I'm Roy. I'm a friend of yer Daddy's," I wanna give her a bigger smile but I might frighten her with my rotten teeth. "He told'ja about me, right?"

She looks at me, real serious, the way kids do. "Are you a junkie, like Daddy?" she asks, just like that. It makes me sad for Rocky that she thinks of him like that. But it means I was right to come here; now I know I'm doing the right thing fer him and not just fer me.

"No, Honey, I'm just a good friend of his. I'm Roy… y'know… Roy?"

She frowns and shakes her head. So… despite what he's always said, Rocky never told her nothing about me and that makes me sadder and, I gotta admit, a bit angry at him too.

"Do you know where my Daddy lives?"

"Yeah," I say. I wonder where she is going with this.

"Will you take me there? I miss him on school days and I want to go see him. Mommy won't take me."

The door opens wider and everything changes. Sam takes one look at me and her face takes on a scared look. Ellie's part way out the door but Sam grabs her and pushes her behind her back, real protective. Sam pushes the door almost all the way closed. "Can I help you?" she asks.

Ellie peeks out at me from behind her mom's hip; she's looking scared now. I hate that I am frightening her but I got no choice, I gotta be here, fer Rocky and fer me. With my knees creaking, I stand back up.

"Hi. I'm Roy, Rocky's friend." Sam's face is blank. "Cal's friend, that is."

"How can I help you Mr…?"

"Jus' call me Roy, eh." I give her a big smile but this seems to scare her even more. The door closes a fraction and I can't even see little Ellie now. "It's like this, Mrs. Rogan, Roc—, I mean Cal, uh, can't be here to take Ellie out today, eh. So I thought I better come over and tell ya."

"Why? Is something wrong?" The door opens a sliver and I can see that she is real worried about Rocky. Maybe she still loves him or something.

"I don't wanna say nothin' in front of…" I indicate Ellie with my eyes and Sam gets it.

"Ell, why don't you go upstairs and see Rosa," she says.

"Mommee-ee!" Ellie don't wanna go. She pushes past her Mom and looks up at me. "Why isn't Daddy coming?" she asks me.

I smile at her. "You go on upstairs, honey. I need to talk to yer Mommy first and then she can tell ya, OK?"

She thinks a bit then gives me such a big smile that it brings a grin to my own face. "OK, Roy," she says and runs off down the hall.

Sam softens. "You have a way with kids," she says. And that makes me even sadder, knowing that I was never a father to a little kid, growin' up like Ellie. Still, no time to think about that, I'm here fer a reason.

She looks long and hard at me and makes a decision. She opens the door wide. "Why don't you come in Mr., uh, Roy." I'm impressed. Most people in this neighborhood'd be scared to let the likes of me into their fancy homes but it gives me another thing to worry about.

I rub the soles of my boots hard on the doormat before walking in and then again on the mat inside the door. I'm praying that she don't ask me to take my boots off inside the house. My socks are full of holes and prob'ly pretty ripe.

She glances down at my feet and starts to say something but I think she guesses what I'm worrying about. Bless her, she decides not to embarrass me.

"Come in," she says again and I follow her down the hallway, hopin' not to get her carpets dirty. She calls upstairs, speaking in Spanish to someone but I don't know what she says. "Why don't you come into the kitchen, Roy." Sam leads me into the biggest friggin' kitchen I ever seen. "What happened? Why isn't Cal here?" she asks.

"I'm sorry to tell ya but he's been in an accident."

"An accident? Is he hurt?"

"Yes, he is. He got into trouble with a gang of drug dealers and they beat the f—, uh, beat the heck out of him. He's in St. Paul's. I don't rightly know how bad he's hurt but it's pretty bad I think. It happened midday yesterday and he was still unconscious this morning."

Her face is pale and I can see that she's starting to tear up. I hope she don't start crying. "Why did they…" She stops. "I have to go see him," she says. "Will you come with me? You can tell me what happened in the car." She heads out into the hallway. "Wait a sec while I get my keys," she says.

This is good. Now I can be alone with her; get her round to my way of thinking. Together we can get Rocky off the street, which'll be good fer him, and make him drop his damn investigation into Kevin's murder, which'll be good fer me.

I let my eyes wander around Sam's kitchen; it's bigger than some apartments I've been in. There's a heavy wooden table in the middle of the room with piles of photos on it. Rocky told me that Sam's a photographer so I can't resist having a quick look at them.

They're all black and white and they're of people on the downtown east side. As I go through them, I recognize some of the folks in 'em: a coupla heroin addicts that Rocky knows and some of my drinking buddies. Somehow Sam has given 'em, I dunno, a kind of beauty, like she caught 'em in a good mood or something. Then I see one that gives me a start. Smiling straight into the camera is my old buddy Tommy, looking at his most cheerful. I know when this photo was taken. It was a few days before he died. Right after he was given the—

"Who the hell…?" Strong hands grab me and my legs are kicked out from under me. Suddenly I'm on the floor with all the wind knocked out of me, looking up into a hard face. Bastard's got one knee on my chest and has me by the throat; one fist is drawn back ready to smash into my face. If he hits me that'll be my teeth gone. I can't breath. "What are you doing in my house?" he asks.

I try and answer but it just comes out as a gurgle.

His fist pulls back another six inches. I know he's gonna nail me and with my head on the ground it's gonna hurt bad. I'm between a rock and a hard place, as they say, *and* I'm

142

gonna take another goddamn beating on account of Rocky. Why the fuck did I have to come here?

Then Sam comes into the frame and grabs his arm. "For Christ sake, George, he's a friend of Cal's. I invited him in."

She stops him hitting me but nothing else changes. He's still kneeling on my chest and holding my throat. I see blackness creeping in around the edges. And still he don't move.

Then I know that he's enjoying it. He's gettin' off on watching me suffocate. Sadistic bastard. It's starting to get dark. I hear Sam from off in the distance. "For God's sake George," she's sayin'.

Then he lets go and stands up and I'm laying here gasping for air like a fresh caught fish. My chest and my throat both feel like they're badly damaged but I got a far greater worry: little Ellie's come downstairs and is standing in the doorway looking down at me and I can see she's terrified, poor little soul. But I don't know if she's terrified of me or him. In a way I hope it's me, 'cos she's gotta *live* with him. I shouldn'a come here, stirring up her life like this, poor kid. I won't come again.

Fortunately, Sam swoops across the kitchen and scoops up Ellie and takes her into the hall. I'm glad she dealt with Ellie first—a kid shouldn't hafta see violence in her own home—except that it's left me with George. He stands, looking down at me for a bit, then, real quick, he reaches down, grabs the front of my coat and pulls me to me feet. He shakes me and I feel the lapel rip; he done it on purpose. Bastard! He ain't that tall, shorter than me in fact, but he's strong and hard too. I don't know what I feel the most: anger or fear.

He takes my arm, none too gently, and leads me to the front door.

"Don't ever think about coming back here again," he snarls as he pushes me out.

My anger wins out over my fear. I look him right in the eye. "Any man who acts like that in front of a little kid ain't worth shit in my book." I don't care what he does to me. "He ain't a man at all," I tell him.

I hold my breath, waiting for the inevitable but instead of reacting the way I expected, he just gives me one of the most creepy smiles I ever seen before he slams the door in my face. I can't resist flipping him the bird through the fancy woodwork. Bastard! I get a horrible feeling that I ain't seen the last of George.

Well, I guess this was mission impossible. Rocky ain't gonna listen to me. Sam was my only hope of getting him to stop being a cop and investigating Kevin's murder.

I take off out of the driveway and along the street towards Marine Drive. It's cold; I hope I don't have to wait too long for a bus. When I get back to the east side I'm gonna get pissed and stay pissed; this whole trip has just stirred up too much stuff for me. I'm glad I told Sam about Rocky but apart from that I shouldn'a come here. It lifted my spirit seeing little Ellie and talking to her but that bastard George ruined it all. It breaks my heart but it's better I don't go see her again.

I'm almost to Marine when one of them fancy black SUVs pulls up next to me. Shit! I just know it's George! I dunno why the bastard's out to get me. Back at the house, Sam'd stop him from doing anything real bad to me but here, I'm a sittin' duck. Here in West Van, no one's gonna question someone like George dealing with someone like me.

I break into a run. At the corner of Marine, I see a number 250 bus coming. If I can just get across the road in time and jump on it, I'll be safe; even if he follows the bus I can get off at Granville Street downtown, where there's always a lot of people about. Safety in numbers. I just need to get across Marine Drive.

144

But the lights are against me and there's a ton of traffic on Marine. I glance back at the SUV and see the black-tinted side window slide down. I have an image in my mind, from some movie prob'ly, of a gun, with one of them silencers, poking out and shooting me. Then I think of the look on his face as he was chokin' me and it don't seem so movie-like. That sadistic SOB'd kill me in a heartbeat. Despite the cold, I feel myself break into a sweat.

The lights are still against me and the traffic's too heavy for me to risk running through it. The bus is real near; it'll be past the lights soon. I'm not gonna make it on time.

Then the lights start to change.

"Roy. It's me, Sam."

I squint through the SUV's windshield and see that it's her at the wheel. I walk back and check through the open window; she's alone. Relief floods through me and I feel my stomach rumble.

"I'm sorry about George," she says. "He's a good man but sometimes he has a temper." I don't like that she's making excuses for him. "Please let me make it up to you and give you a lift back to the hospital. We'll visit Cal together."

I climb in. It's real nice; it smells of leather and brings back memories of the seventies when I used to have some jack in my jeans and drove a Pontiac GTO.

"What happened to Cal, Roy? Why did they beat him up?" She pulls onto Marine.

"It's prob'ly 'cos they know he's an ex-cop who's put some dealers in jail," I lie. I don't want her to know the truth about how Rocky makes his money. "But the why ain't what's important here, Mrs. Rogan. What's important is that he gets off the streets, goes into detox and rehab and gets himself clean."

She reaches over and squeezes my shoulder. "Call me Sam, Roy; I'm not Mrs. Rogan any more." Bless her. Most people don't want to touch someone like me. "You know, for years, I've tried to get him to go into detox but he always has an excuse. It's a lost cause. I gave him two years to sort himself out, stop using and become a real father to Ellie but he's done nothing. I can tell you, he's never going to do it; I've given up."

I can't do it alone. I gotta get her on side. With the two of us pushing him…

"He's got this idea in his head that his buddy Kevin was murdered and that it's all up to him to solve the crime. He thinks if he can do that, then they're gonna let him back into the police department, which is bullshit—excuse my language—'cos they're never gonna let a junkie back in. But as long as he believes that, he's gonna use it as an excuse to not get clean. He says he's got to solve it first. But if he don't get off the streets, they're gonna kill him fer sure and leave your little girl without a father. You gotta help me, Sam."

"He's hardly a father to her *now*. One four-hour visit, once a week." She shakes her head.

"But that's better than no father at all! Anyways, if he got clean, it could all be different."

She shakes her head again and stays silent for a long moment. "Can I ask you something Roy?" she says.

"Sure."

"Why do you care so much?"

I can give her one of the reasons. "I known Rocky a long time. I was his snitch, ya know, when he was still a cop. I helped him put quite a few dealers in jail. Anyways, since he's been living on the streets, I been helping him out 'cos, uh… well… I'm kinda responsible for him taking heroin in the first place." I don't think I could have confessed that to anyone other than Sam. "So I reckon that if I can get him into detox and rehab, well, I'll have done my best to make amends."

She looks across at me and smiles. "Don't blame yourself for him being an addict. Cal has always made his own decisions. You're a good friend to him, Roy. I'm not sure that he deserves you." She thinks for a bit, then takes a deep breath. "Maybe there is one more thing I could do to apply some pressure to him. God knows it would be good if we could get him to drop this so-called murder investigation and go into detox. But I've got to tell you, I don't hold out much hope."

I stifle a sigh of relief.

"But you'll try right?"

She nods. She bought it. Thank God, 'cos she must never know the other reason why I want him in detox and rehab. That's a secret I hope to take to my grave.

Chapter 24

If ever there was a paradox, this is it. Here am I, sent by Mr. Wallace—the man to whom I owe my very life—to protect Cal and help him find Kevin's murderer. Yet, for the greater good, I need to have Cal accept that Kevin's death was suicide and to accept it without me leading him there and being disloyal to Mr. Wallace. The one way I can control what happens is by controlling Cal, or at least by knowing what he is up to.

As I look down at his battered, sleeping face, I can not help but remember the young Cal Rogan, armed with his Master's degree and his idealism, donning the uniform of the Vancouver Police Department for the first time. If only he could have stayed loyal to the uniform, instead of taking those filthy drugs until he became a degenerate, just like all the other scum on the streets. What a stupid waste of a life.

"Arnold?" His voice is weak and his eyes are hardly open. He looks around, trying to orient himself. "What happened?" he asks.

"Apparently, you were beaten up."

"Oh." He thinks for a moment. "Oh, yes… In the alley." He looks like he is searching his memory for the details.

"You've been unconscious for almost three days."

He stares at me for a while and then asks, "How did you know I was here?"

"A dickey bird told me." I do *not* want him to know the answer to that question.

"Where do you Limeys dredge up these expressions?" he asks.

I ignore the insolence, with some difficulty it must be said.

"Well, you being in hospital is not advancing your investigation is it?"

That annoys him.

"No Arnold, it isn't. That's why I need you to help me get out of here right now. I have a new lead I need to follow."

Interesting… I make a mental note to find out about this lead. "That's all very well, Mr. Rogan, but if you leave here now and go back on to the streets, you are likely to run into the same people who put you in here in the first place. Next time, they might not be so gentle and you may end up in the morgue instead. Don't you agree?"

He doesn't reply, so I press my advantage. "If you reconsider Mr. Wallace's offer of that rooming house, you will have a safe place to live and a good base of operations. You will be a lot less likely to run up against your enemies again."

He shakes his head but he doesn't refuse the offer. I just wait for him to respond.

"I'll take it if you get me out of here today," he responds sullenly. Good. The sale is made; now we are just negotiating the terms.

"I spoke to your nurses. They assured me that you are far too weak to even sit up in bed today. But if you agree to take the room, I will come back tomorrow and see what we can do about getting you out of here. Deal?" It's a lie; there is no way he will be able to leave tomorrow.

He nods.

"In your room you will find three bags of groceries, clothes, toiletries and change for the washer and dryer. I've even provided a decent backpack so that you don't have to keep your possessions in a garbage bag."

He raises his eyebrows. "You were pretty sure that I would accept," he says.

From my breast pocket, I take the business card with the address of the rooming house and hand it to him. As he lifts his hand from the blanket to take it, I withdraw it six inches, just out of reach. "The new lead you want to follow up, what might that be?" I ask.

Gainsaying the nurse's assurances to me, he snaps himself upright and grabs my wrist in an unexpected, iron-hard grip. He slides the card from my hand. "All in good time, Arnold, all in good time," he says. "I'll tell you when I'm good and ready."

He holds my eye for a long moment before letting go.

I concede the point, for the present. Now to make one of my own.

"Is your reason for being here connected with your investigation of Kevin's murder or your, uh, lifestyle choice?"

He sighs, "Did you know that, according to Kevin, addiction is a neuro-chemical condition not a 'lifestyle choice'."

Yes, I've heard that worn old excuse before.

"So Mr. Rogan, did they beat you up because of your investigation into Kevin's death or because of your 'neuro-chemical condition'?" I can not keep the sarcasm out of my voice.

"The latter," he grunts.

"Are you sure of that?" I plant the seed.

It takes root. I can see the shock on his face. He looks up, searching his mind for something, and then a frown of frustration crosses his brow.

"How…" The cogs are turning.

I turn and leave before he can ask the question that I see forming in his mind.

Chapter 25

I just played the amnesia card which was not too hard because I'm still having difficulty with some of the details; I don't remember anything after the gang started beating the heck out of me and I know I'm missing something important. Sarge wasn't buying it, he's been around far too long for me to fool him. However, he did agree to ask Steve Waters to visit me. We'll see if he does.

And we'll see if Steve brings Stammo along with him.

I squeeze the morphine dispenser but can not tell if is working or withholding.

Arnold's visit keeps buzzing around in my head. What the hell was all that about—

"Cal?"

Sam's voice stops my train of thought.

"Hi Sam." She looks great, in a wool sweater, tight-fitting jeans and boots.

In one smooth, elegant motion, she pulls up a chair and sits. She takes my hand and kisses my cheek. "How are you feeling?"

"All the better for seeing you," I grin.

She takes a piece of paper out of her purse and my stomach turns over. The only papers that pass between Sam and me are divorce papers, guardianship and custody agreements and letters about my drug addiction with copies to her lawyer.

She unfolds it and holds it up for me to see.

"Ellie sent you this picture. She says that it will make you feel better."

My heart melts as I think of her painting this. I imagine her bent over a desk in her bedroom, a bedroom I have never seen, her tongue peeking out of the side of her mouth.

It is a very complex work for a seven year old, a pastoral scene with rolling hills and an orange sun shining out of a blue sky. A variety of farm animals are grazing or standing beneath trees. A different colored bird, yellow, green and purple, is perched on the head of each animal. In the middle distance, looking down from the top of a hill, is a city with houses and buildings all dominated by a tall skyscraper. It's familiar but I don't know why and, for some reason, I feel that I should.

Several roads bearing brightly colored cars and trucks converge on the city. At the top of the skyscraper is a design with three bright colors, matching the colors of the birds. I've seen the design before somewhere, perhaps in one of her other pictures. The whole thing is strangely compelling.

"Wow."

Sam places it on the window ledge so that I can enjoy it from the bed then comes and sits back down and takes my hand again. It feels great.

"Are you in a lot of pain?"

"I don't know, I'm on morphine."

That causes a cloud of concern to cross her face; she knows that morphine and heroin are kissing cousins.

"At least you're conscious now. I sat here and talked to you most of Saturday and Sunday, hoping that it would get through to you; I didn't know if you would ever wake up. George was mad at me for spending so much time here but I was so scared Cal."

"I'm fine Sam." God, I love this woman. She sat vigil beside my bed. Why would she do that unless...

"You don't look fine," she says, but not unkindly. "Here's what I think you should do. You said they've got a bed for

152

you in detox on Saturday, right?" I nod. "That's five days from now. Why don't you stay here in the hospital until Saturday and then go straight there. I'll come over and drive you, if you like. You'll have somewhere warm and safe to stay and—"

"I can't, Sam. I need to use those five days to solve Kevin's murder."

Her face saddens. "Oh, Cal."

"Sam, I can't prove who killed Kevin from inside the hospital or inside detox."

Now her face hardens. "Cal, listen to me and listen *very* carefully. I meant what I said last week. If you are not in detox on Saturday, I am going to cut you out of Ellie's life." Her voice drops a couple of decibels and so does my stomach. "I've talked to my lawyer. Because you have done nothing to sort yourself out since we signed the custody agreement almost two years ago, I have grounds for refusing you access to her."

She takes a deep breath. "I wasn't going to tell you this." She pauses, undecided whether to continue. Then another deep breath. This can't be good. "George has business interests in Toronto, he already spends two or three days a week there and he wants me to move there with him. I'll do it in a heartbeat if you let me down on this. Do you understand?"

Ellie in Toronto? That's over two thousand miles away. The blood runs from my face and I feel nauseous. I just know that George would love to take Ellie away from me, too. Without Ellie, I would lose my compass. She is the one thing that keeps me in the real world. The thought of never seeing her cheery little face, hearing her laugh and of not watching her grow up grinds in my gut. I look up and swallow hard to keep any tears at bay. I look at Sam and I know this is hard for her too. But I know Sam; she is

153

nothing if not determined. But then so am I and I am determined to bring Kevin's killer to justice.

"Sam. I will be in detox on Saturday no matter what. I won't risk losing Ellie. She means more to me than anything. I promise you. But that's why I need to get out of the hospital as soon as possible. You see, I think I know who killed Kevin. Kev was working with a street guy. I don't want to go into all the details, but some bad stuff happened and I think he killed Kevin. I even think this guy Roy was responsible for me getting beaten up like this. I don't have all the details worked out but I can wrap it up in a couple of days, tops."

Sam's grip is crushing my hand. Her body is rigid and I can see the whites above her irises. "Roy?" she whispers.

The hairs on the back of my neck stand up. "Yes."

"Jesus, Cal. He's been to the house. It was him who told me you were in here. He said he was your friend. He was talking with Ellie. Oh my God, do you think she might be in danger from him?"

"Roy? At *your* house? How would he know where you—"

"Cal. Does Roy pose a threat to Ellie?" She's yelling at me now.

"A threat? To Ellie? No way. Roy would never hurt Ell —"

Then the elusive memory comes flooding back. The gang. One of them said something. The alpha male, I think. What was it?

OH MY GOD!

She sees my face and screams, "What—"

"Fuck, Sam, I just remembered something." My tone cuts her off. "At the end, just before I lost consciousness, I'm pretty sure that the guy in charge said to me, *Your kid's next.*"

"What d'you mean? What guy? D'you mean Roy?"

154

The words come tumbling out. "No, not *Roy*. The people who beat me up. The drug gang. They're bad news, Sam. They don't come any worse than these guys…" I pause, summoning what little courage I have to help me continue. "They know my name and they know about Ellie; they threatened to hurt her."

It takes maybe two and a half seconds for it to sink in then she's on her feet, the chair squealing backwards on the linoleum floor.

"What did you say?"

I repeat it, word for word.

For a long time she is lost for words. She sways and grabs the back of the chair to keep her balance, her mouth opening and closing. I start to speak but realize it is just an excuse that is forming in my mind. I feel the disgust she must be experiencing.

"Cal, how could you," she explodes. "Your irresponsible behavior has put my child, *our* child, in real danger." She processes some more. "Oh my God! I've got to…" she grabs her purse and hauls out her cell phone, stumbling as she rushes from the room.

Now the pain is not just physical.

I need to get well. I squeeze the control in my hand twice. No! NO! I must stay lucid. There has got to be something I can do. Something to protect Ellie and Sam. Maybe call Steve. Or what about that guy I used to know on the West Van force. What was his name? Dave? Don? Doug, that was it, Doug Bailey, a great guy…

I have to get out of here now.

I pull back the covers and start to struggle upright when the morphine hits and it's too late. I fall backwards and find myself drifting into Ellie's picture, leaving the rest of the world to deal with my mess.

Chapter 26

I open my eyes to Tuesday morning and my former partner.
The nurses uncoupled me from the morphine dispenser last
night—doctor's orders they said—and I am jittery again. The
pain killer is wearing off and the a throb in my side is
sharpening up nicely, trying to outdo the headache from that
final punch. Worst of all, the withdrawal that the morphine
has held off might distract me from my goal for this
meeting.

"Hey Cal. How you doing?" Steve asks. It occurs to me
that he has taken twenty four hours to get here. Back in the
day, when I was a cop, he would have been here in a
heartbeat. But things change, I guess. I look around and see
that Stammo is not with him.

"Hi, Steve. Thanks for coming… alone too." It feels
awkward talking to him one-on-one. We worked so many
cases together that we developed a flow of communication
between us that is no longer there.

He gives a half grin and nods. Despite the awkwardness,
I'm glad he's here.

He examines the mess that is my face. "Someone sure
did a number on you." The awkwardness is there for him
too.

"You should see the other guy," I joke. I want to talk to
him about the danger that Ellie and Sam are in but first I
need to rebuild some of the rapport that we used to have, if
that is even possible.

"Who was it?"

"A drug gang; seven of them."

"You're kidding." He looks at me suspiciously. "What did you do to earn this?"

I realize how important it is to me to have the approval of this man. I'm too embarrassed to tell him the truth: that it was in retribution for my stealing from them. If that was not bad enough, I can't get out of my mind Arnold's suggestion that the beating was somehow connected with my investigation of Kevin's murder. Why would he say that?

Steve is scrutinizing me; I have taken too long to answer his question.

"Maybe they found out that I'm one of the cops who put their colleagues away," I say. The half truth trips from my lips.

Steve can spot a lie a mile away. His eyes narrow. "Can't be," he says. "If it's the same gang, they don't kill cops. It's one of their rules; the repercussions are too big." He looks hard at me. "Come on Cal what was it really."

"Steve, I don't know if you've noticed, but I'm not a cop any longer. And I'm not technically dead either."

He relents and smiles, "But you're still a sarcastic SOB, eh?" Despite the humor, I still feel that I am under the microscope here. I resent the fact that I am no longer a trusted colleague and that he is treating me more like a suspect. But I know that my resentment is born of the shame I feel at my transition from cop to junkie. Steve can not be enjoying this any more than me. He deserves better from me; I need to level with him.

The smile fades as he sees the look on my face. "Steve, I need your help," there is a catch in my voice. "Just before I passed out, one of them said to me, 'Your kid's next.' I need to get protection for Ellie and for Sam, too. Could you phone Doug Bailey, our old buddy in the West Van force, and see if he can convince his colleagues to get off their fat asses and mount a protective surveillance on Sam's house?"

157

"I was wondering when you'd get around to this." Steve says drily. He already knows about Ellie! Now I feel like an idiot obviously wasting time, joking with him, trying to build rapport. "It's already done. Sam's new husband is a well connected guy over there. Apparently, he spoke to the Mayor of West Van who kicked some ass himself and got them twenty-four hour protection. For a while, anyways."

"Thank heavens for that." I feel a flood of relief. "Oh and FYI, Steve, he's not her husband… Yet." Still, it's nice to know that George has his uses. "How did you know?"

"I didn't get Sarge's message that you were in here until last night. Soon as I heard, I called Sam to see if she knew. She told me about the threat to Ellie and that her husband had pulled all the right strings to get protection from the West Van police, plus he's hired a private security firm to provide bodyguards."

Now I need to change the subject and I need to tread with care. I want to find out how much the cops know. I don't think I care if Steve knows that I am doing a freelance investigation of Kevin's murder but I don't want him to know what I know. I need to be the one to solve this murder and then present all the evidence to him, and to the Department, on a platter.

But there's nothing to stop me getting him to do a little legwork for me but I have to tread with care. Part of me wants to be completely honest with him but I need to protect Kevin's reputation too. "Steve? There's a rumor going around the downtown east side that there's been a spate of deaths among heroin addicts and alcoholics. Have you heard anything about that?"

"No. Why do you ask?" His eyes are slits.

"Roy told me that a couple of his drinking buddies had died and someone else told me about some addicts that had died for no apparent reason. Seven people in the course of a week."

"What the fuck's going on Cal?" he says. "I can read you like a road sign. You're not telling me something and I think you need to. And no bullshit this time." I can read him like a road sign too and I know he's mad.

"I can't accept that Kevin's death was a suicide. I have been investigating it as a murder." He opens his mouth to speak. "I know, I know. I'm not a cop any more but I know that Kevin Wallace did *not* commit suicide. Anyway, in the course of the investigation, I've discovered this rash of unexplained deaths."

He looks a me, his face expressionless, until I can't hold his gaze and turn away. "And you think these deaths are connected to Kevin's?"

"They might be."

He digests this before speaking. "You know the stats as well as me, Cal. Deaths in that neighborhood fluctuate all the time. I think it would take more than seven deaths to make a blip on the screen. I'll ask around and see if anyone's heard anything, if you like."

"Thanks, man. I appreciate it."

"So who d'you think killed your buddy?" he asks.

I hesitate. I'm worried that if I tell him too much he'll investigate it himself and, with his greater resources, solve it before I do. I tell him this.

"Jeez, Cal. You think I'd take something like that away from you. We were partners, for Christ sake. I'm disappointed in you man. Anyway, the coroner has ruled that it was a suicide so I can't investigate it without authority and I've got enough work on my plate right now, so fill your boots. If you can prove it was murder and who did it, go ahead. You were a great cop. Hell, you were the best I've ever worked with. If anyone can prove it, it's you." Despite these words, he is still irritated at me.

"Thanks Steve, that means a lot to me. I'm sorry, I should have told you right off."

"Yeah, you should have."

We sit silent for a while then he asks, "So who *do* you think did it?"

In my gut, I really don't want to tell him what I know but after his last speech, I can't hold back. "There's a couple of suspects but the only one with a really strong motive and cunning enough to do it and stage it as a suicide is Roy."

"Roy?" he's incredulous. "You mean our old snitch? That Roy?"

"Yeah."

"Well, he's cunning enough but what possible motive could he have?"

"I can't tell you that, Steve."

"Oh fuck you Rogan. Either you trust me or you don't, but none of this 'I can't tell you' shit." He stands up and he is pissed right off.

"Wait a minute Steve, you talk about trust, maybe you should trust me on this." He looks at me and shrugs but at least he doesn't leave. "The reason I can't tell you is that if I *did* tell you and if it turns out I'm wrong, then a good man's reputation would be destroyed and his family devastated. Let me just follow this up with Roy and I'll let you know what I discover."

"Sure. OK" he sits back down, looking a bit ashamed at his outburst. "Just keep me in the loop OK?"

"Yes, I will. Thanks for understanding."

"So when you told Sarge you wanted to see me, what was it about? Not Kevin's murder?"

Now the moment's here, I'm scared to ask him the question I so desperately want to ask but am so afraid of what the answer might be. Maybe I should wait until I've solved Kevin's murder. But that's a rationalization; I'm just chicken.

So I lie. "To get protection for Ellie and Sam."

He catches me in the lie with the same ease that I used to catch out the scum and lowlifes when I was a cop. "Bullshit. Sam told me that you only remembered the threat to Ellie yesterday afternoon when she was visiting. Sarge told me that you asked to see me in the morning when he came here to question you."

He stands up and pulls on his coat. His face is bright red. "This is just like when you started using. Every other word out of your mouth was a lie. Now it's *every* fucking word. I don't know what to believe. Don't waste my time, Cal." He turns to go.

"Steve, wait. Please."

He stops and turns back. Maybe it's something in my voice.

"There's something I really need to know." Now that the moment is here, I am frightened to put it in words in case I should jinx it. Here goes. "Steve, if I could get clean and maybe solve Kevin's murder, do you know if there's any chance I could get back into the department?" I ask.

"C'mon, Cal. Don't ask me that."

"Please, Steve."

He softens a hairsbreadth. He knows how much this means to me. "I don't think so Cal. I can't see them letting an addict, even an ex-addict, back in." He sees in my face the devastation that I feel. He sighs.

"But what do I know?" he relents. "Do you want me to ask someone, find out for sure?"

I nod.

After a while, he nods too. "Sure. No prob."

I notice a slump in his shoulders and in this moment, I know that no matter what, Steve and I will never have the old relationship back. It has been damaged beyond repair and it took this encounter, in a stark room in St. Paul's Hospital, for us both to realize it fully.

He turns and leaves me alone.

161

Alone. Alone with my thoughts. Alone with my fears. Alone with my increasing pain. I can't tell if it is from the beating or from the onslaught of withdrawal. Either way I've got to get some more of that morphine. I press the button to summon the nurse.

As I wait, my eye falls upon Ellie's picture. It is amazing. Despite the bright colors, there is a dark quality to it. But maybe that's a reflection of the darkness in me, *for now I see through a glass, darkly*. I look at the tall building and this time I recognize it. It's the Wall Centre, downtown. And those three slashes of color: I know what they are and where I've seen them before. Then it hits home. One connection… another… then a great leap in the dark. The thoughts click into place like Lego blocks.

With stunning clarity, a whole new avenue of investigation opens up before me.

Chapter 27

I'm on my way to see Ellie. I need to talk to her before I track down Roy. I want to ask her about her picture. Is what I suspect true? Or are my newly aroused cop instincts a phantasm? I have to know. If I am right it may add an interesting new line of questioning and even lead to a different theory of the crime.

They were mad when I checked myself out of St. Paul's two days before they planned to let me go. I think they might have tried to keep me forcibly if I hadn't been twelve inches taller and carrying fifty pounds more muscle than the hospital's elderly, east Asian rent-a-cop. I am relieved to be out of there and pumped about continuing my investigation into Kevin's murder but I feel bad about using my size to intimidate an old guy who was just trying to do his job. Unlike some of my colleagues, I never did that as a cop; I would like to blame it on my burning need to get out of there and talk to Ellie but I know it was just my burning need to get my hands on some heroin. Maybe I have a lot further to go than I thought.

I walked from the hospital to the West End, needing to avoid the downtown east side. I have to be extra vigilant from now on; I can not risk my mission by having another run in with the gang.

It did not take me too long to find a West End dealer who would sell me a gram and all the fixings. I fixed up in an alley off Denman. I hate to do it in public but I needed it right away; I couldn't even spare the time to find a coffee shop restroom. This is the level to which I have degenerated. Yet I still want to be a cop again—go figure.

Another worry is the infection in my left arm. It is getting worse and making it even harder to find a vein. If it gets any worse, I am going to have to learn to shoot up left handed.

I bought myself a pay-as-you-go cell phone and spent a further two hundred bucks of the money from Kevin's wallet in a budget clothing store. It feels good to be dressed in clean, new clothes, even if they are cheap. The clothes that I was wearing when they brought me into the hospital, filthy, ripped and covered in my blood, are in a dumpster and my garbage bag of 'good' clothes, that I dropped in the alley, will be long gone: converted to cash, spent on crack and smoked in a pipe, all for some crack head's one minute high.

Although there is no reason why she should, I am praying that Sam will let me see Ellie, even if it is Tuesday. I decided not to phone first and risk a refusal—it is better to ask for forgiveness than for permission—because I need to ask Ellie about her picture nestled in the inside pocket of my jacket. Yet even this is a source of guilt: the motivation for this trip comes from the cop who desperately needs to speak to a witness, not from the loving father who just wants to see his daughter. Will I always be torn like this?

Sam does a double take when she opens the door but recovers quickly.

"What are you doing here, Cal?" Her tone is wary. She glances up the driveway and I know her well enough to recognize that it is fear I see in her eyes. Fear that I have been followed here, perhaps?

"I discharged myself from St. Paul's. I thought as I missed Saturday, that I would drop by and see Ellie. I need to ask her something, something important. She's home from school, right?" My voice is light, trying to alleviate her concern, but I realize that I sound far too casual. "I really need to see her Sam," I say from my heart.

She looks at me for a moment, weighing the parameters of a decision, then starts to say something, catches herself and instead says, "OK, wait here." Good.

She closes the door and I hear her speaking in Spanish to the maid: short, sharp orders, not at all like Sam. She reappears wearing a brown suede jacket. "Let's go," she says striding towards her Porsche SUV.

"Where are we going," I ask but get no reply.

She is silent as we drive down to Marine Drive and turn east. We are past Dundarave before I ask, "Are we going to collect her from school?" Nothing. "A friend's house?"

I look over at her. Her jaw muscles are rippling as she grinds her teeth. She doesn't trust herself to speak. She keeps silent all through West Van. We pass Ambleside and Park Royal and she sweeps up on to the Lion's Gate bridge, for once clear of traffic.

"Where are we going?" I ask, knowing the answer.

"Shut the fuck up, Cal." Sam never swears. I shut the fuck up.

Silent along the causeway and Georgia Street; silent through a left turn onto Hamilton.

I am not going to be seeing Ellie today and I know that despite my desire to know about her painting, I am longing to see her happy little face and hear her innocent laughter. I may or may not solve Kevin's murder and I may or may not get back into the VPD but she will always be my little girl.

Silent along Hastings.

Hastings and Main.

She comes to a halt outside the Carnegie library. The sidewalk is a-throng with addicts, dealers and drunks: a view of the real Vancouver pointedly not televised to the world during the 2010 Olympics. One old timer with a long, yellow-stained, white beard is vomiting into the gutter, not ten feet in front of the car. An addict, stripped to the waist, is at the foot of the library steps, gyrating in the strange dance that crack has imprinted onto his neurons. A gaunt, pimpled youth is furtively buying something from another addict. All happening in clear line of site of the Main Street police station.

Several pairs of resentful eyes are drilled in on the Porsche.

"Get out of this car, Cal." She stares straight ahead, her taut knuckles gleaming white against the black leather of the steering wheel.

"Sam—"

"Out. Now."

My hand reaches for the door handle.

"Don't you ever come near me or my daughter again, you bastard," she says through her teeth. "Thanks to you, we have to get Ellie out of Vancouver. George and I have accelerated our plans for moving to Toronto. Ellie and I are going on ahead. We're leaving in ten days, ten days during which she will have a bodyguard 24/7. Now get out of this car and out of our lives."

"Sam, please—"

"No, Cal. No more. Just go. Get out there with the other degenerates."

A giant auger is drilling out a void in my gut as I slide out of the SUV and close the door. Does this mean that I will never see Ellie again? My need to find Kevin's killer crumbles to nothing in the face of this eventuality.

Sam is frozen at the wheel of the car. A white marble statue in designer clothes, with tears streaming down her cheeks and dripping off the line of her jaw. Then she is gone in a roar of exhaust and I try to hold her image in my mind, to photograph it indelibly and permanently onto my memory, to keep a picture of the only woman I have ever loved. I watch her until she disappears into the distance, one more vehicle in the Hastings Street flow.

I look around at the denizens of 'Wastings and Pain' as the intersection is often called. *Do* I belong here? Am I now trapped in this circle of hell? Am I forever to be one of these poor lost souls that Sam, with her newly won, wealthy, West Van eyes, can see only as degenerates?

Hell, a few years ago that was what I used to call them as I sat in the comfort of my police cruiser. Now I am one of them.

But right now too many eyes are on me. This is the danger zone. I pull Arnold's business card from my pocket. The address on the back is only four blocks away. I put my head down and head east towards my new digs in Strathcona, so very glad that Arnold gave me a second chance.

Although I wonder why he did. And I wonder if there is any way that Sam will.

Chapter 28

It's a worse dive even than Beanie's, the dim lighting hiding the unsanitary condition of the place.

Roy, instantly recognizable by his battered leather hat, is sitting hunched over a table, by himself, his back to me. It's taken me all morning to track him down and I'm going to have to handle him carefully.

"Hi, Roy." I say quietly.

In an instant he's on his feet, stumbling slightly as his foot catches in the chair leg.

"It's OK Roy, I'm not mad. I understand."

The naked fear on his face melts into a disbelieving wariness.

"Sit down, I'll get you another beer."

I head back to the bar, my back to him, praying that my trust will be reciprocated and that he will not run. Or maybe just the lure of another beer will keep him in place. I order and pay for a pint of his favorite brew without looking back at him. I get a bottled beer for myself because there's no way I'm going to drink out of one of the glasses here. I am not too sure about drinking out of the bottle, even though for such a crappy place the beer is an excellent local brew—go figure.

When I turn, he is sitting down again but this time on the other side of the table, watching me. As I approach, he examines the mess that was recently my face, then slips a glance at the emergency exit door at the back of the bar.

"I'm sorry, Rocky." He says, even before I have lowered myself into the chair, cringing at the unclean, sticky feel of the arms.

"What happened Roy?" I reach forward and squeeze his forearm. The gentle gesture works.

"They made me do it, Rock. Me and Nelson. I was talking to Nelson outside the Irish Heather, he was running on the spot, you know the way he does when he's talking to ya. And they pull up in this big black car. The one in the fancy leather jacket, he gives the orders and the others force me and Nelson down the alley."

The words are tumbling out on top of one another. "They sez to Nelson that if he don't find you and bring you back there, they're gonna kill me and then find him and kill him too. Poor old Nelson's not playing with a full deck but he understood what they was saying and off he runs. Then the big guy on the crutches hustles all the crack heads out of the alley and they made me stand there and tell 'em when you arrived.

"I'm sorry Rock, there's nothing I could do about it."

"It's no problem Roy." I say.

He seems sincere but I can't be sure.

"It was me called the cops for ya. Thank God I had a quarter in my pocket fer the phone." He says.

I remember the scream of the sirens as they were kicking the crap out of me.

"Thanks, Roy. You probably saved my life."

He smiles, takes a long draft of his beer and relaxes back in the chair. Maybe I can catch him off guard.

"Roy, did you kill Kevin?"

He takes in a sharp breath and his eyes lock on to mine.

"How did you know?" His voice comes out as a whisper.

It's my turn to stare with eyes wide open. Roy just admitted to killing Kevin! My only two remaining friends and one killed the other. What is this? A Greek tragedy?

169

The desire for revenge is powerful. Roy's rage at the death of his buddy Tommy and the deaths of Kevin's other guinea pigs must have driven him to the ultimate conclusion: an eye for an eye. But Kevin… my best and oldest friend, the man whose parents were my second parents, the only friend to stick by me as I spiraled down. Roy snatched his life away and with it took my one link to normalcy. Revenge. Roy is going to learn something about revenge.

He reads the rising storm and leaps to his feet, fear written on his face.

"No, no. I didn't kill him." His voice is a panicked squeak. "What I meant to say was how did you know that I was *planning* to? I *wanted* to. But I didn't *do* it, honest Rock. Honest to God." His eyes cut for a second to the back door.

Now I don't know what to think. I have heard hundreds of protestations of innocence in my career but I can not tell if his outburst is the truth. I want it to be but that does not make it so. But then this is the first time I've investigated the murder of a friend. My emotions are in the mix, clouding my observation. I can't see the truth for the feelings. In my confusion, I want to grab him and shake it out of him but as I start to move, the one true part of me takes over, the cop.

Deep breath. Sit down. Deep breath.

"Sit down Roy." He glances again at the back door, I can see him calculating the odds.

"Sit *down* Roy." He shrugs and slumps back down into the filthy chair. I want out of this disgusting place so badly but now's not the time to make the move.

The cop is back in charge. "So Roy, if you didn't kill Kevin, where were you that Saturday morning?"

He looks at his beer for a second then picks it up and takes another deep draft. He keeps his eyes averted and as he puts the glass back on the stained table top. "I'd rather not say, Rocky. Don't make me."

"Roy, where were you?"

"Please, Rocky. Ya don't wanna hear the answer"

I just look at him and wait. His eyes do the trapped animal routine for a while and then he resigns himself to the inevitable.

"OK. OK. I'll tell you." He finishes his beer in one swallow. "Just get me another one, will ya, Rock?"

I get up and go to the bar but this time I don't take my eyes off him for an instant. He moves in his chair and I tense, ready to chase after him if he makes a break for the back door.

When I return, he downs half the beer. He's had enough to loosen his tongue but he's still on the right side of sober. Just.

"OK. Here's the thing... I been kinda following ya.

"I gotta lot of friends, ya know that, but yer the only one that still has a part of his old life. Your Saturday trip to see Ellie was a part of yer life that I didn't know nothing about and I figured ya didn't want me to know about it neither. Ya always said ya was going to arrange for me to meet her but ya never did. I always felt hurt by that."

For a moment I am surprised that Roy expresses his hurt at the fact that I have never taken him to see Ellie. Then I realize that I am doing just what everyone else does when they encounter a junkie or an alcoholic. I forgot that despite the rough exterior, Roy is as sensitive and as vulnerable as any other human being. Living on the streets does not entirely lessen a person's humanity.

He picks up his beer glass but puts it down again without drinking. "Anyways, I got curious and about a year or so ago, I started following ya." He averts his eyes. "At first I'd just trail ya to the bus stop and then one day, a number 4 and a number 7 came along at the same time, you got on the first one, so I jumped on the second one and when ya got off at Arbutus I got off too and followed ya to Kevin's. When ya left, Kevin stayed in his little patch of front yard, watering the plants. I waited a bit and then went over and talked to him. He was a nice fella, friendly. Not many west-siders would take the time to talk to a guy like me. He even gave me a couple of bucks."

More beer vanishes down Roy's throat. "So every week I would follow ya and every week I got to know more and more of your route until finally I managed to follow ya over to West Van, to Ellie's house." Her name wrenches the feelings of loss in my gut.

"So once I knew where she lived, when you left on a Saturday to go to change at Kevin's house, if the weather was OK, I'd go over to West Van and hide out near the house and follow ya and watch ya with her.

"One time, I almost came up and talked to ya but I figured you'd be mad, so I didn't."

I can not keep the amazement out of my voice. "You've been stalking me?"

"Not stalking, just taking a friendly interest. I never meant no harm, ya know that Rocky."

"But why, Roy?"

"I toldja. I wanted to see that other part of yer life. I'm glad I did. It gave me faith that maybe you can get off the heroin. Ya gotta, Rocky. That lovely little kid needs a proper Daddy, not some junkie living on the streets."

His revelation has knocked me off course. I don't know whether to be touched by his interest in my other life or disturbed by the fact that he's been stalking Ellie and me. I'll process it later.

"So are you saying that you were following me that Saturday when Kevin was killed?"

"Yeah, I can prove it too. I can tell ya what happened, eh. You went to Ellie's house and spoke with her Ma for a bit. She handed ya something, money I think. Then ya walked down to the docks, had a talk with her and she looked at something in the water. You walked along the beach for a long time and I couldn't see everything ya done, 'cos I had to stay out of sight. Then you looked in a bunch of them fancy shops and went to have lunch at some Italian place."

Roy's description is just too detailed to be fabricated but the clincher for me is a sudden memory of being with him in the Yaletown pub. I remember his words. *It's gonna be hard but you've gotta do it. For yourself and for that cute little daughter of yours. You'll be able to get back on your feet and then you can take her to a fancy Italian restaurant anytime you want.* The memory of the words holds no comfort to me, I may never go to an Italian restaurant with Ellie again, but it adds the ring of truth to Roy's tale. How else would he have known about the Italian restaurant?

There's just one thing more I need to know.

"How did you know about Kevin's drug testing?" I ask.

Roy looks with longing at his empty glass so I get him another.

"OK. A coupla months back I was sitting on a bench in Pigeon Park with some guys and up walks Kevin. You know how tall he was; he stood out like a nun in a whorehouse. He looks around a bit, kinda scoping out the various junkies and I kinda waved and he recognizes me from that time I talked to him. He walks over and we get talking, eh.

"After a bit he takes me for a beer at Beanie's and he tells me about this drug he's developed and would I help him find some people to test it out on. He offers to pay me for helping and he says he'd pay the people who tried the drug twenty-five bucks a time.

"It seemed like a sweet deal, so I rounded up a bunch of people I know: some drinking buddies and a few heroin addicts. They may have been a bunch of drunks and junkies but they was good people. Normal, nice people who had regular lives before the booze or the drugs took over. Well, shit, ya knew most of 'em yerself."

As much as I don't want to, I believe what he is saying.

"It was great at first, me and a bunch of folks was making some good money and some of 'em wasn't craving like they used to. It was amazing... Then it happened. The drug started killing us off. I was scared at first, I thought I was gonna die too. I was scared to go to sleep at night in case I didn't wake up. But after a while I got as mad as hell. And when Tommy died, that was it."

He's grinding his teeth.

"What did you do?" I ask.

"I was so mad I decided I'd kill the fucker. I planned it all out with a couple of buddies. We decided I'd have to lure him down here into one of the alleys and then we'd do him." He gives me a sheepish look. "I know he was yer friend an' all and I thought about that; I did. Robbing you of yer only other friend wasn't right but when it came down to it, he was still a murderer.

"Anyways, I phoned him up—I knew his number from when I'd been helping him—and told him that I was gonna go to the police if he didn't cough up a thousand bucks. He was shit scared and agreed right away. I told him to meet me outside the Irish Heather at five o'clock on Saturday evening. The plan was to take him into the alley and a couple of the guys was gonna hit him with a length of re-bar or two-by-four and I was gonna finish him off with my good old knife."

He sighs. "We waited until after six, but of course, he never shows up. Someone beat us to it. So anyways, one of the guys had a bottle so we went off to Oppenheimer Park. On the way there, I ran into you outside Sunrise Market but you was off to fix yerself up at the Lion, so you probably don't remember."

More beer vanishes down the throat and he chuckles. "I know he was yer friend and all but when ya told me about how ya got that thousand bucks, my thousand bucks, outta

174

his wallet, I thought I was gonna bust a gut. It made me think that maybe there *is* some justice in the world, after all."

I'm bobbing like a cork on a storm of emotions.

Roy's last words have made me so angry that I want to grab him and wipe that smile off his face. Yet at the same time I'm relieved that he is not responsible for Kevin's death and that we can go back to the way we were before.

Except that we can't. Roy was in my cop world and then in my junkie world whereas Kevin and Ellie were in my other world. Now those lines are blurred. Where will our relationship go from here?

And on top of it all, I have now eliminated my prime suspect in Kevin's murder. Do I have to face the possibility, in fact the probability, that Kevin killed himself? Is my dream of solving the crime and getting back into the police force just another junkie dream? Or is there something that I'm missing? Then I remember Ellie's picture.

"Rock?" Roy breaks into my thoughts. "Y'ain't mad that I followed ya when ya went to see Ellie eh?"

I shake my head and sigh. "No Roy, it's OK. You didn't mean any harm." I feel a real pain in my heart. "Anyway, I won't be going over there any more. Next week Sam's taking Ellie to live in Toronto and she has said that I can't see her any—" Suddenly, out of nowhere, tears are streaming down my face and I'm racked with sobs. I have been pushing my thoughts of Ellie to the back of my mind and now it's all breaking through. Roy reaches his filthy old hand across the table and pats my forearm in comfort but it just makes me sob all the more.

Chapter 29

With trepidation, I type *george walsh finance vancouver* and click *I'm Feeling Lucky.*

Google's faith in my luck pays off. It's right there in front of me.

The logo of Walsh Investment Corporation Ltd. comprises the three bright slashes of color, yellow, green and purple, that I have seen before in two places: last week, I saw it on a business card poking its head out from under a box of tissues on Sandi's desk at QX4; two days ago, I saw it in the hospital, in a picture drawn for me by my darling Ellie, a picture that features the Wall Centre building bearing the logo of her soon-to-be stepfather's company.

The thought of Ellie opens the big wound. When Sam takes her to Toronto, I may never see her again. Would the gang really come after Ellie? I have to admit that from what I know of drug gangs, they will do anything; mercy is not in their vocabulary. It wrenches me inside to know it is safer for Ellie and Sam if they move as far away from me as possible. But I must not think about this right now. I just need to focus on what I'm doing here. I can think about Ellie later.

I click my way around Walsh's website, which I grudgingly have to admit is pretty impressive, until I find a page entitled *Current Investments.* It has company names listed alphabetically. Holding my breath, I scroll down, recognizing a few of the names and logos of companies that George has invested in. Close to the bottom of the list is QX4.

"Gotcha!" Oops, I said that out loud, very loud, loud enough to shatter the peace and earn sharp looks from at least two of the inhabitants of the downtown public library.

There is a link to QX4's website and I poke around there until I find a link to *Management and Board*, which takes me to a listing of the Board of Directors and there, halfway down the page, is George T. Walsh. One more click and I read the information on my ex-wife's intended husband, beside one of those phony, posed photos that business people seem to love.

> *George T. Walsh (Chairman) is CEO of Walsh Investment Corporation. He joined the QX4 Board in June 2008. George has a Bachelor's degree in biochemistry from MIT and an MBA from Stanford and he brings a wealth of business and financial experience to QX4. Walsh Investment Corporation is the largest single shareholder in the Company.*

Brad told me that 'the main investor' invested something like eight million dollars in QX4 and that before it went public, he owned fifty percent of the company. And it's George!

What if George discovered that Kevin had been doing illegal testing of the QX4 drug and that he had killed some of his subjects. George would know that if the information leaked out, it would ruin QX4 and he would lose everything he invested. It would seem logical that George might have killed Kevin, or had him killed, to cover it up. Or would it? Could Sam's fiancé be a killer or am I so close to this that I'm seeing what I want to see?

I click back to the listing of the Board and the name beneath George's catches my eye: Arnold Young. It's a common enough first name but I click on it anyway and there it is, Arnold's photo. What the hell is he doing on the Board of Directors of QX4?

> *Arnold P. Young (Director) is a Director of Wallace Holdings Inc. which was one of the early investors in QX4*

177

and was instrumental in helping the company transition to the public market.

The surprise at seeing Arnold's photo is tempered by the brief bio. My first guess is that Mr. Wallace invested in Kevin's company when Kevin first started to work there and that since he has been ill, Arnold has been sitting on the board of directors in his place. Still I should check this out with Arnold or, better still, with Mr. Wallace himself. Maybe Arnold's association is not as obvious as it seems. Is this why he didn't want to tell me his last name, knowing that I might Google him and find this connection?

Thinking of Arnold brings back the memory of his visit with me in the hospital. I still can't make any sense of his implication that the gang beat me up because of my investigation into Kevin's murder. I need to find out where he got such an idea.

Regardless of George's or Arnold's possible involvement, I have uncovered two lies. Or, to be accurate, one lie from two people. Both Sandi and Brad hid George's name from me. Sandi claimed *I don't even know their names* when I asked her about QX4's investors. Brad said that the major shareholder was an off-shore corporation. *You'd never find out who the person is behind it.* Yet it has taken me no more than fifteen minutes to discover that George is the big investor in QX4. Why would they both tell a lie so transparent? And why would they want to keep George's name from me anyway? Especially Brad.

My gut tells me that there is a major clue here so I need to think this through…

Sandi first. If she killed Kevin in a fit of jealousy she might want to divert my focus away from herself by telling me about Kevin doing the illegal drug tests to support the idea of him killing himself. So why keep George's name from me? Maybe to implicate him as an alternative suspect at a later date, in case I did not buy the suicide story. But that doesn't ring true… unless there's something going on between her and George. What if they were having an affair and Sandi told George about what Kevin was doing? Could they be in it together?

And Brad. Why did he try and keep me in the dark about George? I can see Sandi lying to me but Brad's a friend. Sandi asked me not to tell him about Kevin's illegal testing and he said that he didn't know about it when we met for lunch. Even if he was lying about that, why would he lie to me about Georges involvement in QX4? It doesn't make sense… unless Brad is somehow mixed up in Kevin's murder in a way which might become apparent to me if I knew about George being the big investor. But what?

Despite what I have just discovered, all I feel is frustration at creating more questions and less answers.

Maybe I'm full of it. Just because George is an investor in QX4 does not make him Kevin's killer. Maybe Kevin did commit suicide and I'm just chasing a will-o-the-wisp trying to find a non-existent murderer. Maybe my burning need to get back into the VPD by finding a murderer, whose existence they deny, is warping my judgment. Or maybe, even worse, I just want to nail George because, with him out of the way, I could have a shot, admittedly a long shot, at winning back Sam.

None of it makes any sense. It *is* all a junkie delusion. In two days I'm going into detox and then into rehab. I should put all this behind me and get on with the reality of my life.

It is time to make good on one of my promises.

I phone the detox help line: yes, they still have a spot for me and they are expecting me on Saturday afternoon and, yes, they have had a cancellation and I could come in sooner, this evening if I'd like.

Although I have probably lost Ellie and Sam forever, I still promised them that I would do this. And I'm ready. I am so weary of this life on the streets. This is the promise that I need to keep.

I get up from the computer, mentally wash my hands of Kevin's murder and make my way out of the library. I can walk to my room in Strathcona, pick up my stuff and be at the detox center by six, six thirty.

As I trudge eastward, I think over all that has happened in the days since Kevin's death. My world has been stood on it's tail but maybe for the best. And then, from the mass of memories flooding through my head, one image bobs to the surface and persists: an old man with parchment skin looking up at me from what will soon be his deathbed. *Find out who did this, Cal, no matter what the consequences.*

I made a promise to Kevin's father. I promised to do my best to find the murderer if there is any possibility that one exists. I owe this to him.

I stop, wrenched between my two diametrically opposed promises with their attendant desires and, after an age of indecision, I do what we Canadians do so well.

I compromise.

I'll spend the next two days investigating with an open mind and see where it leads. If I'm no further ahead by Saturday afternoon, I'll keep my appointment with the detox center.

I turn around and, with a spring in my step, head for the buses on Granville. I have two days. It's time to start again from the beginning.

Chapter 30

The watery November sun is just visible in the west, dropping behind the roof of a house on the next block. Its light illuminates the undersides of the heavy black clouds that are rolling in from the southwest, bathing the street in a surreal light which matches my mood.

It feels strange to be here again. Like returning to a childhood place that is at once familiar and yet fundamentally different. I do not like this feeling which is probably what has kept me from coming here sooner; this should have been the first stop in my investigation.

All of the townhouses in the row are identical and as I press the doorbell, I am surprised not to hear the opening bar of the 1812 overture. Mrs. Komalski's doorbell emits a plain and sensible two note chime, more appropriate to her personage.

On the few occasions in the past that I have communicated with Kevin's neighbor, when I picked up his key from her, she has made it clear that she does not approve of me. Her radar had me pegged as a junkie from day one. It is possible that she is not in and, more than likely that if she is, she will not open the door to me, especially if she gets a look at my face.

My one chance of her talking to me is that Mrs. Komalski is the gadfly of the condo association and the local gossip. I am betting that there is one thing that you can rely on from a gossip: if there is information to be exchanged, she will be in there trading. Or will she?

The door swings open and I am looking at her sharp face, the set back eyes circled by dark rings, sitting atop a gaunt frame.

It takes her a moment to recognize me and when she does, I can clearly read the conflict on her face; my police training has not forsaken me. My battered face frightens her but, on the other hand, Kevin's death must be the best grist her gossip mill has ever processed and here on her doorstep is someone who may just have some juicy tidbit of inside information.

"Mr. Rogan." I am impressed that she remembers my name. "What can I do for you?"

"Good afternoon, Mrs. Komalski. May I have a word with you, please?"

Her "About what?" is said warily. She makes no move to invite me in.

"About Kevin's death."

"I've already spoken to the police about that." She retreats a step and the door closes six inches, only her curiosity keeping her from closing it all the way.

It's a thin line. I need to get it right. I no longer have a badge that will guarantee me ingress.

"Yes, of course. But there are some things that the police don't know. I'd like to discuss them with you." This sparks a raised eyebrow.

"Go on." She still makes no move to invite me it.

If I want to get into the house and sit down with her, I need a lever. "Standing out here on the step is not really the right place to discuss Kevin's murd— um, death."

The indecision on her face is almost comical but, as I knew she would be, she is hooked by the curtailed word. "Yes, well…" The smile that appears on her face is a rare event indeed. She steps back and opens the door. "Come in. Please."

The house is identical in plan to Kevin's but bears no other similarity. Every square inch of the hallway walls is covered with paintings, photos and the output of various arcane crafts. I recognize macramé in several places. Unlike Kevin's house, it does not smell of sandalwood but of cat food.

She doesn't lead me upstairs to the living room—the likes of me do not warrant entry to the upper floors—but to the back bedroom which she has turned into an office and cluttered with bric-a-brac. She clears a newspaper from a straight-backed Victorian chair and indicates that I should sit.

Above my head and about six feet to the west is the couch on which Kevin died. I think of his punctured corpse and know that I must get this right. I owe him.

"So were you saying that Kevin was murdered?" No subtlety here. No beating about the bush for Mrs. Komalski.

"I believe so, yes."

"But the police said that it was suicide." She is perched on the edge of an office chair, swiveled away from its desk. She is leaning in towards me.

"Really. Did they tell you that themselves?"

She sniffs. "Huh!"

I raise my eyebrows but she doesn't continue.

"I'm sure you must have been an important witness for them," I prompt her.

"They came to see me… eventually," she admits. I nod encouragement. "I knew something was amiss on the Saturday. First, I was woken up at about seven-thirty by a whole lot of shouting. We don't approve of that in this development. The walls are thick here so I couldn't hear what was being said but she was real angry.

She?

Before I can question her, Mrs. Komalski continues, "Then it all seemed to quieten down." I picture her, one ear

183

to an inverted glass pushed against the wall, desperately trying to catch any items of conversation.

"Anyways," she continues, "a few minutes later I heard Kevin's front door slam, I looked out the window and I saw her march across the street and into that fancy car of hers."

My suspicions are confirmed. Sandi *was* there and she had a big argument with Kevin. That likely explains the engagement ring on the floor. How it must have hurt poor Kevin to have it thrown in his face.

"Did you tell all this to the police?" I ask.

"Yes," she sniffs, "although they didn't seem to pay much attention. Just going through the motions, they were. I also told them that I saw *you* arrive while I was having my morning coffee."

She pauses waiting for my reaction. I imagine her sitting, coffee cup in hand, in the bay window of the living room upstairs—a vulture on her bough, scouring the scene for a juicy morsel.

I smile encouragingly and she continues. I know that the next time she stops I will have to give her something in return. "Well that was normal, you always arrive at the same time every Saturday, as regular as clockwork. I could set my watch by you. When I told them about you, the skinny one that smelled of cigarettes seemed interested but the other one just sat there."

"Told them what about me?"

She ignores my question. "The newspapers said the police think it was suicide, why did you say it was murder?" It's *quid pro quo* time.

"I've known Kevin since the eighth grade," I say, "and we were close. He was my best friend. I just don't believe he would kill himself."

"Well, that's hardly proof," she sneers.

I'm not going to tell her about the illegal drug tests, so I just say, "Well there are some business reasons that may have been a motive and there was a note that the police took for a suicide note but it turns out not to be one. What you just told me about an argument that morning reinforces my belief that it was murder."

There is a smirk on her face that I can only describe as triumphant. "What do you mean, 'business reasons'? Was he doing something illegal? Embezzling, maybe…" she leaves it hanging.

She is no fool. Although she is off the mark, she is not too far off.

"Did anyone else come to the townhouse?"

"I don't know, I went off downtown, shopping with my sister. When I got back, I was having a nice cup of tea when I saw you hurrying down the road with a green garbage bag but you were back in a flash and the next thing I know the place was crawling with police and ambulances and I don't know what else."

"Did you tell the police that I took out that green garbage bag?"

"Why? What was in it?"

"Just clothes."

"Whose clothes?"

"Mine."

She processes this and decides it's OK to answer my question. "Yes, of course I told them." So Steve and Stammo already knew about that?

"So you didn't see anyone else?" I ask.

"I already told you I didn't."

I'm pretty sure I'm not going to get anything more out of her, so I stand. "Thanks for your time, Mrs. Komalski." I offer her my hand; best to leave on good terms in case I need more information later. "The information about the argument with Sandi is very helpful."

She ignores my hand and leads me to the door, a very obvious smirk on her face. I am down the steps and halfway to the gate before she says, "Who said it was Sandi?"

"Sorry?"

"Who said it was Sandi?" My confusion widens the smirk. "Who said it was Sandi that had the big argument with Kevin that morning?"

"You did."

"No I didn't, you just assumed it."

She is right. A cop should never assume; maybe my police training *has* forsaken me: a depressing thought. "So who was it?" I ask.

Her grin has assumed shit-eating proportions. She just looks at me, keeping me waiting for what seems like an age.

"I don't really know if I should tell you," she says. "It's not like you're a police officer. Well, not anymore." She is enjoying this.

As I puzzle out how to get this last item of information from her, she emits a laugh laced with derision.

"His stuck up bitch of a mother, in her big, fancy, chauffeur-driven limo, that's who."

She shakes her head as she closes the door.

Chapter 31

The thought that I might be about to speak to someone directly involved in Kevin's murder makes my pulse race.

He opens the door and his eyes widen at my battered face. "What the hell happened to you?"

He ushers me in as I reply. "Last Friday, I got the snot beaten out of me by a drug gang. I was in St. Paul's for five days, in a coma for two of them."

"What did you do to deserve that?"

With difficulty I ignore the implication that it was my fault... even though it was. Anger is not helpful in an interrogation... unless it's feigned, like it will be in a moment. I have forty-eight hours until I have to show up at detox so I go straight to the matter at hand. "When we met for lunch the other week, you told me that the majority of QX4 shares were owned by an off-shore corporation and that I'd never find out who the big investor was." Brad is already blushing; he knows what's coming. I raise my voice a couple of decibels. "I found out in twenty minutes flat on Walsh's and QX4's websites that George is the big investor, so I want to know why you lied to me?"

He hesitates for a second. "Isn't it obvious?"

"No Brad, it's not fucking obvious. Enlighten me."

"For Christ sake Cal, there you were suggesting that Kevin might have been murdered by someone at QX4 and you wanted to know the name of the big investor in the company. I know how you feel about your ex-wife's fiancé. If I'd told you that it was George, you would have gone about causing a lot of embarrassment for Sam, George, QX4 and for me. I just wanted to divert you."

As much as I don't want to, I have to admit that it's good enough reason but I'm still going to take advantage of the fact that he is embarrassed about lying to me.

"I want you to tell me everything you know about George Walsh."

"Cal, this is crazy. George couldn't have anything to do with Kevin's death." Brad is angry, more than I would have expected; good, I'll use it.

"Humor me. It'll make up for the fact that you lied to me the other day."

"No. No way. It's not going to happen." His anger is ratcheting up and I wonder why he doesn't want to talk about George. "You could hold a gun to my head."

That is exactly what I am going to do.

I draw the metaphorical gun: "Did I tell you that I confirmed what Sandy told me, Brad. You know, about Kevin conducting tests that killed his guinea pigs. It happened. I know the name of one of the victims and I even have a witness."

Brad pales but does not try to deny it.

I chamber the round: "You knew all along, didn't you? But you lied to me about that too."

"Listen, Cal—"

I click off the safety: "So either you are going to tell me everything I want to know about friend George or I am going to contact the pharmaceutical branch at Health Canada and I'm going to tell them exactly what Kevin did."

He is on his feet and looks like he wants to go for me physically. I know he won't dare go that far but he is apoplectic. "You can't do that Cal, you idiot. It would financially ruin a bunch of people and put the folks who work at QX4 on the streets. They could never get jobs anywhere else after this."

It's working. I shrug.

"And what about Kevin's reputation. Think what it would do to his parents." He knows that carries a lot weight with me and I hope that he does not realize that it makes my threat as metaphorical as the gun.

"Kevin's dead, he is beyond being hurt by this. His father wants me to find out who killed him, he said *no matter what*, so that's what I'm doing." I stand up. "Either you talk to me about George or I'm talking to the Feds and, while I'm at it, I might as well talk to an old buddy of mine at the Globe and Mail."

He doesn't respond so I turn towards the door; it is a calculated risk: if he calls my bluff I will lose this round.

No reaction.

At the door, I say, "Last chance, Brad."

Still nothing… until I start to open the door.

"OK. OK. Come back and sit down," he says through his teeth.

Without turning, I ask, "You'll tell me *everything* I want to know?"

"Yes… Yes."

I close the door. I do not want him to see the relief on my face so I head for the kitchen and grab two glasses and two bottles of Hop Head IPA from the fridge and go back to my chair.

"Tell me about him." I hand Brad a bottle and a glass.

Brad pours too fast and the beer foams up. He puts the glass down with a sigh and starts. "George is the brightest businessman I've ever met. He's a completely self made millionaire. His father was a steel worker in Hamilton and his mother worked as a secretary. He started his first business when he was thirteen, buying and selling bikes. Then he graduated to cars. He bought them in bad condition, got a bunch of guys from shop class to fix them up and then sold them. He made enough to put himself through university and grad school in the US."

Despite that he must be angry that I have coerced him, as he speaks, his old enthusiasm returns.

"George has definitely got the Midas touch. Just about everything he invests in makes money. You saw the website for Walsh Investment Corporation. Just about all of the companies listed there, the ones that he has invested in, are stellar performers. He has even invested in a couple of airlines and made money. If you only knew how difficult it is to make money in the airline business. Not even Warren Buffet will do it... Anyway, he's not much older than you and me and he's worth millions. He's a very positive guy. He really is the living proof of what you can do with a positive mental attitude."

"Yeah, sure Brad. If that worked we'd all be rich." I have let my street-won cynicism get in the way. This remark has attacked the very core of Brad's belief system.

He lashes out. "Yeah, well, maybe if you took it seriously, you wouldn't be a—" He cuts himself short. The flashpaper of his anger burns itself out. He takes a deep breath and looks at me with something uncomfortably like pity. "I'm sorry Cal. I know you can't kick heroin with just positive thinking. I shouldn't have said that."

He has shown himself to be a bigger man than me.

Before I can apologize for my own insensitive remark, he says, "You know how you used to go to Kevin's every Saturday to change. I want you to come here instead. I'll give you a key so you can come any time you want."

I feel a rush of gratitude. Brad and I have been distant since the day I started using and the pain at the loss of his friendship has always been acute. I am about to tell him that I don't need a place to change since Arnold is renting a room for me but I can not bring myself to spurn his offer.

"That would be great, Brad. I really appreciate it."

He smiles, almost shyly. "Great. Come next Saturday, I'll have a spare key cut for you tomorrow."

Now I know first hand why a cop is never allowed to interrogate someone he knows: the emotions, either good or bad, will always get in the way.

"I'm sorry about what I said about positive thinking. It wouldn't hurt me to think a little more positively sometimes," I say, even though I can not bring myself to believe in that positive mental attitude stuff.

"No prob."

Now I need to get my interrogation back on track. I use the awkward silence. "How did you meet him?" I ask.

"George wanted to take QX4 public and he was unhappy with the broker he was using. He happened to mention it to Sam and she suggested that he meet with me. We hit it off and he decided to give the business to my firm. The fact that I was close to Kevin was part of the reason, too. It was a *huge* feather in my cap at work. It was fantastic working with him. He has an amazing mind. He told me how he chooses companies to invest in; I learned a *lot* from him.

"He owns distribution, high-tech and manufacturing companies and he's a controlling investor in transportation companies and even some offshore agricultural enterprises: coffee plantations, sugar cane and so on."

"This guy sounds too good to be true. What does he do at night, go out and fight crime?" I say with a chuckle.

My sarcasm doesn't please him. "Cal I'm trying to forget that you blackmailed me into talking about George's businesses. You being sarcastic doesn't help matters."

Now I feel like a I am having to choose between my friendship with Brad and my need to get to the bottom of George's involvement in QX4.

"Sorry," I say.

"He's not perfect." He sounds defensive now. "He told me that his formula didn't seem to work with retail companies. Apparently he owns some convenience stores, a chain of dollar stores and even some foreign exchange outlets but they hardly turn a profit. Just between you and me, I'm working on a proposal with our Mergers and Acquisitions department to sell off these companies for him. If he goes for it, my firm will pretty much have to make me a senior partner and then…"

Although the friend should be, the cop is not interested in Brad's ambitions; I need some more specifics but I let him finish before saying, "When Kevin died and the shares of QX4 dropped by, what was it, sixty percent, that must have dropped ten million off the value of his shares. How did George take that bit of news?"

"He was great," This is not what I expected to hear. "I thought he was going to blow a gasket, but he just said to me, 'You know what, Brad? In business, shares fluctuate but if you're focused on the long term, you don't sweat the ups and downs along the way.'" Brad looks a little rueful. "I guess when you've got that much money, you can afford to be cavalier about a million or two here and there."

I'm not buying this. "Bull*shit*. It's not a million or two. You're telling me that he dropped *ten* million and just shrugged it off?"

"Yeah."

I look hard at him but he shows none of the signs of lying: no dilated pupils, ticks or sweating. I don't know a lot of rich people, come to think of it I don't know any, but I can't imagine anyone taking a ten million dollar loss so stoically. But then again, maybe I'm looking at this all wrong.

"How did *your* firm take the fact that Kevin killed himself and put their client's shares in the toilet." I ask. I want to try out a theory that is forming in my mind.

"Neutral. We made our money when we took them public and during the first year of trading."

"So Kevin's death didn't effect you financially?"

"I wouldn't say that." He sighs.

I am surprised by the depth of the sigh.

"What happened?" I ask.

He waits for a beat. "The deal was that I would tell you everything I know about George, not about my own affairs."

Now I am caught between my need to know and my newly reforged friendship. I decide not to push it; I do not want to lose Brad again. Then the memory again comes unbidden into my mind: the memory of Kevin's father : *Find out who did this, Cal, no matter what the consequences.* I can not ignore his voice.

"Sorry, Brad. I just changed the rules."

"Fuck you!"

"I'm sorry. I really am but I owe it to Kevin's dad to find out all I can." I am not going to repeat my threat to go to the feds. It's empty, anyway. I just shrug and wait while he conquers his anger.

Finally he says, "OK. But you've got to keep this confidential."

"Sure."

"Give me your word, Cal."

I reach forward and offer him my hand. "You have my word. I promise," I say and really mean it.

He shakes my hand. "Thanks... You see, I'm personally in a really difficult position. I've done something that is technically illegal. If it came out, I would lose my job, maybe more"

"I swear, not a word."

He looks down at the carpet. "When we took QX4 public, I made a very healthy commission, over three hundred grand." Wow, three hundred grand on one deal, no wonder Brad can live in a nice condo like this one. "Knowing George's track record, I figured that QX4 shares would go through the roof, so, on the quiet, through a broker I know in Calgary, I spent all my commission on

193

shares, which isn't completely legal, because of my insider knowledge.

"Of course, the shares did well and I got greedy, I started to borrow money to buy more shares using the shares I already had as collateral. The shares went up and up and every few months I'd borrow more money and buy more shares. In the end, I had a seven hundred and fifty thousand dollar debt but it didn't matter because as long I could cover the interest payments and as long as the shares were doing well, everything was great.

"At one point I thought seriously about selling them. The shares were worth one point six million. If I'd have sold them then, I could have paid off the loan and still had eight hundred and fifty thousand. I would have almost trebled my original three hundred thousand." His voice is laced with bitterness.

The numbers boggle my mind. "You'd have had almost a million bucks. Why the hell didn't you cash in?" I can not imagine someone taking such a risk but then again maybe that's why I never had a big condo in Kits; if I had, it would have gone on heroin anyway.

"Greed, I guess. I was holding out for that million. George had told me that he thought the shares were going to double again in the next year..." He falls silent.

"Then, Kevin died?" I ask.

"Yeah. Kevin died on the Saturday. By the close of trading on Monday, my shares were worth six hundred and forty thousand. That's one hundred and ten thousand *less* than the loan. The bank were on the phone by Wednesday morning, asking how I was going to pay back the loan."

"What did you do?"

"I remortgaged the condo to the hilt, I got a hundred and seventy grand from that. The BMW was next, I sold that for fifty grand. That still left me with a loan of over half a mil. I couldn't sell the shares on the open market because that would have depressed the share price even more, so I went to George and offered them to him at a discount.

"He did an amazingly generous thing. He told me to keep my shares and then called my bank and told them that he would personally guarantee my loan."

From what I have seen of George, I can't imagine him doing this without some motive; it has given him a big hammer over Brad and I wonder what he may use it for.

It is difficult for Brad to tell me this story. He is a not someone to make himself that vulnerable. However he's given me the opening I was waiting for. "When do you think QX4 will get back on track?"

"Not sure. If Kevin's illegal drug testing ever comes to light then the company's toast, no matter what. My shares will be worth nothing and I'll still owe George half a million. But if Sandi can fill Kevin's shoes and fix what's wrong with *Addi-Ban* and if the Feds ever get round to giving approval for the human trials…" He shrugs. "Maybe the shares will bounce back then. I don't know."

Brad's story has changed my view. He probably hasn't even thought about it but he has cleared himself of any involvement in Kevin's death. No matter what, Brad would never do anything to ruin himself financially. It's just not in his positive thinker's DNA.

But far more interesting is the fact that George didn't sweat the loss of ten million dollars on Kevin's death. That I do not understand. But in the next forty-six hours I am going to find out.

Chapter 32

The sound of the doorbell drags me out of the strange, dark places through which my mind has been wandering. Thoughts of Cal and of George, so different in almost all ways, yet both so driven: George by his need to grow his business empire and Cal by his need to see justice done. Up until a week ago, I was so sure of my decision to marry George. I certainly love him and he provides the security and stability that Ellie so desperately needs and, in truth, so do I. But when Cal came here for dinner and to talk to Ellie, my longing for the old Cal nearly made me throw everything away. If Cal hadn't turned down Ellie's suggestion of staying the night, I am not sure what might have happened. Could I really swap what I have now for the chaos of life with Cal? The answer seems so straightforward yet I just don't know.

But ultimately, I don't believe that Cal will ever get straight, he will probably die on the streets and, regardless of what I may think or of what yearnings may beset me, my first and only consideration is Ellie and her safety and well being. No matter what, she will be safer the further away she is from him.

It chimes again. Three o'clock. Who could it be? Not Cal, oh please, not Cal. It is exactly two days since he rang this bell wanting to see Ellie. My anger at that visit triggered another attack and has left me weaker than before. So why does the thought that it might be him make me feel like a giddy schoolgirl? I pull myself to my feet and make my way down the hall. My legs feel unsteady; the doctors tell me I'll soon have to start using a cane.

Through the peephole in the front door, I can see a figure in a brown coat with a black hat. It's Roy. I can feel the adrenaline flooding my system. Cal said that he was a suspect in Kevin's death. I feel suddenly vulnerable. George is out of town again and Ellie's bodyguard is with at her school, preparing to bring her home. Why is he here? Oh my God, maybe something awful has happened to Cal.

I have to know.

I fix the security chain in place, open the door against it and give him my widest smile.

"Hi."

"Hi, Mrs. Rog— uh, Sam. It's me, Roy. Y'know Cal's friend, eh." He gives me a crooked grin showing teeth like battlements. He looks harmless enough, more of an old rogue than a murderer really. But I can't trust looks.

"Is Cal OK?" I ask.

His smile drops and his brow knits. "Physically, I guess he's OK." He is silent for a moment. He looks away and then back at me and his eyes hold a world of sadness.

"Ya prob'ly gonna say that this here's none of my goddamn business but I'm gonna say it anyways." He looks away again, steeling himself to say what he came here to tell me. "What I wanted to say, was that, well, Roc—, Cal, he doesn't…" His words peter out. Then, "I'll just say it. Rocky loves that little girl more than anything or anyone. I know ya gotcha reasons and all, but I'm asking ya if ya can find it in yer heart to let him see her one more time. I dunno what it'll do to him if ya don't. He says yer taking the little one off to T'ron'o and he's worried that he's never gonna see her again. He just wants to say a proper goodbye."

Damn it! Just when I'd forced myself to cut Cal out of our lives, Roy comes calling and sets my resolve crumbling. For some reason, I am hit by a wave of sympathy for this old man and I just can't believe that he would be here to hurt

Ellie or me. "Would you like to come in Roy?" I trust my intuition, slide off the chain and open the door.

He starts to move forward but then checks himself, looks down at this clothes and his battered old boots. "I better not," he says, blushing. "Last time yer husband wasn't too keen on me being here." Now it's my turn to blush. George's attack was completely unacceptable, especially in that Ellie saw the result, just a couple of days after Cal had told her that violence was never a solution.

I almost tell him that George is not here but think better of it. Just in case…

"I promise nothing like that will happen again in this house." I tell him and reach out, take his arm and, keeping hold of it to avoid stumbling, I draw him down the hallway into the kitchen. I indicate one of the stools by the counter and he sits down. He is not altogether comfortable and I have a feeling that he does not like to be indoors. I suppose he's homeless, sleeping on the streets. Poor old devil.

"Would you like a tea or a coffee, Roy?"

"Ya don't have a beer, do ya?" He licks his lips.

I get him one from the fridge. "Roy, why do you care? Why would you come all the way over here to persuade me to let Cal see Ellie?"

"Well, I known him a long while, eh. And like I told'ja before, I feel kinda responsible for him being an addict. An' I like him, y'know?" He pauses, considering what to say next, I suppose. "I know what it's like when a kid gets separated from a parent. An' I don't want that to happen to Rocky… or to the little one." A small tear is forming at the corner of his eye.

When I'm downtown, there are a bunch of Roys, right there on the streets, sitting on the sidewalk or leaning up against a wall, almost invariably holding out a paper coffee cup or a battered baseball cap and asking for money. And I do what I guess we all do. I avoid eye contact and speed up my pace until I am safely past them.

Up until now, I have only been able to see the humanity of the dispossessed through the lens of my camera, as though I were seeing them from behind a screen or through a two way mirror, safe and removed, somehow unreal, just conceptual. Now, for the first time, I see with my own eyes that there is a very real person beneath the shabby clothes and dirty skin. A person who has seen many sides of life but a person none the less. A person who cares about others, a person with a history. Someone who has loved and lost, not some faceless degenerate.

Roy, sitting here in his shabby old clothes was once an innocent kid, like Ellie, laughing, running and playing. What happened? I would love to know what twist of fate brought him to where he is now. For a frightening instant, I think of Ellie in fifty years, ending up like Roy and know that, however unlikely that may seem, it is in fact possible.

But Roy's heartfelt plea is not enough. Cal's actions, whatever they might have been, have caused a gang of drug dealers to threaten Ellie and I can not let that pass. I would do anything to protect her, *anything*. I just can't risk it. I won't.

I realize that Roy has been watching me like a hawk. "Ya gonna say no, ain't'cha?"

Now a tear is forming in the corner of *my* eye as I nod.

He takes his beer and makes his way back into the hall. I walk him back to the front door and as he shambles down the steps from the porch, he turns back and says, "Find a way. Please. Just give him his last goodbye visit with the little one, won't'cha."

God help me, I don't know what to do.

Chapter 33

Time is running out. Kevin has been dead for two whole weeks now and I only have twenty-nine hours left to find out who killed him. No matter what, I am going into detox tomorrow afternoon. I have been trying to get hold of Arnold ever since my meeting with Kevin's neighbor. Even when I finally succeeded, he has taken his time in getting here.

He is uncomfortable in these surroundings where his tailored pinstripe is so wildly out of place and draws the lupine stares of the local denizens. It is one of the reasons that I suggested we meet here. This interview will be on my turf and on my terms even if it means enduring the sights, sounds and smells of Beanie's Eatery pub.

"Thank you for coming," I say as he takes his seat like a fastidious matron settling upon a gas station toilet.

"Mr. Wallace's instructions were explicit: that I was to help you in any way that I can," he says. "Although, if *Mrs.* Wallace should discover that we were meeting, I can not imagine what she might say."

"It's one of the reasons I suggested meeting here," I say. "I think it *somewhat* unlikely that she's a regular." I find my tonality and sentence structure taking on a British orientation in reflection of his.

Arnold's smile is frigid. "Mr. Rogan, I want you to understand my position here. My loyalty is first and foremost to Mr. Wallace but, over the years, that loyalty extended to Mrs. Wallace and then to Mr. Kevin. So when I am caught between the opposing desires of Mr. and Mrs. Wallace, I find it uncomfortable in the extreme."

I reward this revelation with silence.

"Why did you want to meet with me Mr. Rogan?"

"I want you to tell me what you did on the morning that Kevin was killed."

"Am I to take it that you regard *me* as a suspect?"

I ignore his question. "What *did* you do that morning Arnold?"

He stares at me, his face a mask, and I wait... until he starts to rise. "If you don't tell me Arnold, I will have to go to Mr. Wallace and tell him that you are not cooperating with me."

He holds for a moment, on the edge of decision, before sinking back into his seat.

"I rose at five, as always. I spent thirty minutes riding the stationary bicycle and then another thirty lifting weights. After my ablutions, I dressed, went to the kitchen and made myself breakfast: eggs, bacon, sausage, toasted rye bread and orange juice."

My antennae are twitching. When someone is too precise in their answers, it is often a subterfuge to cover something that they do not want to reveal. I need to listen carefully.

"I was washing the dishes," he continues, "when Mrs. Wallace entered the kitchen and told me that she would be wanting me to drive her at seven fifteen. She didn't say where."

"What time would that have been?" I ask.

"Eight minutes to seven." There's that precision again. "I finished up in the kitchen and took the Rolls to the gas station at Granville and Forty-first, filled up and returned to the house where I parked in front. Mrs. Wallace came out, at just a few minutes before seven fifteen, and asked me to drive her to Kevin's townhouse. When we got there, she went in for about twenty minutes and when she came out, she asked me to drive her home. We were back by eight and, after parking the car in the garage, I retired to my room and spent the rest of the morning working."

Working at what I wonder.

"So you see Mr. Rogan I do not have an alibi for the time of Kevin's death," he says with a smile.

"What was Mrs. Wallace's disposition when she came into the kitchen?" I ask.

"Mr. Rogan, you have to understand the delicacy of my situation. I am a trusted employee and I refuse to gossip about my employers."

He's pissing me off now. "Arnold, we have some choices here. One, you can answer my questions; two, we can both go to Mr. Wallace and I can ask him to tell you to answer them, which I suspect will be distressing to him; three, I could ask Steve Waters, who is in charge of the case at VPD, to ask you officially. I think you know which is the best option here."

He looks at me and raises an eyebrow and I am sure that he is going to call my bluff. But before he can speak, Beanie's bouncer—a squat bull of a man whose IQ is inversely proportional to his neck size—makes his presence known with, "Ya can't sit here without a drink in front of ya."

I nod at the bouncer, get up and decide that I'll get more flies with honey than with vinegar. "Please Arnold, you know how much this means to Mr. Wallace." Leaving him to think, I walk over to the bar and order two bottles of pedestrian, manufactured beer. They are not going to be consumed but they are the price of admission.

I walk back to the table and suppress a grin at the picture of Arnold sitting at the grimy table in his perfectly tailored suit, hair immaculate, his rear on a chair that had seen better days in the nineteen sixties, ignoring the open bottle of beer I put in front of him.

As I sit, he raises an eyebrow. "I call, Mr. Rogan." My bluff shatters on the table but I can not leave it at that.

"It was Mrs. Wallace who told you what Kevin had done, wasn't it?" I ask.

"What do you mean?" he asks.

"What did you do in the army Arnold?" I ask this because I know the answer.

Surprise and anger are mixed on his face. "How is that relevant?"

"Humor me."

"I was a captain in the military police."

"You must have done some interrogations in your time and so you know that asking 'what do you mean?' is a classic delaying tactic, a ploy to give you some time to consider whether or not to tell me the truth."

His face reddens.

"So I'll take it as read," I continue, "that Mrs. Wallace *did* tell you and I'm guessing that she told you during the drive back home from Kevin's." He releases a fractional nod and I change my tone, no longer confrontational. "How did it make you feel Arnold?"

"Hurt that he had betrayed the honor of his family so profoundly." His emotions are naked on his face and there is more than hurt there. I wonder what it is. Let's see if he answers the next question with as much candor.

"Was Mrs. Wallace angry too?"

"Well firstly, I didn't say that *I* was angry."

"Was she?"

He thinks for a while. "No. She was devastated."

"When you got back from Kevin's did Mrs. Wallace go out again?"

His eyebrow flickers for an instant, registering his surprise at the implication. He looks up and I can tell that he is weighing options. I take an absent-minded mouthful of the beer and wish that I hadn't. I watch him, trying to read what might be going through his mind, until finally he speaks.

"I refuse to be a spy on my employer for you, Mr. Rogan," he says with a sad smile.

"You know as well as I do that Kevin was murdered, don't you Arnold?"

He stands, holds my gaze for a long, distasteful moment of his time. "You're barking up the wrong tree."

"So enlighten me," I say.

"You went to QX4," he says. It is not a question; how could he possibly know that I have been there? "That is a far better place to focus your attentions."

He turns to leave. "Don't ever ask me to come to a place like this again."

"Arnold, wait!"

He turns back, maybe at the note of desperation in my voice.

"What did you mean in the hospital when you asked if my investigation was the reason those drug dealers beat the hell out of me?"

He smiles, like a professor encouraging a slow student. "That's for me to know and you to find out. You were a detective; go and detect." He turns and walks away, his parting shot: "You really should."

Although this meeting has supplied another small piece of the jigsaw puzzle, I am left with the feeling that Arnold has manipulated me into doing what he wants.

Chapter 34

He's big, hard, aware and vaguely Schwarzeneggerian and, in flagrant violation of Canada's gun laws, he is carrying a Glock 16 concealed in a shoulder holster. He looks both menacing and competent. I am happy that he is never more than a few paces away from Ellie and feel a grudging gratitude toward George for supplying her with a bodyguard; the words *your kid's next* are never far from my consciousness.

"Pick me *up*, Daddy," she says.

I pick her up and she perches on my forearm, her arms around my neck. She glances back at Sam, ten paces behind, her sweet little face worried. "Daddy," she whispers softly, "I don't want to go back home. I want to come with you to your new house."

We are on Marine Drive and almost at the turn off to George and Sam's house. There is a bus stop with a blue tubular metal bench. I sit down with Ellie on my lap and look back at Sam. I wonder for the hundredth time what persuaded her to change her mind and allow me this one last visit with Ellie. She looks pointedly at her watch—my four hours are nearly spent and I sense that I am not going to get a single second beyond the allocated time; I know this is painful for her too—shrugs and occupies herself by looking in the window of a women's clothing store.

The Terminator is five feet away, arms crossed, scanning up and down Marine.

"Why don't you want to go home, sweetie?"

"Because I want to come with you."

"One day soon, sweetie," I prevaricate.

"But I want to go with you *now*, Daddy."

I'm relieved to see that Sam is not in evidence. She must have succumbed to the draw of the store.

"Is there something happening at home that's upsetting you?"

I decide to take her shrug as an affirmative.

"What is it, sweetie?"

She looks up at me and the tears welling in her eyes break my heart. "The other night, I got up to go pee and I heard Mommy and George talking. I'm frightened that Mommy may wake me up one morning and take me to Toronto. Then I'll never see you again like Jenny Oliver never sees her Daddy." She breaks down into sobs.

I cuddle her tight, rocking from side to side, and kiss the top of her head. What can I say to her? My anger at Sam for not being forthright with Ellie is rising to fever pitch only to be cut off by the sound that always catches a cop's attention: the loud rumble of a motorcycle exhaust, a sound copyrighted by the Harley-Davidson motorcycle company.

My head snaps to the left and I see, about a hundred yards away, two men on bikes coming along Marine. One is a giant of a man, his face obscured by a triangular bandanna. The other is looking right at me. I look up at the bodyguard; he is eying them but making no move for his gun. I get a sudden feeling of unease about this guy.

I get ready to cover Ellie with my body and pray that Sam stays in the store.

My eyes are drilled in on them, looking for any untoward movement, any indication of impending violence. As they draw closer, I can see them more clearly. The smaller rider is well shaven and has short, well groomed gray hair under his tiny, just-legal helmet; the giant is not wearing a bandanna, it's a knitted scarf: two middle aged businessmen, trying to look like bad boys, out for a Saturday ride.

Paranoia, self destroyer. I flex my shoulders to get the kinks out and I cuddle Ellie tighter.

Then another shadow falls over us: Sam's. "It's two o'clock. Time to go now," she says as she plucks Ellie from my lap and stands her up.

She starts to walk off and I can see that Ellie is pulling back from her. Rather than risk a scene, I take three quick steps to catch up and grab Ellie's other hand. "I'll walk you both home," I say to Ellie.

Sam shrugs and Ellie just stares ahead as we walk in awkward silence. The pain in my heart becomes worse with every step. Will this really be the last time that I am with my daughter. At least Sam is walking slowly—she seems to be limping—so I use the time to rehearse what I am going to say next.

We arrive at Sam's front door and the bodyguard, without word or sign, squeezes his frame into a Ford Taurus and drives off. I wonder why he is going. Does George think that Ellie is only in danger when I am around?

George's car is parked in its usual place. Unbidden, unwanted but not unexpected, my cop brain clicks in and I want to ask Sam about George's investment in QX4, hell I wouldn't mind talking to him myself but I guess now is not the time.

As she inserts the key Sam says "'Bye, Cal," without looking at me.

"Wait, Sam. You need to listen to this." I say. "You too, Ellie."

Sam looks at me; she's trying not to cry. "What is it Cal?" Ellie just looks at the floor.

I crouch down to Ellie's height and put my arm around her but address myself to her mother. "The detox center called and confirmed they have a place for me. I have to report there today at four." Do I detect a softening in Sam's demeanor?

"What that means sweetie," I say to my daughter, "is that I have to go into that hospital we talked about for a week and then to another place for a little while longer." Her face is blank. "It means that I won't be able to see you for a few weeks"—the evasion claws at my gut—"but when I do, things will be much better." I give her a hug, which she does not reciprocate, and stand up.

Sam pushes the door open. "That's good news Cal." The words should be encouraging but they are delivered in a flat, neutral tone. "Come on Ell." She takes the little hand and draws our daughter into the house but Ellie breaks away and attaches herself to my leg.

"Daddy, don't go. Take me with you. I don't want you to go to that hospital. I want to be with you. Please don't go, Daddy. Pleeeaaase."

I reach down and pick her up but can not find the words. I hold her tight. She is the reason I am going into detox yet she will not be here when I get out. I get an insane desire to just turn around and run away with her in my arms but we have nowhere to go. "Listen, sweetie. I know it's difficult to understand, but it's something I have to do. It's just a while then I'll be seeing you again." I know that Sam will make a lie of this in a week but it is up to her to tell Ellie.

With a volte-face that only a child can pull off, she says, "No you won't." She squirms out of my arms and runs into the house. "I don't care. I never want to see you again. Go away." I feel the spear in my heart.

Sam looks at me, shrugs and shakes her head as she closes the door. For an instant, I see George in the hallway. My anguish turns to anger and focuses white hot, re-forging the spear to turn against him. I'm damned if he is going to see her every day for the rest of his life. He's the guiding force behind their move to Toronto, somehow I am going to stop him, somehow I'm going to get Sam and Ellie back whatever it takes. *Yeah, sure. A junkie can pull that off.* The reality deflates my anger leaving an emptiness that I have never before experienced.

I turn from the doorstep and walk off with my fears roiling inside me. I have been telling myself that I can't go into detox and rehab while Kevin's murder is still unsolved. But what do I have? Roy has a rock solid alibi: me. Brad was never a logical suspect; he loved Kevin as much as I did and he has no motive: Kevin's death has near bankrupted him. I can't believe that Sandi did it in a fit of jealousy; it's just not credible. Arnold is an enigma but ultimately, he would do nothing to harm the Wallace family. And George, if George did it I can't see any logical theory of the crime.

Even Blondie's comment, *Your kid's next* doesn't make sense to me. Rather than try and find out what it means, I should just follow his advice. Ellie's safety is more important than my need to solve the puzzle of Kevin's death. I just have to accept that I am an *ex*-cop.

All my excuses are gone. There is nothing I can grasp at as a reason for not doing it. But I am petrified at the thought of the detox process. It's days of suffering through the crippling pain of heroin withdrawal, once described to me as having an extreme cramp simultaneously in every muscle of your body. And for me it will be even worse, I will be suffering from the withdrawal of Ellie to Toronto.

The thought of never using heroin again is agony in itself. Like every other addict, the neurochemistry of my brain, once exposed to the drug, demands it over and over and over again. I have no choice in the matter of my craving. If it were easy to stop using, no addict in the world would take drugs rather than live a normal life. And when I get out, Sam and Ellie will be two thousand miles away.

I turn out of Sam's driveway and head towards Marine Drive and the journey that will see me in detox in less than two hours. Each step darkens my despair.

In contrast, the clouds have cleared and the November sun is shining down on me and glinting off the cars coming towards me. One of them is a black Mercedes CLS, the AMG version. I look appreciatively at it; it is a fine piece of machinery… then I recognize the driver.

He is handsome with long, well groomed, blond hair and is wearing a leather jacket. It's the man from the alley. *Your kid's next.* I follow the car with my eyes and watch with mounting panic as it turns into Sam's driveway.

Chapter 35

I speed dial Sam's number and scream back towards the house. As it rings, I think about the VPD issue Browning 40mm that used to sit in a holster on my side. It would feel good in my hand right about now.

"Hello—"

"Sam, it's me. Whatever you do, don't open the front door."

"Cal, what are you talk—"

"Sam. Listen to me." I hear her doorbell chime through my phone and run faster. "For God's sake don't open that door. Those guys that beat me up and put me in the hospital, the guy in charge, the one that said 'Your kid's next' just drove into your driveway. That's him at your door. Don't open it."

Sam's voice has dropped into a harsh whisper. "Cal. Don't be ridiculous. I don't know what you're trying to do but it's *not* going to work."

I have got to convince her.

"Sam, please listen to me—"

"Enough, Cal." She hangs up.

It takes me thirty seconds to reach the house, panting hard. God, I'm out of shape. I stand by one of the stone pillars that flank the entrance to the driveway and sneak a look at the house. The black Mercedes is parked nose to tail with George's Bentley, definitely not positioned for a quick getaway. If he were here to kidnap or kill Ellie, he would not have parked that way. But this relieves my anxiety hardly a whit.

My training screams at me. *Call for backup.* In one second I scan the street looking for the cops who are supposed to be providing protective surveillance as a result of George's request to the mayor of West Van. There's not a Ford Crown Victoria parked anywhere. I check all the other cars and can see no sign of any occupants. A part of protective surveillance is to be seen, to be a deterrent. There are no cops here.

I have no choice. Twenty long strides down the driveway and I'm ringing the door bell and hammering on the door with my fist.

The door flies open and Sam's fury explodes out. "What the hell are you doing Cal?"

I see Ellie at the other end of the hallway. She looks frightened. "Sam," my voice has dropped to a whisper, "you've *got* to listen to me. The man who just arrived here in that car is the same one who had me beaten up." My voice drops several more decibels. "He's the one that said, *your kid's next.*"

The exasperation on her face tells me that I'm not getting through to her. "Cal, for God's sake don't be—"

"Sam!" I can't keep my voice in a whisper any more. "Either you and Ellie come with me right now or I'm calling the police." I reach into my pants pocket, pull out my cell and flip it open.

"Cal, you're out of your mind. What do you think you —"

"Is there a problem?" Sam is cut short again but this time by George. He is coming through a door on the right of the hallway.

It is only the third time I have met George; I've always wanted to avoid contact with the fiancé of the woman I still love. He is not tall, not more than an inch over Sam's five eight, but he has an air of command that reminds me of Kevin's father. His expensive gym-bought physique is

212

dressed in beige pants and a royal blue golf shirt. He walks to the door and stands beside Sam; his arm drapes itself around her shoulders and my skin crawls.

"Cal." His eyes hold mine. A pleasant smile is on his lips but his eyes are completely neutral. I would not want to play poker with this man. A pause… "Cal, you may not know this, but I love your daughter like she were my own. While she is in my house, she is safe from any harm. In fact… she is safer here than anywhere." He has come straight to the heart of the matter.

And I believe him.

Behind him, I see Blondie. He walks across the hall and crouches down beside Ellie. He tousles her hair and she gives him a huge smile. My whole being aches to take him out with my bare hands but I don't. I don't do anything. Although it hurts to admit it, Ellie *is* safer here than with me.

I hold George's gaze and, for an instant, we each know the other's mind.

He turns and, followed by his guest, goes back into his study.

Sam's voice is puzzled. "Cal?"

I ignore her, my mind racing to make sense of what has just happened. George is in some way connected to the gang. Blondie's threat, *your kid's next*, was clearly empty because Ellie is safe here. So why did he make it? To scare me off? Probably, but from what? Certainly, not from stealing from him and his associates, they would just kill me for that. And what is the nature of George's association with this gang?

"Cal, I think you need to go." Sam's voice breaks my chain of thought.

I look at her and at Ellie standing behind her. Can I take George's assurance of Ellie's safety and, by extension, Sam's? For the moment I have to—there is no way I can persuade her and Ellie to leave with me right now—but no one is safe in proximity to drug gangs. Their huge profits are a magnet for some of the worst psychopaths in history.

"Cal!" Her voice breaks in again. My poor Sam, when she knows what George is mixed up in, she will be devastated.

I crouch down and Ellie runs into my arms to give me a big hug. I have to tear myself away from her and from Sam for a moment but my priority has changed.

I need to rescue them from this house.

Chapter 36

I do not have to wait long. From my place of concealment, standing behind a ten foot stack of timber in the yard of the renovation opposite George's house, I watch as the black Merc pulls out of the driveway. Moments later the front door opens and George is there. He stands in front of his house and looks around the garden. His gaze pans outward and at one point he is looking straight at the point from which I am observing. He is taking deep breaths, as though to calm himself.

Then he moves briskly to his Bentley, gets in and drives off. This is better than I could have hoped for but I wonder for how long he will be gone.

As soon as he is out of sight, I extricate myself from my hiding place and make my way, for the third time today, towards Sam's front door. I flip open my cell and redial. It's picked up after two rings.

"Sam. Don't hang up. You need to hear what I have to say. In a moment, I'll be knocking on your door. Make sure you answer." I hang up. I'm betting that her puzzlement about what happened between George and me will motivate her to want to talk.

She opens the door within seconds of my knock. She is dressed in a sheepskin jacket and her finger is on her lips in a gesture for silence. In the background I hear two voices singing in Spanish: Ellie's and the maid's.

Sam pulls the front door closed behind her with a gentle click, snatches my elbow and leads me round to the side of the house. We are standing on a graveled path that runs between the house and the high laurel bushes that isolate them from their next door neighbor. She pulls cigarettes and a lighter from her jacket pocket and lights up. I haven't seen her smoke since she gave it up when pregnant will Ellie.

I am feeling jittery and I find myself sniffing. My shoulders ache. I sense that when the symptoms take hold it's going to be bad. The thought of enduring this, getting more and more acute for almost a week, frightens me more than another beating from Blondie and his boys.

She draws the smoke gracefully and gratefully into her lungs, holds it for a beat and lets it out with a contented sigh; I guess we all have our addictions. "OK, Cal. What is all this nonsense?"

"I told you Sam. That man who just left with your future husband is the guy who beat me up and threatened Ellie's life. I know this is all new and it's difficult to get your mind around but I need to get you and Ellie away from here right now."

She puts her arm around me and puts a hand to my cheek. "Cal, listen to me. You were badly beaten in that alley. You should still be in the hospital but, pig headed as always, you discharged yourself. Your mind is playing tricks on you. David is a partner of George's in one of his businesses. He has been over to the house lots of times. He's a nice man. He almost always brings a little something for Ellie."

"Sam, you listen. David, as you call him, is a drug dealer and he's right up there in the organization. He is *not* a nice man."

"Come on, Cal. He was wearing three thousand dollars worth of clothing. He's always perfectly groomed and he doesn't look anything like one of those awful people."

Why can't she understand? "For God's sake Sam, you know I was involved with these gangs when I was in the Department, d'you think I don't know what I'm talking about. Everyone thinks of drug dealers as a bunch of

216

yahoos and a lot of the soldiers are. But the guys at the top are very bright, *very* sophisticated business people who wear designer clothes and ride about in expensive European cars. I would have thought that you would be very concerned that your soon-to-be husband is mixed up with them."

I wonder if George is coming back yet. What will he do if he finds me here talking to Sam?

The tip of her cigarette glows a bright orange as she takes another deep draw. "This is getting us nowhere, Cal. I just don't believe what you're saying. I think you believe it but you're mistaken. You were beaten up, you were in a coma for two and a half days and then you were on painkillers and *then* you discharged yourself. On top of that you're a heroin addict. I think you're just hallucinating this nonsense.

"Either that or you're looking for some reason, any reason, to get out of going into detox and rehab so you're fabricating a crazy conspiracy theory as the excuse."

I am feeling drained. I know I'm not going to get through to her. She is convinced that I'm either hallucinating or lying or some of both. Hell, maybe she's right, but I have to get her and Ellie out of here. But how? I can not force her physically and let's face it, why should she take the word of a junkie anyway?

"Sam, you have to listen to me—"

She places a frustrating finger on my lips and looks at the Piaget on her wrist. "Cal. It's past three thirty." Her voice is soft now and gentle. "You said that you had to be at detox at four. Why don't I drive you over there? We could get there by four fifteen, latest. What do you say?"

I can't fight any more. Try as I might, she just can't accept what I'm saying. As much as I don't want to, I just have to trust George's assurance that she and Ellie are safe here. I capitulate, "Sure, Sam. That would be great."

She reaches out and squeezes my bicep. "Come on, let's go."

She turns towards the front of the house and suddenly tries to grab my arm but misses and pitches forward onto the graveled path. Electricity fires through my spine. She's been shot. I didn't hear anything but the way she fell, the shooter is at the back of the house. I turn and check but can see no sign of him.

"Sam, are you OK?"

I crouch down beside her, shielding her body against another shot from the same direction, my back crawling, waiting for the impact of that second silenced bullet. She is lying face down and her body is shaking uncontrollably. I heft her body up to the wall of the house for better cover.

"Sam! Where are you hit?"

I roll her on to her side, not knowing what to expect. I remember with dread the time that I shot an escaping suspect and watched him drop to the ground and twitch just like Sam is twitching now.

I am torn between staying with Sam and getting in the house to shield Ellie.

A quick check reveals no obvious gunshot wounds but her face tells me why she is shaking. She is sobbing.

"Sam! Listen! Where are you hit?"

I ask again but she just shakes her head, unable to speak. I help her into a sitting position and she locks her arms around me, the tears streaming off her face onto my thigh, leaving a pattern of wet drops on my pants. I can not stop myself from kissing the top of her head and holding her tight.

I put my hand under the back of her sheepskin jacket and feel her back for the wetness of a wound.

Nothing.

I can see no blood anywhere.

There is no wound.

Paranoia, self destroyer.

I breath deeply to get my heart rate under control.

"Sam. Tell me what's wrong," I plead.

She brings herself under control; the sobbing slows and she tries to talk between sharply inhaled breaths. "Oh, Cal... I didn't want to tell you like this." She draws in a deep but shaky breath and sighs. "I have been diagnosed... with M... with MS."

My first thought is relief that she has not been shot but the relief is instantly shattered. MS is incurable. Does this mean that it's terminal? Are Ellie and I going to lose Sam in a year or in five years? Why hasn't she told me this before? And why the hell was she smoking? That can't be good.

"Oh, Sam. Why didn't you tell me?" I ask but she just shakes her head.

After what seems an age, she speaks. "Help me up please, Cal."

I help her to her feet and a pain lances through my arm as she rubs against the infection that has been steadily growing for the last two weeks. For the hundredth time I pray that it is just an infection, that the contaminated needle did not carry anything worse than just a few germs.

She reaches up and kisses my cheek. "It's passed now. I'm OK. Let's get you into that detox place." She takes my hand and leads me into the garage. Compared to what Sam faces, the impending agony of detox seems trivial now.

Chapter 37

As I walk through the doors, I hear the throaty exhaust of the 4.8 liter engine as Sam's SUV wings her away. I sniff twice on the walk along the stark hallway to the circular reception desk. My joints are aching now.

Sam's revelation has floored me. I only know a little about multiple sclerosis and it's nothing good. A distant cousin of my mother had MS. I called her Aunt Aida and she was the only one of her relatives that we kept in touch with. We would see her every year or so and I would mentally chronicle the deterioration in her health: she would stumble and drop things on one visit, walk with a stick on the next, then with crutches, then in a wheelchair. The last time that I saw her she could not feed herself.

Is this the prognosis for my darling Sam? And Ellie? I have no idea whether it is hereditary.

On the drive over here, Sam has revealed a lot. She kept the information from me because she didn't want me to turn my back on drugs for her sake rather than my own. She said she knew that I had to get clean from my own desire to do so. And of course I let her down there too.

Her biggest prayer was that I would get clean and start to take on more responsibility for Ellie with the hope that when Sam reached the later stages of the disease, I would become Ellie's primary caregiver. Me, not George. But I've blown that now.

It was Sam who asked Kevin to stop enabling my addiction by not letting me use his place on Saturday mornings. Now I can make sense of Kevin's words. *Cal, I need your help on something… It's a bit difficult to talk about this but…*

But now it's too late. Now she is going to take Ellie to Toronto and when George joins them there in a few weeks he will become Ellie's de facto father. Sam's words ring in my head. *I can't wait for you to sort yourself out, Cal; George will become Ellie's legal guardian when I am too ill to take care of her.*

When I tried to protest that George was somehow linked to illegal drugs, she lost it with me. She pulled the car over and screamed that I was a paranoid junkie, that George was a good man and that he would be a wonderful father to Ellie and that my psycho fantasies were no concern of hers and how dare I speak about her future husband that way. This was just why she did not want me to see any more of Ellie, in case I filled *her* mind with this nonsense. Her outburst deflated her and then she just looked old and tired.

We continued the journey in silence but I could not help noticing that the hand that held the steering wheel had a tremor that would not go away.

"Are you Mr. Rogan?" The man behind the desk breaks into my thoughts. His good looking black face has a kind smile and I suspect that a quirky sense of humor sits behind those alert eyes.

"Yes." I smile back at him and turn around to see if perhaps Sam has returned.

When I turn back, he rises and says, "OK. You're a bit late but no problem. Let's get you checked in here." He knows that I am experiencing withdrawal and he wants to get me settled quickly.

"I just need a moment first," I tell him. He nods and indicates a row of chairs along the wall.

I slump into a threadbare but comfortable armchair and feel a profound sense of failure. I have failed as a father and am losing my daughter because of my inaction; I have failed as a human by procrastinating over dealing with my addiction; I have failed as a detective, too. I promised Mr. Wallace that I would find Kevin's murderer but not one of my erstwhile suspects—Roy, Brad, Sandi, Arnold and George—has both motive and opportunity. I guess I should phone Arnold and ask him to inform Mr. Wallace of my failure. Arnold will enjoy that, I suspect. He never believed that Kevin was murdered. Except...

Except what he said to me in the hospital.

So Mr. Rogan, were you beaten up because of your investigation into Kevin's death or because of your lifestyle?

The latter, I told him.

Are you sure of that?

It didn't make sense then but now that I know there is a connection between the gang that beat me up and George, the man who controls Kevin's company, it puts Arnold's question in a different light.

But there are more questions than answers. Why would a major drug dealer like Blondie have a business relationship with a man who controls a company that is developing a product that could put drug dealers out of business? Or is Sam right: is Blondie an investor in one of George's companies and is George unaware of Blondie's gang connection? And why would George kill Kevin if it caused him a ten million dollar loss? Surely he wouldn't. Yet Brad said that George wasn't phased by the loss.

I am starting to believe that Kevin's murder was part of a bigger picture, a picture that I can't see.

The questions gnaw at me. My gut tells me that Arnold is right and that somehow George and the drug gang are involved in Kevin's death. But how? The cop in me burns to know the answers to all the questions. I glance at the front door of the detox center; the answers are out there. I can't solve a murder from inside detox, can I?

I stand up and turn towards the door but one thing holds me back.

222

Ellie.

If I don't go through with detox and rehab, I may ruin any chance I might have had to be with her again. But, then again, Sam will not let me see her now and in a week she will be in Toronto with Sam and George, in what Sam considers safety. I guess if George does love Sam, he would never let anything happen to Ellie. But what happens if Sam is not there? Will Ellie still be safe?

My best bet is to go through with the detox and then rehab. I can also have the doctors look at my arm, give me some penicillin for the infection. If I am clean maybe I can go to Toronto, maybe...

I am teetering on the edge. Do I get out of here and take a run at finding Kevin's murderer and maybe, just maybe, discover that George is implicated, or do I make the safe and sensible choice and stay here?

Then it hits me.

Safe?

Why have I been so stupid not to think to this before? There is no way that George would want it broadcast that he and a drug gang have some sort of relationship. That's why he and Blondie both headed out so soon after I had been there. They are trying to hunt me down. The fact that I have uncovered the link between them has marked me as a dead man. Sam is bound to tell George that I am in here. For all I know, she already has and there is a posse of gang members on their way now.

That clinches it. There is no safety for me here. I need to be out there and I need to nail George for Kevin's murder before he and his colleagues nail me into a coffin.

And deep inside me, in that place where even I can't lie to myself, I know that the Beast is calling the shots. Getting out of here and solving Kevin's murder is absolutely the right thing to do but it will also give me an excuse to continue using.

I go to the guy at the front desk.

"Look, I can't check in right now."

His look tells me that he has heard a hundred junkies say the same words.

"Mr. Rogan, it's gonna be tough. I know, I was here as a patient a few years back and I remember how I felt at—"

"No. You don't understand. Something has come up that I have to deal with. Something that has put my life in danger. There are people who want to kill me who will soon know that I've come here and who…"

His look stops me in mid sentence. He thinks it's just another junkie's paranoid fantasy. Why not? It sounds like one to me, too. Before he can speak, I turn round and head back down the hall and out the front door.

Outside, I call a taxi and then phone the Wallace residence to give Arnold some very specific and detailed instructions.

Chapter 38

The cabbie is one of those irritating, talkative drivers who think his commentaries are all part of the service. He's taking away from my much needed thinking time, as if thinking wasn't hard enough when you're sinking deeper and deeper into withdrawal. I shouldn't have used my dwindling funds on a taxi but I want to get there fast.

"What do you think about the Canuck's chances this season?"

"I don't follow hockey." It's a lie but it shuts him up for a while.

The puzzle about why they didn't kill me when they had me in the alley may be solved. I suspect George got them to hold off on going all the way for Sam's and Ellie's sakes. But now that I've made the connection between George and Blondie, that bet is off for sure. If they catch me again, I'm dead.

"Who d'ya think's gonna win the election?"

What election?

"I'm guessing it'll be the one who gets the most votes." Hopefully that will shut him up.

I can't go back to my rooming house. Sam knows where it is. She waited outside, on the way to detox, while I packed the things I needed into the nice new backpack that Arnold provided when I moved in there. By now she will have told George about where I went and where the rooming house is. What I need to do now is—

"Guess who I had as a passenger the other day?"

"Listen buddy. Just drive, will you."

I need to find out everything I can about George. His connection with the drug gang means that he could easily have had Kevin killed. I can't quite work out the motive but on that Saturday, I remember that George's car was not parked in the driveway when I picked up Ellie. He could easily have been at Kevin's.

But, wait a minute—

"Do you wanna go along Fourth or Broadway?" Delivered sullenly.

"For Jesus Christ's sake, I don't give a fuck, just shut up for once in your life and take me there." That should do it.

When I went to pick up Ellie, the Bentley was gone, he could have left at any time before I arrived. When I got back to his house, the Bentley was back. Easily enough time to—

The driver has pulled over to the curb. "Get out of my cab. I don't have to take that kinda talk from anyone, 'specially not some junkie who's just come out of detox."

I look at him and can see a Madonna and child statue on the dashboard and a rosary hanging from the rear-view mirror. My little outburst crossed the line for him, big time, but I need him to get me over to the Wallace's residence so that Arnold can do what I asked.

"Look, I'm sorry. I shouldn't ha—"

"Get out." He's not going to budge.

With as much dignity as I can muster, which isn't much, I get out of the cab pulling my backpack behind me. The moment the door closes, he floors the gas and squeals up the ramp onto the Cambie bridge, leaving me standing on Second Avenue across from the Cambie Street police station. I could stand here and try and flag another cab except that my driver has probably put out an alert using that fancy little computer terminal all the cabs carry. If he has, it's for sure that no one is going to stop and pick me up. He'll likely have blacklisted my cell phone number too. I'll have to walk up the hill to Broadway. There's a Starbucks there. I can shoot

226

up in the washroom and then get a cab from a different company or take a bus.

As soon as I cross the street, I see him.

He's about to get into a green Pathfinder which is parked between two police cars. My immediate thought is to avoid him but I don't know why; maybe it is because of the tension at the end of our last encounter. I am about to deke across Cambie and out of his line of sight, when he looks up and sees me. After a brief double take, he smiles. We walk towards each other and he transfers the file he is holding to his left hand. We shake hands, which feels awkward, considering that we know each other so well.

"Hi, Cal."

"Hey, Steve."

When we were colleagues in VPD, we spent hours in each other's company and always had lots to talk about. Now, we are both at a loss for words. After a moment, he breaks the silence.

"It's funny that I should run into you right now. You're the reason I'm here."

A frisson of concern runs down my spine.

"How come?"

"I'm following up on our conversation at the hospital."

My heart beats just a little faster. He has been talking to someone about the possibility that I might be able to make it back into the VPD. Now that the moment is here, I am afraid to hear the verdict.

"And...?" I hold my breath.

"You were asking about unusual numbers of deaths on the downtown east side." I expel the breath and nod, relieved yet let down. "Well, I thought I'd look into it and there *have* been more than normal recently. The Department is concerned about it. When Pickton killed all those prostitutes a few years back, we took a lot of flack for ignoring the situation for too long. Next thing we knew, we'd

227

got the biggest mass murderer in Canadian history on trial. Well, the new Chief has an order out that if there's any sign of unusual patterns of deaths or missing persons they have to be investigated thoroughly. He's even created a task force to look into the statistics."

This is not what I wanted to hear. A task force will almost certainly uncover Kevin's illegal testing of his *Addiban* drug; if that becomes public it would be devastating for the Wallaces.

"Anyway," Steve continues, "after I spoke to you on Tuesday, I decided to talk to someone I know on that task force. He invited me over here today to talk to him. He told me there have been a lot of mysterious deaths recently and all of them are showing the same unknown chemical compound in their systems. The count's up to fifteen now."

Fifteen! I try to keep my face straight. When I talked to Sandi about Kevin's rogue drug testing, she said that only seven people had died. Roy talked about a bunch of people dying but I don't remember him using specific numbers… but fifteen. That's half of the subjects in Kevin's trial. Maybe they are all going to die and Roy's one of them. I can't let my shock show on my face. I sniff, twice.

Steve is looking at me closely. "How did you hear about it?" he asks.

"From Roy." I say as casually as I can, trying to mask that my need to get up to Starbucks—and into the washroom where I can fix up—is soaring. "One of his good buddies, a guy called Tommy, died suddenly and Roy said he'd heard of some other deaths. I was just curious."

I can see that Steve suspects I know more than I'm telling. Hell, he was my partner; he *knows* I am. He opens the folder he's carrying. "What was this Tommy's last name?"

"Connor. At least that was what Roy and I knew him as."

He scans a sheet. "Yes, he was one. Connor, Thomas, age 62. He's the fifth one, died on October thirtieth."

"Could I see the list, please Steve?"

He shakes his head. "Sorry, Cal." He closes the folder.

I hold his eye and I can sense that he is becoming uncomfortable. "Come on, Steve."

He thinks for a second, looks around him then shrugs and hands it over. I smile and nod my appreciation; I know that he is breaking the rules for me. I scan it and recognize two names: Spider Norton was a heroin addict that I met a couple of times, so was James Capp. Before I hand the list back, I do one more quick scan. There's something here but the heroin craving will not allow my mind to focus on what it is.

"Can I keep this Steve?" I ask.

"You know the rules, Cal. *That* I can't do."

I look him in the eye and hold his gaze. It doesn't work this time. "You know what trouble I'd be in if I gave this to you."

"Please Steve. It may be relevant to Kevin's murder."

"You're still pursuing that?"

"Yes, of course. And I'm getting close on something. This list might really help."

He weighs the balance and I win.

"OK, OK," he says as he hands it over, "I've got another copy in the file here; I got it for Nick."

"Hey, thanks, man." I stuff the paper in my pocket.

I have to get up to that Starbucks before I start groaning from the pain but I just need to know one more thing. "When you came to the hospital, I asked you to check something out for me. Did you get a chance to do that?"

"Yes, I'm going to meet with someone in Human Resources first thing Monday morning. Why don't you give me a call after nine o'clock and I'll let you know what they say."

"That's great, Steve. I really appreciate it."

He nods. "Cal I talked to a couple of the guys, without mentioning you by name, they all said… Well, don't get your hopes too high, eh."

He extends his hand. "I gotta go." We shake again and he turns towards his truck, then suddenly turns back. His face is serious. "Cal. I probably shouldn't be telling you this either but what the heck… I thought I'd let you know that Stammo sent your jacket off for DNA testing. The results could be back early next week."

That's the least of my problems. "No worries Steve. I told you, it's Roy's blood."

I wince at the pain of hoisting my backpack over my shoulder and head up Cambie towards Broadway, trying not to stagger. The craving for that next fix is obscuring everything now, even my desire to check the names on Steve's list.

Chapter 39

Noon is fast approaching and I have seen no warning signs: no men sitting in parked cars; no expensive vehicles cruising the area just a little too slowly; no parked Harleys. I have done all the tricks to check myself for a tail: coming here by a circuitous bus route; making sudden changes of direction and looking for equally sudden changes in the people around me; checking reflections in shop windows; running across the road and into the public market, then hiding near the entrance to check for someone following me.

He insisted we meet here at midday but I can no longer trust that he is operating as a free agent.

From my vantage point in the Starbucks, I see Roy in the stream of people coming out of the SeaBus terminal. He ambles towards Chesterfield, rain dripping off his leather hat. I hold until the last of the passengers is through. A quick scan reveals no obvious sign of a tail, so I head after him.

On the short walk to Sailor Hagar's pub, I can observe no changes from when I walked this way fifteen minutes ago: no new cars parked; no pedestrians standing incongruously in the rain. I have adjusted my pace to match Roy's. He does not look around for anyone but just trudges along, his gaze on the sidewalk a few paces in front of him. When he climbs up the steps to the entrance, I take a diversion and comb the streets for two blocks around the pub.

When I finally enter the place, dripping rainwater, I know that the only danger is if they are using Roy as bait and plan to arrive while we are in here. If he is being used, I wonder how willingly he is cooperating.

I scan all the tables. Although it is just after twelve, most are occupied but only two people catch my eye: a burly guy in a Harley t-shirt with a ring of thorns tattooed around his neck, sitting alone at a table in a corner and watching a soccer match on one of the big screen TVs; the other, a wiry, hard looking man of about fifty sitting with a group of people who look like they are all from the same company.

Roy is sitting in the farthest, darkest corner. As I approach I catch the tail of an animated conversation with the buxom server who has brought him his beer.

"I'm sorry sir, you have to either pay for the drink now or give me a credit card so that I can run a tab for you."

"For God's sake," Roy responds as he hungrily eyes the beer in front of him, "my buddy's picking up the tab. He'll be here any minute."

She decides to settle the matter by retrieving the beer but Roy is too fast for her. He snatches up the glass and half empties it before her hand is half way there. I can not help grinning.

"It's OK," I say. "I'll be paying."

She turns and checks me out. I guess I pass the test because she sports a smile, bursting with whitened teeth. "No problem. I'll run you a tab." There is no mention of a credit card. Another example of how the world is stacked against the poorest. People take one look at guys like Roy and make a thousand instant judgments, most of which are just plain wrong. I know. I did. But living on the streets changed all that; there I learned that the quality of a man is not to be judged by his looks or his clothes or his circumstances. Men like Roy and Tommy Connor are as much pillars of their community as Mr. Wallace is of his.

"I'll have a brown ale," I say, giving no indication of my thoughts.

232

Another big, false smile. "I'll be right back."

"Thanks, Rocky," Roy chuckles and takes another deep draft of his beer. "We was too fast for her, eh."

I laugh at his glee. It's the first time I have laughed in a while. The laughter takes on a life of it's own and a tendril of my mind knows that I can't stop. Roy is immediately infected and we sit rocking like a boat of fools adrift on a sea of mirth.

Eventually we get ourselves under control until Roy espies our server, returning with my order, and says, *sotto voce*, "Look out. Here comes tits and teeth." It starts us off again and I can hardly thank her between guffaws. Roy struggles hard to get the words out to order another pint… but, being Roy, he succeeds.

When at last I stop, I realize that I have been teetering on the edge of hysteria and that I am close to tears. One wrong word will push me over that edge. A deep breath helps center me.

"I needed that, Rock. I dunno when I've had a good laugh like that." He's wiping away the tears with hands that are leaving streaks of dirt on his leathery old face. He empties his glass and sighs contentedly.

I sweep the bar and see that ring of thorns and wiry are both still in place.

"So, Roy, why did you want to see me?"

The question slaps the humor from his face.

"We're in real trouble, Rock. They're looking for ya and they mean business. If they catch ya they're gonna put ya in the morgue for sure this time, eh."

"How do you know?"

"They tracked me down, the same guys as beat ya up the last time. They told me that if I didn't help 'em I was a dead man. They even gave me a goddamn fancy cell phone telling me I had to call 'em if I saw ya; that if I didn't, that was it. What are we gonna do?"

If I needed any further proof of George's involvement with the guys who beat me up, this is it. Making the link between George and Blondie has sealed my fate. If they find me, they'll kill me. And poor Roy's in the middle. For some reason he's risking his life to meet me here and warn me. I need to make the right moves to protect us both.

I look all around for our server and when I catch her eye I signal that we would like to order some food. I'm not going to be eating but it gives me a chance to scope out the bar again. Out of the corner of my eye, I catch ring of thorns watching us. As my gaze sweeps past him, he looks away.

"Roy, when you called me did you use the cell phone they gave you?"

"Yeah, Rock. Why?"

"Show me the phone. Hand it to me under the table."

He slides it out of his pocket. It is a new model iPhone. There's only one reason that they would give him such an expensive phone: they have set it up with apps that are monitoring his calls and tracking him with GPS.

"OK, listen Roy. This is important. I want you to go right now into the can, phone them and tell them that I'm here."

"But Rock—"

"Listen Roy. They already know I'm here. Whatever you do, *don't* look around, but we're being watched. They're already here. If you don't call them right now and tell them, they're going to know that you double crossed them. You know what that means."

Roy's face pales under the grime. "Are you sure, Rocky?"

"Yes. Just go do it while I order us some food. Tell them that you lured me here for them and that I just arrived. Tell them that you are calling them now because you wanted to make sure I showed up before you bothered them. Tell them exactly that, OK?"

Roy just nods and heads to the washrooms.

234

Now, I need to work out how I can get myself out of this. I'm going to be outnumbered so there is no way I can fight my way out; they're likely to be armed anyway. What I need is cunning. And I have it. I check my watch; it's a cheap digital but it should be accurate and in the plan that is forming in my mind, timing is critical.

While the waitress takes our food order, I get the chance to check out the opposition. The wiry, hard looking guy is sharing a joke with a couple of people at his table and I'm pretty sure that he really is their co-worker. Ring of thorns however has his eyes on the washrooms. I would accuse myself of being paranoid except that he has the look, the look that I have seen on too many criminal faces over the last fifteen years.

Roy returns and slumps down in his seat. "OK, I done it. But I ain't happy about it," he says.

"OK Roy, that's good." I check my watch. "Listen, in exactly four and a half minutes, I am going to make a run for it. I want you to stay here and finish your beer and eat the food that the waitress is going to bring. About five minutes after I leave I want you to start looking about for me. Maybe call the waitress over and ask if she saw where I went. Get up and walk about like you're looking for me. Check in the washroom. Then you phone again and tell them that I must have taken off. You got that?"

"Yeah, sure." He's looking worried.

"Eventually, they're going to come and talk to you and ask you what we talked about. Tell them about how we were laughing about the waitress and then tell them that we were talking about your buddy, Tommy. Now this is important. You've also got to tell them that just before I left, I told you that there was a guy with a tattoo around his neck who I thought was watching us. That way they won't think that you tipped me off. You got all that Roy?"

"Yeah, yeah, I got it."

Three and a quarter minutes: I slip my hand into my pocket, take out three twenty dollar bills and slide them under a menu. "Grab hold of this money when I walk away from the table. Use it to pay the bill. Call me on my cell tonight but make sure that you do it from a pay phone. OK?"

Roy just nods.

Sailor Hagar's has only one entrance, so I'm guessing that they will be waiting for me out front. I check my watch. 12:22. I take the time to rehearse Roy on what he is going to say and do over the next ten minutes. After exactly three minutes I stand up and say, "I'm going for a smoke." I do a brief mime of smoking and hope that I'm not overdoing it. I turn and head for the back deck and see out of the corner of my eye that ring of thorns is on his cell phone.

During the winter months the back deck is covered in plastic sheeting and provides scant cover for smokers to huddle over their addiction. As I go through the door, I pat my pockets like I'm trying to locate a package of cigarettes. The door swings closed behind me. A quick backward check confirms that the right hand side of the deck is out of the line of sight of ring of thorns. I head there and, to the consternation of two young woman, who look too young to either drink or smoke, I pull back the plastic sheeting and swing first one leg and then the other over the railing.

The surface of the deck is about ten feet from the pavement below. In one movement I slide my hands down the vertical bars of the railing until they reach the bottom so that I am crouching, then I let my body drop until I am hanging from the bottom of the railing. I look down and let go, land awkwardly and stumble forward, falling onto the asphalt.

I should have at least a five minute head start.

The screech of brakes is very close. I forgot that the deck is over the entrance to the pub's underground parking. I look up and see the hood of a Ford Expedition looming over me, six inches from where I am lying. I don't know who is more shocked: me or the elderly man driving. As I leap to my feet, he honks his horn angrily. The smoking teenagers are looking over the railing and laughing; they must be thinking I'm doing a 'dine and dash'.

I try to silence the driver with frantic hand signals but he just hits the horn again, long and loud, several times.

I hear a shout from above, "At the back." The Harley t-shirt is shouting into his cell phone. There goes my head start.

12:26: I take off through the teaming rain, running down the alley towards Chesterfield. The alley is empty and the end is clear, for now. I push myself harder. Halfway down, I glance back and see two men have just turned into the alley and are running after me. If my exit is cut off they will take me easily.

Right now one of the gang will be walking Roy out of the pub so he will not be calling the police for me this time.

Despite my speed the end of the alley gets closer way too slowly. I don't fear another beating. Their orders will be to take me alive and relatively unharmed; they want to be able to question me at length somewhere where we will not be disturbed. My insides turn to liquid at the knowledge of how they will do this to me; it squeezes an additional burst of speed out of my muscles.

After an eon, I charge out of the alley and hare across Chesterfield, narrowly avoiding going under the wheels of a bus on its way down to the Quay. I lengthen my stride as I run downhill towards Esplanade. There are three men heading up the hill toward me.

12:27: another check over my shoulder. My pursuers are closer and I catch a glimpse of Blondie's black Mercedes pulling onto the street behind them.

One of the men in front of me, the only one without an umbrella, reaches inside his jacket. If it's a gun and if he's prepared to use it in broad daylight in a busy shopping area, I'm dead meat.

Behind him, the lights at Esplanade are just turning red against me. If I can get past him, that's good because they will also be red for the Merc. He pulls out his hand and I catch a glimpse of metal but it's not a gun. My stomach tightens, I can not handle the thought of the knife blade sliding into my viscera; I would almost prefer that it were a gun. My only hope is that with all these people around, he won't dare…

It's an iPod; I'm flooded with relief until I check over my shoulder. One of my pursuers is gaining on me.

12:28: I dash diagonally through the traffic on Esplanade —drawing honking and the finger from several drivers—and up onto the pedestrian walkway that leads to the SeaBus. The Mercedes can't follow me here.

My chest is heaving as I draw great gulps of air into my lungs. I put my head down and dash past the long architectural horror that is the ICBC building. The wet sidewalk is slick here and I slow down a fraction to avoid slipping. Just before I reach the end of the walkway, I sneak a look back. One of my pursuers has fallen way back but the other is gaining on me; he's small and wiry and his legs are pumping like an Olympic sprinter.

Back at the far end of the walkway, I can see the blond head and leather jacket of George's buddy, shouting into his cell phone. At whom, I wonder.

12:29: I dodge around the end of the building and head for the escalator. I get a flash of a movie where the hero slides down the handrail. I think not. The escalator is stationary, out of service. I dash down three steps at a time.

Now it's all in the timing. If I've got it right, I'm home free, otherwise…

The pavement comes up to smash into my body. At the speed I have been moving, I have misjudged the step from the stationary escalator onto solid ground. I curse at the pain that lances through me from my partly healed rib. I can hardly draw breath but I have to get up... Now... But I can't. A quick check reveals my tail just arriving at the top of the escalator. I can sense his feeling of victory as he see me on the ground.

I force breath into my lungs and somehow struggle to the vertical.

I hobble across the plaza as fast as I can and see the display that tells me the next SeaBus is leaving in fifteen seconds. I'm screwed, unless there's a margin of error.

Ten seconds: I accelerate down the covered gangplank, the pain is on the point of blacking me out.

Two seconds: I run pass the ticket machine.

Zero: almost at the turnstile.

Minus two: I'm through the turnstile—thank God for the honor system—and the terminal doors start to close.

Four hard paces and I just squeak through the terminal doors. The seaman who operates them raises his eyebrows at me in disapproval as I dash across the aluminum gangplank and into the ship. I collapse into a seat, chest heaving, as the ship's doors close behind me.

The flat tones of the safety announcement are music to my ears as the ship starts its glide out of its bay into the waters of the Burrard Inlet and I silently thank Translink for the unfailing timeliness of the SeaBus. I look back and see my pursuer, staring impotently at me through two sets of doors. I have just the strength to raise my hand, grin and wave goodbye to him.

The SeaBus will make the crossing in about twelve minutes. Not even the five hundred horsepower of Blondie's Mercedes is going to get him downtown that fast.

Despite the pain that tears at my ribs with each indrawn gulp of breath, the flush of victory courses through me. Every moment since I walked away from detox, I have doubted my decision but this tells me I did the right thing. The gang's considerable efforts to lay their hands on me tell me that they and George are deeply involved in Kevin's murder. I just need to find out how. And I will. I am going to nail them all.

I lean back in the seat and, with a pang, my exaltation is blunted by the thought that Blondie may take out his frustration on Roy; then it is eclipsed when I see their faces, two rows away.

I have been outguessed and outmaneuvered: on the left, Goliath, now without his crutches; on the right, the hard looking face from the alley, the one whom I stabbed in the neck with a discarded needle.

They look pleased to see me. How nice.

Chapter 40

A massive overdose. That's how I would do it. Leave the body in some flop house, another careless, dead junkie; it happens all the time. Even as I contemplate my own death, my mind toys with the promise of the orgasmic high that a massive overdose might deliver.

But I'm not doing it. They are. It's gone beyond the fact that I stole from them. These guys want to know what I know about their connection with George—which, I realize is virtually nothing—and are going to enjoy trying to extract that information from me in the most painful way they can. I know how it works; in the past I've seen the mutilated bodies of their victims, fingers and toes broken, eyes and genitals torn away. I feel my sphincter tighten and a trickle of cold sweat go down my back.

I have to hand it to Blondie, his planning was flawless. He predicted that I might make a run for the SeaBus and stationed two of his soldiers at the terminal. They followed the orders he shouted into his mobile and boarded the vessel ahead of me. My captors have been joined by three others; I recognize the guy I knocked out in the alley and the bodyguard from yesterday, the one that looks like Arnold Schwarzenegger, supposedly hired to help protect Ellie from them. With a brass-knuckled hand, the latter pulls back his jacket to show me the military knife that he is carrying.

As we take the walkway over the railroad tracks—like the President of the US surrounded by his Secret Service detail —my mind is working overtime. For sure they have a car waiting at the entrance to the terminal; if I enter that car, I'm a dead man.

I have to find a way out. I don't want to die but the thought of Ellie's pain, left as an orphan and doomed to grow up with George as a father, is what fuels my determination.

But what? I am surrounded by five hard guys. Goliath alone, walking behind me, could pick me up by the scruff of my neck and hold me helpless at arm's length. Brains not brawn will win this day.

By the time we walk though the swinging doors onto the marble flooring of the terminal's main concourse, I've still got nothing. I sweep the area with my eyes. There are people everywhere: hurrying to and from the SeaBus and SkyTrain; buying tickets from the machines or just lining up at the Starbucks. There are two security guards, one standing by the front door, the other far away, standing in front of the bar of the Transcontinental restaurant drinking water from a plastic bottle. They are unarmed, of no use to me.

In desperation, I consider shouting 'Bomb!' but that is not an option; my guards will have me on the floor and hustle me out of there, telling the crowd that they are the police and I'm a terrorist, the current zeitgeist working in their favor. As we walk towards the front doors of the terminal, I see a black Chrysler 300 glide into view and stop at the curb.

My available time is dilating.

We are through the terminal doors and I cast about looking for something, anything that I could turn to my advantage. A number 50 bus is pulling up at the bus stop. The driver honks at the Chrysler to no avail. A homeless guy, pushing a supermarket cart loaded with his possessions, stops in front of us and starts shouting verses from Revelations at the hard guy that I jabbed. He screams, "*By these three was the third part of men killed, by the fire, and by the smoke, and by the brimstone.*" My guard detail stops in a moment of confusion just as a VPD cruiser appears, going east on the other side of the street. That cruiser is my one chance.

Now!

As I spring forward, one of Goliath's meaty hands grabs the back of my jacket, immobilizing me, the other clamps over my mouth. "No way, José," he chuckles in my ear.

The moment passes. Schwarzenegger hustles the vagrant along the sidewalk and in seconds I am being forced into the back seat of the car. My options are now severely limited.

Needle guy is on my left and the Terminator on my right. In the driver's seat is a fat guy with straggly gray hair. He is slouched down in the seat, his right arm stretched along the back of the empty passenger seat, his left wrist draped over the top of the steering wheel. He smells of sweat and peppermint.

With an ugly grin from Goliath, the car pulls away from the curb, turns up Granville for a block and then heads east on Hastings towards Main. I don't know where they are taking me but I'm betting it is not too far. We leave downtown and enter the five blocks between Abbott and Dunlevy which are the center of Vancouver's drug trade and the crime that goes with it. I wonder how I will withstand their interrogation. I have been told that everybody caves under torture but I have no solid information about George, the gang and Kevin's murder; it is all just suspicion. How long will they linger over their ministrations, trying to unlock information from my mind, information that is not there? How long before I am screaming for mercy?

My heart accelerates.

I see a slim chance, my only chance.

A block ahead two uniformed police officers are on the sidewalk interrogating a tattooed man with a plethora of piercings, his hands cuffed behind him. Their cruiser is double parked. Traffic has slowed as two lanes merge into one to pass the cruiser. We are now in the left hand lane and approaching the incident.

I stay relaxed, I do not want any tension transmitted to the guys pressed on either side of me.

Wait… Wait… Wait… *Now!*

I reach forward and grab the headrests of the front seats. In one movement, I pull my upper body over the seat backs. The sloppy driver is completely unprepared. My left hand grabs his right knee and forces his leg forward. The car leaps ahead as his foot pushes down on the gas and with my right hand I drag the wheel to the right. My guards are trying to pull me back into my seat but their efforts are countered as we plow into the back of the police car and the world goes white as the airbags deploy.

The impact of the crash has thrown me into the front seat. As the airbags hiss their way to flaccidity, I open the door and wriggle out onto the pavement. The uniforms are running over, a white man and a tall East Asian woman. I stagger towards them and shout, "I'm a member! Cal Rogan, badge number 56113. There's a man in that car with a prohibited weapon."

They buy it and draw their guns. The female officer keys her radio and calls for backup. They stand at the back corners of the Chrysler and the male officer shouts, "Get out of the car *now* with your hands in sight."

They are completely focused on the occupants of the car as I fade back onto the sidewalk, out of their line of sight, praying that neither of them turns round.

I turn and stroll towards Carrall Street.

If he doesn't already know it, the Schwarzenegger clone with the brass knuckles and military knife is about to learn they are listed as prohibited weapons and possession of such is an indictable offense under the Criminal Code of Canada.

Hasta la vista, baby.

Chapter 41

I have the information he wants. The least he could do is give me his attention now but he is talking on his mobile. So typical of his generation. He catches my eye and saunters over. He nods at me as he sits down and mouths "On hold." As if I care.

"Hey Steve," he says into the phone. Steve? That's the name of his old VPD colleague, I think. "When I ran into you on Saturday, you said that you were meeting with someone in Human Resources first thing this morning. Did you get a chance to?"

What could that be about?

After a brief reply from the other party, he says, "So… is there any hope?" He is grinding his teeth. So that's it. He wants back into the Department. I doubt there is any chance of that. Unless… Hmm. Hold that thought.

"Sure…" His voice has taken on an uncertain tone. After a small delay he adds, "Sure, I could come over there in an hour… No, I'm meeting with someone right now. I'll be there around ten, OK?… Yeah. Ten, ten fifteen latest."

He closes the phone, a puzzled look on his face.

Finally he has the courtesy to address me.

"Hi Arnold. Sorry about that."

I nod.

"How is Mr. Wallace?" he asks. The question surprises me but I am pleased that he asks it before we get down to business.

"No better. He is in a lot of pain but, except at night, he is refusing the morphine. He says that he needs to keep awake and alert. He is waiting to hear from you that you have found Kevin's murderer." I wonder for the thousandth time how I will cope with the death of that wonderful man.

He nods sadly and takes a sip of the coffee I purchased for him. More to cover his feelings, I think. "Arnold, thanks for getting the new digs so quickly for me. They're great and it's good being a bit removed from the downtown east side. I feel a lot safer there."

I nod again.

"So were you able to get the information?" he asks. A big part of me wants to tell him no… oh, so very much. Even though Mr. Wallace was adamant, maybe it's time for me to make my own decision. I think about it.

"Yes, actually I was." I can not break the habit of loyalty. I reach down, slide the paper out of my briefcase and hand it to him. "As you know, right after Kevin's death, the value of QX4 shares dropped by sixty percent. Well, I analyzed the trading patterns of the shares *after* that drop. I noticed that every two days or so a fairly substantial purchase was made. None were enormous but in total the purchases over the last two weeks have amounted to twenty million shares; that's ten percent of the company."

"Who bought them," he asks. There is a light in his eyes, the look of the hunter.

"Obviously, I too was interested in that. Most of the trades were made by a small brokerage firm in Toronto."

"Is there any way to find out who the buyer was, Arnold?"

I am enjoying this. "No. The shares are held in the name of the brokerage. There's no way to know who the buyer is…" I pause for three seconds and watch the frustration write itself all over his face. He turns away and gazes out of the window, teeth grinding again. "…normally."

When it hits, his head snaps back.

"It just so happens that an old army chum of mine is a partner there. He owes me. After a bit of persuasion, blackmail if truth be told, I got him to tell me who was buying all those shares. He told me that it was a company based in the Cayman Islands. The trades were all initiated by the company's Cayman lawyer."

He knows what that means. His face drops; I find it quite comical. "So you don't know who the actual buyer was." He purses his lips and exhales a silent fricative expletive.

I relent of keeping him hanging. "Please, Mr. Rogan, give me more credit than that. Mr. Wallace is very well connected, even in the Caymans. He made a couple of phone calls and within an hour he knew who was the behind the company. Would you care to guess, Mr. Rogan, who made those buys of QX4 stock?"

"George Walsh?" His face has lit up.

"Yes." I smile. A rare event which I enjoy... occasionally.

"So what Walsh is doing," he says, "is buying QX4 shares while they are cheap, so that he will make an even bigger profit when they go up again at some point in the future."

I see the return of the hunter and trump his comment. "Quite so. However, Walsh is not going to make a big profit at 'some point in the future'. That future is now."

"What do you mean?" he asks.

"After the Toronto Stock Exchange closed on Friday, QX4 put out a press release saying that they had received Federal Government approval to move on to human trials of their drug. At six A.M. Pacific time this morning, when the Exchange opened, the market reacted to this news by buying QX4 shares heavily."

I take out my Blackberry; now he can wait for me. I check e-Trade and it is as I thought.

"The last trade of QX4 shares brought the price to within five cents of the price they were before Mr. Kevin's death. By the end of trading today, the twenty million shares that Walsh purchased piecemeal over the last three weeks will have almost doubled in value. He'll make back all of his losses and an additional profit of some three million dollars."

I can almost see the cogs and wheels turning in that clever head. What a waste. He had so much potential before he started taking that filthy muck.

"You realize what this means?" he says. "George killed Kevin to drive the price of the stock down, so that he could buy more stock at fire sale prices and make a big profit when it went up."

Not quite.

"That doesn't fly," I tell him.

"Why?" There is annoyance in his tone.

"Killing Mr. Kevin could have killed the company. His death could have ruined their chances of ever getting government approval and without approval for the human trials, the shares would never have recovered. I checked if there were any sales of shares before his death. That would be more incriminating: Walsh sells shares at a high price before Mr. Kevin dies and then buys them back at less than half price after his death. Unfortunately, although there were some sales of shares in the two weeks prior to his death, the amounts were insignificant. All Walsh did was take advantage of the fact that the shares had slumped by buying more shares cheaply. Insider trading, perhaps, but not proof of murder."

He stares across the coffee shop, eyes focused in the far distance, his front teeth pushing down on his bottom lip. I think he's getting there.

Finally he speaks. "OK, here's a couple of thoughts. First, if it had become public knowledge that Kevin was conducting unapproved and illegal testing on humans which resulted in the deaths of fifty percent of the subjects, then that would have ruined QX4 permanently. The government would have been all over them, they would never have got any more government approvals and there would have been lawsuits by the relatives of the victims. There would have been no recovery from that. All the investors would have lost everything."

"True." He *is* getting it.

"However, if Kevin dies, commits suicide, the shares take a big dive but they can recover. So, if Walsh knew about Kevin's testing, it would be better for him to kill Kevin than risk it becoming public knowledge."

"Yes." I nod my approval. "From Walsh's point of view killing him is the lesser of two evils. You said you had a couple of thoughts, Mr. Rogan. What was the other one?" I wonder if he can make the next step.

"Over the last three weeks Walsh bought twenty million shares of the company and then, guess what, the company announce that they have got approval for the human trials and the shares bounce back to what they were before Kevin's death. That's just a little too convenient for my taste. What if Walsh already knew about the government approval *before* Kevin's death? He could have killed Kevin, knowing that it would make the shares crash temporarily but also knowing that he could buy a bunch of cheap shares through a company in the Caymans and then announce the good news about the approvals."

I can not hide my surprise. I hadn't thought of that angle and it is an interesting one, to say the very least.

"Let me see what I can find out." I tell him.

Instead of gratitude, he has a shocked look. His face pales. "Oh my God," he whispers.

"What?" I ask.

He is shaking his head. "What if they feel compelled to start human tests. They could trigger a whole new round of deaths."

He's right. Well I can do something about that and I tell him how.

He looks much relieved. "Thank you, Arnold. And please thank Mr. Wallace for me. Tell him I will come and see him soon." He gestures to the paper on the table with the details of the share transactions. "May I keep this, please?"

"Of course," I say. He folds over the paper and puts it in his jacket pocket.

Now to use my newly acquired knowledge. "You know my own feelings about Mr. Kevin's death," I say. He nods, a look of caution on his face. "Well, Mr. Wallace does not accept that he killed himself and is adamant that you continue your investigations. If you are successful, he said he may just be able to apply his influence with the Mayor and the Chief of Police to smooth the way back in."

His look of amazement quickly transforms into one of gratitude. Before he can speak, I say, "Would you also call me and update me on any developments. I want to keep Mr. Wallace up to date."

"I will, I promise."

The inducement of that last little white lie cemented it. He is now firmly moving in the direction we want him to go.

Chapter 42

Intuition is a funny thing. It is hard to tell what is an intuitive leap of faith and what is just a lousy guess. On the way here, my instincts were screaming at me not to meet Steve at the Main Street police station. I can not decide if this is the result of intuition or whether being there is just too painful a memory, reminding me of the career that I loved and lost. Either way Steve was not happy when I called him to change the venue for our meeting.

I walk into the Bean Around the World on Powell Street. It is my favorite coffee place in the entire city. So much better than the fancy place where I just left Arnold. Steve is already there, at a table, sitting with his back to the wall, talking on his cell. I get a medium sized dark coffee from Stu, the owner, and nod to Bob, the manager of the Lion Hotel, eying me warily.

I go join my ex-colleague. He looks very uncomfortable as he closes his phone.

"So Steve, what's up?"

I can tell from his face he doesn't know which way to approach what he wants to say. My heart sinks. I know he has talked to VPD's Human Resources Department about the possibility of my reentering the force if I can clean up and get straight. Clearly he is not the bearer of good news. As much as I don't want to hear the verdict, I decide to make it easy for him.

"They said 'no', I guess."

He looks confused for a moment and then realizes what I mean.

"Cal, that's not what I wanted to talk to you about. It's something else." Alarm bells go off. When we talked on the phone he said it was exactly what he wanted to talk to me about. He takes a deep breath and continues. "I shouldn't be telling you this sitting here but, hell, we worked together for a lot of good years and I owe you the truth." He hesitates again. "We've been doing some digging and we discovered that your buddy Kevin had reached the end of his rope supporting you. That he was planning to stop enabling you and cut you off from using his place to clean up every Saturday morning."

I do not deny it. I have seen too many guilty men get in deeper by protesting too much, so I try another tack. "I thought you guys were treating Kevin's death as a suicide. Why would you be asking about my relationship with Kevin?"

"I told you that Stammo sent your jacket off for DNA testing—"

"Yeah and I told you that it was Roy's blood."

"There was blood from two different sources. One from an unknown male, which I assume was Roy's," he pauses, undecided about something, then the moment passes and he continues. "Anyway, the other exemplar, which was newer and on top of the first, was a hand sized smear of Kevin's blood."

I can feel the blood drain from my face. What is Steve saying? It is just not possible. How could Kevin's blood be on my jacket? There has got to be a mistake. I look at Steve and know for a certainty that there is no mistake and I can see in his eyes that he may be judging my reaction as one of guilt.

"Cal, I'm telling you this as a courtesy because I know you and I can't imagine that you killed your best friend. But Stammo is all over this like maggots on a week old corpse. I want you to do the right thing here. Let's drink our coffee, walk over to 312 Main and have a chat about it. Let's sort it out together."

I rein in the thousand thoughts that are chasing through my head. They all come down to one choice. I can go with Steve, call some Legal Aid lawyer and fight this charge through the system, while detoxing in a cell, or I can make a run for it and somehow prove that George is the murderer, not me.

As I procrastinate, I look out the window and see a black Ford, a Crown Victoria. Stammo is getting out of the passenger side and the shit eating grin on his face makes my decision for me.

As I stand up, I say, "I really am sorry Steve," and push the table into his lap, spilling coffee all over him. I spin around, dash between the counter and the back wall of the shop and run down the thirty foot hallway that leads to the back alley. Yet another alley beckoning me. I am praying that Steve expected me to come quietly and has not stationed a couple of uniforms out back.

That prayer goes unanswered.

As I barrel into the crash bar and open the back door, it bangs hard against someone and I hear a yelp of pain. On my left I see a surprised Sarge, no more than four feet away, and on my right lies the crumpled body of the kid, not unconscious but still disoriented from his encounter with the door. Serves him right for standing too close. Sarge makes a grab for me but I dash to my right, too fast for him.

I burst out of the alley and turn north on Gore Street. I shouldn't be running like this. I know I'm innocent and I still have faith that our legal system would exonerate me. But I also know it is the Beast inside that keeps me running. I can't face the agony of going cold turkey in a jail cell so I'm running again, from the gang, from the police and from myself.

I have one chance and even that is a risky one. A block and a half away, at the end of the road, is a fence that surrounds the railway yards and the docks. If I can just make it over that fence. I have a chance. Then I remember one of my first days on the job: the mutilated body, the dismembered legs lying on the railway tracks, the horrified train driver and the blood, so much blood.

Halfway down the block, I check over my shoulder. Sarge is chasing me and talking into his radio. He is too out of shape to have any hope of catching me. As I dart across Alexander, another back check reveals that Stammo is rounding the corner from Powell, a full block behind me. I've got a fighting chance here.

"Stop, Rogan. Stop right now." Stammo shouts. I thank heavens that this is not the United States. In Canada, cops are very unwilling to draw weapons unless there is imminent danger to someone, especially when there are civilians on the streets. But will Stammo make an exception in my case? My back muscles tense awaiting the thwack of a 40mm round.

As I approach the fence, I risk another quick look back. Stammo has passed Sarge but has not even reached Alexander. In contravention of department rules, the stupid bastard has drawn his gun and is running with it. He's too far away for an accurate shot, even for him, and I am grateful that he is a smoker.

But Steve is not far behind him and Steve can run. If he catches me, am I prepared to fight it out with him? And I know the answer: it's not up to me, the Beast will do anything to avoid being caged, screaming in pain in a cell. I dread having to find out how far I might go if Steve catches me. As I jump and scramble up the fence, I hear the sound of an approaching train. I vault over the top and land in an off balance crouch. My right ankle twists under me and a jolt of pain sears up my leg as I stumble and fall on the track closest to the fence, the most used one. Panicked, I roll away from the fence and off the track. Maybe the train I can hear will shield me from my pursuers. No such luck.

On the next track is a stationery train. Cursing, I crawl under a freight car loaded with containers, imagining what would happen if the train starts. The wheels will slice my limbs like a sharp knife through a ripe tomato.

I leap to my feet yelling out at the pain in my right ankle. There are five empty tracks and on the sixth track is a freight train moving west, towards the downtown shunting yard. It has slowed to about fifteen miles per hour. It's my ticket out of here.

I step forward and hear the shriek of a train whistle.

Just in time I see the freight train lumbering eastward and it's right on top of me. Heart hammering, I shrink back as two hundred tons of engine pass only inches in front of my face. My ankle collapses and I trip and fall backwards into the freight car I just crawled under.

I check over my shoulder and see that Steve and Stammo are less than fifty yards from the fence: approaching accurate shooting range and Stammo is the best marksman in the VPD. The rail yard may have been a tactical error. There are few civilians here, which raises the likelihood of Stammo firing. As I get up, I see Steve pass him.

I have only one option. I run east as hard as my sprained ankle will allow, screaming at the pain and trying to match speed with the slowly accelerating train beside me. I grab a handrail and, with a leap, I clamber up the steps on to an empty container car. Without any handhold, I limp gingerly across the gently swaying platform knowing that I am making a near perfect target for Stammo. I dare not look back; a slip here is certain death. During what seems an age I make it across and jump one footed onto the rail bed on the other side, the momentum of the train sending me sprawling in the gravel. The train has taken me over a hundred yards along the track. I can not see where Steve and Stammo are.

Three tracks away, the west bound train is almost past me. It is slowing but still moving faster than I can run with my ankle. I half limp, half hop across the tracks and just miss the last car on the train. I try to ignore the pain and hare after it.

The unmistakable ping of a ricocheting bullet tells Stammo is firing at me over the empty container cars of the eastbound train. I've been shot before and my skin crawls at the memory.

Steve is picking his way across one of the cars of the eastbound train, just like I did. But the trains are moving apart at a combined speed of thirty miles an hour, fifteen yards every second.

Lungs bursting and foot screaming, I push myself to the limit. I am only a couple of feet from the end of the train but I know if I can't make it or if I slip and fall, I will be taken. I hear another shot from Stammo's Sig Sauer.

With a supreme effort, I catch up to the caboose, grab the handrail and somehow drag myself onto the platform. I stay prone to make a small target, gulping air for my fibrillating heart. Within ten seconds, I am out of range of Stammo's fire and although Steve has jumped off the eastbound train there is no way that he can catch me; he has given up the chase. In a few minutes I will be under the SeaBus terminal downtown.

Myself, well mounted, hardly have escaped but now what?

I have nowhere to turn. There will already be an APB out on me; Roy is a leaky sieve; I dare not show my face in the downtown east side where the gang will be on the prowl; I can not even see my lovely Ellie without walking into a trap.

On top of that, I can feel the pain in my shoulders match the pain in my ankle and I have to buy heroin.

There seems to be only one choice.

Chapter 43

Everything has changed. I have it. I have it all. The potential disaster of Kevin's blood on my jacket was a gift: the definitive proof that Kevin *was* murdered. George knew that I changed my clothes at the condo and that my jacket would be there; nothing could be easier than framing me by smearing Kevin's blood on it.

After my escape from Steve and Stammo, I bought from a dealer in the West End and, stopping only to purchase stationery supplies, headed back to the new home that Arnold arranged for me yesterday. It's a safe house now but for how long?

Somehow, the adrenaline of the chase, combined with the effects of the heroin, honed my mind to a razor's edge. My room back there is still festooned with more than twenty flip charts all marked up with brightly colored felt tips. I charted everything I know about Kevin's murder, about QX4 and Sandi, about George and his business dealings and the gang.

One set of charts shows all of George's businesses that I found on his website and from my talk with Brad.

I stared at those charts for an hour.

The manufacturing and distribution companies, the airlines, the convenience stores, the agribusinesses all seemed like an unrelated mish-mash until, with a spinal rush of electricity, it all fell into place. They are interrelated in a most unusual way that points to one stunning conclusion: George is not associated with the gang.

George *is* the gang.

For the first time in my life I have one goal and one goal only. I have to prove that George and his gang buddies killed Kevin. If I can do that, I can see them put away and clear my own name and maybe, with Mr. Wallace's help, somehow get back into the VPD. I have no other path.

Accepting this is freeing. No decisions to be made; just get on and do it.

One thing seems not to fit. I reviewed the list of the people who died from Kevin's drug. When Steve gave it to me, my withdrawal symptoms masked a nugget of gold: Palmer, Jason, age 19, died October 31. Poor kid died on Halloween. I did not see it at first. The name might be a coincidence but it is definitely worth checking out. Something else I must do later today.

Oh, and yes, I must find the time to deal with another question that is still niggling at my mind: the one thing that, try as I might, I can not make fit: Arnold's comment that my beating by the gang may be connected to Kevin's murder.

My thoughts are interrupted by a drop-dead gorgeous secretary. She gives me a warm smile and leads me through a corridor to the plush interior of the office.

As soon as she closes the door behind me, I say, "I know Kevin was murdered and I know who killed him," I do not get the reaction that I expected. Instead of irritation at my continuing pursuit of the murder theory, I get a bemused look, although it is not quite acceptance. I decide to press on. "When I tell you, you're not going to believe it at first but I want you to hear me out. Will you do that?"

"Sure…" The word is drawn out, as much a question as a confirmation.

I desperately need his help, so I need to convince him right now. I decide to start at the beginning.

"We've known Kevin since grade eight, in fact *you've* known him since elementary school. We were the

258

three amigos. I don't think that even his parents knew him as well as we did."

Brad shrugs and nods.

I continue. "Can you really believe that Kevin killed himself, Brad? In your heart of hearts?"

"But the evidence, Cal. The autopsy and the—"

"Just put that aside for a moment." I am trying hard to curb my feelings of irritation. "If there were no evidence, no autopsy, no coroner's verdict, would you believe that Kevin was capable of killing himself? that he could stab himself in the chest with his own knife?"

He struggles with the idea. "I don't know… I guess not." But he is not convinced.

"I've never believed it. Now, I'm sure that it was murder and I know who did it."

I wait. I am determined to make him ask.

He does. "So who, already?" Now it's Brad who is irritated.

"It was George Walsh."

Brad takes a breath and throws his eyes heavenward. He turns his head away from me and blows the breath out audibly through his lips, shaking his head. The dismissive gesture hurts but I press on.

Before he can speak, I say, "You promised to hear me out, Brad. I've got some evidence and with your help, I can prove it."

"OK. Prove away."

I ignore the skepticism in his tone. "We know that Kevin was conducting illegal human trials of his anti-addiction drug. Sandi confirmed it and so did my buddy Roy. I've seen the police's list of the people who died and I recognized a few of the names."

"The police know about the drug testing?" He sits bolt upright in his executive chair and his face pales. *Now* I have got his full and undivided attention.

"No, but they know that a number of street people have all died recently and all of them have the same unusual chemical in their blood."

He leans forward and puts his head in his hands. "Shit! If they find out about it, QX4 is a dead duck. Everyone will lose everything. I'll be ruined. Just when the shares have bounced back, I'm going to lose it all again."

My sympathy for him is limited. "The fifteen people who died are a whole lot more ruined." I comment.

"Fifteen! I thought it was seven," he is on his feet, working hard to keep his voice down.

"It was, up until the time that Kevin died. Since then, another eight have been found. That's fifty percent of the people being tested."

Brad's face has gone from pale to the color of the parchment skin of Kevin's father. "No Cal. That's one hundred percent. You told me that Kevin had thirty subjects. He would have split them into two groups of fifteen. To one group, the control group, he would have given a placebo. The real drug would only have gone to the other group of fifteen. Everyone who took the damn drug died."

We both pause for this to sink in. Instead of being appalled by the enormity of the tragedy, I feel relief. Roy must have been in the control group. My nagging worry that he might follow Tommy and the others is put to rest. He's going to be around to bug me for a lot of years to come.

Hiding my desire to smile at the thought, I continue, "I think George found out about the results of the testing, either from Kevin or Sandi. He realized that if Kevin started telling people what he had done, then QX4 would be ruined for ever; it could never recover. So he decided that it would be better to take a hit on the stock price when the news of Kevin's death was announced."

Brad thinks about it and starts to nod to himself. Time for my next salvo.

"Right after Kevin's death, QX4's stock price dropped sixty percent, so what did George do? Bit by bit, through a company in the Cayman Islands he bought another twenty million shares at fire sale prices, then lo and behold, last Friday the company announces that it's got approval for human trials and the shares rocket up and good old George has made another killing"

Brad is getting animated. "What?! George bought more stock? How do you know that? And how do you know about all that Cayman Islands stuff?" he asks.

"Arnold found out, with Mr. Wallace's help."

He processes this. "It doesn't make sense. Why would he buy those shares? He didn't know that QX4 was going to get approval from the feds. For all he knew, the approval was never going to come through because of Kevin's death."

I can now trump that objection. "Arnold called me on my way over here. He found out through one of Mr. Wallace's contacts in the Federal government that the approval to run human tests was couriered to QX4 on the Thursday *before* Kevin died. They would have received it on the Friday morning. I'm betting that George knew about it and decided to kill Kevin rather than have word of the illegal testing get out. Plus he could make a nice little profit into the bargain."

Brad's face takes on a green hue as it all sinks in. He makes one last ditch, but halfhearted, attempt. "But businessmen don't solve business problems by killing people. We talked about this before. You said you had only ever once heard about it happening. It just... I mean..." His objection peters out.

I can now take the last trick of the slam.

I lay it all out for him. The circumstantial evidence that leads inexorably to the fact that George is running the drug gang.

And, as implausible as it might seem, he buys it. I'd better not burst the bubble by telling him who the police's prime suspect is.

Now all I have to do is get him to help me prove it.

But first, one of the anomalies needs investigation.

Chapter 44

The security guard, like Worcester, is *malevolent to me in all aspects*. Since Sandi refused to see me, I told him I would wait and did not take no for an answer. He wants me out of his reception area but is not big enough to try and eject me himself and, I suspect, wants to avoid the embarrassment of having to ask the police to do it for him. He has glowered at me for the last forty-five minutes. But it is evening and I know she will have to leave eventually.

But his trial is ended as Sandi sweeps out of the elevator. I pull myself out of the stylish and uncomfortable knock-off of a Mies Van der Rohe chair but before I open my mouth she says, "I have nothing to say to you Cal."

She strides towards the front door, opening a blue and white golf umbrella bearing the QX4 logo. As I go to follow her, the guard's hand locks on my upper arm and I am surprised at the strength of his grip. Rather than struggle with him, I call, "I want to talk to you about Jason."

She turns and her face is wreathed in fury. The last name was not a coincidence.

For a moment she is unable to talk but brings herself under control and nods at the guard. "It's OK. Let him go." She walks through the rain to her car, followed by me with the guard at my elbow. She clicks the remote and says to me, "Get in."

The guard is not a happy camper. "Honk your horn if you need me, Miss Palmer." He gives me a hard look and is not impressed with the phony grin I flash him, but he walks off anyway.

I get into the car. Sandi is staring straight ahead, sitting with her hands white knuckled on the steering wheel, bringing herself under control. The rain is beating a tattoo on the convertible roof, flashing me back to a memory of my days as a Boy Scout, under canvass in the rain. The sound calms me.

"Sandi," my voice is gentle. "I'm sorry to come to your place of work like this; it's just that I didn't know how else to get in touch with you."

Silence.

"I know about Jason. Was he your brother?"

Sandi nods; I suspect that she can't trust herself to speak.

"I'm very sorry."

Nothing.

While I was waiting I had the time to plan my approach. "Sandi, I know you don't like me very much and I know that I'm not a cop any longer and that I have no standing in this. Legally there is no reason for you to talk to me." She is still silent but I know she is listening.

"I still believe that Kevin was murdered and at some point I am going to have to go to the police and tell them what I know." I notice her jaw tighten. "But the motive may have nothing to do with the issue of his doing illegal tests of that drug." This out-and-out lie catches her attention and she half turns to look at me. Is the emotion on her face hope? Or am I seeing what I want to see.

"I know that if it came out that Kevin had been testing the drug on human guinea pigs, it would ruin the company and I don't want to do that. So if you could answer just a few questions for me, I can follow my other leads and it need never come to light."

She takes a deep breath and turns away from me to look out of the driver's window. After a long moment she says, "OK."

"So Jason was an addict?"

"Heroin." She turns and faces me. "An older guy got him hooked when he was sixteen. After years of his lying and stealing from them, my parents gave up on him and threw him out of the house on his nineteenth birthday. I tried to help him when I could but…" Her voice tapers off but I know all the implications of what she is saying: the constant pleas for help; the barrage of lies, broken promises, unpaid loans and theft. Every junkie's gift to his family and friends.

"Did you know that he was one of Kevin's guinea pigs?"

"Not at first. When Kevin broke it to me that he was doing the drug tests, he conveniently omitted to tell me that Jason was one of his subjects. Jason always carried a card in his wallet with my home and cell phone numbers, so when he was found, the police came to me to tell me that he had died. Even then I didn't put it all together; even though by then I knew that six of Kevin's subjects had died, it never occurred to me that Jason was one of Kevin's guinea pigs. I was devastated. I went to tell my parents and they completely broke down. They blamed themselves. If they hadn't thrown him out…" Tears trickle down her face, mirroring the rain on the windshield.

In an attempt to give some consolation I say. "They couldn't have stopped him, nor could you. Addiction is just too strong a force," She just stares ahead.

"It was the Friday, the day before Kevin killed himself," she continues. "After I had gone to see my parents, I went over to Kevin's to tell him. He wasn't there, so I let myself in and waited. I waited hours. He didn't get back until midnight. When he walked in, his face was deathly pale and he looked like he hadn't slept in days. I told him that Jason was dead and he just said, 'I know.' Even as I started to ask him how he knew, the answer hit me." She turns and looks out the window and I can tell from the movement of her shoulders that she is crying.

265

I give her time to recover her composure before I ask, "What happened then?"

She reaches into the glove box and takes out a package of tissues. She wipes away the tears and blows her nose.

She looks me in the eye and says, "I lost it. I attacked him. I tried to scratch his face but he held my wrists. Then I tried kicking and I caught him a couple of times in the shin. I swear to you Cal, if I'd had a gun I would have shot him. Finally, I just collapsed onto the floor." She pauses. "I don't know how long I lay there but when I finally stopped crying, I got up and looked at Kevin. He was sitting on the couch with his head in his hands. I took off the engagement ring he had given me only a few weeks before. I threw it at him and walked out."

Either Sandi's telling the truth so far or she is the world's greatest actress.

"I'm sorry, Sandi but you know I have to ask. Did you go back the Kevin's on Saturday morning?"

"No, Cal. I didn't."

"Where were you on Saturday morning?"

"I was at the office."

"On a Saturday?"

"Yes, on a Saturday. I don't work for the government you know."

"Were you alone?"

She holds me in a glacial glare. "No, as a matter of fact. I was in a meeting."

"Who with?"

"You know what, Cal? Fuck you!" she explodes. "As you reminded me, you're not a cop any more. You don't have any standing and I don't need to give you an alibi. In fact, maybe you should give me *your* alibi. Did you know that Kevin was going to cut you off? Not let you use his place any more on Saturdays. Maybe you got so pissed off that *you* killed him. Now, get out of my car."

266

To emphasize her desire, she hits the horn four times and the security guard comes jogging out through the doors with a colleague; it must be change of shift.

"One last question," I ask. I have to get the answer before the guards come and drag me out of the car.

She is struggling to hold her temper in. "No, Cal," she says calmly.

The rent-a-cops are three cars away. Last chance.

"Please, Sandi. It's really important. Why are—"

"GET OUT OF MY FUCKING CAR!" she explodes.

I've got all I'm going to get from her for now, so I open the door of the car and face the security guards, right there, looming above me. I raise my hands to them, palms outward, in the universal signal for compliance, and get out into the rain, then turn and walk briskly through the downpour and out of the parking lot.

So Brad was right. Kevin was going to cut me off. Although I can understand why Kevin would want to do this, my understanding does nothing to ease the feeling of betrayal that I feel. My only friend from my old life was about to abandon me. But before I can start feeling sorry for myself, my unanswered question returns to my mind.

If *Addi-ban* killed her brother, why the hell is Sandi still working at QX4?

Chapter 45

I've always hated stakeouts—the boredom, the length of time spent for one minute of evidence—but this one is different. This one is personal. Everything hangs on it: the proof that George is Kevin's killer; peace of mind for a dying man in a mansion in Shaughnessy; exoneration for me and, with George out of the picture, maybe, just maybe, there will be a chance for me to regain my family.

I have not left Brad's Toyota in seven and a half hours. I have avoided eating and drinking but my bladder is full and I can not keep it in check much longer. A few hours ago I fixed myself up, masked by the pall of rain shrouding the car. I am praying that nothing happened while I was on the nod.

In another couple of hours the store I am watching on Robson Street will be closing. What if I am wrong? What if it *is* all circumstantial, just coincidence. Will I come back and do it again tomorrow, then the next day and the next? And for how many days will Brad let me have his car?

As the minutes drag by, the pressure on my bladder becomes unbearable. If I have to come back tomorrow, I will bring an empty juice bottle with me but, right now, I have to risk it. It will take three minutes max but, in a stakeout, it can all happen in three minutes. Three stores away from my stakeout target is one of Vancouver's ubiquitous Starbucks. I can wait no longer; I get out of the car and run through the rain hoping that I don't have to beg a barista for a washroom key.

Three minutes later, I burst out onto Robson and stop dead. There is a black BMW 7 series double parked in front of the target, right between me and the Toyota. I can not see the driver but my old buddy Goliath, looking out of place in a thousand dollar business suit, is getting out of the passenger door.

I freeze.

If either of them sees me, they may very well stop their activity and I will not get the evidence I need. They might even turn their attentions on me and decide to take me down.

I'm only thirty feet away from them and any unnatural movement will draw their attention. If I turn towards them, they will see me. If I turn away, I will miss seeing what goes down. If I just stand here like a statue, one of them is sure to spot me. I decide to just cross the sidewalk and head over to the other side of Robson but this means crossing right in front of their car... and that's when I see my salvation: a tourist in full rain gear peering at his plastic covered map. I stroll across the sidewalk to him.

"Can I help you?" I ask. Out of the corner of my eye I see Goliath limping through the rain into the store. He has an expensive leather briefcase clutched in his huge paw.

"Oh, ja. Thank you. I am looking for Stanley Park. It is not far?" The accent is distinctly Scandinavian: a hardy Swede or Norwegian seeking a walk through the park in a downpour.

Keeping him between me and the windshield of the BMW, I tell him, "Just keep going along Robson in this direction and the park is at the very end." I point to Lost Lagoon on his map, "You'll be right here. It's about a fifteen minute walk."

"Thank you so much," he says and, without any warning, strides off down the street leaving me naked to the view of the driver.

A trolley bus has pulled up behind the double parked Beamer and its driver is not impressed; he gives a blast with his horn which elicits an obscene gesture out the car's window. In the hope that my adversary has his attention distracted for long enough by the bus, I stroll casually across Robson and walk into an expensive clothing store.

I can watch the street unobserved through the window and within seconds I see Goliath back on the sidewalk, hands empty, no briefcase in sight.

It was a drop off.

My heart rate is up; it's the thrill of the hunt. How I've missed this. How could I have lived without it for the last two and a half years. It's better than heroin. Heroin is no longer a high, it's a need. *This* is a high.

But before I can enjoy the high, the low sweeps in: Brad lent me his camera so that I could document the evidence, the same camera that I left sitting on the back seat of the Toyota. I've seen what I hoped against hope to see but it might as well not have happened; I have zero proof, zip, nada.

Accompanied by a second horn blast from the trolley bus, the BMW takes off down Robson. Now I've blown it. No photograph, no evidence. Unless…

I dash out of the store and holding my hands extended, palms outward, I stop the slow moving traffic as I dash across the street and scramble into Brad's Toyota. The driver of a red Corvette hits his horn as I pull out from the curb and cut in front of of him. There are five cars and a trolley bus between me and the BMW and I can't see my quarry.

The traffic crawls eastward and the bus turns left onto Burrard but the BMW is gone. I glance up Burrard to my right and it is not there. There is no sign of them ahead. I have only one hope. If I've lost them, I will be back again tomorrow and the next day and the next, until they decide to do another drop off.

I accelerate along the short block, hang a left onto Hornby and I feel my breath come out in a long sigh as I see them stopped at the traffic lights at Georgia.

Keeping several cars back, I follow them down Hornby to West Hastings. A couple of blocks along, the driver parks illegally and Goliath takes an identical briefcase into an identical store but this time I capture it all in the camera's memory. Within seconds he is back in the car and they are off along Hastings, away from the glossy high-rises of downtown to the rat infested edifices east of Main.

Just as I hoped, the BMW pulls into a parking spot. On this section of Hastings there are two or three convenience stores on every block. The denizens of this neighborhood are, in the main, either drug users or poor immigrant families, neither of whom have much money to squander on the inflated prices of convenience store merchandise. Until now, I have always wondered how they manage to stay in business. Now I know.

I have parked a few spaces ahead of the Beemer and in the passenger side mirror, I see my buddy go into a dingy store, the barred windows covered in faded posters advertising various items of junk food. This time Goliath goes in with a bulging envelope in each hand; I turn and fire the camera's shutter, click. In less than sixty seconds he is out, minus one envelope, and limping through the rain in my direction. Click. He walks right past me and goes four doors ahead to an even sadder, more fly blown emporium. Click. He is out in an instant, hands empty. Click.

This is great. God, how I wish I were a cop again. This would be a career maker. Maybe it will be a career re-maker. I laugh at the irony. If I worked for the department now, I would not be able to do this stakeout: I am doing it as part of an investigation into Kevin's murder and, as far as they are concerned, the Kevin Wallace case is solved.

I put the camera down on the passenger seat and the movement catches his attention. For an instant we are locked eye to eye and then recognition dawns on his ugly mug. He is less than twenty yards away and he breaks into a lumbering jog in my direction, yelling something to his buddy in the car. If they can take me, I'm going to be found dead in an alley, another victim of a heroin overdose.

I start the engine, put it in drive and give a quick glance in the driver's side mirror. Good, the street is clear and better, the BMW driver has got out of the driver's seat. He is fat where Goliath is massive. He waddles past the parked cars towards me. I have to time this just right.

Wait…

Wait…

The driver is level with my back bumper just as Goliath yanks open the passenger door.

"Get the fuck out!" he yells.

One more second and I crank the wheel and hit the gas. On my right, the passenger door handle is snatched from Goliath's paw and on my left, his fat friend, who had just pulled level with my window, is nudged off his feet by the car as it swings out in front of him. Serves him right. If he had waited in his car, he could chase me and there is no way Brad's Toyota could outrun the 535 horses under the hood of the BMW.

I have bought myself the time I need. I hang a right and lose myself in the side streets of Strathcona.

I've got what I wanted. But is it enough?

Chapter 46

Cal is like a force of nature. Once started, there is no stopping him. He's got a great mind, always did have; not like Kevin—Kev was a *bona fide* genius—but what Cal has is this amazing intuition.

Despite my skepticism last night, I did some digging and I have to admit that he is on to something and it could be a way out for me.

I hand him the half used bottle of penicillin that he asked me to bring. He nods his thanks and, without looking at the instructions, washes three capsules down with a gulp of his beer.

"So, what happened?" I ask.

The question brings a big grin on his face. Something's happened, for sure. "You first," he says.

No way. I want to find out if he has discovered anything concrete before I open up about what I know.

"Come on, Cal. You're the one that has been doing the stakeout; what happened?"

He takes a maddeningly long time to chalk up his cue and break. A striped ball goes in the side pocket. He pockets two more, then misses an easy shot. Why are we doing this?

"I was right, wasn't I, Bradley?" he ignores my question and he knows it irritates me when he calls me Bradley. "What did you find out?"

I miss the green ball completely. I hate this game. I know Cal's stubborn streak; he's going to make me talk first.

So I do. Why fight the inevitable? "I talked to George today. He told me that he wants to diversify Walsh

273

Investments' portfolio and felt that he has too much invested in QX4 stock. He says he's found an institutional buyer for seventy-five percent of his shares.

"You were right. He knows that QX4 is toast over the long term and he's going to get out as quick as he can. If he can pull it off at a decent price, he'll walk away with about eighteen million bucks."

I can't keep the bitterness out of my voice. If QX4's shares collapse, I will lose everything and be in debt to George to the tune of half a million dollars. As fast as I can I've been selling my QX4 shares in small blocks that won't attract attention. If I can sell most of them before they collapse, at least I will be able to pay George back. If Cal's suspicions about him are true, he's not someone I want to owe money to. Maybe I'll even have a little left over for myself.

"You're next. Tell me all." Now it's my turn to find out what he has been up to today.

He pockets two balls with one shot, lucky bastard, then misses a tricky long shot. He looks at me, a big smile on his face, then takes a long drink of his beer. He's playing the showman here and it is bugging me. He sees it in my face.

"OK, OK," he says. "I was right. George's retail operations, the ones that you said were not making any profits, are one great big money laundering machine."

He tells me about his stakeout. "If I took this to the police, they could take him down for money laundering. We always guessed that the only way we would get to the guys at the top would be to bust them for money laundering or tax evasion."

"So how do you know they are money laundering?" I ask.

"Their drug profits are all in cash, so clever old George has bought a bunch of retail outlets that traditionally take in cash. Downtown foreign exchange stores and all convenience stores take in a lot of cash and can easily change it into non-cash items like money orders, travelers checks and checks written to phony suppliers. It's brilliant."

"So what are you going to do?" I'm terrified that if he brings down George before I can get rid of my shares, I'm toast. I can't positive-think my way out of that.

"Are you guys fucking playing or what? There's people waiting for this table." He's a short guy, dressed like a biker and he looks tough as nails. Cal looks like he's going to make a big issue of it. "We'll—"

I cut him off, fast, "Sorry man. We're finished, you go ahead." I take Cal's cue and rack both of them and hustle him away from the pool table to the bar.

"What are you going to do?" I reiterate, "about George?"

"Nothing for the moment." Thank God for that. "I want to get George for Kevin's murder but at the moment, all I've got is circumstantial evidence. I need to find solid proof. Right now the police think I did it."

"*What?* You? Why?" This is a huge surprise, I thought they had ruled it suicide.

"Someone, I'm guessing Sandi, told them that Kevin was planning to cut me off from going to his place on Saturday mornings, like you told me. They figure that's good enough for a motive. I was at Kevin's house just before he was killed and to top it all, they found his blood on my jacket."

"How did you get Kevin's blood on your jacket?" I can feel my heartbeat.

"I didn't," he says defensively. "It was my street jacket. I left it lying on the bed in the spare room at Kevin's with my other street clothes while I went over to see Ellie. George must have known that and smeared blood on my jacket to frame me. Anyway, my old partner tried to arrest me, or at least, take me in for questioning, but I escaped."

"When?"

275

"Yesterday morning." He looks more than a little sheepish.

"Why the hell didn't you tell me this last night."

"I'm sorry. I should have. I just didn't want anything to defocus you from the idea of George being the killer."

"Cal, if you want me to help you bring George down for Kevin's murder. You can't hold out on me like that; you have to keep me in the loop on everything, OK?"

"Yeah, absolutely. It won't happen again. I promise." It had better not because it's non-negotiable.

We sit in silence for a while.

"I found out some other stuff about George, too," I volunteer.

"What?" he really wants to know.

Now it's my turn. I take two slow swallows of the last of my beer and order another couple from the barman before answering.

"After last night, I looked deeper into George's business portfolio and you were right. Take the airline. It's a charter airline and it's *very* profitable. All the aircraft are hybrids, they have cargo space and passenger space. But what's really interesting are the destinations. He has contracts with the Canadian and US governments to fly people and supplies to and from Afghanistan.

"Think about it. You take some people—they could be security people, aid workers or politicians or whatever—and a bunch of supplies to Afghanistan, all in the same plane. On the return journey, you maybe bring back some other people but you are not likely to be bringing any supplies *back*, so the cargo hold is empty. So…"

I leave it hanging. I don't need to tell Cal that the biggest cash crop in Afghanistan, to the tune of four billion dollars a year, is the poppy from which the highest grade of heroin is made.

But I've not finished.

276

"What makes it such a sweet deal, is that his planes usually fly in and out of Canadian Air Force bases, which means he probably circumvents the normal customs processes.

"And that's not all. His airline also has contracts with several Canadian and US mining companies which have properties or joint ventures in South America. He ferries people and supplies from here directly to the mine sites. On top of that, he has big investments in a number of coffee plantations down there. It's the perfect cover for importing cocaine.

"I told you he was a business genius. He's got a vertically integrated drug business. It's a criminal business hidden inside a legal business and it doesn't pay a penny in tax or make charitable donations or do anything other than make money for George."

I thought Cal would be delighted with this—it rounds out his theory about George to perfection—but if anything he looks puzzled. He is shaking his head.

"What?" I ask.

He doesn't answer. He's holding out on me again.

"OK, Cal. What's up here? I thought you'd be all over this."

"No, it's great. It's just that there's one thing bothering me about George. Something that just doesn't fit."

"What's that?"

"Why would a big time drug dealer invest millions in a company that is working on curing addiction and potentially putting him out of business?"

I can't help laughing out loud. Cal's a super-bright guy and a great cop but he doesn't understand how a businessman like George thinks.

Now it's his turn to be irritated. "What are you laughing at?" he demands.

"What does a wealthy business do when a small competitor comes along?" I ask.

He shrugs.

"They get control of the competitor. If George is the big time dealer we suspect, spending a few million to get effective control of QX4 is nothing."

"Yes, of course. I never thought of that. To George, risking ten million bucks is zip."

He thinks about it and I can almost see the cogs and wheels turning over in his head. Something else is brewing up in there. I wonder if he is going to tell me.

He is nodding to himself and taking an infuriatingly long time to speak.

Finally. "He didn't even risk it," he says. "You know what? When he found out about Kevin's illegal testing it was the answer to his prayers: the death knell for QX4. But instead of telling the world, George killed Kevin to keep him quiet, giving himself time to get his money out. And you can bet when he does, he will leak the story and QX4 will be history and no longer competition for the drug trade."

He's right. It's a powerful motive for George to want to kill Kevin.

Cal laughs. "Oh, this guy is going down if I have anything to do with it."

And if I know Cal, he will.

I can feel events taking motion. I never thought I would say this, but no amount of positive thinking is going to change matters. I have got to get my money out of QX4 before the axe falls.

Chapter 47

The report runs to twenty handwritten pages.

It has taken me most of the evening to write and it details all that I have learned about George's trading in QX4 stock, my surveillance of what I am sure is a money laundering operation, and Brad's and my speculation about George's other businesses. Inside the report, in plastic sleeves, are the photos I took with his camera.

The report does not mention any names or companies and there is no mention of Kevin's murder. That will come later.

But is it enough? This is my one shot to put things right and if it fails, I will end up in jail for a very long time and George will get away with murder and fraud and have a lot more money in his pocket. But if I can pull it off, George is the one who will spend most of the rest of his life in prison.

I allow myself to savor the thought for a moment, swill it around on my palette as it were, but the finish is taken off by the effect this will have on Sam. She doesn't know what George is and she must love him; if she didn't love him she wouldn't be with him. It's not for the money. Oh, I'm sure that she likes having nice things but money has no hold over Sam. And Ellie, what will this do to her? Will having another male ripped from her life ruin her for all her future relationships with men. That worries me a lot. But I can't let George get away with Kevin's murder. The thought of Ellie brings a smile to my face and, as I reach for the phone to call her, it rings. On the cheap pay-as-you-go plan, there is no caller ID but I have a good idea who it is, one of those psychic father and daughter things.

"Hello, sweetie."

"*Uh, hello. This is St. Paul's Hospital calling.*" It is a woman's voice, uncertain; it sounds middle European, Polish maybe. "*May I ask who I am speaking to?*"

It sounds genuine enough but I'm not altogether sure.

"My name's Rogan," I say cautiously.

"*We found this number on a piece of paper in the wallet of a patient. The name Cal was also written on the paper.*"

With rising alarm, I say, "Yeah, that's me."

"*The patient is an older man, in his sixties or early seventies. Do you know who that might be?*" In the background, I hear a ring, like the sound of an elevator reaching its destination, then a voice paging a Dr. Armin. It really is St. Paul's.

I stall for time, my thoughts racing. "Was he wearing a long tweed coat that has seen better days and a battered old leather Stetson?"

"*I don't know sir, I didn't admit him. If you hold, I'll find out.*" The hospital sounds continue in the background. It's got to be Roy. I feel sick to my stomach. If they are calling me, they don't know who he is, so he must be unconscious. That can only mean one thing.

"*Hello, sir. Yes, he was. Can you tell me his name please, sir?*"

"Sure, yes. It's Roy."

"*And his last name?*"

I almost say 'I don't know' but stop myself just in time. If I admit that I don't know his last name, they will certainly not let me see him or tell me anything about his condition. The first surname that pops into my head is 'Rogers' but I can't say that, so I borrow from Tommy. "Connor, it's Roy Connor. How badly is he hurt?"

"*Are you a relative sir?*"

"Yes, I'm his nephew. What ward is he on?" Claiming Roy, the free spirit, as a relative feels odd. But OK. More than OK.

"He's not. He's in the operating room. He was badly beaten."

"Do you know when he will be out of the OR?"

"No sir, I don't."

"Where was he brought in from?" I ask.

"He wasn't. He was found on the sidewalk in front of Emergency, a couple of hours ago."

I say, "I'll be right there," and close the phone.

Those bastards. They'll stop at nothing to get to me.

The note is phoney. Roy may be an old drunk but he has an amazing head for numbers. I am betting he has never written down a phone number in his entire life. Plus he never, ever refers to me as Cal. For some reason known only to him, I will always be Rocky as far as he is concerned. The gang have beaten Roy to within an inch of his life and put that paper in his pocket. Then they dumped him at St. Paul's and they will be staking out the area, ready to grab me when I show up there.

I feel my options closing down, blocking me in; I am like a spelunker crawling deeper and deeper into a dark, narrowing fissure. I find myself gulping for air. I think of Roy and what has been done to him. *This thing of darkness!* But Shakespeare is no comfort now.

Roy has always looked after me on the streets; now it falls to me to reciprocate. Of all the things I might do—even though my best laid plans to nail George may gang off to glae—I will choose to do the right thing, *though it be folly.*

Pausing only to take another hit of Brad's penicillin, which doesn't yet seem to be having any effect on the sore on my arm, I pull on my jacket and head out.

Chapter 48

Cops spend a lot of time in hospitals. We know the routines. I'm going to make use of those routines to avoid the trap set for me.

I am crouching in the bushes behind St. Paul's, arrived at by a circuitous route through the west end and across the park at Nelson and Thurlow.

I do not have to wait more than a few minutes. The back door crashes open and two nurses step out. They are discussing a patient, an old man with a twinkle in his eye and roving hands; under other circumstances, that might be Roy. As they walk down the short concrete path to the sidewalk, lighting their cigarettes, I slip through the slowly closing door and let it click shut behind me.

The ER is packed with east side people in all stages of disrepair. When I was in uniform these were the people whom I would have interviewed, consoled or arrested. Now we are ships passing in the night. I go straight to the nurse's station and address myself to a pleasant looking Filipina, talking to a colleague sitting in front of a computer terminal. She has a pink ribbon holding her hair in a ponytail.

"Hi, I'm looking for my uncle, Roy Connor. Someone called me about half an hour ago and said that he was in the Operating Room."

She does not need to check the computer. "Oh yes. He's just out of the OR now and is in intensive care. I'm glad you're here. The doctor wants to see you."

I follow her through the emergency ward, steeling myself for what I am going to see. "How bad is he?" I ask.

"The doctor will give you the details." An ominous answer.

We go through some double doors. There is a glassed off room with a single bed in it. The shrunken figure on the bed is connected to the surrounding devices by an incomprehensible array of tubes and wires. I lick my lips; my mouth has gone dry.

"Is that him?" I ask.

She nods and the gravitas of her expression tells me all the things that I do not want to hear.

"Can I go in?"

She nods. "I'll go and get the doctor." She reaches out and touches my arm.

My mouth goes dry as I look at him. He is barely recognizable. His mouth is covered by an oxygen mask and his forehead is swathed in a bandage. There are four sets of stitches on various parts of his face, forming bridges between islands of raw skin and black bruises. His left arm is in a fiberglass splint. The machines to which he is connected are hissing and beeping. I move to his right side and take his good hand. It feels cold, colder than it should.

"Hello. I'm Doctor Patel." He has an air of competence and authority that belies the twenty-three year old look of his face.

Without letting go of Roy, I extend my other hand to shake his. "I'm Cal Rogan. I'm Roy's nephew. I'm his only living relative."

This seems to satisfy him.

"Mr. Rogan, I won't mince words. Your uncle was very badly beaten, as you can see."

"But he's going to be all right." It's a statement not a question. Roy is the toughest old bird I have ever known. He has weathered more storms than the good doctor could possibly imagine. I have known him for a lot of years and I am going to know him for a lot more. It may take him a while but he is going to be back on the streets and giving me heck.

His face offers no comfort. "I am afraid that the external wounds are not the concern, here. He was hit repeatedly to the body causing damage to his kidneys and liver, and worse, causing him to have an MI: a heart attack. I mean no disrespect but might I ask if Mr. Connor is uh... a drinking man?"

"Yes. Roy's an alcoholic. He has been a heavy drinker for at least forty years."

He nods. "I thought so." He gestures to me to sit on the chair beside the bed. "You should prepare yourself for the possibility of the worst case scenario; the drinking has obviously weakened his heart. He is sedated now and he should regain consciousness some time tomorrow but it is uncertain whether he will last the next forty-eight hours. I'm sorry."

I can't speak. I just nod my thanks. He nods back and leaves.

My emotions are in turmoil. Part of me is devastated by the thought of losing the man who has become my closest friend—I can't imagine life without Roy—but underneath the fear, a part of me knows, and knows to a certainty, that Roy will beat the odds and prove the doctors wrong. I smile at him and squeeze his hand.

The Filipina nurse comes in. "You can stay here as long as you like," she says, "but there is a policeman outside who would like to talk to you."

"Thank you, nurse." I manage to say.

She turns to leave.

"Nurse," I ask, "the doctor said that he is sedated, is there any chance that he will wake up before the morning?"

"I doubt it very much," she says. "He will remain sedated for at least another twelve hours." She gives a kind smile and leaves.

I check my watch, it is nearly midnight. As much as I want to stay, to be beside him when he wakes, I can not miss the appointment in the morning. It will mark the beginning of the end for George Walsh and, with luck, bring down his gang: the lowlifes who did this to Roy.

I squeeze his hand. "I'll see you tomorrow Roy," I whisper, knowing that he will understand, and think I see a shadow of recognition pass over his face. Or is it just my hope-fueled imagination?

I leave the room and look around. The uniform, whose job it is to interview, console or arrest me, is probably standing on the other side of the double doors leading out of the ICU. In the opposite direction, I see an emergency exit with a crash bar.

I head out into the night, retribution on my mind.

Chapter 49

The place is huge. If it were in the city, twenty-five miles to the west of here, it would cover an area eight blocks wide by four deep. The perimeter is over two miles of heavy-grade, chain-link fence topped by tightly rolled razor wire, surrounding its charges. This morning's thick, gray cloud cover washes out most of the color, giving the place a harsh, surreal look. Despite its forbidding aspect, this is the best place that I could think of for this particular meeting.

There are rows upon rows of old cars, arranged roughly by make, thousands of them. Some are standing, rusting on their wheels; some are in piles, compressing under their own weight; some have been crushed into blocks the size of a file cabinet and piled, like huge Lego pieces, into high walls. Once upon a time, each one of them was the delight of its first owner. Now, imprisoned in this place, they are destroyed dreams.

On this bitterly cold morning, it is the perfect place.

My phone rings.

"We're at the front gate. Now what?" My heart beats a little faster. They have arrived.

"Park your car and walk in on foot," I tell them. "Go past the office and head for the back of the lot, towards the big crane with the magnet. When you get there, call me again." I close the phone, turn and give the thumbs up to Brad sitting in the warmth of the Toyota, outside the fence. He smiles and reciprocates.

I can't smile. Too much depends on this meeting.

It takes five or six long, dragged out, minutes before my phone rings again.

"OK. *We're standing by the crane.*"

"Good. Come round the back of the crane and walk between the rows of Ford Tauruses until you get to the back fence, then turn left." I close the phone and wait for the men who want to arrest me to come into view. It takes less than a minute.

Stammo is in the lead. I can see the grim smile on his face and the handcuffs in his hand. He hasn't come here to talk. He is going to take some convincing. I can only hope that Steve, two feet behind him, will be more reasonable but his expression does not give me any comfort. He looks like he is still mad at my escape from him on Monday.

As soon as Stammo sees where I am standing, his face breaks into a scowl and he makes an angry noise in the back of his throat.

I am on the outside of the big-assed fence.

He is on the inside. He looks up at the razor wire; there is no way he can get to me.

He is *really* pissed. I should not antagonize him but I can not resist throwing him a happy grin. He marches fast at the fence, grabs it and shakes it in his frustration, glaring at me through the wire.

"You murdering mother-fucker." His breath steams in the cold air. "Don't think you can get away with this. We didn't come here to play some stupid little game. I'm going to take you down for killing Kevin Wallace."

"Oh, you mean the suicide?" That's me, innocent.

"Don't give me that crap, asshole," he shouts in his frustration.

I can not resist Macbeth. "Nicky," I use this form of his first name because I know it irritates him. "*That is a tale told by an idiot, full of sound and fury, signifying nothing.*"

Drawing from his own great storehouse of witty quotations and repartee, Stammo says, "Fuck you, Rogan." He looks up at the razor wire again, spits and lights a cigarette.

Steve's face is neutral. I guess it is the best I can hope for at this point.

We eye each other through the fence.

I address myself to Steve. "First thing, I want to say that I'm sorry about Monday. Running like that was stupid. I should have just called a lawyer and worked it out with you guys. I wasn't thinking straight." It's BS but it's what Steve wants to hear.

Stammo is in like Flint. "You weren't thinking at all, you moron."

"OK, OK." I can't tell if Steve is mad at me or Stammo. "Why are we here, Cal?"

Now for the moment to truth. I rehearsed this speech twenty times in the car coming out here but it still sounds lame to me. My fear of blowing it is in the forefront of my mind.

"When I was still in the department, you and I spent a lot of time going after the drug gangs and we had some real successes. But way more than half the time, their lawyers managed to get the big cases thrown out of court based on some mickey mouse Charter of Rights technicality." Steve is showing nothing and Stammo is shaking his head.

"Well, I've got some evidence that if we follow it up, we can nail an entire gang, including the guy at the top, and I mean the very top, with money laundering. If we get lucky, we can also bust a major drug smuggling and processing operation. We'll send a bunch of very bad guys to jail."

Stammo grunts, "Bullshit," but Steve knows me better.

"What've you got?" he asks.

From an inside pocket I take a photocopy of my report, roll it up tightly and push it through the chain-link. Steve unrolls it and starts reading, as he finishes each page he passes it to Stammo. I am holding my breath and I have to force myself to breathe. I watch their faces and something tells me that they are buying it: the occasional unconscious nod; a lifted eyebrow.

It takes them ten minutes to take it all in.

"There are no names." Stammo says. There is accusation in his tone.

"What kind of stunt are you trying to pull here, Cal." The disappointment in Steve's voice shatters my flimsy hopes.

"Fuck, Steve, let's go." Stammo turns to me. "Start running Rogan because as soon as we get back to our car we are coming after you." He turns and stalks off the way he came.

Steve looks at me and then follows his partner, shaking his head. I am shocked that I have lost all credibility with the one guy on the force whom I thought would listen to me.

"Steve, Nick, wait!" I wanted that to come out confidently but it smells of desperation.

Stammo stops and turns. Steve marches on but, as he passes Stammo, the latter whispers something. Steve shrugs and they turn back.

"Names," Stammo grunts.

"Sure. If you agree to my terms, I'll tell you ev—"

"Names first."

With a shock, I realize that I only have one name: George. I remember Sam mentioning Blondie's first name, David, I think. Of the others I have no idea. I feel my position eroding beneath my feet.

"Last chance," Stammo says.

Here goes. "The guy at the top is George Walsh."

"Your ex-wife's fiancé?" Steve asks. There is no sign of the expected incredulity in his voice.

"Yes. I know it would be easy to say that I am making this up because I have an ax to grind about him marrying Sam but I'm not."

"Are you one hundred percent sure about this, Cal?" Steve asks.

Nowhere near a hundred percent. "Yes, I am," I say.

Steve leans in and whispers something to Stammo who looks at him hard and then nods.

"So what are your terms, Rogan?" Do a hear a glimmer something in Stammo's voice? Maybe he can't resist the opportunity for glory that will fall out from any major gang bust.

"You put any thoughts of arresting me for Kevin's murder on the back burner. You let me in on this. I work with you and when it's all over, you tell everyone, from the Mayor on down, that I brought this to you. That's the deal."

"And if we don't agree." Stammo is being the tough guy but I can trump him.

"Then I'll take it to the RCMP. I'm sure they'd love to take a bust from right under the noses of the VPD."

The mention of the Feds seals the deal. No local cop likes to lose a bust to the Mounties.

Steve and Stammo eye each other and I see the micro movement of Stammo's head. They've bought it.

"OK, Cal. You've got a deal but, no matter what, we are not going to be able to forget about Kevin Wallace's murder?"

"No prob. If we haven't unearthed Kevin's murderer as part of the investigation, then I'll just turn myself over to you guys and we'll see where the chips fall."

Stammo starts to object. "How do we know that—"

"Wait a minute!" Steve interrupts him. "Are you saying that this money laundering is somehow connected to Kevin's death?"

"Yes. It's how I unearthed it all. The guys who we're going after killed Kevin."

After a moment's thought, Steve says "OK. Works for me. We can live with that,". He turns to Stammo. "I worked with Cal for years; I'll take his word on this."

Stammo shrugs but I detect a falseness in Steve's tone and, for the first time in my life, I wonder how much I can trust him.

"Right. Let's get this show on the road." Steve says. "We'll get our car, drive round the back there, pick you up and go downtown."

"I've got a ride." I point to Brad. "I'll see you there later. I've got to do something first. Roy was badly beaten up last night, by the same guys we're going after. The doc says he may not make it but you know Roy, he's a tough old bird. I'm pretty sure he's going to be OK. But I want to drop in and see him before I come over to 312 Main."

"How badly was he beaten?" Steve's concern is written on his face, together with something else that I can not quite fathom.

"Badly. Lots of internal damage and it triggered a heart attack," I tell him.

"Shit! Those bastards." In the old days, when Roy was my snitch, Steve knew him well and they hit it off. But there is something more here. Steve looks at Stammo, a question on his face. Stammo is undecided. He looks from Steve to me and back again. He shrugs and after a moment nods.

"What?" I ask. What's going on here?

Steve looks around, like he's trying to get out of something.

"What, Steve?" I ask again.

"When we sent your jacket off to the lab for DNA testing of the blood, we also sent your DNA from our files, for elimination purposes."

"Sure," I say, "it's standard practice." I don't know why they are telling me this but I am getting an uneasy feeling about it.

"Well the results came back that there were two samples of blood. Kevin's and an unknown male."

Where is this going? "You told me all this," I say, "and I told you it was Roy's blood. He cut his hand the previous night."

Steve is silent and in that brief instant, I know exactly what he is going to tell me. I can feel electricity coursing up my spine as I grab the chain link fence to support myself.

"Cal. There's no easy way to say this but... if that *was* Roy's blood on your jacket, then Roy's your father."

Chapter 50

Why couldn't I see it? The words keep running through my head. The enormity of Steve's revelation has shattered half the beliefs I hold about myself. My severe mother and the freewheeling Roy are my parents! I can't make sense of that picture. How can it be and *why couldn't I see it?* And why would my mother never tell me? Anger toward her flares in me at the thought... but, for some reason, I don't feel angry at Roy.

Roy is Ellie's grandad... and somehow *that* fits: the happy-go-lucky gene skipping a generation.

Now I know why Roy has always tried to take care of me on the streets. But my paternity begs a lot more questions than it answers. Questions that I will start asking in just a few moments. Especially the big one. I find I am looking forward to seeing him in a whole new way. A good way, I think. For many sons, their fathers becomes their friends but how many can say that their friend became their father? I smile at the thought as I walk into the ICU.

But the smile washes from my face. I am too late. He is gone. His bed is empty. I feel my stomach drop through the floor. Despite what the doctor said, I was so sure that he would pull through. Why didn't I stay with him last night and sit beside my friend as he died? But then perhaps Steve would not have told me about the DNA results and I might never have known. I force back the tears forming in my eyes at the irony of learning my paternity and then losing the opportunity of ever getting to talk to my father before he died.

An irrational anger stirs me. Why did he die before I could talk to him? Why couldn't he just hang on long enough to acknowledge me as his son? So like Roy to run away from that responsibility. I hate this anger but can not suppress it. To distract myself, I look around.

In the way that only a hospital can, they have erased all traces of Roy's sojourn here; it is as though it were a dream that I sat here and held his hand for the only time in our history together.

"Can I help you?" Her voice is severe. I am trespassing in her domain.

"I was looking for Roy. Roy uh… Connor."

"Are you a relative?"

"Yes. I'm his…" My voice breaks. I can not release the word.

She softens but her face confirms my fear. I dread what she is going to say.

But she surprises me.

"He was transferred to the cardiac ward on the sixth floor of the Centennial building."

A wave of relief courses through me and I thank the God whom I don't believe in. "How is he?"

"I'm not sure. You would have to ask them up there."

The elevator ride is interminable. It stops at every floor; gurneys roll in and roll out; visitors get on and get off, their faces a chart of their loved one's conditions; nurses and doctors armed with clipboards and stethoscopes enter and exit, dropping fragments of information about their patients.

"I'm looking for Roy Connor," I say to a nurse at the sixth floor nursing station.

She gives the sympathetic smile and asks the inevitable question. "Are you a relative?"

"Yes." This time I think I can say it. "I'm uh… his son." Why couldn't I see this? Was I so stupid that I missed something?

"Just a moment." She picks up the phone and dials, smiling at me as she waits for the answer. "Dr. Duffus, Mr. Connor's son is here." She hangs up. "He'll be right out."

"How is… my father?" The word is surreal but somehow joyful, like the first time you talk to a stranger and refer to your new bride as your wife.

"I'm afraid I don't know his exact status." She equivocates.

"Mr. Connor?" I do not at first react to the name. "Mr. Connor." The English voice belongs to a good looking man in his fifties. "I'm Barry Duffus. I'm your father's doctor." His smile is friendly and, in a surge of intuition, I know that Roy is in good hands; it gives me a big boost of hope.

I shake his hand. "How is he Doctor?"

"Come with me. We'll talk as we walk." He starts down the corridor. "You father had a massive heart attack. When we x-rayed him, we discovered that his internal organs have been compromised over the years. His heart is very weak. It's good that you're here now."

"But he will recover." It is as much a statement as a question.

"It's… unlikely," he says. "I'm sorry."

And yet, despite his pessimism, I know that Roy will pull through this and that somehow we will form a new relationship and new lives long into the future.

He opens the door to a small ward. Two of the beds are empty. All that I can see in the third bed is the shaggy gray head of a body which is curled under the covers in a fetal pose. This is the room where they bring people whom they think are going to die.

Roy is propped up in the fourth bed, eyes closed. The covers are rolled down to his waist and his upper body is naked. He is breathing heavily with the help of a transparent oxygen mask. The straggly gray hairs on his chest do nothing to mask the bruises. His face is misshapen from the punishment it has taken and for the first time I study that face, looking for similarities to my own. Our noses are about the same size and shape and our eyes are not too different, although his are blue and mine more green. Even our lips are the same shape. The question comes again: *Why couldn't I see it?* It was all in front of me all the time.

Dr. Duffus breaks into my thoughts. "Although he will feel cold and clammy to your touch, he'll complain of being hot." He smiles sadly. "I'm sorry that there's nothing more that we can do for him." He shakes my hand in both of his and leaves.

"Roy... Roy, it's me, Rocky."

The eyes flicker and open. It takes them a minute to focus. "Hello, Rocky," he croaks. He licks his lips. "Get me some water, Rock. I'm parched. I'm burning up here." He chuckles. "I think I must be standing too close to the gates of Hell." His sense of humor is still alive and kicking and it further buttresses my hope against the doctor's prediction. This is not the end of Roy.

I sit on the edge of the bed and reach across for the water on his night stand. I hold the bendy straw to his lips and he takes a small sip. "Thanks."

I take his hand in mine. There is a clip on his index finger from which a lead runs to a monitor. He gives my hand two squeezes, smiles and nods. I feel the questions bubbling up inside me, all the things I have to know.

"Why didn't you tell me, Roy?" I ask.

"Tell you what, Rock?" He asks the question with an innocence that stirs a whiff of anger in me.

"Why didn't you tell me that you were my father, for God's sake?" My voice has risen several decibels.

"Who told'ja that?" There is a denial in his voice; perhaps he doesn't know. "Father. Huh." The addendum or, more accurately, the way it is delivered, puts paid to the denial.

"Don't give me that bullshit, Roy. You know as well as I do." My voice is a shout and the body in the other bed stirs.

In the long silence, a cloud passes over Roy's face. "How did'ja find out?" he whispers.

"DNA. When they checked out the blood on my jacket." I have my anger under control now.

"Oh." He takes four labored breaths.

"Why didn't you tell me Roy? Things could have been so different." My anger dissipates and I wonder where it came from in the first place.

"Ain't it obvious?" There is anger in his voice now. Am I missing something here?

"Not to me, Roy. No."

"Figure it out." He closes his eyes and is breathing more easily.

But I can't figure it out. Why would a man deny his only son? The thought hurts. "Tell me Roy, please."

Two deep breaths, his voice hardly more than a whisper. "I didn't want'cha to know that your father was a pathetic old drunk."

"You were never pathetic to me. You were my best friend." I squeeze his hand and hold back the tears.

He nods. "I wanted to protect ya. You'd achieved so much; I was so proud of ya. I didn't want to bring ya down. You was better than me."

"I don't understand. If you didn't want to 'bring me down', why did you—"

With a surprising force, his hand crushes mine, cutting me off. "Listen," he says. He is breathing more quickly now and I see him struggle to get it under control.

"I'll tell ya everything," he says. "Don't interrupt. Just listen for once. OK?"

I just nod, not trusting myself to speak.

297

He takes deep inhalations forcing his breathing to slow while he puts his thoughts in order. It takes several agonizing minutes before he starts to speak.

"I was twenty-two when I met yer mother and I was living in a hippie commune on Fourth Avenue. Kits was Vancouver's Haight-Ashbury then, not the yuppie place it is now." Each sentence is punctuated by his labored breathing.

"I met her at a free concert down on Jericho Beach. She was beautiful. She actually had flowers in her hair. It was love at first sight." He smiles at the memory. "I wanted her to move in with me but she wouldn't. She was nineteen, lived with her parents and worked in a Hungarian deli. Her folks was old country and there was no way they was ever going to let her date some uneducated hippie. For her it was part of the excitement I think. The secrecy. Y'know, dating someone who'd make her parents freak out."

I am having difficulty seeing my severe mother in this picture but she is there. I know Roy is telling me the truth. His breathing has evened out; maybe he's over the worst now.

"We was together for almost a year but it was bound to come to a bad end. I was making a living dealing acid. A friend of mine was a chemist, he manufactured it and I sold it up and down Fourth. It wasn't like drug dealing today. No one ever got addicted to LSD; it was just a bunch of people experimenting and having fun, eh?

"I was making a lot of money but spending it like water." The thought of Roy having money to spend like water makes me shake my head in amusement. "I dropped acid now and again but I was drinking heavy and your mother didn't approve. Then it happened. She came to me and told me she was pregnant. She said her parents would freak and that she wanted me to pay for an abortion." He stops for a moment, his breathing more labored again.

The shock of this bit of information raises the hairs on the back of my neck. In complete opposition to my beliefs about a woman's right to choose, I think, *"My mother wanted to kill me."* I can not shake the thought off or rationalize it away with logic. My stern but loving mother wanted to kill me. I feel cold descending on me.

Roy gets his breathing under control. "Abortions was tricky back then," he continues. "There was no clinics like now. There was some doctors who would do it but mostly it was done in dirty, backstreet rooms by woman who didn't know what the fuck they was doing.

"Anyways, I didn't believe in it. I was living the hippie life and we believed in love and peace and flower power: all that shit." As he struggles again for breath, I imagine him in sixties clothing with beads and flowered shirts and a full head of shoulder length hair. A grin spreads over my face as my emotions continue their roller-coaster ride.

His breathing evens out again. "So I told her we should have the baby and live together. She got real angry and stormed out."

He gestures towards the water and I give him another couple of sips. He winks at me. "A beer would be real nice right now, Rocky." I laugh. Of all the things he might have said, this is the one that tells me he is going to pull through. Doctor Duffus has no idea what a tough old bird Roy really is. I make a mental note to smuggle in a six pack tomorrow.

"I'm glad I wouldn't let her do it." He squeezes my hand and gives me his crooked old smile. I wonder if my mother would have gone through with the abortion; I'll never know now. But he has answered one question that has bothered me my whole life. Why did she never tell me about my father? It is plain to me now. She never once lied to me but if she had told me this story, she would have had to tell me that she wanted to terminate her pregnancy and me with it. She could never bring herself to do that. I feel a great flood of sympathy for the frightened nineteen year old, pregnant by her irresponsible boy friend.

After a minute, he continues. "So she went home and told her parents and they threw her out of the house. Just like that. She came back one last time, begging me to help her get the abortion and when I told her I didn't think it was right, something seemed to break in her." Another pause for some deep breaths. "I don't know if I understand it myself but she seemed like she all of a sudden turned into a block of ice." He thinks for a moment then adds, "No. Not ice. Steel. She walked out and said she would never speak to me again." I recognize my mother in those words.

"At first I couldn't handle losing her. I really loved her. I want you to know that, Rock." The unwelcome tears try and force their way into my eyes. He squeezes my hand again and I reciprocate, knowing that I have always loved this old man, despite our occasional ups and downs. "I went to the deli where she worked and tried to talk to her but she refused to say a word to me. So one day, after the deli closed, I followed her. She was living in a little apartment in Marpole. I discovered later that she shared it with a couple of girls. I never approached her again but I just kind of keep tabs on her. When she got close to her time, I hung around outside her apartment one day and waited for one of her room mates to come out. I gave her a hundred bucks, which was a lot of money in them days, and made her promise that she would come and tell me when you was born, eh?

"She kept her promise and I snuck into the hospital, Grace Hospital is was called in them days, and saw you for the first time in that room they put the babies in. I looked through the window and saw you. Baby Rogan it said on the little blue card. Even though it was her name, not mine, I don't think I've ever felt happier." A tear trickles down his cheek and he signals for more water. I was born in the same hospital as my darling Ellie and I've been absent for much of *her* life. The sins of the father, visited upon the son?

"Can you open a window, Rock. It's boiling in here," he asks and then seems to forget about it. "I went into her ward in the hospital and she let me talk to her. I told her that I loved her and wanted to be part of her life and your life. She said OK. I guess she just didn't see any other way out."

He is having to take a labored breath every few words and I worry that his exposé is tiring him too much. As much as I want to hear more, I can't bear to see him struggling . "Why don't we take a break Roy? Give you a chance to get some sleep and heal a bit more. I can come back later and we can carry on then. I'll bring some beers along too."

His hand holds mine like a vice. "No. I wanna tell you everything now. You waited a long time to hear this and I won't have you wait any longer. I'll be all right. I can have a nice sleep later and enjoy that beer this evening."

True to his word, his breathing seems more even. "I rented an apartment and got it furnished and we all moved in. I was still making good money dealing acid so we was OK. She insisted on having you christened California. She said she always wanted to go there. I said it was a stupid name but she put her foot down."

"I wish you'd changed her mind. I hated being called that. I always insisted on going by Cal but some kid would always find out and sing that Chilliwack song 'California girl, California girl.' I got in more fights over that…"

He chuckles. "Some chance. You know yer mother once her mind was made up."

I do indeed.

Even the chuckle has worn him down. He takes a full minute to breath deeply before he can continue. "Once you was about eighteen months old, she started going out to work nights, cleaning offices. I told here she didn't need to do that but there was no telling her." I recognize my mother in those words, too. "I used to stay at home and look after ya. We'd play with your toys or watch television for a bit then I'd put you to bed." I try hard to stir a memory of this. I want to remember. But no memory of the father I never knew will come.

More deep breaths. "After you was in bed I'd usually drink myself to sleep." A thought lights up his face. "I remember that ya loved that cartoon about the squirrel and the moose, so I started calling you Rocky. It annoyed the hell out of your mother; so I did it all the more, eh." Another piece of the puzzle clicks in place. "I even started calling her Bullwinkle and did she ever get mad." This time his chuckle turns into a cough and it takes him a long time to recover.

The thought of having had a normal, warm, though somewhat quirky family life stirs in me a strong feeling of loss.

"Why did you leave, Roy?" I ask.

He shakes his head and stays silent, struggling for breath.

The crushing sadness of being the kid without a father, for years being the kid who didn't even know who his father was, comes screaming back into my soul.

"Why?" I demand, giving his hand a rough shake as the pent up anger of my childhood loss comes pushing to the fore. "Why, Roy?"

"It all fell apart." Ragged breaths are heaving in his chest. "My buddy who was making the LSD got busted and so I lost my source. I had nothing to sell and anyways people was losing interest in acid. When I started hanging round the house all day, your mother got a day job as well as her office cleaning job and for a while I looked after you full time, a regular Mr. Mom, until one day I got drunk and fell asleep with a cigarette in my hand. When she came home after her daytime job, I was asleep on a smoldering chesterfield and you was upstairs in yer crib hungry and crying, with a full diaper. She threw me out. Got the police and had me removed. Court order, the whole nine yards."

He is interrupted by the arrival of a young nurse. While she is tending the old man in the other bed, Roy takes the time to marshal his strength. She comes over, listens to Roy's heart.

"Is there any improvement?" I ask.

"Not really." She gives me an awkward smile and leaves.

He continues his story. "She never talked to me again. I tried sobering up and I'd go round to see you but she wouldn't even open the door. For a few years, I managed to work at different jobs, some of 'em a bit crooked, and every so often I'd leave an envelope of money on yer doorstep for her. But then…"

His voice peters out. He looks like he can't go on. His eyes have closed, his hand feels like ice and his breath has become heavier. I press the call button beside his bed and the nurse is there in seconds. She listens to his heart and watches the monitor. She signals for me to come with her but I will not let go of his hand. I won't leave his side until either he's better or…

I look at her and at my hand holding Roy's and she seems to understand. She comes and sits on the chair beside me, pats my forearm and whispers. "He doesn't have long now. I'm sorry." She waits for a moment. "Do you have any questions?" she asks. I shake my head and she leaves. Despite her words, something in me knows that he will get through this.

There is so much I want to say and to ask but it will have to wait until later; I just hold Roy's hand in both of mine and think about what might have been.

"I'm sorry, Rock." His eyes are still closed and he is crying.

"What for, Roy?"

He takes three big breaths. "The heroin."

I catch my breath. He is referring to the night after the trial that sent two gang leaders to jail, thanks to Steve and me. After the celebratory party, I went to the downtown east side and found Roy at his hang out, Beanie's Eatery. We were both hammered.

"It's OK Roy. I just don't understand why?" The accustomed anger, which accompanies memories of that night, comes flooding in but I don't want to be angry with him right now. "Why did you do it?" I ask as evenly as I can.

His voice is a whisper and I have to lean closer to hear. "Do you remember… what we… talked about…? In Beanie's…"

It all comes back in an unwelcome rush.

"Roy, why don't you just stop drinking? You've got a lot on the ball; you don't have to live like this."

He gets mad. "You don't know what you're fucking talking about. You can't just stop. It's easy for you to say but you don't know what it's like." He slams his hand on the dirty table.

And I, in my hubris, drunk beyond caution, on the high of success, say the wrong thing. "Bullshit, Roy. That's just a lame excuse. You don't want to stop drinking. You're just like all these junkies around here. They're bums. They'd rather live on welfare and do dope than sort themselves out."

"Who you calling bums?" He spits the question at me.

"Anyone who hasn't got the strength of character to just stop doing the thing that's gonna kill them." My logic is irrefutable.

"You couldn't stop." Roy throws it out, not as a statement but as a challenge.

"Of course I could." It is a pissing contest now.

"You really believe that?" he asks.

"Yeah. Absolutely." I finish my beer in one long draft, as if to emphasize my point. I have no doubts. I've seen it time and again on the streets. "Junkies are all lowlifes. A normal person isn't going to get

hooked taking one shot of dope once in his life. That I know for sure. I have more character than some bum, for God's sake."

"OK." Roy has that sly look that sometimes takes over when he is drunk. "You come with me and we'll see."

He takes me to the alley. The alley that terrifies me.

There's a dealer. It costs me ten bucks. The dealer shows me how to do it and throws in a clean syringe and all the fixings. Great marketing he thinks... but I know better.

Sure I'm nervous, I've seen the effects. But that was on degenerate junkies, not Cal Rogan, ace detective, Master of the Universe, buster to drug gangs.

But I hesitate. Unsure for a moment.

Roy is laughing and gulping from a bottle of no-name vodka. "I knew ya couldn't go through with it," he jeers. "You know as well as I do that not even the great Cal Rogan will be able to stop once he's started."

"Fuck off you old drunk," I shout at him. "I could stop any time I wanted and you know it."

"So do it, Detective... Fuckin'... Rogan."

His contempt triggers something in me. I am not some degenerate junkie. So, armed with the courage and lack of inhibition imparted by the beer and with the sure knowledge that I am a Master of the Universe...

I do it...
Then I've done it...
Then I'm done.
Then I think of Ellie and Sam.

"You hurt my feelings... Called me a bum... an old drunk...I just wanted to... lash out at ya... I'm sorry," he gasps and I understand. *How sharper than a serpent's tooth it is, to have a thankless child.* A wounded father stirred with a cocksure son: a recipe for disaster.

Once again the anger dissipates. "It's OK, Roy. It wasn't your fault. It was bound to happen sooner or later."

And it is true. A part of me has hated Roy for so long because he introduced me to heroin but I know in my heart that he is not the reason that I took that first needle. He brought me to that water, it was my choice to drink. I wanted to try it, wanted to know what it was all about.

He is fighting for every breath now. His lips are moving and I lean closer.

"I don't have... nothing... to give you... except... your name... Be Rocky... and remember... me." The breaths are racking his body. "Tell... Ellie... her grandad... loves her." He has not the strength to say more.

I squeeze his hand. "Just try and sleep now, Roy. We can talk again this evening."

It's my fault. The only reason he is here is that the gang wanted to draw me out. By getting him to help me, I gave them license to use poor old Roy as a pawn in their game. He deserves better. Roy may have been absent in my childhood and he may have been the catalyst to my addiction but he has been a true friend to me since I have been a junkie. Without him, I would not have survived on the streets.

My earlier anger, in fact the anger which is never far from the surface, was not directed at Roy. It was directed at me, at the mistakes I have made with drugs, with Sam, with Ellie and now with Roy, with my father.

"I love you Roy... Dad..." and I do truly love this quirky old man with the battered leather hat. I let the tears flow down my face and fall on our clasped hands.

His head nods a fraction and I feel the slightest pressure from his fingers.

I weigh the scales of our relationship. "You were a good father to me." This time there is no response.

Then he gives one deep, deep sigh and the monitor beside his bed screams at me.

He is gone.

Chapter 51

I see Brad first. He has been here in the ER waiting room while I have been with Roy. His face changes as he looks at me. He knows. He gets up and walks to me. "I'm so sorry, man." He envelopes me in a hug and my grief wells up, stronger than ever. I sob in his arms. I cry for the friend I have lost, the father whose death I precipitated, the grandfather whom Ellie will never know and the gaping hole that his passing has left inside me.

Brad just holds me, without speaking.

Then, through the tears, I see a face that I know. On the day of Kevin's death, he smashed into my room at the Lion Hotel and for his trouble earned a shattered elbow from Goliath. He is on his phone standing guard near the door.

The words of Laertes come unbidden into my head: *Let come what comes; only I'll be reveng'd, Most thoroughly for my father.* And a white heat subjugates all other emotions. These bastards killed Roy. Rage rejects reason and he is the focus. I rush past Brad and go for him. His eyes widen as he reads my face. His last two encounters with me have brought him nothing but pain. He stamps on the rubber mat in front of the doors; they hiss open and he hares through. As I come out the doors, he is halfway across the tarmac area where the ambulances park. *I love you Roy. You were a good father to me.* Now I am going to avenge you.

His feet are leaving a trail through the light carpet of snow that must have started falling while Roy was dying. He looks over his shoulder towards me and the change of posture is fatal. His foot slips on the snowy surface and he

307

falls, landing inevitably on his broken arm. His cry of pain spurs me forward. He is struggling to get up when I reach him. He is on one knee and his good arm, which allows his face to receive the full force of my kick. His head snaps back and his body slumps. I draw back my foot for a second kick, this time to his ribs but, just in time, I catch sight of his cohorts.

The hard faced one is close and I see the knife in his hand. It's Roy's knife! He is going to regret this theft. That knife was part of Roy. I am determined that he will be buried with his knife in his pocket.

In the background I glimpse Blondie and two others running towards us. But I ignore them as training takes over —in a Scottish accent. *Go in close on a man with a knife, laddie* —I step towards him as he slashes up towards my stomach. I block the blow with my left forearm and then pivot and grab his wrist with my right hand. My blocking arm slides under his elbow and my hand drives the knife hand down as I jerk his elbow up. The loud crack and his accompanying scream drown the sound of the weapon falling to the ground. Still holding his wrist, I disengage my left arm and drive the elbow into his face. He drops to the tarmac and I turn. They are upon me.

Blondie is leading the trio from behind, but he is my goal. Whoever delivered the fatal blow to Roy's chest did so on his orders.

I crouch down, grab Roy's beloved knife—now my talisman—and flow upwards towards the nearest target. A slash of the knife towards his face causes him to jerk his head back so hard that his feet slip in the snow and he lands on his back with a loud exhalation. Another score for Roy. I slip around him with my eyes locked on to Blondie. A battle lust that I have never before experienced courses through me and makes me invincible. He can see it in my eyes. I bring the knife up to belly button height and he takes a step back.

As I advance, a hand grabs my ankle and pulls hard and, on the snow dusted surface, I am down. Too late, I remember von Clausewitz: over ninety percent of battles are won by the side with the bigger numbers.

A foot stamps on my wrist causing both the knife and my invincibility to clatter away. I roll on my side just in time to see Blondie produce an aluminum baseball bat from behind his back. In the heightened perception that battle endows, I see bloody marks on it and know that this was used on Roy. My rage ramps up a notch and I know I must control it or risk a fatal error. He brings the bat up over his head, both hands clamped firmly on the grip and steps into the blow. I tense my muscles ready to roll away from its trajectory.

"FREEZE!" The shout from behind me causes Blondie to check his swing and look up. His eyes widen. "DROP IT!" He lets the bat fall from his upraised hands. I roll over to follow the line of his gaze and see the gun pointed at Blondie's chest. Not just any gun. A Steyr .357 semi automatic. Even more surprising than the presence of the weapon is the identity of the person wielding it.

"Get up Cal. Quick." I am not about to argue.

"Wait," I tell him.

I retrieve Roy's knife. It will stay with me until it goes into the ground with him.

Not taking his eyes off Blondie, Brad describes a wide circle around the stationary group, moving towards the road. In his inexperience, he almost positions me between himself and Blondie but I move quickly ahead of him. When we reach the sidewalk, Brad slips the gun into a shoulder holster under his rain jacket and points to the car parked on a meter. We dash through the snow to his Toyota, get in and take off down Burrard. I look back. Blondie has just appeared on the sidewalk, too far back to read Brad's license plate. He is not going to follow, he has to deal with his fallen soldiers.

I look across at Brad. He is staring ahead through the snow with an almost maniacal grin on his face.

"Where the hell did that come from?" I ask.

He chuckles. "I've had if for ages. Never thought that I'd get to use it but hey, like Al Capone said: *You can go a long way with a smile. You can go a lot farther with a smile and a gun.*"

I find myself laughing at Brad's positive-thinking take on what's just happened, but I can't stop. The laughter becomes uncontrollable and then turns to tears. Reaction, I guess.

I finally stop and take a couple of deep breaths. "When I saw you standing there with that in your hand, I nearly laughed. I don't know who was more scared, you, me or Blondie."

"Me. It was definitely me." He is laughing again.

"Let me see it." He pulls it out of his holster and hands it to me. It's not a Steyr, as I first thought, but some sort of cheap knockoff, not in great condition either. The safety catch is still on and I don't remember him switching it. I'm guessing that it was on all the time.

"When did you get it?" I can not get over the fact that Brad actually owns a weapon that will stop just about any man in his tracks.

"D'you remember when we were kids and we used to watch those Dirty Harry movies?" he says. I nod. "Well I always wanted a big assed gun like Clint Eastwood. You remember after I graduated I went to work in the States for a year? When I was down there, I bought it, second hand. Smuggled it in when I came back home. I never told you or Kev. I always figured you guys would take the piss out of me and with you in the VPD you'd probably have made me turn it in."

"Have you ever used it?" I still can not believe that Brad has a gun.

"Once. I took it to a gun club while I was still in the States and fired it at a paper target. To tell you the truth, it scared the crap out of me. I've never used it since. But when you told me about George and his connection to the gang, I thought it wouldn't be a bad idea to have it along. And I was right."

I look at him. He reminds me of Billy Rosewood, Judge Reinhold's character in Beverley Hills Cop, and I start laughing all over again. Brad has taken my place; now *he* is the one offering protection and carrying a gun.

"So before you brought it out, did you clean it and load it with fresh ammo?" I ask.

"No, I didn't have time."

"Man, you have got to hand that sucker in to the police. You'll kill yourself if you try to use a gun that hasn't been touched in, what is it, fourteen or fifteen years."

The thought of him firing that weapon has washed the laughter out of me.

"Brad. Thanks for what you did back there. You saved my life. They were going to kill me, for sure."

"Hey. No prob. The three amigos, remember."

And I do. Kevin, Brad and me three completely different characters, joined at the hip.

We are silent for the drive over the Burrard Bridge and, now drained of all emotion, I think of my last moments with Roy.

As if sensing my thoughts, he says, "Those bastards killed your father, didn't they?"

I told Brad about the DNA results on the way to the hospital. Brad never met Roy and it sounds strange to hear him refer to Roy as my father. Strange, but good, it somehow helps fill the void of Roy's death.

"Yes. And they're going to pay for it."

"Good."

We relapse into silence until we get to Brad's apartment. As he pulls into his parking spot, he says, "I want you to keep the gun, clean it up and all that, and if you get a chance, blow that Blond bastard's head off with it."

I shake my head and hand it back. I want to see Blondie rot in a high-security prison for the rest of his life, not get a quick bye to the next world.

And I start thinking about how I'm going to put him there.

Chapter 52

Another stakeout. This one in an office above a ritzy clothing emporium, right opposite the target. At least I am not hampered by a full bladder but there is plenty to worry me. Steve has done well, the senior members in the VPD authorized him to pull out all the stops on this one and, only two and a half days after our meeting at the junk yard, we are supposedly ready to move in.

That's one of the things worrying me. It's too fast, way too fast. One false move, one illegal search, one thing out of place, one detail missed and any case we build against George and his gang may get thrown out of court. Hell, it may never get into court in the first place. To my amazement, Stammo has been with me on this, he also thinks we are being precipitous, not that he would use that word, but Steve and the bosses are gung ho, adamant that we do it sooner rather than later.

And that's not all. Everyone wants to nail George the drug dealer to such an extent that my priority, George the murderer, has ceased to be a consideration.

But as much as the cop in me thinks it's too fast, the father in me is impatient. If we can arrest George today, Sam will almost certainly not take Ellie off to Toronto tomorrow. There will be nothing for her to run from... except, perhaps, from me.

The boredom of the stakeout exacerbates my worry.

I look through the window.

They look like any other young couple in love, laden with festive, designer-styled store bags, taking time off work to do their Christmas shopping together on Robson Street. An echo of Sam and me when we were first married. Except that this couple only stay within one block, sometimes on one side of the street, sometimes on the other. We can see them window-shopping from our vantage point across the road. They have been doing this for the four hours since the stakeout began and I am worried that someone in the foreign exchange store will notice them,

As if in response to this thought, a young-ish man wearing a red ski jacket leaves the store.

Close beside me, Lena, the tech on the stakeout, takes a photo, then another. She's very cute but unfamiliar with the concept of deodorant. The man is a new face; he did not walk into the store during the time we have been here so he can not be a customer. He looks up and down the street. I watch him like a hawk. If his eyes seek out the window-shoppers, they will have been made and any deliveries to the store will already have been canceled. But his gaze does not linger on them. He takes a package of cigarettes from his pocket and strolls down the street in the opposite direction, ignoring the displays in the shop windows which he must have seen a thousand times before.

Steve's high-tech encrypted radio squawks, "Target black BMW approaching from West." We have a list of possible cars, including Blondie's Mercedes, George's Bentley and the black Chrysler that I smashed into a police cruiser a week ago, but they are using the same vehicle they used three days ago.

The couple stop admiring the high-tech wonders in a window two doors down and make their way to the target. They enter the store just as the BMW double parks outside.

Then comes the first glitch.

When I staked it out on Tuesday and members of Steve's team staked it out on Wednesday and Thursday, it was always the hulking Goliath who dropped off the leather briefcase.

He has been identified as Guy Chang, a man with a string of drug related convictions with known ties to gang activity. An easy link for a jury to accept. But today it is a different guy wielding the briefcase; a face I've never seen before. The change of routine makes me even more uneasy. Did someone spot Steve's men doing the stakeout yesterday? Will the gang have made a switch and filled the briefcase with innocuous papers rather than incriminating bundles of cash? Lena is taking a stream of photos.

He enters the store and within thirty seconds he is out and sliding back into the passenger seat. This time she gets several shots of his face. The driver pulls ahead, not knowing that he is on his way to Stammo and another team, waiting opposite the foreign exchange store on West Hastings. Similar teams are posted around the eleven convenience stores that have so far been identified as owned or franchised by Walsh Investment Corporation.

Steve beckons to the uniform who is the forth member of our stakeout team. "Let's go, Tom." I follow them to the head of the stairs and Steve turns.

"Not you Cal. You're not a member, we can't risk civilian lives here."

I am floored by this. I brought this to him, I've been included in the operation from the start, I've even sat in some of the meetings with the senior staff and now he's *excluding* me? Plus the plans for the next phase of the operation make his excuse about risk ludicrous.

"Come on Steve—"

"Sorry Cal, not negotiable. Stay here with Lena."

He and Tom hare down the stairs and I wonder if Steve has another agenda here? Does he worry that I am getting too much of the glory? Or is there something else?

I look at Lena and she shrugs. So I follow them down the stairs.

I enter the foreign exchange store fifteen seconds behind Steve. The window shopping couple have worked fast; their badges are clipped to the front of their coats and the woman has her weapon drawn. The store's employees are lined up along one wall and the male officer is frisking them, removing their cell phones. There must be no outgoing communication from anyone in any of the locations where arrests are being made.

Steve is at a desk behind the thick glass of the secure area of the store, examining the leather briefcase. I walk through and he glares at me then cuts a look at the restrained suspects and decides not to make an issue of my presence here.

Inside the briefcase are wads of used notes of all denominations. I can not begin to guess how much, but it is certainly thousands of dollars. He fetches a large paper evidence sack from one of the couple's shopping bags, and slides the briefcase into it.

The employees are now all cuffed with plastic ties. They are strangely silent; no one is objecting or questioning what is going on. It speaks to their guilt; innocent people would be voluble in this situation. Or is there another reason? Were they perhaps expecting this raid? The unease in my gut ramps up another notch.

As the female officer goes into the back of the office to open the emergency exit and let in the uniforms who are stationed in the back alley, I see, out of the corner of my eye, the front door opening. The employee in the red jacket, back from his smoke break, steps part way through and takes in the scene. It takes him less than a second to know exactly what is happening. He spins around and runs.

I shout, "He's getting away," as I hare across the front area and out through the door. I see a flash of red as he runs east on Robson and I give chase. If this guy gets away, with one phone call, George will know what is happening and go to ground. With his resources, he will be out of the country in an hour. We will never be able to track him down and, worst of all, I will be back on the hook for Kevin's murder.

Red jacket looks back over his shoulder and sees me. He starts to run faster but I am still gaining on him. Heroin may be bad for the body but cigarettes will slow you down more. The crowds on the sidewalk are getting heavier as we approach Burrard, impeding us both. I shout, "Stop. Police." It feels like a cliché but it gets the attention of the pedestrians in front of me some of whom move out of my way. I am gaining on him even faster. I shout it again.

As he turns the corner on to Burrard, I see that he has pulled out his cell phone and is trying to dial as he runs. Willing all my strength into my legs, I accelerate towards the intersection and as I turn the corner, I am faced with another pedestrian horde lacking one thing: a red ski jacket. I look ahead and there is no one running.

As I slow my pace, I almost trip over the jacket, discarded on the sidewalk, a potential prize for one of downtown's many homeless. I scan the crowd ahead for someone without a jacket but can see no one. Somehow he has eluded me and is probably right now on the phone to his bosses. I have been nervous about this stakeout from the start and here is the glitch that will ruin the whole operation. I let him through my fingers and I dread telling Steve and Stammo.

As I turn back towards Robson, the screech of brakes draws my attention and I see my quarry. He has run the gauntlet across six lanes of traffic to cross Burrard and is less than thirty yards away. But now it is my turn for a lucky break. The traffic lights are changing and as the vehicles grind to a stop I weave my way between them. He is on the other side of the street and thinks he has escaped detection. He moves into the doorway of a high fashion shoe store and dials his cell phone. I break into a sprint, I have to reach him before the connection goes through.

As I swing into the doorway, he is opening his mouth to speak. My arm jabs out and I dash the phone from his grasp and clap my hand over his mouth. Before he can break free and shout a warning to whomever he has called, my foot comes down hard on the cell which breaks into several pieces.

He goes limp and, from force of habit, I reach behind me for handcuffs which, of course, are not there. I pull out my own cell and call Steve.

It feels amazing to be acting like a cop again. I am standing straight with a big smile on my face, for the first time believing that I can find a way back into the department, permanently.

I can't live without this job.

When Steve arrives, he cuffs the perp and checks his watch. "OK, Cal. Phase two," he says. I open Roy's cell phone and dial.

Now my previous unease becomes plain, old fashioned fear.

Not as much for what we have to do, as for where we have to do it.

Chapter 53

I have to agree with Steve that tactically and psychologically this is the right location, but it makes my skin crawl with trepidation. Even before making my very first heroin buy here, I have always feared this alley and so far my fears have been prophetic: it was here where I woke up a month ago on the morning that Kevin was killed; it was here where Blondie and his crew beat the snot out of me and put me in St. Paul's. It could have been here where they dealt Roy the blow that proved fatal. The early evening darkness does not mask the horror of the place; it heightens it.

It is teeming with life: crack heads on the pipe, heroin addicts on the nod. Like me. Just like me. My feelings of being a cop reborn are eroded to nothing here.

A group of aboriginal youths wander past smoking pot. An emaciated girl asks me if I want to party, desperate for ten bucks for another rock of crack.

And the smell of decay pervades all.

A man walks into the alley. His face is not familiar but his look is: hard and vicious. As soon as he sees me standing by the green dumpsters, he stops and opens his phone. He talks for no more than three seconds, then closes the phone and waits... and watches.

I feel my phone vibrate. It's probably Steve telling me that they are arriving but I do not answer it in case it spooks the watcher.

The headlights come first. Then simultaneously two cars pull into the alley, one at each end. They crawl slowly towards me, pitching on the pothole riddled surface.

With the innate sense of the hunted, the addicts fade out of the alley, except for two heroin addicts on the nod and two ragged bundles of clothes that conceal sleeping drunks. But I see them differently with my newly regained cop eyes.

The cars stop about thirty feet on either side of me and the occupants get out. It is old home week: Blondie, as well dressed as ever; Goliath; the man in black, his elbow back in a sling; the hard faced guy whom I stuck with a needle not twenty feet from where I'm now standing; two others who contributed to my beating and my guards from the SeaBus terminal, including Schwarzenegger. But the guy who dropped off the cash today is absent. They approach and stand around me in a semi circle at a radius of ten feet.

"So, Rogan," Blondie says, "what do you have to tell me that is so important that I'm going to let you go after you've told me?"

The paddy wagons should be screaming into the alley right about now. With a sudden rush of fear, I wonder if I should have answered the phone when Steve called. Maybe there is a problem or a change of plan. With a flash of terror, I have the thought that Steve is going to abandon me to the gang, let them kill me and then have them cold for murder. And in a warped way it makes sense: he collars Blondie and the gang and does not have to prove that I murdered Kevin. He's the judge, Blondie's the executioner. I feel a cold trickle of sweat flow down my back.

My heart accelerates when Blondie's response to my silence is to bring up a gun and level it at my chest. My mind is screaming at me to look up to the roofs of the surrounding buildings for evidence of the SWAT team that may not be there. They should stay concealed but a part of me would like to catch a glimpse of them, just to know for sure that they *are* there, that I have not been abandoned.

With a spine tingling rush, I know why I have always feared this alley: it is the end of my story; someone else will have to finish it from here.

"Well?" he asks.

"I know all about your operation," I extemporize. "the money laundering, everything."

"In that case, I should just kill you right now and let the knowledge die with you." To underscore his point, he raises the gun until it is pointing between my eyes. It gives me some cold comfort: a head shot is more difficult to make.

"Except that I have written it all down and placed it with a lawyer." I am starting to sound like a TV show from the eighties. "If I don't call him he'll deliver it to the police."

Blondie's laugh is genuine, he is not buying this. "Is that all you've got?" he chuckles.

My mind races to come up with something. When he stops laughing he is going to start shooting.

"GO!"

The voice is coming from high above me.

Simultaneously I see Blondie propelled backwards and hear the sound of the sniper rifle that shot him.

With screaming sirens, two paddy wagons block the alley. SWAT team members in body armor, with bulletproof shields, march towards us. I am in the crossfire. I pull one of the dumpsters away from the wall and crouch behind it.

"DROP YOUR WEAPONS AND LIE FACE DOWN, ARMS EXTENDED." A voice says through a bullhorn.

There is the sound of running feet then silence. I venture a peek from behind the dumpster. The gang are all lying face down on the filthy surface of the alley surrounded by armed cops. Blondie is lying with his back against the wall, the blood stain spreading out across the front of his designer shirt. Two of the ragged bundles, who were pretending to be drunks, are standing on either side of him,

321

their guns trained on him; one of the 'heroin addicts' is talking into his radio.

I come out from behind the dumpster; I came through this alive. Blondie's eyes lock with mine and I smile broadly, then give him a big wink. Big mistake. With the last of his strength he raises his gun.

I see the muzzle flash and hear a fusillade of shots so close together that it is difficult to distinguish them. As I start to spin, I see his body twitching under the impact of the bullets. I didn't get my wish for Blondie; he got his quick bye to the next world.

I slam into the wall and collapse to the ground. The pain in my chest is excruciating and I am having to fight for every breath. Hamlet's words run through my head: *A villain kills my father; and for that, I, his sole son, do this same villain send to heaven.* For a dying man, his aim was superb. He got me in the chest, to the left, a heart shot. I feel the strength draining out of me.

The concerned faces of the SWAT team members, running towards me, fade to black.

My last thought: *Thank God for Kevlar.*

Chapter 54

It is a tight fit in the back of the Lincoln Town Car; with Stammo on my left and Steve on my right, each corner makes me ache from the huge bruise on the left hand side of my chest and I'm feeling claustrophobic. It reminds me of being in the back of the gang's Chrysler. The comfortable leather seating and the accompanying smell are no compensation.

I try to focus on Steve who is debriefing the Deputy Chief of the VPD, sitting in the front passenger seat, while the V8 engine whisks us silently across the Lion's Gate bridge towards the Walsh residence in West Van. There is no siren, just a red light on the dashboard flashing a warning to let us pass.

My big worry is that George has got word of the bust of his money laundering operation and has flown the coop.

"From the bust this afternoon," Steve is saying, "we counted the money and there was fifteen grand in cash dropped off at each of the foreign exchange places and an average of twenty-three hundred at each of the convenience stores.

"We arrested the CEO of the foreign exchange company and the slimy bastard caved right away and gave Walsh up, claims he was being forced to do it. What's really interesting was that the operation was much bigger than we thought. The company has seventeen branches: Toronto, Montreal, Calgary and here. There were drop offs every day. We did the math. They were laundering at least ninety million bucks a year."

Even these details do not allow me to focus my mind away from my worries about Ellie, in that house with George.

"The convenience stores are a little more difficult to tie down. We raided six of them. Unfortunately they are all owner operated in a loose franchise arrangement that Walsh has with them. The owners don't know anything except they had to take in the cash and write checks every week to three or four different companies, at least one of which we traced back to Walsh. From what we can piece together, there could be forty or fifty stores involved in Vancouver alone. They could account for another forty million a year. Maybe more in other cities, we don't know yet."

The deputy whistles. "So we could be talking a hundred and thirty million bucks a year money laundering scheme."

"Maybe more," Steve opines. "We haven't even looked at his chain of dollar stores. We'll know more in a few days."

The numbers boggle my mind. No wonder George can afford that five million dollar house. I do the math: he bought it with just two weeks of laundered revenue.

"It's a big win in the War on Drugs, sir," Stammo the sycophant adds.

I can't resist asking. "Oh crap, Nicky. Didn't they tell you?"

His annoyance at the use of the diminutive is vanquished by his curiosity. "Tell me what?" he grates.

"It was in all the newspapers. The War on Drugs is over... Drugs won."

The Deputy Chief chuckles and I earn a vicious dig from Stammo's elbow. He manages to hit both my ribs and the infection in my arm. It makes me gasp but it was almost worth it.

"You're right, Rogan," says the Deputy. "Nothing we do is going to stop people taking drugs; in fact, I think because they're illegal it makes them more exciting to a lot of people, kids especially." He sighs. "And all the hard-to-come-by millions in budget money we have to spend on interdiction…"

There is a weariness in his tone which generates a strange and uncomfortable thought in my mind. I was a cop for thirteen years, most of that time risking life and limb fighting the criminals who run the drug trade and so the illegality of drugs is programmed into me. Even as a junkie I have never questioned it. But George and his gang are making at least a hundred and thirty million a year, in spite of the fact that their business is illegal. No, that's wrong. It's *because* drugs are illegal that they can sell them at such huge profits.

"Do you agree with the Mayor that drugs should be legalized, sir?" I ask.

"It doesn't matter what I think or what the Mayor thinks, for that matter. It'll never happen in this country."

"Why not, sir?" Even Stammo is intrigued.

"The US would never let us. They would close the borders on us."

I can't believe that we are having this conversation. "Why, sir?" I ask.

"Too many powerful special interests down there who don't want to hear anything about legalization. Legalization in the US would put seventy percent of criminal lawyers out of business; the corporations that run the prisons would go broke overnight; police departments, DA's offices and at least four federal agencies would face huge budget cuts and layoffs. Then the unions would get in on the act. It's a long list. Add to that the profits from the drug business are so frigging huge the gangs could afford to pay every Senator and every Congressman a million dollars a year bribe and not even notice it. I'm even betting one or two…" He stops abruptly. "Enough said."

We are silent as the car circles off the bridge on to Marine Drive. I try to process what it would be like if drugs were legal and you could buy heroin from, say, a liquor store or a pharmacy. It would be a fraction of the price too if the gangs were out of the picture.

"How are the ribs, Rogan?" the Deputy cuts into my train of thought. The discussion on the politics of drugs is over.

"Nicely bar-b-cued, sir." They hurt like hell but I have to make light of it. It is a macho world in the VPD.

"Waters tells me you unearthed this money laundering scheme because you were investigating your friend's death. Is that right?"

My heart speeds up. I want this man to know my part in this. "Yes, sir."

"Is there any evidence that Walsh killed him."

"He's certainly got motive, but that's it so far."

Steve says, "If it wasn't Walsh, it could have been his gang, doing it on his orders."

The Deputy says, "Some of the foot soldiers may be prepared to talk with their leader dead. SWAT guys had no alternative to shooting him, did they."

"No, sir," Steve, Stammo and I agree in unison.

I already know that Blondie or his boys didn't kill Kevin. It had to be George himself. But I keep my own council for now.

After a long silence—during which, no doubt, the Deputy was weighing the implications of what he is about to say—he turns in his seat to face me. "You did good work, Rogan. I'm impressed."

"Thank you, sir. I appreciate it." In my very soul, I want to ask him what are my chances of reentry into the Department. For about a minute I wrestle with how best to word it but in the end I do not dare; I am too afraid of what the answer might be.

We hit a bump in the road which sends a stab of pain through my ribs. I think back to the alley and the confrontation with Blondie and his gang.

"Steve," I ask, "did you call me on my cell when I was in the alley back there?"

"No, why?"

"Someone did."

I squirm around to pull the phone from my pocket and check the voice mail. It was Brad; I dial his number. One good thing that has come out of this mess is my new relationship with my old buddy. Kevin's death has brought us together and his rescue of me from the gang has deepened the return of the old camaraderie. He has called me every day to see how I'm doing and I've got to say that his positive thinking attitude is the only thing that still lets me believe that I will make it back into the VPD.

"*Hey, Cal, how's it going?*" he asks.

"Great. You'll be pleased to know that the gang who killed Roy are all under arrest, except for the leader. He's dead."

"*So what's next?*"

I don't want to tell him details of the investigation in front of a car full of cops; it would be regarded as a breach of security. I just say, "I'm going over to Sam's house, right now."

He gets the implication. "*You're going to arrest George?*"

"I hope so."

"*That's great news. Let me know what happens.*"

"I will, for sure. Anyway, I've got to go. I'll give you a call tomorrow."

"*Go get 'em, hombre,*" he says and hangs up. I have to grin.

We arrive in Dundarave village at nine fifteen. It is deserted except for three VPD police cars and another black Town Car, in which is seated the Chief of Police of West Van. Now I know why we came here with the Deputy in his

327

Lincoln. He is here to smooth any inter-jurisdictional feathers.

Steve checks his radio. One of the surveillance teams at George's house confirms that George is still inside. Good. My worst fear that George would get word of the busts of his lieutenants, evade the surveillance team and run for cover is abated.

"OK, guys. Go do it," says the Deputy to Steve and Stammo.

"Sir," I interject. "I know I'm a civilian now but I want to be there when he's arrested. I'd like your permission to go with them."

Before the Chief can respond, Steve says, "I don't think it's a good idea sir."

"You know my daughter lives there, sir." There is a note of pleading in my voice. I think George's surprise arrest should be straight forward and without violence. But 'should' is a unreliable concept.

To my surprise, Stammo supports me. "If you don't mind me saying so sir, but I think Rogan has earned the right."

I can see the Deputy balancing the options. He doesn't want to make this decision.

So he doesn't.

"Mr. Rogan," he says, "you are a civilian and I can't really tell you where to go or what to do. Unless you have committed a crime, I don't have any jurisdiction over you."

He smiles at Steve, opens the door of the West Van Chief's car and gets inside.

Chapter 55

George Walsh, I have a warrant for your arrest. I await, with mounting anticipation, the look on George's face when he hears those magic words. Then the anticipation is vaporized when in a moment of panic I think that Steve may have forgotten the paperwork. Now the time is here, I'm getting nervous.

The prospect of seeing George led away in handcuffs is definitely enhanced by the fact that this may just be my ticket back into the department. With the Deputy Chief's remark in the car and the possibility of a good word from the Mayor to the Chief, maybe I have a chance. Not that a couple of kind words mean that much. Steve never did tell me what the department's policy was on rehiring; he tried to arrest me instead. But the hope is all I have to hang on to. Brad would have a positive thinking line here, I'm sure.

In a guilty little corner of my mind, I am also happy to see George removed from Ellie's life and, for that matter, from Sam's. But the icing on the cake is that with George gone, Blondie dead and his gang in custody, Sam surely wouldn't remove Ellie to Toronto, would she?

I catch myself sniffing: the start of withdrawal symptoms. Another thing to make me jittery. Thank God this will soon be over and I can use the last of the heroin secreted in the zipped inner pocket of my jacket. We are in the home stretch now.

There is no answer, so Steve rings again. We wait for a seemingly interminable twenty seconds but the door stays closed. Stammo raps with his fist and calls. "Mr. Walsh. Open up please. It's the Vancouver Police Department."

Silence.

Then a crash: the sound of something heavy breaking. My God, what's happening in there?

Steve is the first to react. He shouts at the uniformed sergeant stationed at the entrance to the driveway, "Bring the ram. Now!" Three times Stammo tries to burst open the door with his shoulder before the sergeant runs up. Stammo grabs the heavy battering ram and with one mighty swing, hits the door in the area of the lock. It flies open and we race inside.

I shout, "Sam. Sam, where are you?"

Silence. Then a sound, coming from the living room, part hum, part growl, makes the hair on my neck stand up. I rush down the hall. There are two bodies on the living room floor. Both are trussed in duct tape. Rosa seems to be unconscious but Sam is thrashing about making the noise that we heard. Beside her, toppled onto the floor, is a small antique table and the remains of a ceramic flower pot and its contents.

I rush to Sam and roll her onto her back; her face is covered in tears. "Sorry Sam. This is going to hurt but I can't wait for a paramedic to do it properly." I start to pick at the edge of the duct tape across her mouth and she nods her understanding. When there is enough material to afford me a decent grip, I rip it from her mouth. She screams at the pain and starts sobbing.

"Sam. Sam! What happened? Where's George?"

"No. No. I can't tell you."

"Why? Why can't you tell me."

"He made me. I can't say… He…" She is sobbing uncontrollably.

I pick her up and place her on the couch. "Someone get a knife from the kitchen so that we can cut her wrists free." I point in the general direction.

"Now Sam." I am forcing myself to stay calm. "Tell me what happened."

"No. No. No. No. Nooooooo." I recognize the mounting hysteria.

I can not bring myself to slap her so I shake her hard and it seems to work.

She looks like a haunted animal for a moment and then it all bursts out. "He took her. He took Ellie. A hostage, he said. Oh Cal, he took Ellie…" she ends in a wail and descends into sobs.

My whole body is alive with electricity. I think of Ellie, terrified, somewhere out in the night with a man who will stop at nothing, a man who controls a vicious gang of drug dealers. I want to run up to Ellie's bedroom and see if this is all some nightmarish mistake. I start to move but my training takes over: stop, breath, focus… and my mind is clear. Except for the fear.

Sam is still sobbing. I sit beside her on the couch, take her shoulders and shake her again, gently this time, to get her attention. "Listen Sam. You have to stay calm so that you can tell us what happened."

"Cal, you have to find her."

"I will, I promise." I remember something from my training: you never promise a victim that you will get a good result because you may too easily be proven wrong. I shake the thought from my head. "You have to tell me exactly what happened."

I realize that I have taken charge of the situation and, more strangely, Steve, Stammo and the Deputy Chief are letting it happen. I don't have time to assess what this may mean.

331

She takes a couple of deep breaths. In the background, I can hear someone on a radio calling for paramedics. "He got a phone call. Right after, he looked worried. I asked him what was the matter and he yelled at me to shut up. He has never spoken to me like that before."

"When was this?"

"I don't know." Her eyes have a haunted look, then flicker with a memory. "It was nine o'clock. George always likes to watch Larry King on CNN at nine. He was annoyed that the phone had rung just as it started." I look at my watch it is nine twenty-five.

"OK, that's good, Sam. How long was he on the phone?"

"Not long. Not more than a minute or two."

"Then what happened?"

"Well, he was obviously thinking about something. After he yelled at me, he paced up and down for a moment and kept looking at his watch. Then he stalked out of the room and I thought that maybe I had done something wrong but he was back in a minute or two." While she is talking, the sergeant comes in with a paring knife and sits on the other side of her. He starts to cut the duct tape off her wrists. She flinches at the touch. "He just walked in, and without any warning, he pulled me out of the chair and punched me in the stomach. He grabbed me by the hair and forced me on to the floor and put the tape across my mouth. Then he tied my hands behind me." My blood runs cold. If George could turn violent towards Sam, what might he do to Ellie?

"As he was starting to do my feet, Rosa walked in—she must have heard all the noise we were making—George just grabbed her and punched her in the stomach then in the face. After he had finished with me he tied her up too."

As she is talking, I am calculating times. Two minutes on the phone, he thinks for a minute or two and then goes and gets the duct tape. It must have taken him five minutes to immobilize and duct tape both women. That takes it to about ten after nine.

"What about Ellie?" I ask. For the first time I face the real possibility that I might never see her again.

"He went into the hall and I couldn't see him for a moment then I saw him head up the stairs, he had his coat on and he had Ellie's coat in his hand. I knew what he was going to do. I tried to shout out but I couldn't." Her tears are flowing again but she is keeping it together.

"In no time, he was back downstairs with Ellie in his arms. She was still more than half asleep." She is sobbing now. It must have taken George at least two minutes to get Ellie, put her coat on and bring her downstairs; he is less than fifteen minutes ahead of us.

Her sobs reach a crescendo. "Sam. Sam!" I say. "You've got to stay focused now."

"He said she… she was his hostage and if the… if the police came after him he would… kill her." This time she can not bring her sobs under control.

I look up at Steve but he is already ahead of me. "Do you know what sort of car he drives?" he asks.

"A dark green Bentley convertible," I reply for her.

Immediately Steve is talking into his radio. "Find out the registration of a dark green Bentley convertible registered to a George Walsh and put out an APB on it."

"No. No." Sam is shaking her head. "He didn't take the Bentley. He took Ellie and went out onto the deck and into the back yard."

Why would he do that? Why leave on foot when he had a perfectly good car?

Steve supplies the answer. "He must have guessed there might be surveillance out front, so he decided to sneak out the back." I make a mental note to trace the call that George received at nine. I have a mounting suspicion that there may be a leak in the police department, either Vancouver's or West Van's.

"But we had surveillance in the lane out back too." Stammo says. He turns to one of the uniforms. "Come with me." They go through the doors to the deck and disappear into the dark beyond.

I put my arm around Sam. Steve asks her, "Where do you think he might go, Sam?"

The options are limitless. He is a man with enormous financial resources and underworld contacts. He could literally disappear and resurface anywhere in the world. We are never going to be able to second guess where he might go and where he might take Ellie.

Out of the corner of my eye, I see the West Van Chief come into the room; he is a large, unattractive man who brings to mind a memory of Jabba the Hut from Star Wars.

"I don't know," Sam responds to Steve's question. "He could go anywhere. He has a private plane. He keeps it at the airport."

"What type of plane? Do you know the registration letters?" I ask.

"It's called a Citation, but I have no idea of the registration."

Before Steve can react the Deputy says, "I've got it," and opens his cell phone. It needs his level of seniority to give orders to the YVR control tower.

"And he's got one of those fast boats. You know, what they call cigarette boats. We used to joke about it being a drug dealer's boat."

"Where does he keep it?" I ask.

"At the Royal Van Yacht Club." Where else? Steve gets immediately on his phone.

While the Deputy, closes down the airport to departing private aircraft and Steve dispatches a police car to the yacht club. I try and put myself into George's shoes. He is a smart man. He must have known that this day could come; the day when the noose tightens around his operation. He would have a contingency plan.

What would I do in his position? First, he wouldn't use any form of transportation that could be tracked back to him. So the private jet and the cigarette boat will be dead ends. Without doubt, he would have another identity: passport, driver's license, valid credit cards. He would also have a reasonable amount of cash with him both to cover his trail and to buy a new identity if the one he is using gets blown.

"Sam," I ask, "think carefully now. When George left, did he have anything with him: a briefcase, a bag, even a large envelope."

Before Sam can answer, Stammo bursts back in through the door to the deck. "He's got the unmarked car. The guy on surveillance is unconscious in the back alley and his car's gone."

The Deputy Chief mouths an obscenity and Jabba the Hut has a smug look that says 'if you'd had us do the surveillance, this would never have happened.' But this may be good news. It's just possible that George doesn't know all VPD cars are fitted with GPS.

The Deputy opens his phone but Stammo says, "It's alright sir, I already called it in." Good work, Stammo.

The paramedics come in. Stammo directs one out to the back lane and the other starts dealing with Rosa. The room is getting crowded and Sam has a confused, far away look on her face. I bring her back by asking, "Sam, apart from Ellie, did he have anything with him? It's important."

She thinks for a moment. "No, definitely not. He was carrying Ellie in one arm and I could see that the other hand was free when he opened that door."

A cautious man would not keep alternate identities at home where they could be found by a wife, a nosy cleaner or even a child. I start with the obvious. "OK, Sam, that's good. What's the address of his office."

"It's in the Wall Centre the uh… Twenty-third floor." The same building as the head office of the foreign exchange operation. I check my watch. George would have taken the police car fifteen or maybe even twenty minutes ago. At this time of night, he will be downtown by now.

"Got it." Stammo opens his phone again and dials. Maybe I misjudged this guy.

I am starting to feel sure that the first thing that George would do is pick up his alternate identity or maybe identities; it would be smart to have more than one. His office is an obvious choice but obvious may not be best.

"Sam. Does George have any other properties? Is there an apartment downtown or a house? Does he own any apartment buildings, maybe? Anywhere you can think of that he might go?"

"Not downtown. We've got a house on Salt Spring." Her use of the word 'we' makes me realize how devastating this is for Sam. She has not only lost our daughter but she has been utterly betrayed by the man she loved. As much as I wanted Sam to be rid of George I hate that it has to be like this and to my chagrin, I know that it is my efforts that have precipitated this whole mess. There is no way she will ever forgive me for this.

I look at Steve. He nods at me and says, "I doubt that he would go there but better safe than sorry." He talks to the Deputy Chief who dials his phone and talks to the RCMP detachment on Salt Spring Island.

Stammo's phone rings. He listens for a moment, grunts his thanks and closes it. "The patrol car is in North Van. The GPS says it's parked on First Street. It's right outside a garage, an auto repair place."

We all know what this means. George has switched cars. I am betting that the car he is using is not registered in his own name. The trail just got a lot colder.

Stammo says, "I'll try and track down the owner of the garage. See if he can give us an ID on the car."

I feel my phone vibrate then hear the ring but I do not have time for it right now.

I can not think of anything else to ask Sam and I have no idea what to do next. My fears for Ellie fill the vacuum. What will George do with her? If he tries to leave the country on a scheduled or a charter flight, he will not be able to take her with him. He *could* just let her go but that does not compute with what I know about the big shots in the drug trade.

I sniff and realize that the withdrawal symptoms are starting to strengthen. All the activity of the last ten minutes has kept them out of my immediate consciousness.

Time is running out for Ellie and time is what I'm losing fast. My daughter needs me and, within an hour or so, I am going to be a basket case, unable to think clearly. Maybe I should just go and shoot up now. Maybe just one point; just enough to keep me going. Just enough to take the pain away. No one will notice. Maybe Steve, or Sam, but no one else.

NO! I push the Beast behind me. This time Ellie must come first. Somehow I'll get through. I have to hang in there. For Ellie. If I can.

"I think his office is the best bet." Steve interrupts my thoughts. "Let's go. You coming, Cal?"

"Sure." I put my arms around Sam and kiss her forehead. "Sam, I'm sorry." I whisper. She just nods her head.

As I run for the front door, I hear Sam say, "I'm sorry too, Cal."

With all my heart, I long to hold her, comfort her, tell her that I love her and that everything is going to be alright.

I turn and look at her in that instant and know that I have already lost her and that it is Ellie I must hold on to.

I turn back and run after Steve.

Chapter 56

I'm like a prisoner. We're in one of the VPD cruisers. Stammo is driving with Steve beside him and me in the back, behind the metal screen. Steve is checking his voice mail and I remember the call that I got. Not many people have my number and two of them, Sam and Steve, were in the room with me. It wouldn't be Brad again and with Roy gone that only leaves—

I'm an idiot. Why didn't I realize this when it rang at Sam's house. I struggle to get the phone out of my pocket, flip it open and hold down the '1' key. My heart is beating a tattoo against my rib cage. As soon as I hear the recorded voice, I enter my password: 1005, Ellie's birthday.

"You have one new message." '1' again.

"Daddy?" Her whisper stops my heart. *"George has taken me away from Mommy. I'm in this room and I don't like it. I'm scared, Daddy. Come quickly. Please."*

There is a long silence and I strain to hear more. Anything. *"To delete this message press '7'."*

I hang up. "Steve, Nick, I just got a voice mail from Ellie. She said she was in some room and—"

"What's the number she's calling from?" Steve interrupts.

"I don't have caller ID." Oh God.

"Who's your cell phone carrier?" he asks.

"Fido."

Steve starts dialing.

A real anger suffuses me. If I had thought through who the call was coming from while I was in Sam's house questioning her, a lot of time would have been saved. We would already be at George's office, or wherever he is holding her, and she would be safe in my arms right now. If something happens to her, I will never be able to forgive myself.

Stammo turns on the flashing lights and the siren and accelerates down Marine. He too pulls out his cell and speed dials someone. "Get hold of the guys on the Lion's Gate Bridge and tell 'em to turn the middle lane red in both directions *immediately*." I can forgive Stammo anything now. The Lion's Gate bridge from West Van to Vancouver, has three lanes; at this time of night, it is always one lane into Vancouver and two out. By turning the lights red on the middle lane we can sail through.

Within two minutes, we are pulling onto the bridge—doing sixty miles an hour and still accelerating—Steve has given my phone number to a supervisor at Fido and, after what seems a never-ending delay, he has the phone number from which Ellie called.

"It's a land line," he says. Thank God; tracing a cell phone's location is an inexact science. Ellie must have been calling from a phone in the place where she is being held. Steve enters the number into the computer in the cruiser and immediately has an address.

We have crossed the bridge and are turning off Georgia on to Denman as Steve calls in for backup. He gives the address and requests they don't use lights or sirens.

WHAT?!

"Steve. What was that address?" He repeats it. I was not mistaken.

"That's my buddy Brad's address," I tell them.

"Why would Walsh be going to your buddy's house?" Stammo's voice is dripping with suspicion.

"I don't know," I reply. "Brad works for the broker who took QX4 public." I realize that maybe they don't know what

QX4 is. "They're a company that George owns a big chunk of."

Steve jumps in. "So… could this Brad be part of the whole money laundering thing with Walsh?"

"No way. I've known Brad since I was thirteen."

"So, if Walsh is on his way to pick up a false identity, why would he go to Brad's house?" Steve's tone is sounding more like Stammo's.

"I have no idea." And I don't.

"Could he be holding on to Walsh's other IDs for him?" Stammo asks.

"Why would he do that," I ask. Stammo just shrugs.

"Does Brad have any weapons?" Steve's question makes my blood run cold.

"Oh my God! Yes. He's got a cheap knockoff of a Steyr .357 semi automatic." My little Ellie is in that apartment with that weapon.

"Fuck." Stammo and Steve say it in unison. Then Steve is on the radio updating his instructions for the backup team.

Stammo is driving like a mad man along Pacific headed for the Burrard Bridge. Surely Brad would not let anything happen to Ellie. He has known her since she was born. Besides, George could have no idea about the gun. Why is he at Brad's anyway? Nothing is making any sense.

And all the time my body is reacting to the effects of heroin withdrawal. The pain is getting worse but my mind is clear. For the moment anyway.

We cross the bridge and turn right off Burrard on to Fourth; Stammo turns off the siren but keeps the lights flashing. Steve has finished on the radio. He turns to me, face grave. "Cal. I want you to stay in the car while we deal with this. You—"

"No way, Steve," I interject. "My daughter's in there. I brought you Walsh on a platter and that gives me some rights here. I want in."

341

"Ellie is in there, with your buddy, with a big-assed gun and with a ruthless criminal. There is no way you can be objective. Plus, you are not armed and you were injured by that Blond bastard less than three hours ago. Also you have started sniffing all the time and I know what that means. I'm sorry, Cal. It's not going to happen."

"Steve, you can't stop me from coming with you." I am pleading now.

"Remember where you are, Rogan," Stammo says.

He is right. I am in the back of a police cruiser, with doors that can not be opened from the inside and a wire mesh screen that cages me in.

"Guys, please." But it's no use.

Stammo turns off the lights and pulls onto Brad's street. There is a cruiser already there and probably one around the back. As they jump out of the car, I plead, "Steve. Watch out for Ellie. Be careful." He nods to me as he runs towards the front door of the building. It has already been opened and he disappears inside. All I can do is watch, impotent, through the windows of the police car.

I scan all the windows of Brad's condo. I am getting twitchy. I can not remember if Brad's unit is at the front or the back. I am just watching for any sign. A light comes on. Not in a window. It is at the top of the ramp down to the underground parking; it must be a security floodlight working off a motion sensor. The gate to the parking garage is opening and, through the bars, I can see a maroon Toyota.

It is Brad's.

In desperation, I try the doors but they are securely locked. Grabbing and shaking the steel mesh has no effect.

The car pulls up to the top of the ramp. Because of the floodlight, which is shining in my eyes, I can not see who the driver is but in the passenger seat, I can see Ellie's face, white and frightened, staring towards me through the passenger window. Before I can tell if she has seen me, the car drives slowly off.

Forcing myself to control the rising panic, I pull out my cell phone and dial Steve's number. I can still see the Toyota driving up towards Broadway.

I slide across the seat to the window and, with all my strength, drive my elbow into the glass. A pain like an electric shock travels through my arm but the glass is intact.

The Toyota has come to a stop at Broadway, left indicator light flashing.

Steve's phone is ringing at last.

I take my eyes off the target and lie across the seat, with my head against the left side door. I put my feet on the right side window and push with every ounce of strength in my body.

All the injuries I have sustained in the last two weeks, combined with the withdrawal, make me scream out in pain. But I use it and push harder until with a bang, the window shatters.

Steve's phone is still ringing as I put my hand out of the cruiser and open the door from the outside. In seconds, I am in the front seat. Yes! Stammo left the keys. There is no sight of the Toyota.

I hear Steve's voice on the phone as I accelerate. "Steve. I'm in pursuit—" But the voice is his recorded voice mail greeting. I close the phone and throw it on the seat beside me.

Barely slowing, I turn on to Broadway, causing two drivers to hit their brakes hard.

The traffic is heavier than normal for this time of night. But I have an advantage. George knows he must drive cautiously—now is not the time for him to get stopped by a traffic cop—whereas I am in a police cruiser. However, I dare not use the siren or lights until I have him in sight. I don't want to give him any advanced warning.

343

We are coming up to the traffic signals at Burrard and they are red. Risking detection, I put on the flashing lights and pull left into the oncoming lane. As I sweep by the waiting cars, I check them all out but there is no sign of my target.

I snap off the lights as I cross Burrard. Up ahead, the cars are stopped at Pine. As the lights change a car pulls out into the fast lane. A maroon Toyota! He crosses Fir, signals left and pulls into the left turn lane for Granville Street. He comes to a stop behind a trolley bus. The filter light goes green as I pull up behind him and the bus pulls forward.

I can not take him yet.

He checks his mirror and our eyes lock; his open wide as mine narrow.

The bus is making its ponderous turn on to Granville. He guns the Toyota past the bus and races down the hill towards the bridge. But he is no match for the 4.6 liter V8 in the cruiser. I put on the lights and the siren and pull in behind him.

Where the traffic was heavy on Broadway, it is light here. I grab my cell and press 'Send' twice.

Steve answers immediately. *"Cal, where are you?"*

"I'm on the Granville Bridge, following George. He's in a maroon Toyota." I give him the number plate. "He's got Ellie with him." George pulls into the right hand lane and I follow. "He's taking the Seymour exit. I need backup."

"Gotcha." I hear him talking into his radio. I put the phone on the seat beside me and leave it open.

Why doesn't George pull over? He must know he can't escape. He's just putting Ellie in danger. Now to make matters worse, I can see that he's talking on his cell. At the speed that he is driving, if he hits another car, he will kill them both. If I stop pursuit, he may slow down and reduce the danger. But then he could escape taking her with him.

We come down the ramp on to Seymour. The lights turn red at Drake. A brown UPS truck is starting to cross in front of George. He hits the brakes hard and turns right, cutting in front of the truck. I follow but the truck is between us now. The Friday night downtown traffic is heavy on Drake. The oncoming lane is blocked and, despite my lights and siren, no one can pull over to let me through. The UPS truck lumbers ahead to Richards before it can pull over and let me past.

George has taken advantage of the gap in the traffic and is already across Homer. Where the hell is he taking Ellie? He's nowhere near his office. Does he maybe have an apartment in Yaletown that Sam doesn't know about? He just catches the green light at Pacific and screams into a right hand turn.

By the time I get there it's red. I slow down and as I cross against the red, I'm sideswiped by a speeding red Camaro. The force of the impact pushes me into the median and the cruiser stalls. I scream Ellie's name in frustration as I see the Toyota vanish eastward down Pacific.

I need to tell Steve. I grab for the phone but it is not on the seat; after the impact, it could be anywhere in the car. I scrabble around on the floor in a rising panic but it's nowhere.

A good looking young man opens the passenger door of the cruiser. "Are you OK, officer?" he asks.

I slide across the seat and out of the car. "Give me your cell, quick," I exclaim.

"Sure, it's in my car." He runs towards a silver BMW parked in the middle of the eastbound lane with it's four way flashers on. The car is an M5 about fifteen years old.

I follow him, catching a quick look at the Camaro. Its nose is buried in the side of the cruiser and the airbags are deployed.

345

He retrieves his phone from the center console and hands it to me.

I don't take it. "Call 911 and tell them that an officer is in pursuit of a maroon Toyota. Tell them to check with Detective Steve Waters. That's important. You got that?"

"Yeah, sure." He starts to dial and I jump into his car. "Hey, what are you doing?"

"Just make the call," I shout, "and tell them your license plate number."

I do a lightning check of the cockpit. It's a manual transmission and the key's in the ignition. I fire it up, slam it into first and fishtail down Pacific, the momentum causing the driver's door to slam shut.

I'm praying that George will see that I am no longer in pursuit and will slow down to a normal speed. I fly though the lights at Davie and Cambie, wracked by fear that he might have turned off. It doesn't make sense for him either to double back or to head down to False Creek; I have to play the odds. I weave through the traffic as best I can but it's Yaletown on a Friday night. Finally I get to the stadium and the road opens up into three lanes.

Then with a shudder I know that I'm going the right way. I know where George is heading. And he's taking my baby with him. But why? Why is he going there?

I push down on the gas and the car leaps ahead like an eager stallion. I flash by the other traffic, I must be doing seventy-five miles an hour and my fear for Ellie is pounding through my veins.

And as I approach Abbott, I know that I'm right. A block ahead, I see the Toyota turning left onto Carrall. I slow the BMW down and follow at a normal pace.

I can see that George is still on his phone. Who can he be talking to? And why is he heading towards the alley? There are three cross streets before we get there. The lights are bound to be red at one of them. Then I'll have him.

346

I run through a plan in my head. As we come to a stop, I'll jump out and in two seconds have his door open. One quick punch to the side of the head to disorient him and then I'll reach in, turn off the engine and remove the key. Then George and I will have a little conversation.

The first set of lights are green.

Then the second.

The third turn red as he approaches them.

He stops and removes the phone from his ear and looks down to dial it. Great! He won't see me in the mirror.

I fling open the door of the BMW and all hell breaks loose.

A bicycle, laden with two giant plastic bags full of drink cans, smashes into the door and the cyclist flies over the top with a shout. A dumpster diver and his recycling. One of the plastic bags rips open and there are evil smelling cans everywhere.

George's head snaps up and again our eyes make contact. But this time, instead of surprise, I see rage.

I leap out. Throw the bike aside and race for George's door. I can't yank it open. He has locked it. Then the door handle is wrenched out of my hand as he accelerates through the red light.

Somehow he makes it across Hastings.

I turn back. The owner of the bike is on his feet swearing at me in Technicolor.

I ignore him and get back into the BMW.

There is no traffic in the right hand lane and George dashes down the half block and turns right into the alley. I catch a glimpse of Ellie's face looking back towards me. Even at this distance I can see the fear.

The dumpster diver, however, is not prepared to be ignored and plants himself in front of the car, swearing and pointing at me. I hit the horn and edge forward but he refuses to budge. I want to just floor the gas and run him over.

I jump out and grab my wallet. The last of the money that I stole from Kevin is in there. I give it all to him and push him out of my way.

Then I'm in the BMW, the lights are green again and I scream across Hastings and turn into the maw.

The Toyota is slewed across the alley, half way down, just this side of the dumpsters. The lights are off and in the dark I can not see if George and Ellie are in it. Any fear I have of this place is obscured by my need to protect my daughter. I drive down to within six feet of Brad's car. In the BMW's lights the interior is illuminated. It seems empty.

I get out and scan the area before approaching. The usual lost souls are in the alley, looking malevolently at the vehicles which have invaded their territory.

Four steps and I am at the Toyota. I call, "Ellie? George?"

Silence. Even the crack heads are quiet.

Somehow George has escaped. Maybe through the back door of one of the buildings. This is his escape route. Has he taken Ellie or has he decided that he has no further use for her? Would he feel the need or the desire to silence her?

My nerves tingling with fear, I reach the door of the abandoned car, dreading what I might find crumpled on the floor. As it opens the interior light comes on, providing him with a signal.

Then George stands up and is pointing Brad's .357 in my face.

The safety is off now.

He is on the other side of the car, his left hand clamped cruelly over Ellie's mouth.

"Let her go George. She shouldn't see this."

He has a moment of indecision. I guess that he has spent most of his time managing the gang's enterprises in the background, staying away from the sharp end of the business; Blondie would have laughed at me as he pulled the trigger.

George nods. "I'm sorry, honey, for taking you from your Mommy and for…" his voice, unexpectedly kind, trails off as he releases her.

With waves of relief rushing through me, I tell her, "Go and get in the car behind me sweetie and lie on the floor. OK?"

She whispers, "Yes, Daddy," and runs around Brad's car. I hear the BMW door open.

"Back up against your car." I do as he says.

He comes around the Toyota without the gun wavering an inch from its aim at the middle of my chest. I could really do with that Kevlar vest now. Then I remember that I still have Roy's knife in my pocket. It would be justice indeed if this knife brought George down. My hand creeps toward my pocket.

He extends his arm and the gun is pointing at my face. Amateur!

He smiles, "Goodbye, Cal," and pulls the trigger.

The noise is deafening. I feel like I have been punched hard in the shoulder and I spin around to the sound of broken glass tinkling on the pavement.

My fall to the ground is slowed as my head makes sharp contact with the side of the BMW.

When I open my eyes, I don't know if I have been unconscious. My head is spinning and all time sense is gone.

I roll on my back and look at where George was standing but he has vanished.

I must get to Ellie. I push myself back onto my feet.
Which is impossible.

The .357 bullet should have shattered my shoulder beyond repair making my arm about as useful as spaghetti.

Then I see George lying on the ground, covered in blood.

I can not stop the victory whoop from bubbling up. Brad's fifteen year neglect of the weapon has resulted in a catastrophic misfire. The gun exploded in George's hand. Part of it hit me in the shoulder and other bits broke the windows in both vehicles... which stops the laughter. Ellie!

I yank open door of the M5. There is glass everywhere but no Ellie.

Adrenaline fires through me.

Wait. Wait. I remember that these days, kids always get in the back seats of cars. It's automatic for them. I sigh with relief and pull open the back door but she's not there either.

I look over at George but he is still unconscious. Did he call an accomplice to meet him here? Has *he* taken Ellie?

"ELLIE!" I shout, hearing the panic in my own voice. "WHERE ARE YOU."

The alley has eaten her up. I look up and down and all I can see are the damned junkies. There is no sign of her. No one is running or acting strangely. I have no clue what to do. My fear is screaming at me. I look again in the BMW praying that by some miracle I overlooked her the first time. Nothing.

I go over to George, maybe if I can make him regain consciousness I can force out of him some clue. I kneel down, grab his lapels and shake him. "George. GEORGE." But he is out for the count.

"Over here," a voice croaks.

I spin towards the sound. It's coming from a darkened doorway. There is an emaciated woman of indeterminate age. She smiles at me, showing two lines of gums, her teeth the victims of a lifelong devotion to crack cocaine. She's crouched down and the arm of her filthy pink hoody is around Ellie's shoulders. Ellie has her arms wrapped around her and her face is buried in the bony shoulder. "There's yer

Daddy sweetheart," she says. "He's all right, see. I told'ja he would be, didn't I?"

Ellie looks up cautiously at first but as soon as she sees that it is me, she lets go of her protector and rushes towards me. I drop to my knees and envelope her in my arms.

Through my tears I look at the woman in the pink sweater and mouth the words 'Thank you.' She nods at me and I can see that she too is crying. Perhaps for the loss of that brief moment when she hugged and was hugged by an innocent child. My heart goes out to her.

The alley has thrown everything it can at me. Heroin, beatings, attempted murder and kidnap. But it couldn't beat me. I've survived. Ellie has survived. Its hold on me drifts away in the chill wind that blows between the buildings.

I hear the scream of approaching sirens. In Vancouver, the sound of a gun shot does not go unnoticed.

As my adrenaline level drops, the withdrawal pains come back with a vengeance. I have to have a hit very soon or I will be screaming. But I don't submit. I won't let it beat me. I won't let go of Ellie. Never again.

We cling to each other until the cavalry arrives.

Chapter 57

Steve and I are enjoying a brief respite, sitting on the designer chairs in the QX4 reception area. We are waiting for Sandi to arrive for work. Although it is a Saturday, when Steve called her she asked him to meet her at the office.

Neither of us has slept and it shows. My right shoulder is throbbing where the chunk of Brad's gun sliced it. Another fragment scored my left cheekbone but that was fixed with four stitches. An inch higher and it would have entered my brain via the eye socket.

We have just come here from Vancouver General. Brad was taken there unconscious last night. Early this morning he told us everything.

When George bailed Brad out with the half a million loan, George asked Brad to hold on to a lock-box for him, as a favor. Although Brad did not know it at the time, it contained three different sets of identities and fifty thousand bucks in cash.

It was a smart move on George's part. If the noose ever tightened on his operation, he knew that his office, houses, plane and boat would all be searched or at least staked out, and perhaps safety deposit boxes in his banks would be too. Where better to keep his stash than with an acquaintance who owed him big time?

When George arrived at Brad's place with Ellie in tow, he explained away her presence by saying Sam was sick and Rosa was away. Ellie told us that he had threatened he would go home and kill Sam if she didn't play along with this story. For that alone, I could kill him. He paid for it when he made the error of putting Ellie in the bedroom, with a phone beside the bed, while he talked to Brad.

Brad handed over the lock-box but in his hurry, George had forgotten to bring the key. But for that mistake, we would never have got to Brad's in time. George needed the contents immediately in order to effect his escape; unfortunately for him, it was sturdy and fastened by a big padlock. They tried unsuccessfully, for some minutes, to open it with Brad's meager collection of tools and so they needed to knock on several neighbor's doors until they were able to borrow a small pry bar. Once it was open, George had checked the contents and stuffed them in his pockets.

And then he turned.

We learned that George knew about Brad's gun because Brad had boasted about it at one time. He paid for his braggadocio. George demanded that he hand over the weapon and rewarded Brad by pistol whipping him into unconsciousness.

Why George left in Brad's Toyota, and took Ellie, is a mystery. Steve's theory is that he saw the police cars and could not get to the car he had taken in North Van. So he took Brad's car and dragged Ellie along as insurance.

As for George, during the night, he underwent surgery and is still unconscious. He is handcuffed to a bed in St. Paul's under police guard. When he regains consciousness, he will be formally charged with kidnapping, assault, money laundering and maybe more. The Crown Prosecutor's office is working on other charges related to organized crime and conspiracy.

There is one loose end. Sam told us that George received a phone call at nine last night which set him off. Stammo traced it back to a disposable cell phone. We may never know who made that call. Steve thinks that maybe one of the gang escaped from the ambush in the alley and called George.

The reason Steve and I are here, waiting for Sandi, is to tie up the case against George for Kevin's murder. I have told Steve and Stammo everything I know about the case and I have held nothing back. It took several hours and is one of the reasons we haven't slept.

While I am still mulling over all that Brad has told us, I see Sandi striding towards the building. As she walks though the revolving door, she spies me. With a look of annoyance she heads for the security guard. Steve gets up and walks towards her with his ID in hand. I follow.

"Ms. Palmer, I'm detective Waters of the Vancouver Police Department."

She ignores him and glares at me. "What's he doing here?"

"Mr. Rogan is helping us in an ongoing investigation. I think it might be better if we all go to your office."

She turns from me and affixes her glare on Steve; then shrugs and leads the way to the elevators.

In her office she says, "Well I suppose you'd better sit down." The very model of graciousness. She also sits and I notice that the chair behind her desk has been adjusted so that she is several inches higher than the people in her guest chairs. Some corporate ego thing, I guess. "What do you want to know?" At least she avoids the *I'm a very busy person* cliché.

Steve has told me, in no uncertain terms, that he will conduct the interview with Sandi and that I am only to speak if he directs a question to me.

"Ms. Palmer, your company announced that it had received authorization from the Therapeutic Products Directorate of Health Canada to proceed with human trials of your new drug *Addi-ban*, is that correct?"

Sandi frowns. This is not a question that she was expecting.

"Yes."

354

"And you announced it on Friday November twelfth. Is that correct?"

"Yes."

"Ms. Palmer, when did you first learn that the human trials had been approved?"

She hesitates. Gives a furtive glance out the window. She is deciding whether to tell the truth. Steve spots it too. "It would be best if you told the truth here, Ms. Palmer."

She snaps him a hard look for a moment... and then deflates.

"We received the approval on Friday October twenty-ninth."

"That would be three weeks before you announced it?" Steve's question is rhetorical. "QX4 is a public company. I understand that you are bound to publicly disclose any news that might effect the share price and that you should do so immediately. Can you tell me why you delayed this particular bit of news?"

"We would have announced it right away but then, when Kevin died, we decided to sit on the information. The company knew that Kevin's death would be disastrous for the share price so we decided to let that happen before we made the announcement. Two announcements at the same time, one good and one bad, might have been very confusing for the investing public."

"Hmmm." Steve is playing it exactly right. "When you say 'we' decided, who specifically do you mean?"

"Mr. Walsh, mainly... in consultation with me."

Clever George. He let Kevin's death push down the share prices so that he could buy cheap, then announce the approvals of the trials and watch his money grow.

"And when did you and Mr. Walsh make this decision?"

"On the Monday following Kevin's death."

Steve is silent, hoping perhaps that Sandi will supply more. She does not.

"On the Friday, when you received the approval from Health Canada, who knew about it?" This is the question. George knew about the approval and he knew about Kevin's illicit drug testing. So he made the decision to kill Kevin. If word of the illicit drug testing got out, QX4 would be finished for ever and George would lose millions. Kevin's death by suicide would only cause a temporary blip in the share prices, one of which he could take advantage.

"Only me. There was a slip up by our mail room. The package was addressed to Kevin but he was off that day; he was very depressed about something." She cuts a sideways glance at me. She wants to know if I have told the police about Kevin's illegal testing. I keep a stony face and she continues. "The mail room boy delivered the package to Kevin's office, this office, when it arrived on Friday morning. It sat here all day until about five thirty.

"I was out of the office in the morning, on personal business." I remember that it was on that Friday morning when she learned about the death of her brother. "I went to get some papers from Kevin's desk and found the courier envelope. I saw who it was from and knew I had to open it."

"What did you do next?" Steve asks.

"Well, I thought I should tell Kevin first but I couldn't get hold of him. So I called George—Mr. Walsh that is."

"How did he react when you told him?" Steve asks. There is another question that I want to ask but I bite my tongue.

"He didn't. I couldn't get hold of him, so I left a message."

"What did you say in the message?"

"I asked him to call me on my cell. I told him it was very important."

"In the message did you say anything at all about the approval?"

"No. I wanted to tell him in person."

"So when did he find out?"

"It wasn't until the next morning." Sandi seems puzzled. She can not make out why Steve is asking all these questions. "When he got my message, he called me back on my cell, but I had it set to vibrate and I didn't notice it ringing. It wasn't until the morning that I checked my messages.

"George's message said that he would meet me at nine in the morning at the office. It was the Saturday morning. That was when I told him."

If Sandi is telling the truth, George could not have known in time to kill Kevin, unless...

Steve is on it. "So you met Mr. Walsh here in the office?" She nods. "And at what time did Mr. Walsh arrive?"

"I don't know. I arrived at five after nine and he was already here."

"And when did your meeting finish?"

"It was after eleven thirty. I stayed here to do some work but I don't know what time Mr. Walsh left. You could check with security, everyone gets logged in and logged out."

"And you and Mr. Walsh were together the entire time from nine-oh-five until eleven thirty?"

"Except for a five minute break, yes."

If this is true, George could not have killed Kevin and, for that matter, neither could my other suspect: Sandi herself. Unless they were in it together and this is an alibi concocted for the benefit of them both.

"What is your relationship with Mr. Walsh?" It's a great question; one I did not consider. It opens up a whole new vista of possibilities.

"He's the Chairman of this company. My ultimate boss." She says it like she is talking to a kid but then realizes the implications of the question. She reddens and glares at him. So much for that idea. Not even Meryl Streep is a good enough actress to pull that one off. Sandi's relationship with George was strictly business.

"I'd like to get on to another subject now." Steve says smoothly. He is a great interviewer. Except for the one question that I think he has missed, he is right on the money.

He continues, "I understand that Kevin Wallace had been conducting illegal trials of *Addi-ban*." He lets the statement hang in the air.

Sandi looks at me, her face neutral. She takes a big breath and nods.

"Ms. Palmer, your brother Jason was one of the people killed by *Addi-ban*?"

She nods again and this time a tear makes its way down her cheek, followed by another.

"I have to ask you this." Steve's voice is gentle. "Why have you continued to work for a company whose drug killed your own brother?"

She is racked by sobs and it takes time for her to get them under control.

"George made me. He said that if what Kevin had been doing got out, then the company would be ruined. He threatened me."

"When did Mr. Walsh threaten you?" Steve asks.

Sandi looks panicky for a moment. She is on the horns of a dilemma. She can not decide. And then the dam bursts it all floods out of her. "That Saturday morning. I didn't know that Jason was killed by Addi-Ban until I went over to Kevin's late Friday night. The next morning I told George about the government approval and about Kevin's illegal drug testing and Jason and everything. I said I was going to hand in my resignation. He told me that I couldn't resign; that I had to take over Kevin's position and that I had to keep my mouth shut about the illegal tests.

"He became very angry. He said no one must know anything and that he knew people; that if I didn't do what he said, he would have me killed."

"Why didn't you come to the police?"

"I thought about it and then Kevin died and I thought maybe George already knew about what Kevin had done and had sent those people to kill him. I was just too scared."

She is sobbing again and Steve and I exchange looks. We have not got what we wanted from this meeting but I think we have got the truth.

Sandi grabs some tissues from the box on her desk and wipes her eyes.

"Thank you for telling us this, Ms. Palmer. You've been very helpful. You might like to know that we arrested Mr. Walsh last night and he is under guard at the hospital. Those people he spoke about are a drug gang. We have several of them under arrest and their leader is dead. I don't think you have anything to worry about now."

She can not take it all in at first but when it does settle, I can feel the waves of relief washing off her.

We get up and we walk to the elevators in awkward silence. She is probably composing her resignation letter in her mind. We are never going to like each other and hopefully we will never have to meet again.

"Can I ask you something Sandi?" I ask.

She shrugs.

"When I first came to see you here, why did you tell me about the illegal tests that Kevin had carried out?"

"Isn't it obvious? George forced me to stay on at QX4 against my will. I figured that if I told you, you would use the information to pursue your investigation into Kevin's death and that you would have no compunction about telling the world. If it came from you, George could not tie it back to me. QX4 would close down and I could leave. I just didn't want you to tell Brad, in case it got back to George from him that I'd told you."

Sandi was manipulating me. I guess I shouldn't be surprised.

It is not until we are in Steve's car, on our way back to Main Street, that I remember the question that came to me during the interview, the one that I thought Steve missed.

Chapter 58

Stammo is doing the interviewing now. And I am the interviewee or, to be more precise, the interrogatee. I have mixed feelings about Stammo, twice in the last couple of days he has stood up for me, in complete contrast to our former relationship, and yesterday he did some things that impressed me as a cop. But we still have that antipathy that has been there since we first met. And then it hits me: Stammo is *fair*. He doesn't like me—and, to be honest, I've never given him a reason to do so—but if he thinks something is not fair, he will speak up for me. When Steve didn't want me in on George's arrest, Stammo told the Deputy Chief that he thought I had earned the right. It's a side of him that I never observed before. We are never going to like each other but at least I can respect him now.

I have had my shot at George and at Sandi but both were misfires. Now I am the target in Kevin's murder and Stammo has played this right. He has kept me waiting in the interview room for a while. Long enough for withdrawal to take a hold. Stammo wants it to distract me; make me slip up.

I want to get back to see Ellie, see how she is coping. But now I am getting this feeling that I am going to spend tonight and maybe a lot of other nights in a cell. Suddenly that possibility seems very real and it scares the hell out of me. Former cops do not fare well in prison. There are a lot of people inside that I put there, they would love to have me on their territory. Unless one theory that I have brewing pans out, I may be heading for old home week at the Fraser Regional Correction Center.

"So, Rogan." He is enjoying this. "Your attempt to implicate Walsh was a bomb and into the bargain, your other suspect, Sandi the girlfriend, is out of the frame. They nicely alibi each other. Unless she's lying her ass off which Steve says he doubts."

"She wasn't." Steve adds. "We checked the logs of the security system and, unless she or Walsh tampered with them, they show their check in and check out times."

"I agree with Steve," I say. I need them to hurry this along, finish this line of questioning.

Stammo continues with a smile, "So with Walsh and Palmer in the clear, that leaves you as the only suspect."

"Except for Walsh's gang." Steve comes to my defense. "Walsh could have ordered it as a hit."

Stammo shoots a glare at his partner. I know the deal here. They must have agreed Steve would take a run at my theory of the crime—that George was the killer, or possibly Sandi—and, if that came to nothing, then Stammo would have a free pass to go after me.

I surprise both of them by saying, "Nick's right. The gang didn't do it."

"How do you know that?" Steve asks.

"Because *he* did it." Stammo answers for me.

I force myself to chuckle, not for humor but to piss him off. "The reason they couldn't have done it was that there was no sign of a struggle at the crime scene. Kevin wouldn't have let a stranger into his place without a struggle. Furthermore, the killer would not have known that my jacket was there so he wouldn't have known to smear it with Kevin's blood."

I give Stammo a false smile when I say this. I'm trying to hold it together but I can't stop sniffing and the ache is in my shoulders is getting bad.

"That's all very nice," Stammo says, "but the fact remains that, one," he holds up a finger, "on your own admission, you were there around the time of the murder. Two, Wallace's blood was on your jacket and three, you had a motive. Your buddy was tired of you changing your clothes at his house every week. He told you this and you freaked out and killed him."

The thought that Kevin was going to cut me off from using his place to change my clothes stabs, sharp in my gut. It goes against the very nature of the man. Kevin was nothing if not loyal. Loyalty was bred into him.

Loyalty, the word sets my mind on a new track so that I almost miss Stammo's next pronouncement. He gives a smug smile. "I go with that Ocram guy. Y'know, the simple solution is the best one."

This time my laughter is for humor.

"It's Occam, you dope. The principle is called Occam's Razor."

Steve's quick reaction stops Stammo from reaching across the table and punching my lights out, or at least trying.

"Cal! You are not helping matters here." Steve is madder than a wasp in a jar.

He's right but I can not keep myself from goading Stammo; it is *so* easy and *such* fun. But if I continue to do it, it will just prolong this.

Steve is not impressed. "It's all very well making smart-assed remarks, Cal, but what Nick says is right. You *are* a viable suspect. The only viable suspect, in fact. So let's cut the crap. If you have something to say, say it."

Good. They have exhausted their questioning.

"OK, OK. I'm sorry." I'm not. But what the hey. "There is one other possibility."

I pause to get their attention.

"Steve, you believe that Sandi Palmer was telling the truth when we spoke to her this morning?"

Steve nods his agreement and I continue, "So do I. You did an A1 job. You asked a couple of questions that I wouldn't have thought to ask. But there was one question that kept nagging at me and I never got the chance to ask it."

"What?" Stammo asks.

"Steve, you remember when you asked Sandi what she did after she opened the courier envelope, the one which had the Health Canada approval in it?"

"Yeah. She said that she couldn't get hold of Kevin, so she called Walsh. So?"

"There was a question I wanted to ask her." I pull out my cell phone. "Have you got her mobile number there?" Steve supplies it and I dial.

"Sandi. It's Cal. I want to ask you one other question... Yeah, just one... On the Friday evening, after you opened the envelope with the approval for the trials, you said that you tried to get hold of Kevin. What did you do to try to get hold of him?" I listen carefully to her reply. "Do you remember *exactly* what you said to them?" She replies in the affirmative and gives me the details. I thank her and hang up.

Then I look at my pay-as-you-go cell phone and another random thought leaps into my mind.

I look at the questioning expressions across the table.

And tell them, carefully and with conviction.

Stammo doesn't want to buy it but I'm guessing Steve knows I didn't kill Kevin.

They leave the room. I hope they don't leave me here for too long. I need to get what's in my jacket and head to a restroom.

But they return quickly and it's a go.

Chapter 59

I bring the Rolls Royce to a halt in front of the Main Street police station. It is as out of place here as a debutante at a soccer match, drawing sullen stares from most of the passersby. One ragged degenerate actually spits at it.

After a longer time than politeness allows, Rogan comes through the brass doors and gets in the car beside me. "Sorry to keep you waiting," he says with what I judge to be a minimum of sincerity. I keep silent.

"Thanks for coming, Arnold."

I check my mirror, pull away from the curb and, without signaling, do a U-turn. As I come to the lights at Hastings, I check my mirror again and it is as I suspected. A black Ford, a Crown Victoria, is doing a U turn behind me.

"Why did you want to see me Mr. Rogan?" I ask.

"First, Arnold, I want to give you an update for Mr. Wallace. Last night, the police arrested George Walsh and several of his associates. However, we discovered this morning that it is unlikely that any of them were responsible for Kevin's death."

After a moment's silence, I prompt him. "Walsh's arrest is good news. So, who did kill Kevin?"

"Arnold, what would you say is your most prized quality?" He has answered my question with one of his own. I know where he is going with this.

"Loyalty and perhaps courage."

"Yes. When I first spoke to Mr. Wallace about Kevin's death, do you know what he said to me about you, Arnold? He said, 'He is *completely* loyal to this family.'"

"That is true, Mr. Rogan."

"How far would that loyalty go, Arnold?" he asks.

I can answer that without any dissembling. "I would happily lay down my life for either Mr. or Mrs. Wallace."

He waits a beat before continuing. "Arnold, you told me that you drove Mrs. Wallace to Kevin's townhouse at seven-thirty in the morning of the Saturday that Kevin was killed."

"And?" I ask.

"At the time I wondered why Mrs. Wallace would choose to go visiting so early in the morning. I also asked how you knew that Kevin had been conducting illegal testing of the *Addi-Ban* drug but you refused to tell me." He waits for me to talk but I decline. He shrugs, "I found the answer to both questions about an hour ago. On Friday evening, Sandi called the Wallace's house trying to find Kevin. You answered the phone and when you told her that Kevin was not there, she asked to speak to Mrs. Wallace. She told Mrs. Wallace all about the testing and about the fact that the test subjects had died. Mrs. Wallace started crying and Sandi said that she heard your voice in the background asking her what was wrong."

I have to admit that Cal's skills as a detective are first class. "Well done," I congratulate him. "Mrs. Wallace did indeed tell me what Kevin had done. We agreed that she should talk to him first thing on Saturday and find out if what Ms. Palmer had told her was true."

"How did you feel about what he had done Arnold?" he asks me.

I can feel the rage boiling up inside me again. I check the mirror and see that the unmarked police car is still behind me. I glance across at Cal and he is watching me like a hawk. A couple of deep breaths calm me enough that I can answer his question.

"Frankly, I was appalled. I felt that Kevin had completely betrayed his family and everything that they stand for. I was beside myself with anger. I could not tolerate the fact that Mrs. Wallace had to bear the burden of what Kevin had done and I will do anything to ensure that Mr. Wallace never finds out."

Out of the corner of my eye, I can see him nodding. "Arnold," he says, his voice not much more than a whisper, "I completely believe that you would die to protect Mr. and Mrs. Wallace and I have to wonder if you would also kill to protect them?"

"Yes, Mr. Rogan, I would." I can not keep the pride from my voice.

"After you drove Mrs. Wallace home from Kevin's house that Saturday morning, you went back, didn't you, Arnold?"

How the hell does he know that? Is it just a guess on his part or did someone actually see me? A lie at this point would not be a good idea. "Yes, Mr. Rogan, I did. I even 'borrowed' Mrs. Wallace's key to the townhouse."

And here comes the big question.

"Arnold. Did you kill Kevin?"

"No, Mr. Rogan. When I arrived there, Mr. Kevin did not reply to the doorbell, so I used the key. He was already dead."

He digests this information and I add, "If he had been alive, I can not say for a certainty that I would not have killed him myself."

"Why didn't you call the police?" He asks.

I have asked myself that question at least one hundred times. "I really don't know."

"Arnold, did you take my jacket and smear Kevin's blood on it?"

His question stuns me. Does this mean that someone tried to frame him? Who would know to do that?

He stares intently at me. I am rarely intimidated but I find myself wilting under his steady gaze.

367

We have arrived at the main pavilion at Vancouver General Hospital. I pull into the drop off area.

"Just two more things," he says. "First, you popped up on the street after my lunch with Brad and then again when I was in the hospital. How did you know where I was?"

I was wondering if he would ask this. "Mr. Wallace told me of his intention to ask you to investigate Kevin's death. So when you came to the house on the day of Kevin's funeral, I put a GPS chip with a transmitter into the lining of your coat. Later, I put another, larger one in that nice backpack that you have with you now."

He looks stunned and reaches for the door handle.

"You had a second question?" I ask.

He recovers his composure. "Yes. Why did you suggest to me that being beaten up by that gang might be associated with my investigation into Kevin's death?"

"Instructions from Mr. Wallace. Why don't you ask him? He's on the twelfth floor, in the palliative care ward."

"Thank you, Arnold." He gets out walks to the hospital door; it looks like he's talking to himself.

I check the mirror. The police car is right behind me. Two officers are approaching me, one from each side of the vehicle. Two others are trailing Cal.

Chapter 60

"How are you feeling?" I ask.

"A lot better than I did this morning. They're probably going to discharge me around four o'clock. Did you get the evidence that you needed on George?"

"No. I'm afraid not. It looks like George wasn't the one who killed Kevin."

"You're not serious." Brad has a look of amazement on his face. "How can you be sure?"

"He was with Sandi at the time of Kevin's death. They are each other's alibi."

"Could they have been working together?" he asks.

"We don't think so and there's other evidence. Besides, I think I now know who killed Kevin and I'm going to need your help to prove it."

"Who?"

I ignore his question. There's something I need to know.

"When I came here this morning with the police, you told us about last night. There was something that you said that has been running through my mind. You said that George knew about your gun and made you give it to him."

In the pause, Brad says, "Yeah."

"How?"

"What d'you mean, how?"

"You are five inches taller and twenty pounds heavier than George and you were on the wrestling team at school. How could George make you give him your gun."

"He didn't force me physically." Brad's voice has dropped to a whisper. "He, uh... had something on me. It was about that money I owed him."

"Are you telling me that George coerced you into handing over a gun because of the loan he made you?" I'm pushing harder now.

"Yeah, it was a lot of money. I couldn't refuse him."

"So much so that you were prepared to give a gun to a man who had my daughter with him?"

"Yes, yes. I'm sorry Cal. I didn't think about Ellie being there. She was in the other room. He really had me over a barrel."

"But it wasn't because of money was it?" I am standing up and am almost shouting now. My show of anger has got him off balance, now is the time to strike. But I don't want to. I know the words will drive an eternal rift between us but I have to say them. Because, for better of for worse, I am a cop ahead of being a friend. "It was because George knew it was you who killed Kevin." I yell.

His eyes are enormous. "Come on Cal, you know I could never kill Kev. He was my best friend." He's breathing heavily and there is a slight dilation of his pupils.

"You almost got away with it." My voice is back to normal. "I was so sure it was George and I wanted to nail him for it. But George—and you for that matter—wouldn't be likely to kill Kevin because of what it would do to QX4's stock price and to the money that he had invested. But then I learned that QX4 had received approval for human trials of the *Addi-ban* drug *before* Kevin's death. So I assumed that George knew about the approval and he decided it was better to kill Kevin and bury the secret of the illegal testing with him. Sure, the shares would take a big drop but as soon as the approval was announced, they would bounce right back again."

"That makes sense," he agrees too quickly. "You need to break his alibi, Cal. It's ridiculous to think I would kill Kev."

"But George didn't know about the approval. Sandi was the first person to learn about it. She tried to reach George but couldn't. But she also tried to reach Kevin. He didn't answer at home or on his cell so Sandi called his mother who didn't know where he was. So then she called you. She told you that she wanted to contact Kevin to tell him that the government approvals had come through. So other than Sandi, you were the only person to know about the approvals. Oh, except for Arnold, but I've eliminated him as a suspect."

"Cal, you're crazy. Arnold loved Kevin; he would no more do it than I would. It's got to be George."

"Yeah, I must admit, I could never really see Arnold as the killer but I had to check it out. Do you want to know what clinches it for me Brad? How I knew it was you?"

"Humor me," he says.

"It's been bugging me since last night. But when I was sitting in the police station this morning, for some reason it clicked into place."

"What did?" He is rattled now.

"George got a call last night, from a disposable cell phone, telling him to clear out of his house. We couldn't work out who called him, Steve assumed that one of the gang members whom we didn't catch had called him. I never bought that. My theory is that only the blond guy at the top knew how to contact George and he was dead. Then I remembered the call I got from you when I was on the way to arrest George. I trusted you and I told you where we were going."

"Why would I tell George."

"You knew that I was obsessed with the theory that George was the killer. And you knew that if we arrested George, we might find out that he didn't do it. But if you

371

tipped him off and he got away, we would think that the murderer had escaped and stop looking. You'd be in the clear *and* George would owe you."

"Oh come on Cal, it's circumstantial. A coincidence."

Oh, Brad. How I wish it was.

"We can ask George when he wakes up."

He says nothing but his jaw is tensing.

"Oh, and there's one other thing. As I walked into the hospital, I got a phone call from one of the cops on the team, a guy called Nick Stammo. He got a court order and went over to your apartment; he found a cell phone. The number was the same number as the phone that called George at around nine last night. I'm willing to bet that when we do the forensics, your prints will be all over it."

He is sweating.

"What I don't understand," I add, "is how you could bring yourself to kill him." A bigger truth I have rarely uttered.

I wait. Thirty seconds, watching the cogs turn in his mind. Then he lets it all out with a long sigh.

"You have to believe me, Cal. I didn't mean to."

I nod, "I know, I know." I put as much sympathy into my tone as I can stomach,

He draws a breath. "Kev called me on the Thursday evening, asked me to come over to his place and he told me everything about his illegal testing and the deaths. He was completely devastated. He couldn't stop crying. He said that he was going to go to the police the next day and tell them what he'd done.

"I couldn't believe it at first but when it sank in, I realized that if he did that, the company would be closed down and I would be ruined financially.

"I told him that he shouldn't be hasty. We should think it over first. I appealed to his generous side. I talked about all the people at QX4, people he had worked with for years, people who would be out of work if he blew the whistle on himself. I got him to agree not to say anything, at least until after the weekend.

"At midnight that night, after I had left Kevin's, I called George to tell him what Kevin had done. He told me that no matter what pressure I had to apply, I had to keep Kevin from saying anything to anyone.

"On the Friday, I called Kevin every hour but he wasn't at work and there was no reply from his home. I even went round there half a dozen times but he wasn't in. Then at the end of the day, Sandi called me looking for him and she told me about the approvals for the human trials. I tried to get hold of him all through the evening but no luck. I even went round there again but there was no reply.

"I hardly slept at all that night. I called him early Saturday morning and he was home. I told him I had to see him right away. He said that you were coming over and that he was going to tell you what he had done. I begged him not to. I jumped in my car and raced over there. I got there just before you did. I was telling him about the approvals from the government when you arrived. While you were in the shower, I laid it all out for him. How he would ruin the company if he admitted to the illegal testing. How he could reformulate *Addi-ban* and just go ahead with the human trials when he was ready. But he just wouldn't budge. When he went downstairs to talk to you, I listened from the top of the stairs and I couldn't believe that he was going to tell you but you didn't have the time to listen."

A wave of guilt crushes me. If I had taken the time to listen to Kevin, he would still be alive. My impatience caused his death. In a way Stammo is right: I did kill Kevin.

"The reason that I hadn't been able to get hold of him on Friday was that after we had spoken on Thursday night he had gone fishing at his parents' cottage at the lake. Try and clear his mind, he said. His fishing stuff was on the coffee table, including his tackle box and that knife you bought him all those years ago. He was rearranging the stuff in the tackle box—you know how obsessively organized he was—and he told me that he had decided that he was going to go turn himself in to the police, that as soon as you got back from seeing Ellie, he was going to ask you to go with him.

"After you left, I was beside myself. He was being so stubborn. I remember myself shouting at him. Didn't he care that he was ruining me financially, just because something had gone wrong and a bunch of junkies and drunks that nobody cared about had died? How could he ruin QX4 and everything he had worked so hard on for all those years? All he had to do was keep quiet and keep working on *Addi-ban*. For Christ sake, the government approvals had come through. But he just kept saying that none of that mattered, that he had killed people and he had to pay the price. I tried all ways to Sunday to get him to change his mind. I even told him about having every penny of my own money tied up in QX4 shares. D'you know what he said, Cal. Do you?"

I just shake my head.

"He said that he would ask his dad to pay me what I had lost. His Dad! I told him I could never handle the humiliation of taking money from Mr. Wallace, cap in hand. I tried so hard to reason with him but he just kept fiddling with the fucking crap in his damn tackle box and saying the same thing over and over and over: 'I have to pay the price, Brad. I have to pay the price.'

"I snapped. I couldn't help myself. It was like watching someone else do it. I snatched the fishing knife out of his hand and suddenly there it was sticking out of his gut. He fell back on the sofa and blood was pouring out of his chest. He tried to grab the knife and pull it out but he couldn't. I just stood there like an idiot and watched him die. He was staring at me. He…"

He looks into the far distance, a wild stare in his eyes.

"What did you do then?" I ask.

"What? Oh… I wanted to just run out of there but I managed to get myself under control. For some reason, I didn't seem to have any blood on me. So I got a cloth from the kitchen and wiped my fingerprints off the handle of the knife. Then I took both his hands and put them round the knife handle and pushed it hard into his chest, so that it would look like he did it himself. It almost made me puke. After, I took the tackle box downstairs—he always kept it in the closet in the spare bedroom—and that was when I saw your jacket lying on the bed. There was blood on it and I just thought that…" His voice tapers off.

We are silent, deep in our own thoughts.

"Cal. Does anyone have to know about this? Can you help me out here? The police think it was suicide right?"

I reach inside my shirt and pull out the tiny microphone and its transmitter. With a crushing sadness, I shake my head. "You know what Brad? You were right. It was all circumstantial. It was your confession that I needed. Positive think your way out of that." As soon as the last sentence leaves my lips, I regret the meanness of it.

"I'm sorry," I say. "You'll never know how much."

Steve and Stammo walk in. The former gives me a smile, the latter a nod. Now we do have enough evidence to get a court order and really go find that phone. The bluff was risky, but it worked.

So, I did it. I solved Kevin's murder. The goal that has been my obsession for the last three weeks has finally been reached. I have fulfilled my promise to Kevin's father and may, just may have earned enough brownie points to find a way back into the VPD. But the victory is Pyrrhic. The elation I should be feeling right now is dust in my mouth. I

375

would give just about anything for it not to be Brad. With Kevin and Roy gone, I really wanted him back as a friend so my mind resisted accepting him as the killer. Arnold's genuine surprise about the blood on my jacket eliminated him and forced me to accept that it was Brad. As Holmes said, *when you have eliminated the impossible, whatever remains, however improbable, must be the truth.*

But why? Why did it have to be Brad?

Chapter 61

The room feels very still. He is propped up against the pillows, his head slightly to one side, his gaunt hands beside him on top of the covers. I sit in one of the chairs beside the bed and take his hand as gently as I can. I am afraid that a harsh grip will turn it to powder, like the wings of a moth.

"Hello, Cal," he says without opening his eyes. "Have you come to tell me who killed my son?" His voice is strong, clear and fluent.

I swallow. "Yes sir, I have."

"Tell me."

"It was Brad." Saying the words hurts.

His eyes open wide and drill into mine. "Brad? Are you sure?"

"Yes, sir. He just confessed to it ten minutes ago."

"But why ever would Brad…" He shakes his head. His voice drops to a whisper. "I suppose that it was about money."

"Yes, sir. It was."

He shakes his head, a gesture of both amazement and sadness.

"I was sure that you were going to say that…" his voice peters out.

"…that it was Arnold?" I finish the sentence for him.

He frowns, puzzled. "No. That's ridiculous. Arnold is incapable of hurting anyone in this family. I was thinking of someone else entirely."

Who can he have suspected? He looks at me, eyebrows raised, wanting details about Brad.

"There were some problems with the drug Kevin was developing and he wanted to stop working on it." Sharing Arnold's concern, I sanitize the story.

He smiles. "Thank you for trying to keep it from me Cal... at Arnold's request no doubt. But I know about the tests that Kevin performed. I know what went wrong, the deaths, everything. *Now* tell me about Brad."

I tell him the whole story. Every sordid detail. At the end, he squeezes my hand.

"Alexander and Cleitus." Even so close to death's door his agile mind has drawn the perfect parallel from Henry V. Despite my Masters in Literature, I will never know the Bard the way Mr. Wallace does.

"Thank you for unearthing the truth, Cal. My wife wanted it covered up but that was never my way."

In the silence, a question pushes itself to the fore.

"Can I ask you something sir?"

"Of course you may." He chuckles. "Ask while I can still answer."

"As you probably know, I was beaten up by a gang of drug dealers. Afterward, in the hospital, Arnold asked me if it was because of my investigation of Kevin's murder."

He chuckles. "Yes, I told him to ask you that. He didn't know why either."

"Why did you, sir? It was partly right."

"When Kevin went to work at QX4, I invested some money in the company and put Arnold on the Board to keep his eye on things. A couple of years later when George Walsh came along with his millions, everyone was very happy to have him invest but I was suspicious of him. He seemed to invest without really checking the company out, which was most unusual. So I checked *him* out.

"A former army friend runs a successful private inquiry agency. He gave me a very thick report on Mr. Walsh. There was no absolute proof of criminal activity but it was clear that he was making a lot more money than his legitimate businesses could possibly generate. My source believed it was almost certainly drugs. I realized we had a viper in our midst. I tried without success to buy him out of QX4 but he would not budge.

"When Kevin died, I felt sure that Walsh was behind it and when I heard that you had been attacked by a gang of drug dealers, I thought there must be a connection. I knew if Arnold planted the seed, you would follow it up. You see, I wanted you to prove independently that George Walsh murdered my son. I wanted that man dealt with."

I realize with a twinge that even Mr. Wallace has manipulated me.

"It worked. He *has* been dealt with."

"What?"

"Walsh. He's been arrested for money laundering and kidnapping. More charges relating to drugs will be coming. The evidence is very compelling. He's going to be spending most of the rest of his life in jail."

"You've been busy, Cal."

"Yes sir."

We sit in silence. It feels peaceful. Mr. Wallace has been a force in my life for the last twenty-five years and has been the closest I have had to a father.

"I found my father, sir."

His eyes open wide. "How many surprises do you have for me today?" he asks. "Who is he? When am I going to meet him?"

"I'm afraid that he's dead. Killed by Walsh's gang."

I tell him everything about Roy and I can not help expressing my grief at his loss and my anger that I never knew he was my father until it was too late. When I finally run out of steam, he squeezes my hand and says, "Cal, when you think of him, remember the good times that you had, have compassion for him and know that he was trying to do what he thought was best for you, as much as he was able."

I absorb his words. Compassion: something that is in short supply on the streets of the downtown east side; something that is needed there.

"You have been more busy than I thought. And you have done well. Exceeded all expectations in fact. I will make sure that it is rewarded."

My heart skips a beat. Does this mean that he will use his relationship with the mayor to get me back into the department? Before I can decide whether or not to ask him, he removes his hand from mine and squeezes my wrist. "Go now, Cal. I need to think about everything that you have told me. Make sure that you call Arnold tomorrow. I do not expect to see you again on this side of the Styx but perhaps we shall meet sometime in the undiscovered country. You were like a son to me and, although I have never said it before and perhaps I should have, I love you like one."

My tears fall upon his silver hair as I lean forward and kiss his forehead.

Chapter 62

The scene is washed by a late November drizzle. The stand of trees looks stark black against the gray landscape. Even the color of the grass seems muted by the standing lines of gravestones.

Roy's grave is close to Kevin's, his eternal bed a gift arranged by Arnold on behalf of the Wallace family.

It is the first funeral that Ellie has ever attended. We stand alone beside the grave, her hand gripped tightly in mine. Water is dipping from her rain hood and my hair. In contrast to Kevin's funeral, we are two lone mourners. The rent-a-minister is gone. The doleful service is over. *When beggars die, there are no comets seen.*

I wonder how long it will be before I am back here to say a final goodbye to another father.

Ellie tugs on my hand. I look down. "Now, Daddy?" she asks.

"Yes," I smile at her.

She steps forward, dragging me with her, and throws the rose into the maw of the grave. It lands on the coffin and in my mind I see Roy's body, dressed in the maroon velvet shroud supplied by the undertaker, his old leather hat at his feet, his beloved knife open and clasped in a gnarled old hand, ready to ward off foes in the undiscovered country.

I look at the gravestone.

Roy
– 2008
He lived life on his terms.

So much never to be known.

So much that we could have done together for years to come.

I look over at Kevin's grave. *Kev, I am so, so sorry.* If I had just taken that one minute to listen to what you had to say on that Saturday morning, you would still be alive, your career in ruins for sure, facing jail time perhaps, but still alive damn it.

And Roy. I put you in harm's way and the fact that we avenged your death provides no solace, quite the opposite in fact.

I feel like the murderer that Stammo wanted to prove me to be.

Of all the things I want to say, I just stick with, "Goodbye Roy... Dad."

We turn away and walk through the sodden grass to the path where Sam waits in her SUV. Sam: yet another victim of the fallout from Kevin's murder. Her reactions to me have been guarded. At some level I think that she blames me for ruining her life by bringing George to justice: another layer of guilt for me to consider. She is still living in his house but knows it can not last. The government may well seize all of George's assets. This may leave her and Ellie homeless and with MS she will be limited in her ability to work.

Ellie and I bundle into the back seat. The car is warm and so we struggle out of our coats before we buckle up. I wince as the seat belt scrapes against the infection that has been growing in the crook of my arm and I worry for the hundredth time about what I may have picked up from the needle I dropped on the floor of the Lion hotel.

"Are you OK, Cal?" Sam asks, looking at me in the rear view mirror.

I'm not but I nod.

I smile down at my lovely daughter and think about my last moments with my father.

"Sam," I say, "will you do me a favor?"

"If I can," she says guardedly.

"I would like it if from now on you would call me Rocky. It was the name that Roy always called me."

"Sure... Rocky." She tries it out.

"Should I call you Rocky too, Daddy?" Ellie asks.

"No, sweetie. You can still call me Daddy. OK?" Her little hand squeezes mine and she giggles.

"Uh, Rocky," Sam is struggling with what she wants to say. "I want you to know that I don't blame you for what happened with George. I made a terrible mistake which I am going to pay for dearly, so will Ellie, but I wanted you to know that you did the right thing. We are going to move out of the house on the weekend, I need to get our stuff out before the government decide what they want to do about George's assets. We are going to move in with my parents until we get ourselves sorted out." I hear the catch in her voice and so does Ellie. She looks at me with puzzlement on her little face.

"Sam, I'll do anything I can to help." I feel the emptiness of my words. There is nothing I can do until I am clean. It spurs my resolve.

Sam heads the car towards the downtown east side and the detox facility on East Second.

"This time it's for sure, Ca— Rocky?" Sam asks.

"Yes. For sure." And I pray that it is.

It has to be.

This time it's not for the chance of returning to the VPD, it's not for Sam or even for my darling Ellie.

It has to be for me.

I squeeze Ellie's hand. She smiles up at me and helps soothe my worry for her and for Sam but can do nothing to ease my rising dread of what I will have to endure over the next little while.

She is thoughtful for a moment and then asks, "When he came to our house he was nice, he made me laugh. I asked him to take me to your house."

"I wish so much now that I had brought him to see you. We could have all gone out together. You and he would have had so much fun. He had all sorts of stories and jokes."

"Tell me some of them Daddy."

Tears are welling in my eyes. I no longer know whether they are for Roy or for Kevin or for Brad.

Or for me.

I smile down at Ellie. "Let me tell you about your grandpa…"

The End

**See the next page for a preview of Oboe,
the second Cal Rogan Mystery**

OBOE

Chapter 1

The thought of crossing this line fills me with dread.

I feel rooted to the ground. I know that once I move I will be changed forever. Steeling myself—or am I just delaying the inevitable?—I look up at the trees. They are old growth, moss covered monsters that have stood here for centuries. With enmity they glare down at me through the forbidding early light, knowing that I am a member of the species that has just profaned their woods. I can not suppress a shudder as I lift the yellow tape and stoop under.

At twenty paces, facing away and clad, like me, in crime scene clothing, heads tilted forward, they look like alien prisoners about to be executed by a bullet in the back. Five of them are standing in a semicircle looking down at the sixth, a man, crouching over something on the ground. Cops at a murder scene often indulge in gallows humor, a futile mechanism to try and erase their horror at the brutal theft of a human life, but as I approach I note that they are silent.

I take my place beside my minder at the left hand end of the group as a distant peal of thunder announces my arrival. In an effort to delay the inevitable, I exchange looks and nods with each person present. Glad of the excuse, they fix their eyes on me. Waiting for the reaction, I suppose.

At last, I force myself to look down.

In my years as a cop and during the time I was living on the streets of the downtown east side, I have seen violent death in all its forms: faces blown away with hollow point bullets; guts spilled through knife slashes; the arched bodies of overdosed junkies; once a blood-drenched garrote victim. I have even seen the murdered bodies of two people whom I loved.

But nothing has prepared me for this, the crime scene that every cop dreads.

The gray light filtering through the forest canopy is just enough to illuminate the body. He is wearing funky yellow and green sneakers and gray sweat pants bearing the red Nike swoosh. They are muddied and ripped. He is naked above the waist and is drenched in blood. He looks to be about nine or ten years old, the same age as my darling Ellie, forcing other images into my mind. There seem to be five wounds forming an approximate circle with his belly button at its center. As if this were not enough, on his face there are two knife slashes forming an X. Each slash starts on one cheek and finishes on the opposite jaw line, with the center of the X over his mouth. Both his eyes seem to have been damaged in some way. There is not a lot of blood on his face and I am praying that the wounds were inflicted after he was dead.

I can not stop my mind from picturing Ellie lying there, violated by some sadist, and I have to turn away, feeling the anger rising. The shiver that runs through me has nothing to do with the cold February morning.

"We'll know more later but I estimate time of death at about six or seven PM yesterday," says a voice in a slightly Quebecois accent. I turn back and see that the coroner is on his feet and I am grateful that I do not have to look downward. "Cause is almost certainly the wound to his solar plexus. The facial wounds were *post mortem* and there is no obvious sign of sexual assault." At this last, there is a sigh of relief from most of us. He nods towards my boss, "I should have more for you later."

2

"Was there any ID on the body?" I ask. He shakes his head.

It is time for the removal of the body and then the crime scene techs can take over. Before I clear the scene, I force myself to take a good look around the area. About five feet from the body is a yellow winter jacket and what I guess to be the remains of a green t-shirt. Nothing else on the forest floor seems to be out of place but, if anything is, the techs will find it.

I somehow bring myself to take a final look at the body. Three lone rain drops fall from the leaves above and I watch them spatter on the boy's bloody torso. Claudius' words spring into my mind, *Is there not rain enough in the sweet heavens to wash it white as snow?*

No, Claudius. There isn't.

I pull out my mobile and call missing persons as I head back towards the trail where the cars are parked. The not so sweet heavens open and, as bad as this day has started, I know it is going to get worse. By the time it draws to its close I will be longing for the sweet release that only heroin can bring.

For details of publication date, visit

www.robertpfrench.com

3

12457518R00210

Made in the USA
Charleston, SC
06 May 2012